Praise for *In Bed with the Earl*

"Exceptional . . . This series launch is an intoxicating romp sure to delight fans of historical romance."
—*Publishers Weekly* (starred review)

"Sizzling, witty, passionate . . . perfect!"
—Eloisa James, *New York Times* bestselling author

Praise for Christi Caldwell

"Christi Caldwell writes a gorgeous book!"
—Sarah MacLean, *New York Times* and *USA Today* bestselling author

"In addition to a strong plot, this story boasts actualized characters whose personal demons are clear and credible. The chemistry between the protagonists is seductive and palpable, with their family history of hatred played against their personal similarities and growing attraction to create an atmospheric and captivating romance."
—*Publishers Weekly* on *The Hellion*

"Christi Caldwell is a master of words, and *The Hellion* is so descriptive and vibrant that she redefines high definition. Readers will be left panting, craving, and rooting for their favorite characters as unexpected lovers find their happy ending."
—*RT Book Reviews* on *The Hellion*

"Christi Caldwell's *The Vixen* shows readers a darker, grittier version of Regency London than most romance novels . . . Caldwell's more realistic version of London is a particularly gripping backdrop for this enemies-to-lovers romance, and it's heartening to read a story where love triumphs even in the darkest places."

—NPR on *The Vixen*

UNDRESSED
with the
MARQUESS

OTHER TITLES BY CHRISTI CALDWELL

Lost Lords of London

In Bed with the Earl

In the Dark with the Duke

Sinful Brides

The Rogue's Wager

The Scoundrel's Honor

The Lady's Guard

The Heiress's Deception

The Wicked Wallflowers

The Hellion

The Vixen

The Governess

The Bluestocking

The Spitfire

Heart of a Duke

In Need of a Duke (A Prequel Novella)

For Love of the Duke

More Than a Duke

The Love of a Rogue

Loved by a Duke

To Love a Lord

The Heart of a Scoundrel

To Wed His Christmas Lady

UNDRESSED
with the
MARQUESS

CHRISTI
CALDWELL

 Montlake

Published by Montlake, Seattle

www.apub.com

Amazon, the Amazon logo, and Montlake are trademarks of Amazon.com, Inc., or its affiliates.

ISBN-13: 9781542021364
ISBN-10: 1542021367

Cover design by Juliana Kolesova

Printed in the United States of America

To Karen.
Thank you for your eyes. Your support.
And most importantly, your friendship.

Chapter 1

When Lewis Tooley was hanged, to the more merciless crowd's delight, and to the less hardened people's horror, the man's head popped right off.

Thomas Winterly wetted himself the moment the bag was draped over his head.

Or there was Mrs. Blythe Starwich, who went purple, and whose strangulation was so slow that even the most ruthless gluttons for displays of violence called out for mercy on the half-mad woman's behalf.

Now, having come to terms with these, his final moments, contemplating each of those possible outcomes for his own demise, Dare felt more . . . a detached curiosity about the end of his life.

Unlike the ribald excitement that always filled the gallows on hanging day, there was a surprising quiet to the crowd. A somberness that didn't fit with the affair.

He did a sweep of the thousands assembled, all faces blurring together, a swath of tattered brown fabrics all blended as one into a blanket of sorts comprised of the masses.

Tears wetted the coal-smudged cheeks of many of the spectators.

It spoke to his ungratefulness, because Dare should be grateful for those tokens, ones that indicated some out there would at least regret his passing.

And yet . . . they were still the tears of strangers. They'd grieve over the loss of what he represented for the people here.

There was one who *might* grieve, however . . . and as he looked out, it was her face he sought. The one who, years and years earlier, had urged him to the Devil and said he was dead to her . . .

The guard grunted. "It's toime, Grey." He prodded Dare sharply at the center of his back.

Dare stumbled and pitched forward, managing to right himself.

He steeled his jaw. He'd be damned if anything but that rope knocked him down.

Hisses and boos went up amongst the audience.

"Free 'im . . ."

Those two words rolled slowly and quietly through the crowd, but then took on a steady beat until the crowd roared with demands for his freedom.

And in the greatest of ironies, his guard shifted uneasily, moving closer to Dare.

"Let's get on with it," the other guard shouted, his call barely rising above the deafening din.

Catching Dare at both arms, they dragged him closer to that dais.

He'd lied. He wasn't at peace.

Sweat slicked his palms and coated his frame. Vomit churned in his belly, and he swallowed rapidly to keep from retching before the thousands bearing witness.

His gaze skittered frantically.

For all the times he'd found himself in Newgate, there'd always been an almost calm understanding that he'd escape. He'd never made it to his last meal and last rites. And this march. He'd never made this march.

He choked on his bile, grateful for the near pandemonium that allowed him that smallest dignity.

His stare landed on a gleeful face amidst the crowd. There was a vague familiarity to the stranger. And yet, for as many as Dare had helped, there'd been triple those whom he'd been unable to. Men and women he'd turned away. Or gang leaders whom he'd foiled.

The man grabbed himself crudely. "Deserve it, ya do . . ." That triumphant spectator's mouth moved, his words clear, even as they were silent amidst the pandemonium.

Yes, there were those who'd relish his death.

Dare's legs knocked against the bottom step leading up to the dais.

And the panic that had pounded like a drum within retreated and faded, leaving him numb once more.

This was what the end was, then. Terror, ebbing and flowing like the tides rushing in and then out.

Dougal, the burlier of the guards, grunted. "It is time to get on with it. Ain't no one comin' for ye this time." A faint hint of regret tinged that announcement.

But then, in the thirteen times Dare had landed himself in Newgate for robbing some nob to give to the poor, he'd come to know many of the guards. Those same men had often helped coordinate the bribe which had seen Dare freed. This time, however, there'd be no escape. That reality did not erase Dare's gratitude for what this guard, and others, had done in his past. He briefly held the other man's gaze and nodded. "Thank you." For all the other men had done before this moment.

The guard gave the slightest, most imperceptible of nods that, had Dare not been studying him so closely, he would have missed.

And oddly, that grounded him. It gave him the courage and strength to place his foot on the first step. Nor did he believe his march, different from the customary shorter one, was anything but deliberate.

No, everyone from the constables on down to the magistrate was making a pointed example of him.

Dare made a slow climb up the last ten stairs he'd ever ascend.

And then he reached the top of the dais.

Drawing in a slow, steadying breath, he stared out at the sea of strangers below. Men, women, and children who'd have no one fighting for their justice and their survival. People there to be exploited.

So much work left undone.

And he proved very much the bastard Temperance had called him out as . . . because he found himself thinking of just one: her.

I wanted forever with you, Dare . . . but I'm not your first love. Your first love will always be your thieving ways . . . and I cannot—will not—be around when you finally fall . . .

His throat jumped.

She'd been right.

She'd always been right about so much. Always honorable, Temperance had certainly been too good for the likes of him.

But I wanted her anyway . . .

He closed his eyes, letting the crowd melt from his mind, wanting her face to be the last he saw. Not as she'd been the last time he'd seen her, but before that. Back when there was her laughter and his, melded together, as harmonious in their joy as they had been in making love—

The guard jabbed him hard in the back, bringing the reverie to an end and Dare's eyes flying open.

A third guard stepped forward with a burlap sack in hand. In one fluid movement, the man shoved it over Dare's head.

Dare sucked in a breath as he was swallowed by darkness. *No.*

A rope dropped about his neck.

Terror plucked at the very edge of his consciousness, and he clenched and unclenched his bound hands, wanting to rip at that weighted cord about him.

And then came the strangest of occurrences.

Silence.

An eerie wave of it rolled through the crowd, punctuated by the periodic wail of a small child.

And he found himself longing for the noise. The one that would keep the world from hearing the hammering of his heart or the ragged, frantic breaths he sucked in through lungs that were too tight.

I'm not ready . . .

"In the name of the king . . ."

The king . . . That monarch who'd never cared about his people. Not the ones who'd most needed his care. Rage swept through Dare, and he welcomed the white-hot rush of it. He opened his mouth and shouted into the quiet, *"Fuck the king!"*

Cheers erupted, a wild, raucous bellowing of approval so thunderous it dimmed the frantic discussion taking place amongst his guards.

"In the name of the king"—that voice at his back shouted once more—"you are hereby ordered to cease . . ."

I don't want to die . . . I don't want to die . . . I don't want to die . . .

It was a litany that rolled around in Dare's head. He was grabbed by the arms and lurched forward, all his muscles coiling tight at that violation, and it was all he could do to keep from trying to fight off those men propelling him onward to his death.

Nay, he'd not die a coward.

Then the enormous weight of the noose was lifted.

Through the haze of panic and the adrenaline that pumped in his veins came confusion.

He was dead.

There was nothing else for it.

"Save 'im . . . save 'im . . . save 'im . . ."

And yet if he were dead, why did the crowds cheer still?

Those cries and shouts pealed through the square.

Where was the silence death brought?

He staggered backward, nearly tripping over his feet at the pace set by his captors. His saviors? It was all confused in this moment.

They continued dragging him down the steps . . . and back still, leading him off. The din of those who'd assembled at the Old Bailey grew muffled and muted, indicating he'd been drawn away from the gallows.

A long while later, those leading Dare abruptly stopped, dragging him to a halt alongside them.

KnockKnockKnock.

The rusty creak of hinges squealed. Dare was shoved into a room.

"Remove that . . . bag . . . this instant." An austere voice in the same clipped English as the king himself cut through the loud silence.

Hands were immediately on Dare, struggling with the knot about his neck.

The sack was pulled from him. A blinding blast of light streamed through the glass windowpanes, and he squinted, bringing his hands up in a bid to blunt the bright rays.

Perhaps he was dead, after all. And he was here to meet his maker and have his sins laid out before being cast into that fiery hell awaiting him.

"And his hands," that same voice ordered.

Dare blinked; slowly his eyes adjusted to the light . . . and to the group of people assembled before him.

The gaoler, Wylie, stood at the center of a trio: an elderly pair who couldn't be a day younger than their seventieth years, both with canes clutched in their opposite hands. And a finely dressed young woman, who just then wordlessly looked Dare up and down.

Dare rubbed at his wrists and assessed this audience of strangers. Searching his mind and memory for past lords and ladies he'd robbed. And yet . . . there was nothing familiar about them. Nay, that wasn't altogether true.

His gaze settled on the youngest person there.

Dark-haired, tall, and sharp-featured . . . there was something familiar about the woman.

Dare searched his mind but came up empty.

Tiring of the silence, he put a question to the one person he was all too acquainted with—Wylie. "Throwing me a party before I meet my maker, are you? That's not a courtesy I thought I'd see from the likes of you."

A hard smile ghosted the gaoler's mouth. "It seems you've more lives than a damned cat, Grey." He waved away the still-hovering guards.

As they marched off, befuddled, Dare searched his still-slow-to-process mind for what the ruthless gaoler was saying.

The white-haired gentleman limped forward and, holding a quizzing glass up to his eye, studied Dare for a long while. "Hmph," he grunted, and let the scrap fall. "It's him."

All the color spilled from the old woman's cheeks. "My God, it can't be!" Her mouth trembled. "There must be some mistake," she cried, those words a plea.

"At least he can speak the King's English," the gentleman said, patting her hand.

Dare kept his focus on him. "Only when Oi'm really trying."

The fancily clad lady wilted. Collapsing into a nearby chair, she grabbed for one of two gold chains about her neck. Uncorking the vial of smelling salts, she inhaled deeply.

"He's making a jest, Beverly," the pragmatic lord, clearly the woman's husband, said. "You remember how he was."

Everything about you is games and fun. You've no sense of responsibility . . . no sense of understanding of what you'll one day inherit . . .

That voice came from a distance, an echo of long ago, words forgotten . . . buried away.

The old man motioned once more to Dare, pulling him back from the past. "He spoke perfectly just moments ago. He's merely trying to get a rise out of us."

Dare rubbed at his wrists to restore the flow of blood. All the while he eyed the gathering, this group of people who had knowledge of him. "Who the hell are you?" Dare put that to the leader of the little trio.

Wylie opened his mouth to speak, but the commanding lord silenced him with a single finger. "Leave us."

"You don't want to be alone with the likes of Grey."

The gentleman thumped his cane. "I said, leave us."

And it was a testament to the man's rank, power, and influence that he managed not only to silence Wylie but also to have the ruthless warden quit the room.

Dare's curiosity stirred all the more . . . as did his suspicion. He'd filched from enough powerful peers to know there was no friend for him amongst that class.

"You don't know who we are?" The gentleman put that question to Dare the moment Wylie shut the door behind him.

Dare eyed the trio. He shook his head. "I don't."

"I am the Duke of Pemberly."

He racked his brain, searching desperately for a reason that this man and his wife should be somehow . . . familiar. A sense of unease skittered along his spine, scraping it and icing it over. "And you think your title should mean something to me?" he asked impatiently, frustrated at being the only one in the dark. "I don't give a damn about it."

I don't care about his title . . . He's not so very scary . . . He's more fun than Father . . .

An odd buzzing filled his ears. He jolted and looked unblinkingly at the duke.

"The names mean nothing to you," the duke murmured, more to himself. He indicated the old lady. "This is my wife, the Duchess of Pemberly."

Dare shifted his gaze over to the old woman.

"Hullo." The lady spoke in a quiet voice.

Get down this instant, Darius, and kiss my cheek . . . Your grandmother orders it . . .

A child's laughter pealed around the chambers of Dare's mind, and he curled his hands tight, fighting the need to dig his fingertips into his temples.

His skin prickled from the weight of the stares on him, and he made himself relax his hands.

Because he didn't want to look too closely at these people. He didn't want to look and see . . . anything.

The duke stared at Dare. Moisture glazed the old man's eyes.

Unnerved, and unable to meet that gaze, Dare shot a desperate glance at the closed door leading out . . . away from these people and the gilded world they belonged to. And yet Wylie would be there. Dare was as much a prisoner now, before these lofty peers, as he'd been with a bag over his head and a noose around his neck.

He made himself look to the last figure present: the young woman. She'd still not spoken, but rather continued to eye Dare cautiously.

Smart lady.

The duke gestured at the woman. "And this is Kinsley, your sister."

His sister.

And the dais may as well have been kicked out from under his feet.

He stared, unblinking, at the young woman . . .

"I . . . don't suppose that name means something to you?" the duke asked with a gentleness Dare wouldn't have believed any nobleman capable of.

It is better that you're gone, Darius . . . I know it . . . You know it . . . Life has gone on without you . . .

And not for the first time that day, his gut churned and tossed.

The duke swallowed loudly. "Hello, grandson."

Hello, grandson.

Dare made himself go absolutely motionless.

All the while, wanting to flee.

To escape.

He was more cornered now than he'd been when his latest cell at Newgate had clicked shut, imprisoning him within its dank folds. And another cool sweat slicked his skin.

"Grandson?" Dare scoffed. "You're a long way from Mayfair, Duke. You don't have any family in these parts." They were the truest words he could have tossed to the old duke. Dare turned to go.

The duke called out, halting Dare in his tracks. "Do you deny who you are? What you are?"

What he was . . .

Your brother is better suited . . . Your brother is better suited . . .

Turning back, he curved his lips into a cold smile. "My name is Dare Grey. And if you're here looking for anyone else? You are wasting your time."

"Wh-what does it mean, th-that he'd deny it?" The duchess's voice crept up a pitch. "He'd rather be hanged than join us, Harold." She wept against her fist.

The duke ignored his wife. "You know what we're talking about, Darius." The elderly lord spoke with a quiet insistence. "We know Connor Steele came to you. We know you're aware of who you are."

Aye, the same detective who had hunted Dare down in the streets and sought to bring him out of East London had been the one to contact his *grandparents*. "He went to you?" he asked, unable to keep the loathing from his lips. Dare had happily sent the man on his way . . . but it appeared he'd been undeterred.

"He did," the duke confirmed. "And it is a good thing." He looked meaningfully toward the doorway Wylie no doubt stood outside, at attention.

Yes, if it hadn't been for that intervention, even now Dare's lifeless body would be getting cut from the gibbet.

He balled his hands tightly and damned the duke for being correct. About so much.

This *was* the world Darius had been born to. The one he'd only briefly considered rejoining . . . and only a very long time ago. Back when he'd been a boy of fourteen.

It is better without you here . . . It is better without . . .

His mind balked at that also long-buried memory. For even then, he'd known the truth: he'd been away from that fairy-tale world too long, been too wicked, and done even more scandalous things—criminal ones, and not just the mischievous stunts of boys. As such, there was no other place for him.

"I can't help you," he finally said, his voice deadened. He resumed his march to the door. He'd take his chances with Wylie over the group assembled here. Dare had reached to knock when the duke called out, freezing Dare's hand midmovement.

"But we can help you . . . Darius."

And given that when he rapped upon the panel, he'd seal his fate with that inevitable trip to the gallows, Dare let his arm fall to his side.

"If you are, in fact, the person I believe you are—my grandson?" This time, there was a question from the duke.

If you are, in fact, the person I believe you are—my grandson?

All he need do was just deny it. To confirm that the other man was dicked in the nob and that Dare had no bloody idea what nonsense had spared him the hanging he'd been moments away from.

A sound of impatience escaped the young lady standing there. "Let us just leave." She clipped out each syllable. "I've already told both of you, this is a waste of all our time."

A memory intruded, made stronger by the disdain emanating from the young woman across from him.

You've wasted your time in coming here . . .

"I trust that would be best for you, wouldn't it?" Dare taunted her.

The young lady's jaw tensed. "If it means protecting the title from a common street thief whom my grandparents are desperate to believe is the grandson they lost, then yes . . . that would be best, indeed." She angled her shoulder dismissively and spoke in more gentling tones to the old woman. "Grandmother, come. I told you . . . Darius is dead."

They prefer you dead, Dare Grey . . . Live your life . . .

And yet . . . if he walked out and sent these people on their way, there would be no life.

Fixing a smile on, Dare looked squarely at his late mother's father, the duke. "Hello, Grandfather. How long it has been."

Chapter 2

Living in the Cotswolds, a small village on the outskirts of London, Mrs. Temperance Swift had discovered there were different rings of hell.

Dealing with old Mrs. Marmlebury, the town's nastiest widow and gossip, was the last and most miserable of all the rings.

Mrs. Marmlebury tapped her wooden fan on the counter. "Are you *listening* to me, Mrs. Swift?"

"Yes, Mrs. Marmlebury." After all, it would be nigh impossible to tune out the old woman, who was deafer than her late husband had been blind.

"Because if you were," the elderly lady went on as though Temperance hadn't spoken, "you should know that I quite prefer pink. I look lovely in the shade. Mr. Marmlebury always said I was a vision in it." She dabbed at her eyes with a kerchief. "God rest his soul."

"God rest his soul," Temperance murmured, bowing her head in the requisite display of contrition and respect. More like God rot it. When he'd been living, the gentleman had made a habit of visiting the dressmaker and assaulting the staff, all under the pretense of "shopping for my beloved wife."

"Mr. Marmlebury insisted it was the only color I should wear."

Temperance bit her tongue to keep from pointing out that the late Mr. Marmlebury had been blinder than a bat, with a penchant for mixing blue and red in his own attire.

Alas, if a client couldn't be reasoned with, then any dressmaker determined to keep her business adhered to the adage "the patron is always correct." After all, ultimately their pleasure and happiness were of the utmost importance.

"I *like* pink. It's not shameful, like red." She glanced pointedly at Temperance's modest vermilion dress. "Would you gather me pink, Mrs. Swift." No one would ever dare confuse the widow's words as a question, but neither could a seamstress afford to make presumptions with clients.

"Of course." Rushing across the shop, Temperance made her way over to the bolts of fabric, the pathetically skimpy selection of pinks. While her client angled a fabric before her wide frame, Temperance considered the choices.

She picked up a pale piece.

Pink.

God, what a hideous, garish color. Any and all shades of it. What was it about pink that so many women should prefer such a hue?

Nay, with warm brunette coloring, Mrs. Marmlebury would be far better suited in—Temperance skimmed her gaze quickly over the drearily limited selection—peach or apricot . . . or even an apple green. Temperance lowered the bolt. Perhaps the old widow could be persuaded?

A small figure slid into position beside her, briefly startling a gasp from Temperance.

"She can't," Gwynn Armitage, a fellow seamstress at *Vêtements Français*, said from the corner of her mouth. Temperance and all the girls who'd been employed here had become adept at hiding their speech while working.

"She can't what?" Temperance spoke in matching hushed tones. She and Gwynn had met in the Cotswolds nearly five years ago when the other woman, a young widow, had just been hired. They'd clashed from the start . . . until they hadn't. Until they'd realized they shared the same frustrations at their lot in life. And somewhere along the way, the two enemies had become sisters in a world where one was fortunate if she had even a single person whom she might rely upon. "I don't know what you're talking about."

"Yes, you do. She can't be reasoned with." Gwynn collected a swath of pink and held it aloft, concealing her mouth and affording them brief privacy from their employer. "That's what you were thinking." She paused. "And you can't. Pink is her decision, and she cannot be swayed. Mayhap if we were real seamstresses in a fashionable modiste shop on New Bond Street. But the Cotswolds? This isn't that place."

Alas, at the end of the long working day, they'd always been practical enough to know that these were the best circumstances they were likely to ever know.

"Mrs. *Swiiiift?*" Mrs. Marmlebury called out. *"Hallooo?"*

From where she stood, helping a more distinguished, plumper-in-the-pockets-for-Cotswolds client, Madame Amelie paused to glance in Temperance and Gwynn's direction.

"Just a moment, Mrs. Marmlebury," Temperance said loudly so the nearly deaf woman might hear her. "I am just searching for the perfect options." She reached for the apple green.

Gwynn pushed it from her reach and gave her a long look.

They locked in a silent war over the bolts.

It had taken a lifetime of mistakes to learn anything of true import; however, one area she'd always had remarkably in order and under control, the one thing that had made sense, was color. Temperance released a frustrated sigh. She made one more appeal. "No decent seamstress worth her weight in bolt would dare put that woman in this color."

"Not Bond Street," Gwynn repeated. "As such, no wise woman intending to keep her post would argue with the late Mr. Marmlebury." She bowed her head in mock solemnity. "God rest his soul."

A sharp bark of laughter burst from Temperance, and even as her customer and employer glanced her way, she had already disguised that mirth for a cough. "Stop," she mouthed.

"Take the pink." Gwynn enunciated each syllable.

"Mrs. *Swiiiift*. I do not have all day," Mrs. Marmlebury whined.

In the end, Gwynn stole the decision. Grabbing the apple-green bolt, she thrust several pink ones against Temperance's chest.

Temperance grunted and collected the armful.

Gwynn waved over at the old widow. "We've found lovely options for you, Mrs. Marmlebury. I trust you'll be very pleased. Mrs. Swift is just bringing them over. Now," her friend added under her breath for Temperance's benefit. She followed that with a hard nudge in Temperance's lower back, knocking her forward.

"Ouch." Over her shoulder, Temperance flashed a frown. "That hurt."

"Do you know what hurts worse than that?" Gwynn answered her own question. "Having no employment or funds to feed oneself or pay for rent or—"

"You've made your point," Temperance muttered under her breath. Yes, her friend was correct. It was the unfortunate circumstance of the street-born that in the position they held, they didn't have the luxury of speaking as freely as they wished. Or of having complete say over decisions that they were best equipped to make.

Nay, she'd learned firsthand with several sackings and docked pay that her words couldn't be freely given. Not truly. Not if she wished to eat and survive and live . . .

There will come a day, love, when you're going to do more than survive . . .

That voice slipped in, an echo of long ago, and yet still so very fresh in her mind.

You're a damned fool still, all these years later, allowing him any real estate inside your mind . . .

"Mrs. Swift? Mrs. *Swift?*"

A kick to her shin, coupled with her name being called, brought her back.

Gwynn gave her a look. "What is going on?" she mouthed.

"I am fine." Temperance retrained all her focus on her client. Returning to Mrs. Marmlebury, she guided the older woman back over to the mirrors. Temperance proceeded to hold the fabrics up, draping the silk over her client's frame so she might see the color against her skin.

She didn't think of Dare Grey often. Oh, in those earliest days, she'd been bereft . . . heartbroken . . . incapable of anything but tears and terror. Then she'd fought the memory of him because it had been too painful . . .

Until it hadn't been.

"You're the last man I should marry, Dare Grey . . ."

"That's no doubt true, Temperance," Dare, the most arrogant thief in London, said somberly. He flashed his devil-may-care grin. *"But I'm also the only man you'll ever want . . ."* He reached for her . . .

The echo of her squealing laughter pealed around her mind.

Even as she'd been distracted, Temperance had also given her friend the truth.

She was fine. Far better off these years than she'd been . . . *ever.* Born to the ugliest drunk in London, one of the hands of gang leader Mac Diggory, Temperance had spent her earliest years in hell, and the only brief respite had come from a London thief.

She'd been hopelessly weak for him, and it had very nearly destroyed her.

This new life was far better.

Or rather, it was the best she could hope for.

Temperance went about draping Mrs. Marmlebury, creating the illusion of a dress for the older woman to assess.

All the while, she let her mind wander.

Where in blazes had thoughts of Dare Grey come from? It had been at least a year that she'd managed to keep him buried. Not that his memory was always an unwelcome one. It wasn't. For the pain had receded at some point, and with all remembrances of him came a stark reminder of what happened when a woman wasn't resourceful, when she allowed herself to care too deeply for someone who wasn't so very deserving, and allowed herself to put feelings and emotions before building a foundation and future all her own.

The tinny bell at the front of the shop jolted her from her musings. Disinterestedly, she glanced over to the latest customer—

Not a customer.

His arms laden with several crates, her brother, Chance, stepped inside. "Ladies," he called out in greeting, and seemingly effortlessly balancing that enormous burden against his hip, he doffed his hat with the other hand.

Her brother was a moderately successful weaver for one of the most successful mill owners in England, and Temperance couldn't have been prouder of how far he'd come from their beginnings in East London if she'd given birth to him. But then, their own mother having died when he was just a babe, Temperance had stepped in to fill that role.

She watched as he moved deeper into the shop. Smiling as he went, he possessed an urbane charm that no one was immune to, not even Temperance's employer, Madame Amelie.

Of course, it did help that he was the favored employee of a more-than-successful textile mill owner.

As the shopgirls called out greetings, Chance flashed his usual charming grin before settling his focus on one.

Gwynn blushed under that look.

Temperance stared on wistfully, proving herself to be a disloyal sister and an even more disloyal friend for the flash of envy she felt at what the pair shared. At what she'd hungered for, for herself . . . and what she'd never have. There was that, too.

But you almost had it . . .

And for a very, very brief while . . . she had.

She went absolutely still at that whisper of a past long forgotten.

Something sharp stung her arm, startling her from that reverie. Madame Amelie had her flicking finger out once more. "You were distracted, Mrs. Swift. You don't get distracted."

No, Temperance was the second in command at the shop, and the reason why she was never a recipient of that notorious flick.

"I will help Mrs. Marmlebury," her employer said. "See to Mr. Swift, if you would." Madame Amelie's fleeting smile was gone in favor of the cool look she reserved for her shopgirls. "And take those crates from him, Miss Armitage."

Together, they hurried over to Chance. "I have them," he said, all eyes for Gwynn.

More sighs went up at that chivalry.

With a wry grin, Temperance rescued the heavy crates from her brother, sagging under the weight of them. She, however, may as well have been invisible to the pair of young lovers as they stared misty-eyed at one another. "Come along, you two," she muttered, starting for the back of the shop. Before realizing she made the trek alone.

Adjusting her hold on the crates of linens, she glanced back at her brother and best friend. "Now."

That barely snapped the romantic reverie as the two, with eyes only for each other, moved in tandem, side by side, down the aisle of the shop. Their hands periodically brushed as they walked, in a discreet but absolutely intentional caress.

Forcing her gaze away from that intimate moment, Temperance marched forward. She reached the doorway that led to Madame Amelie's workroom. Struggling with her burden, she gave her brother a look. "If it isn't too much trouble?"

"It isn't," Gwynn murmured.

Chance smiled down at Gwynn. "Not at all."

Oh, bloody hell. To be young and stupid for love again.

"I meant the door," Temperance muttered, sinking under the weight of the packaged textiles.

Her brother blinked several times and looked over at Temperance. And then the door.

She gave a little nod.

His cheeks flushing red, Chance grabbed the crates from her. "Forgive me."

He needn't have apologized. Temperance well knew how limited their time together was. She knew every moment he shared with Gwynn was fleeting because of their work. Because of where he lived and where Gwynn lived. And Temperance would see they had the opportunity to be together when they could.

The moment they entered Madame Amelie's workroom, Chance set the crates down atop the tidy, organized table. And while her brother and Gwynn became lost in one another once more, Temperance began removing the items he'd brought.

"Orange taffeta?" she asked, cringing. "That's nearly as bad as pink on Mrs. Marmlebury."

"Hmm?" Gwynn said distractedly, not so much as taking her eyes from Chance.

"Nothing. Nothing at all," Temperance said and began pulling out the remainder of the bolts.

Simply put, when they were together, Temperance and the world ceased to exist for the couple.

Yet for her earlier envy, the truth remained—love was a luxury for those of their station. It was why she allowed them whatever time they had together. It was why she didn't mind being forgotten, because they were deserving of happiness.

Temperance paused in her sorting and stared absently at the cheerful yellow satin in her hands.

Happiness wasn't for their lot. And *certainly* not happily-ever-afters. She knew that firsthand, but it did not mean she wouldn't help her brother and her best—and only—friend steal joy where they could.

A short while later, all the bolts having been removed, laid out, and organized according to color as Madame Amelie preferred, Gwynn glanced over.

The dazed happiness had gone from her friend's eyes, to be replaced with the sadness that always came when it neared time for Chance to return to his work in London.

"Hey, none of this," he murmured, touching a finger to Gwynn's chin. "I'll have more deliveries soon, and I've every reason to believe Mr. Buxton intends to one day soon promote me to supervisor of the floors. Then there'll be funds." He cupped Gwynn's chin. "Just until then . . ."

The other woman's voice shook when she spoke. "London is too far."

It wasn't too far. It was, however, far enough, and that was the reason Temperance had fled to this sliver of country years earlier.

Tears slipped down Gwynn's cheeks, and Chance looked hopelessly at Temperance.

"He'll return soon enough," she said, unable to offer any more assurances than that. And she looked away as her brother placed a kiss on Gwynn's lips.

Chance lingered there a moment, his eyes upon Gwynn. "Someday, we'll be together. Forever." And with that, he was gone.

Gwynn stared after him.

"I am so sorry, Gwynn," Temperance said softly. "Someday . . ." Except she could not make herself finish. Because she knew better than anyone else that, in matters of the heart, "somedays" did not exist.

Her friend swiped the tears from her cheeks. "There won't be . . . and there isn't. Not when there aren't funds to be together. Not with each of us reliant upon the work we do on altogether different sides of England." Gwynn stared at the door where Chance had taken his leave moments ago. "This is as good as it will ever get," she whispered to herself. And with that, she left.

This is as good as it will ever get . . .

And how Temperance hated it. For her brother. For her friend.

She'd long ago accepted the disappointments in her own life, of what she'd lost, of what had never been meant to be. But as she removed the now empty crates and stacked them at the back of Madame Amelie's workroom, she wished she could see Gwynn and Chance, with their rare kind of love, find the happiness she'd never managed.

Chapter 3

It had taken seven days.

Seven miserable days of Dare living in Mayfair and being waited on by servants he didn't want, and receiving visits from *family* he didn't consider family, to at last have the sole meeting he cared about.

Seated amongst the same gathering who'd fetched him from the gallows, Dare listened on through the monotone ramblings of the bespectacled fellow.

"The title of Milford goes back nearly seven and a half centuries and was created for William Greyson, a Norman baron . . ."

Ticktock-ticktock.

Dare stole a glance at the fine clock resting on the mantel and narrowed his eyes.

Austrian giltwood. Blue glass. Sometime of the last century. Certainly not the oldest, and yet it could still fetch a nice enough sum to see several wrongly accused freed.

His skin burnt from the feel of eyes trained on him.

Dare looked over.

Lady Kinsley . . . his *sister*—the sister he'd only just recently met—glared blackly at him.

"Its earlier grant was by Henry I to his first wife." The gentleman frowned and consulted his papers. "Many pardons, his *second* wife, Adeliza, of the forfeited honor of—"

"We can stop with all this," Dare cut in. "I don't require a history lesson." Nor did he want one. "Just tell me: How much do I have?" That was what mattered. That and what he could do with the fortune he'd inherit.

The servant's visible Adam's apple jumped. "O-of course, my lord." He shuffled ahead several pages.

For the first time since he'd gathered here with his grandparents and sister, Dare leaned forward in his chair, eager and interested. He cracked his knuckles . . . and waited.

"But . . . in order to understand the current economic circumstances of the Milford title, one must understand the history of England on the whole."

Bloody hell.

Dare sat back in his chair as Mr. Heron launched into an accounting of the kingdom's finances following the Napoleonic Wars. *To hell with this. To hell with all this.* And while the servant ran on with those unimportant-to-Dare details, Dare resumed his mental inventorying of the office.

His office.

A French neoclassical vase. He peered at the gold-and-floral-painted piece and pegged it as newer—somewhere between the late eighteenth century and early nineteenth. With the right buyer, it'd fetch a good sum.

The floor-to-ceiling shelves of books, however, required closer inspection.

"Upon his death, she married William, who became master of the lands . . . Some of these lands have remained entailed. Some unentailed . . ."

Annnd it appeared they'd returned to the twelfth century. Dare consulted the clock once more.

An hour of this hell. And he was no closer to having answers than when it had first begun.

"Busy day?"

That curt query brought Heron's recitation to an abrupt stop.

Dare looked to the source of the interruption.

Kinsley Greyson had her perpetual glare leveled on him.

"I beg your pardon?" Dare asked in cool tones that had managed to send taller, broader men fleeing in the opposite direction.

Mr. Heron looked hopelessly between the siblings, then over at the duke.

"Kinsley," the duke said warningly.

The young lady, however, kept a fierce gaze trained on Dare.

And then, in a remarkable show of bravery, Kinsley rested her palms on her knees and leaned forward. "You're stepping into one of the oldest, most distinguished titles. One that has existed since William the Conqueror."

God, it was as though his father had returned from the grave and spoken through the mouth of his youngest child. And Dare could not resist the sting of resentment and loathing.

"You can spare some time to learn about that important history before asking what is in it for you," the young woman was saying. Fire and hatred blazed from her eyes.

Dare would hand it to the young woman. She'd a greater strength than he had credited any nobleman as having. That realization, however, still changed nothing. The only things that mattered, the only reason he was here even now, were the funds he stood to earn.

Leaning forward, he matched his sister in her positioning. "This isn't *my* history." Not anymore. Mayhap it never had been. "And it never will be."

"That is just fine with—"

"That is enough," the duchess cut in with stern tones. "Furthermore, we don't make productions in front of . . . anyone. You know that." Her scolding came quieter.

Her mouth set stonily, Lady Kinsley slumped in her chair, looking very much like a recalcitrant child. Nay, she was more like . . .

I'm going to ride the rail down, and you can't stop me . . .

"What of Perrin?" His younger brother, who'd done an admirable job in his stead, who'd always done . . . everything right. "I trust he would have done well enough in the role of marquess that you wouldn't have had to come searching for me."

Her Grace pressed a fist to her breast, and husband and wife shared a look.

The elderly pair spoke at the same time.

"You remember."

"He remembers."

They scrabbled for each other's hands. Dare had said too much. He resisted the urge to squirm.

The pair clung to one another and leaned in, touching their brows, forgetting the scolding they'd just given Lady Kinsley about showing emotion.

He glanced about, wondering at his other sibling's absence. Was it resentment at being forced to give up that which he'd inherited? *Either way, why should you expect he would have wanted to see you? Why, when your own parents were better off without you?*

"It doesn't mean *anything* that he remembers Perry," Lady Kinsley pointed out. "He might be making it up."

Aye, with that healthy mistrust, mayhap they were siblings, after all.

Her grandparents turned sharp glares on her.

"That Darius is our grandson and your brother has never been in doubt. He was just a boy when he was taken from us, not some babe where anyone might have been passed off for him, as in those other cases," the duke said sharply. "He is your brother, as much as Perry was."

Was. The past tense which bespoke only the finality of death.

Lady Kinsley's throat moved quickly, and she glanced away, but not before Dare detected the gleam of tears in the young woman's eyes.

"He is dead, then?" Dare asked when no one confirmed with words the fate his . . . brother had met.

The duchess, breaking her own rules, began weeping.

"He is," the duke murmured, stroking his wife's back in an unexpected display for a peer.

He is.

Perry, three years his junior, was dead, then.

Perhaps had Dare come home long, long ago, certainly had he never left, there would have been a crushing weight of grief. There was, however, only a profound regret and . . . a sadness for the brother whom time had made a stranger of. And it only cemented what he'd learned at his mentor-turned-partner Avery Bryant's side: how much greater that pain would have been had Dare been fully a part of Perry's life.

The irony was not lost on him, however; where Dare had been the one to live out on the streets of East London, Perry had remained ensconced in the secure, comfortable family folds in Mayfair—only to be the one to perish.

"Perrin died just two years ago," His Grace murmured.

Dare did the quick math. Perrin would have been only twenty-five years of age. With the spare who'd become the heir gone, it made sense why Dare's *family* had finally begun looking for him.

"Dropsy," Kinsley spat. "My God, you couldn't even ask what happened to him?"

"Would it have changed anything?" Dare asked quietly without malice, but there may as well have been elements of it there for the hatred brimming in the young lady's eyes.

There was only one history that mattered to Dare—his time in East London. The rest was a fanciful fairy tale that may as well have belonged to another, as farcical as it was. He nodded to Heron. "Get on with it."

Tripping and stumbling over his words, Mr. Heron resumed the recitation of his history lesson.

"Following the Napoleonic Wars, the country fell into an economic depression . . ."

These people knew nothing. Dare and his people in the streets had gone without long before that war ended.

"Your father's estates began to suffer mightily, as did so many."

Your father . . .

Dare's entire body tensed. For years, he'd not allowed himself to think of the man who'd sired him, or of the woman who'd given him birth. As such, there was . . . a peculiar detachedness at the servant's labeling of that man whom Dare had spent more years away from than with.

Before the man-of-affairs could resume his drawn-out breakdown of England's finances, Dare cut him off. "And this matters because?"

Heron adjusted his spectacles. "Yes, my lord, I am coming to that."

Dare rather doubted that. The man was incapable of directness.

"However," Heron was saying, "this period proved short-lived. The depression struck, and weavers and spinners were all hit hard." He paused. A thick tension fell over the room. It was the same feeling that had dogged him moments before capture—the knife about to fall. "As were your family's investments."

Dare went absolutely motionless. "What are you saying?" he asked carefully, measuring his words. Modulating his tone.

Heron removed his spectacles. "I am saying there is little left."

Little left . . . ? "How little?"

"In terms of actual monies?" The other man removed a kerchief and mopped at his suddenly damp brow.

Oh, bloody hell. This was bad.

"Many avowals have been called in, and debtors are seeking to secure repayment for monies loaned."

It did not escape Dare's notice that the bespectacled servant had failed to give the number he sought. Nor could there be any doubting the reason why . . .

There was nothing?

He glanced around at the room's silent occupants: the duke and duchess, the young lady. That trio remained impressive masters of their emotions and expressions.

Dare sat up slowly. "Is this some manner of jest?" he snapped.

"I fear not," the duke said in sad tones. "Upon your father's death"— *God rot the hateful bastard's soul*—"the title passed to your brother, who, as you since have learned, passed." At that, the duchess dissolved into a quiet show of weeping, dabbing at her eyes. "He ventured into trade."

And Dare wouldn't safely wager a pence that the older woman was crying about the work her departed grandson had taken part in.

"Aren't there rules amongst you people that lords don't dabble in trade?" Dare asked impatiently. "Dirty hands and all?" Of all people, his brother would have known that.

The duchess gave a pleased nod. "Even gone all these years, he knows as much," she said to her husband. "Your brother couldn't have had the same foresight," she muttered to herself.

"Yes, but it was promising to be lucrative," the duke said with a defensiveness on the departed man's past that not a single member of Dare's former family had ever shown to him.

And the irony was not lost on Dare that this should have proven the one time his paragon of a brother, preferred and always dutiful, had chosen to do something other than that which was expected of him as a lord.

He felt . . . an unexpected wave of sadness that he'd not ever been around to see that different side of Perrin. Perrin, who, in Dare's absence, had also become "Perry," that more playful name not at all suiting the serious boy he'd been.

Feeling a stare on him, he looked and found Kinsley eyeing him with a sad little glimmer in her eyes.

Then as quickly as that softening had come, it was gone.

Kinsley Greyson smiled, and it was an expression Dare recognized all too well. Cold and hard and taunting, it was the same grin he had affected in the streets when dealing with his foes. "Disappointed, I trust?"

"Be quiet, Kin," the duke said tersely. He turned back to Dare. "It bears stating that it was not your brother's ventures that sank the fortunes."

Dare stared at him. Then how else was there to account—

"Him," the duchess seethed.

"A distant cousin inherited after Perrin's passing"—His Grace took over the telling—"and he was—"

"Is," Lady Kinsley piped in.

"*Is* a scapegrace." His Grace shook his head regretfully. "Spent it all. On wagering and women and—"

"Harold," the duchess gasped.

Color filled the older man's cheeks. "Other things. Lavish parties. The finest brandy and other spirits. Not a pence was spared."

Not a pence was spared . . .

If you'd only returned when Connor Steele searched you out . . . Then, however, Dare had been so confident he wanted no part of the nobility. He'd happily banished the detective from London.

And in the ultimate twist of irony, with an untimely trip to the gallows, Dare had found himself forced back to the place he'd sworn to never be, only to find everything that mattered here gone.

Heron cleared his throat. "The entailed, as well as the unentailed, properties are largely . . . bankrupt."

"I gathered as much, Heron," Dare snapped. This would be the moment the rambling servant thought required clarity.

Dare *would* have been resurrected to the role of marquess, only to inherit a bankrupt title. His bloody *luck*.

Suddenly, the hilarity of it all hit him. Kicking his legs up, he propped the heels of his boots near the papers Heron had set out . . .

and slowly laughed. "You brought me back here, and dragged this out a week, now, only to tell me . . ." He looked to the man-of-affairs.

The spectacled, wiry fellow cleared his throat. "There is nothing," he clarified.

"I thank you for saving my neck." He shoved to his feet. "But this has been a waste. I want an accounting of what is mine, free and clear, to sell, and the value of the properties that I'm also free to sell." He eyed the furnishings . . . threadbare and old. But good enough to fetch some funds.

He'd strip the whole estate, take what he could, and then go.

The duchess grabbed her cane and struggled to stand. "What? Where are you going?" She glanced frantically at her husband. "Where is he going?"

Dare ignored the glare Lady Kinsley turned on him. Not that the woman was a sister to him in any way. Nor, for that matter, did Dare intend to remain here.

He started for the door.

"The way I see it, Darius, you have two options afforded you," the duke called out.

Pausing, Dare turned back. "Oh?"

"One . . . you might remain here and become the marquess you are."

That wasn't an option. That wasn't even a consideration any longer. He folded his arms. "I trust option two is completing my walk to the gallows?"

His Grace snorted. "There's some family whom I'd let to that fate. You aren't one of them. I'm not going to let my grandson hang."

And Dare found himself having to mask his surprise at that unexpected display of humor from this duke . . . and that matter-of-fact defense of him. He nudged his chin at the old duke. "Option two, then?"

"You can go back to living the life you've lived"—Pemberly's mouth tensed and moved, as if he were struggling to get his next words out—"picking pockets."

Picking pockets. That was what the whole of the world believed Dare's crime to be. Society—and certainly not those of Pemberly's station—could imagine no grander scale of thievery. One where Dare stole from the wealthiest, the men and women Dare's newly found family likely called friends and certainly brushed elbows with. "I prefer the latter." Dare spoke without inflection. "Though I do . . . appreciate your intervention on my behalf."

"Let him go, Grandfather," Kinsley said briskly. "He's made his decision. You've already wasted enough of your time."

Yes, Dare trusted the young lady would far prefer that outcome to welcoming a street rat into the fold of her family.

Pemberly ignored his granddaughter. "If you carry on with this life, you're eventually going to hang, Darius. I won't always be able to intervene."

Yes, Dare had always known what fate awaited him. It was why he'd sought to avoid true entanglements.

A memory slid in.

I cannot quite decide which is more perilous to my heart, Dare Grey: a life without you or one with you, knowing you'll one day be gone . . .

"I know that," he murmured, forcing back those memories he'd not allowed himself. Since his near hanging, however, she, Temperance, had wound her way back into his thoughts at the oddest of times.

If only I could entice you to stay, Dare . . .

"Perhaps I might entice you to stay?"

For a moment, the past blended with the present, and Dare struggled to sort his way through which was real.

Pemberly stared squarely back. And for all the ways in which the duke was in full command of himself, it was his eyes. That weakness Dare wagered the other man didn't know he possessed. And just then, those intent eyes hinted at the old man's fear—that Dare would walk away rather than hear him out.

Dare, however, had never been too proud to entertain any proposal put to him. It was how he'd built his reputation and created the existence he had for himself. Returning to his seat, Dare nudged his chin. "I'm listening."

Kinsley shot to her feet. "This is madness!" she exclaimed. "You don't need him, Grandfather. Look what the last man who had no place being the marquess did to this family."

There was the faintest stirring of curiosity about the fellow who'd come before Dare. Not enough, however, for him to ask questions.

In the end, he needn't have asked, as the duke provided answers to those unspoken ones anyway. "The woe of distant cousins without any meaningful connection to a title," the old man went on with a sad shake of his head.

"Don't let him manipulate you, Grandfather," Lady Kinsley pleaded. When not even a facial muscle ticked in Pemberly's wrinkled face, the young woman turned to the duchess. "Grandmother, you must make him see reason. He doesn't need to entertain this"—she slashed a hand in Dare's direction—"miscreant."

Dare curled his lips at one corner. "Miscreant." He touched the brim of an imagined hat. "That is certainly the politest of the insults I've been dealt."

Kinsley surged forward. "This is all a game to you," she spat.

The duchess shot the end of her cane up, halting the young lady's charge. "Sit down this instant, Kinsley Daria Greyson."

Daria Greyson.

His chest clenched.

They'd named her after him.

The replacement babe that she'd been.

And he hated there was any feeling or reaction on his part to that truth.

As if she'd caught Dare's notice of her name, Lady Kinsley jutted her chin out, anger burning from her eyes.

"Now," the duchess said when Lady Kinsley, her cheeks flushed red, reclaimed the seat beside her. "No one takes advantage of your grandfather, dear. *No one.*"

The younger lady jabbed a finger in Dare's direction. "But one such as him is not—"

"Enough," the duke commanded. "Now, if I may resume." His wasn't a question. "The cousin to claim Perrin's"—he grimaced—"your and your father's title was a distant, distant cousin. The young man squandered all the funds your brother had managed to restore to the estates—"

"Whoring," Lady Kinsley spat.

The duchess gasped. *"Kinsley."*

"It is true," the girl said defensively, with more of a world-weariness than Dare would have expected of a lady of her situation. "All men are the same."

"Yes, well, it is true, but we needn't speak of it," His Grace said, ending the debate between his wife and granddaughter. "My title isn't yours. Nor will my entailed properties pass to you. However, what I do have . . ."

Dare's ears pricked up. "I'm listening."

Kinsley Greyson scoffed. *"Of course* you are."

Dare ignored the young woman's mutterings.

"You've not had an easy life, Darius. I don't know what your struggles have been, but you deserve more than the bankrupt estate that some spendthrift scoundrel left you. Of course, your father would have been wiser to have his fortunes secured in a way that they were better protected."

Kinsley stiffened but kept quiet through the old duke's blunt insult of her late father.

Their late father?

"Do not blame Papa. He couldn't have imagined Perrin would die."

"A nobleman is always prepared to look after generations of descendants, dear, and had your father done so, we wouldn't be where we are now," the duke said in gentle but insistent tones meant to end any further debate.

Lady Kinsley, however, proved her stubbornness once more. "That isn't true. You've not even given proper time to see the outcome of the investments Perrin made. These matters . . . They take time."

"The debt is enormous, and the creditors have begun calling," the duke said flatly in frosty tones. "Whatever it is or might have been or wasn't matters not." He motioned about the room. "Here we are."

The duke thumped his cane. "Leave us, Kinsley."

Fire lit the woman's eyes, and her tense mouth moved as if she fought the challenge there, but then, with a sharp glare in Dare's direction, she sailed from the room.

After she'd gone, the duke turned to his wife. "If I may speak to the boy alone, dearest?"

And without any of the same obstinance of the granddaughter who'd preceded her, Her Grace filed out.

When Dare, the duke, and his servant were alone, the greying gentleman focused his gaze on Dare.

Dare tensed. Now that the women were gone, the duke didn't have to bother with sensibilities or pretend niceness. Dare knew exactly how the nobility operated.

Or rather, he thought he did. The duke spoke and threw that all-knowing assumption into question.

"I want you to know, Darius," the duke murmured, "I never believed you were dead."

"Why, thank you for that faith," he said dryly. Of course, it begged the question why, if the old duke had been so very confident, he'd certainly not gone out of his way to find him. Dare was unable to tamp down that bitter resentment. Except . . . resentment would have to mean he cared. Which he didn't.

"Each year," His Grace went on, "I set aside funds for when you returned, Darius."

And yet the duke had been more wrong than he'd known. The grandson he recalled, the one he'd held out hope of again seeing . . . Darius Greyson was as dead as if he were gone and buried. And accepting that was easier than thinking that there might have been people who'd actually wished for his return.

In the end, it was far simpler to ask about the money awaiting him than to think about the duke longing for the return of his missing grandson. "How much?"

"Twenty thousand pounds."

And Dare, who'd long been a master of concealment, dissolved into a fit, choking and strangling on nothing more than his own swallow.

Twenty thousand . . .

Dare couldn't even complete the remainder of that amount in his mind.

Leaning over, the duke banged him between the shoulder blades.

It was a fortune.

The kind of funds that would ensure countless men and women and children saved and comfortably set up in situations different from the miserable ones in which they found themselves.

The duke didn't resume speaking until Dare had regained the ability to draw an even breath. "I've a fortune saved and available for you." There was a slight pause. "A fortune that I can give you."

All Dare's senses went on alert. "Oh?" It didn't escape him, the key word that had fallen in the very middle of the duke's sentence—*can.*

Not "would."

Not "intend to."

"Can."

And "can" implied strings attached.

Of course, what did you think? A duke intended to simply turn over a fortune to you?

Even *if* the old man held some sentimentality for the boy he'd once known. "What do you want?" Dare asked bluntly.

His Grace didn't mince words. "For you to look after your sister."

And just like that, the illusive hint of a dream withered on the vine of hope. "She doesn't seem to be one in need of looking after or, for that matter, wanting my assistance."

The duke rested a hand on Dare's arm, reminiscent of the way he had when Dare was a small child. "You know that isn't true. All women require looking after."

There was only a partial truth to the duke's words. In making women property and chattel of their fathers and husbands, society had thrust women into that precarious state where marriage was a prison and yet could also represent escape.

I want to see you protected, Temperance . . . I want to see you safe . . .

The duke continued speaking, and Dare welcomed the diversion from thoughts of . . . her. "If I give you those monies, Darius, you'll be gone."

"Aye," he allowed. And he'd never look back. Because nothing good could come from doing so. Not truly. He'd committed himself to never being bound to any place. "You are not wrong." He'd never bind himself to anyone . . . *Although that isn't altogether true,* a voice taunted. For there had been one person. One act . . . of folly. Of weakness. Dare shoved those thoughts of Temperance far away in his mind. "Why is it so important to you that I return?" he asked flatly. Once upon a lifetime ago, the old duke might have "dear boy'd" him and teased him, but they didn't have that relationship any longer. More, they had no relationship, and never would. The sooner the duke accepted that, the better off he'd be. "What use do I serve to you?"

A frown chased away the smile on His Grace's lips. "Is that how you view the world, Darius? With suspicion and cynicism?"

That was the kindest, most generous way in which he viewed the world. Dare, who'd lived firsthand its cruelty and ruthlessness. "What do you want?" he repeated quietly.

His Grace chuckled and thumped Dare on the back. "I do appreciate your honesty, grandson." His levity was replaced by a tangible worry in the ancient lines of his wrinkled cheeks. "Kinsley has no fortune of her own, and, well, she's an example of the peril an unmarried woman finds herself in when we are no longer here. If you go, I'll be left trying to find an answer to the question of what happens to your sister."

His sister . . . Kinsley . . . All those words, completely foreign. It was a singularly odd way to think of the stranger who'd stepped out of the room, who but for her obstinance bore no hint of a connection to Dare.

"When your grandmother and I are gone, and you eventually hang"—the duke spoke plainly of Dare's death—"your cousin returns to the role of marquess."

The scoundrel and spendthrift . . .

"What are you proposing?" he said flatly.

"Stay around long enough to see your sister married off. She has no fortune of her own, and if the estates revert to your cousin, that cad will likely just let her starve."

Dare took all that in. "In order for me to secure monies that, according to you, were always intended for me, you plan to keep me as a hostage?"

The duke's eyes twinkled. "If you consider living in Mayfair with a houseful of servants to tend your needs and no worries about a hangman's noose awaiting you being held hostage? Then yes."

Tension whipped through him, and, restless, Dare wandered over to the window, looking down upon the clean streets below. Lords and ladies in their finest morning dress strolled down the pavement, while along the cobblestones, young lords and gleaming carriages passed at a steady clip. Lady Kinsley wasn't his concern. She wasn't a sister to him. Not really. And yet . . . even as he wanted that to hold true, there was an unwanted concern about what should happen to her if he walked out . . . "So you want me to stay until she's married?"

"Yes, and, well, I'd hoped you could form a relationship with her while you are here. Get to know her. Squire her about *ton* events. Balls. Soirees. Dinner parties. The customary," he said with a flippant wave of his hand.

The customary? Get to know her? Squire her about? Had the duke even witnessed Dare and the lady's volatile exchanges? "And then what?"

"And then, as I said, after she is married, you may leave. If you want to, of course," the duke tacked on.

Oh, he'd want to.

Only something in the duke's tone gave him pause. That perception a product of learning that when anything appeared too good, invariably it was. "Why do I think there is more?"

The duke's smile was back in place. "Because you are my grandson and far too clever by half, Darius."

"Is she . . . amenable to marriage?"

The duke stretched his arms wide. "Aren't all women, Darius?"

"Dare," he corrected. It was time the old nobleman disabuse himself of the notion that Dare was the grandchild of his remembrances. The one he sought to reel back into Polite Society.

He considered what the duke had presented him with. Of course his *grandfather* was correct. Kinsley was a lady, born of privilege and a distinguished lineage she'd railed at him for not caring enough about. As such, she'd be bound by those constraints. Ones that Dare had never conformed to, and his father had loathed him for his refusal to do so.

"I see you're thinking about it," the duke cajoled. "All you'll need to do is look after her for one Season."

How matter-of-fact the other man was. How very casually he spoke, as if Dare returning to this life would be no different from switching off one set of garments for another. But this? He repressed a shudder. What the hell did Dare know of squiring a lady about the Town? Or being a chaperone who assessed the suitability of potential suitors? He'd been born to this world, but he'd never really belonged to it. His father had made that clear to him often. No, the task the duke asked of Dare required a woman who could deal with Kinsley and help her navigate a—

Dare stilled.

For there was . . . *one* woman. One who'd prove fearless in that role.

Someone who would rather see you dead than ever see you again . . .

The idea turned in his mind, over and over.

And yet . . . there would be good at the end of it. He wasn't so naive as to believe he couldn't do his work from this posh side of London. He didn't want to, but not having what he wanted was something he'd become accustomed to long ago. "I'll do it," he said quietly, because in the scheme of what the duke offered, his living here in this foreign world was a small sacrifice.

One he could always run from if the task proved impossible . . .

"Splendid, boy," the duke said. "The terms will be drawn up by Heron." The servant was already frantically scribbling notes upon a page. "With my support, you'll have entry to any event your heart wishes." Dare's heart wished for none of it. "Anything is yours."

"Except your twenty thousand pounds without me serving in the role of nursemaid to that viper," he muttered.

The duke waggled his eyebrows. "That *viper*, as you refer to her, is in fact your sister." He paused. "That being said, I'm mindful to not place all this solely upon you."

His back went up. "I'm listening." *Again.* The duke, with his ability to dangle just enough intriguing bits of information, was a master of manipulation, and therefore one to be watched . . . and mistrusted.

"It is hardly fair to tie you entirely to someone else's fate and future."

"Isn't that what you are doing, *Your Grace?*" he asked, layering heavy sarcasm within that question.

The duke looked offended. "*Of course not.* Looking after your sister is the duty any brother should and would be responsible for." Dare didn't disagree with him there. "But let us say for whatever reason, she doesn't make a match . . ."

Dare straightened. His earlier reservations, the very question he'd wondered at, reared its head. "And is that a real possibility?"

"Darius, she was born the daughter of a marquess and the grand-daughter of a duke." His Grace spoke in lofty tones. "Do you truly think she's going to have difficulty securing an offer for her hand?"

The immediate answer was yes. If Kinsley Greyson turned on others the venom and ice she had upon Dare, all that would remain in terms of suitors would be those she'd poisoned or frozen.

But members of Polite Society? They weren't most men. They were a very small few, the sorts of men who overlooked anything in the name of their precious bloodlines and craving for even greater connections.

"No," he allowed. "I trust noblemen will overlook . . . much."

The duke laughed. "Indeed they do, Darius," he said, thumping him hard on the back once more. "Indeed they do." He let his arm fall, and moving so that he stood shoulder to shoulder alongside Dare, taking in the same sights below, the duke stared down at the passing lords and ladies. "But in this hypothetical scenario, where those gentlemen do not see your sister for the diamond of the first waters she is . . ."

Dare strangled back a laugh. Surly as she was ruthless, she was many things, but a diamond she wasn't.

Clasping his hands at his back, His Grace continued speaking. "I like to believe I am a model of fairness. As such, there should be other terms in place to ensure that your ability to earn those twenty thousand pounds is within your complete control."

Dare stared at the glass panes. "Oh?"

"There are only two ways to ensure your sister is properly cared for—"

"A husband?"

The duke nodded. "Yes, a husband." There was a long and deliberate pause, and his entire body tensing, Dare looked back. "Or a babe."

Dumbfounded, it was a moment before Dare could respond. And when he did, he swallowed wrong and choked, strangling on his own spit.

The duke gave him another thump on the back.

"I-I hardly s-see how a b-babe can l-look after her."

"Of course it can. A boy babe, that is." With that, the duke gestured to the forgotten man-of-affairs, and some kind of unspoken communication passed between those two, for Heron nodded and began flipping through his folders.

"A boy babe," Dare echoed, feeling like the only one not knowing what was expected of him. Or what was being said, exactly.

"An heir," the duke clarified. "If the estate can go to your son, there wouldn't be a worry about your cousin returning and running it in your stead."

And *then* it hit Dare. An heir. "I am *not* having a child." There was a permanency to babes and children. They represented a greater—nay, the *ultimate*—connection and dependence than Dare was willing to have.

There also required the matter of a wife with whom to have that babe . . .

That was an absolute impossibility.

The duke shrugged. "Then you'll just have to see your sister married."

How simple he made it sound. And yet . . . that possibility? An angry, snarling Lady Kinsley landing some lord? That was a greater possibility . . . a greater reality than Dare having a child.

"Do you have the contract drawn up?" His Grace called over to his busily working man-of-affairs.

"I do," the servant said in his nasally tones.

Adjusting an already flawless lapel, the duke looked to Dare once more. "I've had that last part included, regardless, as a safety measure."

"What part?" Dare asked slowly.

"Well, you cannot have a babe without a wife. That is, not an heir." And with that casual deliverance, His Grace headed for the door.

Dare stood rooted to the floor, staring at the retreating duke's back. *"Whaaaat?"*

His grandfather cast a bemused look back. "You need a wife to have an heir, and as such, I've included those terms in our contract."

"Terms?" He strangled on that lone syllable.

The duke shrugged. "Our agreement is also contingent upon you getting yourself married." He gave a dismissive wave. "That way, if you need to fall back on term two, you'll be able to." The old duke may as well have thrown up London Bridge between Dare and the damned treasure at the end of it all.

At his silence, the duke gave him a long look. "I trust those terms won't pose a problem?"

Those terms, as in Dare finding a wife? The other man may as well have spoken of Dare swapping out his coarse wool pants for a new tailored suit.

"No, Your Grace," Dare said in even tones.

"Splendid. I take it this has been a great deal for you to take in. I'll give you five days to reflect, and then we'll speak further on these terms."

The moment the duke sailed out with the man-of-affairs close at his heels, Dare swiped a hand over his face.

Remaining here in the fancy end of London and squiring a shrewish sister about Polite Society would be a hell all its own.

But producing . . . a wife?

That didn't pose a problem. It proved a damned catastrophe.

Chapter 4

The six-o'clock hour was a seamstress's favorite.

It didn't mean that was when the day ended and rest came. For there really wasn't rest for the seamstress. It was, however, a time when one was spared the misery of an endless stream of thankless patrons and customers.

And then after the shop was tidied came the next set of work— constructing the most recent orders.

It was a harsh profession that left women with bloodied fingers and aching backs and strained necks.

And yet it was one Temperance gave thanks for each day.

Because having lived in the most ruthless ends of London with a drunkard for a father and a washerwoman as a mother, she'd witnessed firsthand the options that existed for the masses.

And at least with her own hands, she was in charge of her fate.

And when she was working, she wasn't allowed to think.

About the past.

About the regrets.

And there were so many of them.

All of them revolving around one.

Over the years, she'd managed to organize her past, to break it up into neat little compartments which she then divided into drawers within her mind that she kept firmly shut.

But sometimes a thought wedged its way in, and the memories slipped around.

And it had taken nothing more than a parting statement from her brother to Gwynn at their last meeting.

Someday, we'll be together. Forever . . .

I cannot promise you forever . . .

Different words. Such a different vow.

"Are you all right?" Gwynn asked.

Temperance started. "Fine." It was a lie . . . one that she'd make true. Eventually. Soon. When she managed to make herself forget him—Dare Grey, a perfectly bold name for a man who'd commanded the Rookeries . . . and her heart.

I will not think of him . . . I will not think of him . . .

Quickening her steps, Temperance noted the bolts of blue fabric that had been hastily pulled and left upon the wrong table. She gathered them up and started across the room. Work was good. Work helped. It brought exhaustion and escape.

It had to.

It always had.

The shop clean once more, Temperance dusted her palms together.

"You're not done," Natalie Forde, the eternal pessimist of the shop, pointed out from the other end of the table.

No, she wasn't. But this was, despite the fatigue and toil of the day, the moment Temperance lived for. The joy she found in creating. It was some small measure of control she had. There, she could lose her mind in another task.

Temperance found her way to her neat worktable . . . and came to an abrupt stop. A groan escaped her. *"Noooooo."*

"What was that?" Natalie asked.

Temperance ignored the question, her gaze locked on the sight before her, one that remained unchanging: three swaths of heinous pink fabric.

Madame Amelie was testing her. There was nothing else for it.

Muttering a litany of frustrated curses under her breath, she sank onto the edge of the stool, and lowering her forehead onto the table, she knocked it lightly against the surface. And in the greatest of ironies, that garish fabric softened each little, deliberate blow.

"Is there something the matter, Mrs. Swift?"

Temperance gasped and jerked herself upright so quickly her already strained muscles screamed their protest.

Madame Amelie swept deeper into the room, the curtains fluttering at her back.

Temperance forced herself to focus on her work. "No, of course not, Madame Amelie." Everything was the matter. It was this gown and this client, but she knew better than to say as much.

"Because it sounded as though you were cursing and banging your head." The woman ignored those false assurances she'd given.

Temperance forced a laugh. "Of course not. Whyever would I be cursing?" Between the resurfaced memories of her greatest mistake and the pink disaster before her, she couldn't even force any believability into that lie.

"I don't know," the tall, statuesque proprietress said dryly. "But why would you challenge Mrs. Marmlebury's choice of pink? There's no explanation for these things."

And it was that underlying droll humor that sometimes reared itself and left Temperance wondering about the stern, driven proprietress.

Madame Amelie narrowed her eyes.

So the woman didn't intend to let go that recent grievance.

Temperance weighed her response. The woman had started as a seamstress herself . . . She'd built a business of her own. Mayhap she could be reasoned with. "These are the fabrics she selected, Madame Amelie." Temperance gestured to the eclectic collection of varying shades of pink. "She wants them all incorporated into a ball gown."

Though what anyone in the Cotswolds would have need of a ball gown for remained to be seen.

Madame Amelie's features remained unbending. "And?" she asked coolly.

And this wasn't the fine end of London, where ladies flitted from ball to soiree to grand dinner fete. She'd never say as much. Not when the woman took such pride in being one of the most successful proprietors in the Cotswolds. As such, Temperance weighed her words.

When she at last spoke, Temperance kept her features calm and placid, a skill she'd perfected as a girl seeking to avoid brutal beatings at the hands of her father, Abaddon Swift. "I've seen your masterpieces, Madame Amelie; I know that you know—"

"Don't patronize me, Mrs. Swift." The other woman cut her off with an impatient tinge in her tone. "I'm not a compliment-seeker, I'm a coin-earner. And you"—she jabbed a finger at Temperance—"earn your coin, and whatever it is you care to design or think you know more of, always remember"—*The client is always in the right*—"the client is always correct."

There it was. A slight variation, but the meaning and the message always the same.

"Tell me, Mrs. Swift: Are you a wealthy woman?"

"No," she said between her teeth, already knowing where this familiar line of questioning went. Nor would she ever be one. She was a worker and would never be anything more.

"Do you have a hidden fortune? A protector, perhaps?"

She paused as a face flashed behind her mind's eye. *Not* a protector. A vise cinched about her heart and squeezed at that organ. It was too fresh.

"Mrs. Swift?"

"There's no protector," Temperance made herself say. She was the one who saw to her own security . . . and to her brother and Gwynn's.

Her employer, three inches taller than Temperance's impressive five feet seven inches, leaned down. "Then I'd suggest you be more focused on earnings and less on what color of pink Mrs. Marmlebury wants this time."

And that was what marked them as different in their craft. Oh, it wasn't that Temperance had the luxury of wealth and security . . . She didn't. She had coin enough to put food in her belly and, come winters, heat the fire some. No, she was not safe. No one truly was. Even so, there was something inside Temperance that couldn't separate from that inherent need—a creative urging that was like a hungering to be fed. For the sense of control it offered, when there was so little . . . of anything in her life.

The tinny bell at the front of the shop jingled, interrupting her musings, and more—Madame Amelie's diatribe. "Who would be here at this hour?" Temperance asked.

"A client is a client, regardless of what time they arrive." The proprietress glanced at the cameo clock affixed to her breast. "See to her."

And ordinarily Temperance would have wept at being torn away from sewing in order to take a client. But this proved a reprieve from the dress she'd be forced to construct. Hurrying through the curtains, she rushed to greet the villager—

Stumbling to a stop, she caught the edge of a table to keep herself upright.

For it wasn't a villager.

It wasn't a patron.

Or even, for that matter, a woman.

It was . . . a ghost. One from her past; a man whose memory haunted her when she least expected it. Only he was here now, before her.

Sweat slicked her skin; it left her flesh clammy and her mouth dry. *I'm seeing things. There is nothing else for it.*

She blinked rapidly . . . and yet the sight remained.

He remained.

A buzzing filled her ears, a thousand hornets set loose around her mind, adding to the hum of confusion there.

Over the years, she'd seen him in the unlikeliest places. Ofttimes in her mind. Others, in the shadows of the strangers around her. And yet she'd blink and he'd be gone, and she'd be reminded all over again of the man whom she'd wed in a night of folly.

But in all the ways she'd seen him, she had never seen him like this. In elegant wool and impeccable garments perfectly tailored to his person. And very much . . . real.

Doffing the high top hat, Dare flashed a pearl-white, devil-may-care grin. "Hullo. We meet again . . . wife."

⚬

For years—more specifically, that last time when she had turned him away—he'd occasionally allowed himself to think of this moment.

Of seeing Temperance Grey again.

He'd let it play out in his mind . . . how he wanted that imagined meeting to go. How he'd wanted their last real meeting to play out. There would have been tender looks and joyous laughter.

Now, as they—two strangers—studied one another, he let himself drink in the sight of her as he'd not when in the bowels of Newgate. Her waist was still narrow, and yet where there'd been something almost coltish in her frame, time had lent a maturity to her form; her hips were slightly wider, her breasts fuller.

Just then, she wetted her full lips, and he recalled all the times he'd kissed that mouth.

What he'd not anticipated was just how potent the desire to again taste that flesh would be.

And suddenly the onerous chore his grandfather had given him didn't seem so very bad, after all.

He took a step toward her, and the wide plank floorboards groaned under his heel.

And with his every movement, Temperance remained absolutely stock-still.

Dare made himself stop, allowing her the space she required.

"You're not real," she whispered.

"I told you, the noose can't hold me," he said softly. How many times had he uttered that very phrase to her? Offered that bold assurance before then going out to fleece a lord?

She used to swat his arm and scold him for his arrogance.

Time, however, had transformed her. She'd always been in control of herself around everyone . . . except him. With him, she'd always been a tempest. Now she was all blank nothingness . . . and his heart ached at those changes. The ones time had wrought. Or mayhap it had been him.

"I *don't understand.*" She released the death grip she had on the table and clutched those midnight strands that, like the woman herself, had always refused to be tamed. Then, suddenly, she let her arms fall to her sides and took a slow, deep breath. "Why are you here?"

That was what she'd ask.

Abandoning her place at the table, she took a jerky step forward but still kept that barrier between them, and that hurt worse than a physical blow.

"I'm here . . . with the intent of picking up where we left off."

"I don't . . ." She slowly shook her head.

Unbidden, he stretched a hand across the table and stroked his knuckles down the curve of her cheek. "As husband and wife," he murmured.

Some emotion sparked in her green eyes. An emotion he couldn't identify. "You're here . . ."

"To propose an arrangement between us," he said again.

Of course, he'd get to all the details of that later. Having lived the life of a thief, he'd come to appreciate timing, and it would be wise to proceed carefully here.

As it was, she was taking this a good deal better than he'd expected. Mayhap there was hope of her cooperating, after—

Her gaze darkened. "You are bloody mad, Darius Grey. I've no interest," she said coolly. "If that is why you've come, you're wasting your time." She turned to go.

Dare hurried over, placing himself at the end of her path, and that managed to halt her.

A moment anyway. She was already starting down the next aisle, gathering up lace embellishments from nearby tables as she went. "Get out of here, Dare."

Why . . . why . . . the chit was . . . working. She'd already perfectly moved on from both his reemergence and his suggestion.

Dare hurried around to the other end of the table. "I'm not leaving." He'd no other choice. The duke had not given him any.

Temperance stopped once more. Stealing a quick glance toward the back of the shop, she spoke in a quiet whisper. "You had a moment of clarity. Mayhap you saw your life all laid out. Mayhap you were filled with regret of what would never be."

Unnerved at how very accurately she'd read those last moments of his life on the dais, he fought the urge to move.

"Trust me, you are wasting your time. I've no desire to be your wife."

He rested his hip on the edge of the table. "Ah, but that wasn't always the case," he said in silken tones.

She snorted. "Save your seduction for some woman foolish enough to fall for it. Ours isn't a real marriage. It never was, and I've little interest in it ever being one." She moved to step around him. "Now, if you'll excuse me?"

She'd not be swayed, then. God, she was still as put out by his silken tongue as she'd been then. The only thing she had appreciated, the only sentiment she had responded to, was blunt directness. He'd been a fool to attempt anything else where she was concerned.

Dare slid once more into her path, preventing her escape. "I don't have a choice, Temperance," he said flatly, getting to the real reason for his being here. He'd come to accept their at-best tense relationship would never be more. "I need a wife, and whether you wish it or not, that is the role you agreed to."

If eyes could shoot flame, he'd have been a heap of ashes before her.

"Are you saying you'd force me to . . . what? Play at the role of your wife?"

"Yes!" That was a perfect way to describe the arrangement. Her eyes narrowed into dangerous slits. "No," he amended.

"Get out," she said once more. "You're wasting both of our time." With that, she hurried to retrieve the bolts of fabric that had toppled to the floor. As she gathered them up, Dare studied her. So focused on the reason for seeking her out and the need to convince her, he'd not, until this moment, thought about just where he'd found her.

All these years, this was where she'd been. He glanced about at the ribbons hanging from the ceiling, and the satin and silk fabrics neatly arranged upon the tables. "It makes so much sense," he murmured to himself.

Arms laden with those long bolts, she set about returning them to their proper places.

"And what is that?" she asked crisply.

"You always sewed."

"I darned socks."

"You stitched my garments whenever I required."

"Which wasn't often," she said, an almost wistful quality to her voice. "You always had funds enough."

Stolen funds.

This, what his grandfather had presented him with, was an opportunity to secure money, free and clear, for him to use as he would . . . without risking his neck.

Dare passed his gaze over her as she flitted about the shop, seeing to her work.

"You were so very good at what you did, Temperance." She gave no indication that she'd heard that praise. "This was the perfect place for you to go. To escape—"

She spun about. "Not another word."

"I am sorry. I should not have mentioned . . ." *Him.* The one who'd hurt her. A monster of a father who'd made her do desperate things, such as marrying Dare. Steering his words and thoughts away from those demons, he tried a different tack. "I should not have mentioned anything about the past," he settled for. "And yet there is no way around speaking of it."

Her full lips formed a hard line.

She didn't say anything, however, and he was encouraged.

Dare strolled slowly toward her. "Nor was it all bad, Temperance," he said quietly. Of its own volition, his hand came up, and he brushed his knuckles lightly along a jawline that was slightly too firm and wide, but that had always managed to lend her a beauty that was unique and interesting for it.

Her skin was satiny soft and warm.

The faintest of trembles shook her slender frame, and there was, since he'd arrived, a moment of triumph. Furious as she was with him and at his arrival, she was affected by his touch, still.

Dare continued brushing his knuckles in a light up-and-down sweep. God, how he'd missed touching her. How he'd missed her. Even as there had always been tension and fire between them, there'd been something more, too . . . He lowered his head, bringing his lips close to hers, and their breaths mingled together, hers bearing the hint of honey she'd always dashed in her tea.

Temperance's long, smoky lashes fluttered.

"There was so much that was good . . . so much that was right between us," he whispered huskily. "A reunion between us wouldn't be all bad. In fact"—he dusted his palm over her lower lip—"it can be good, Temperance. It can be so very good in some ways."

It was the wrong thing to say.

He knew the moment her eyes flew open that he'd gone too far.

Oh, bloody hell.

She grabbed the scissors. "Are you trying to seduce me, Darius?" she hissed.

"Uh . . . sway you? Which is not altogether—"

She brought those gleaming blades up higher.

Rethinking his words, Dare took several hasty—and, by the fire in her eyes, wise—steps back.

Alas, where he'd once been capable of charming her, she met his efforts with only ice in her eyes. "Your time here is done, Grey."

And for the first time since he'd set out to the Cotswolds, panic rooted around his belly. He'd convinced himself that she could be persuaded.

Not that you've done a spectacular job of swaying the damned woman . . .

"I need you, Temperance," he said bluntly, dropping all attempts at seduction and sway. He opted instead for cool, hard logic.

Temperance clutched her scissors close . . . but she did lower them. "Get. Out."

"I'm asking you to hear me ou—"

"Get. Out," she repeated, her voice creeping up an octave.

Footsteps came rushing from the back of the shop. A moment later, a trio of women came staggering into the front room, each seamstress bumping into the one before her.

The severe, Spartan woman at their front looked to Dare and Temperance, her gaze lingering on the scissors pointed upright at Dare's chest. "Whatever is the meaning of this?" she demanded.

"Madame Amelie." Temperance hastily lowered her scissors. It did not escape his notice that she retained a hold on that weapon. She'd always been endlessly resourceful.

As if she'd followed his silent praise and disapproved, Temperance glared at him. "This man, he has no place here. I've asked him to go." Her eyes bored into his. "Which he is."

"Actually, I'm not." God, how much fun it had always been to tease her. It had been ever more fun when she'd laughed and teased him in return. Now, there was only an icy hatred . . .

"Very well." She looked him squarely in the eyes. "I'm telling you now. Leave."

A thoroughly befuddled-looking Madame Amelie looked back and forth between Dare and Temperance. "Whatever is the meaning of this, Mrs. Swift?"

She'd used her previous name . . . different from the one he'd conferred to her upon their marriage, and instead belonging to the monster who'd sired her. It was an inconsequential point to note and even more peculiar that it should sting.

When neither answered, Madame Amelie put a question directly to Dare. "Are you a . . . thief?" She proved shockingly on the mark. Just not in the way she thought.

A smile twitched at his lips. "I'm a marquess." Temperance's eyebrows went flying to her hairline. "The Marquess of Milford." He knew that when presented with the truth of his title, none would ever notice he'd evaded that question.

Murmurings rose amongst the audience of women now watching.

Madame Amelie clapped her hands once. That crowd instantly dissolved, scurrying back through the black velvet curtain.

The woman was instantly all smiles. "Are you a client, then?"

He and Temperance spoke at the same time.

"No."

"Yes?" He flashed a smile at the tall woman. "I *could* be."

Temperance's furious stare fairly singed. It wasn't the first time he'd been the recipient of that heated look.

Madame Amelie sized him up, touching her appraising stare on his garments, the gold chain connected to a heavy gold timepiece. "Forgive Mrs. Swift. Allow me to fetch one of my other—"

"That won't be necessary," he called when she started for the curtain leading to the back. "I would have . . . Mrs. Swift, is it?"

The black-haired minx gnashed her teeth loudly enough that they rattled noisily in the quiet. "It. Is."

"I'm certain any number of your"—he glanced over to the young women who'd slipped out from behind the curtains to watch the *discussion* unfolding—"lovely staff are capable; however, I have very specific requirements that only Mrs. Swift might see to."

Chapter 5

Temperance had been married for just eight months.

That was, eight months before Dare Grey, a thief of everything, not the least of which being her heart, had gone from devoted husband always at her side to his next big theft.

It hadn't been unexpected.

Quite the opposite, in fact, given the terms of their marriage: he would offer her his name as a means of protecting her from her monster of a father, and she'd accept that his life of thieving was his work. She'd understood those terms . . . and accepted them. Having first been best friends, it had made sense. They may have been married only eight months, but they'd been sweethearts for ten years before that. Then he'd gone to rob a wealthy lord in the country, and she'd been left vulnerable, alone to face her father's wrath . . .

In fairness, neither she nor Dare could have anticipated that her father would be more outraged at being thwarted in having control over his daughter than he would be afraid of Dare's influence.

All her muscles seized, and she hurriedly pushed aside thoughts of her father and the night of his last and most violent beating.

Yes, she and Dare had been young lovers, but ones who had never been able to make their lives align because of the work he'd refused to give up and the expectations she had for them . . . as a couple.

And it had been five years since she'd seen him.

Now, she made herself look at him, conversing with Madame Amelie.

How easily he charmed, but then that was why he'd always been able to slip free of the constable or the hangman's noose.

It took a moment to register that the pair had stopped talking and now looked squarely at her.

Something was expected of her . . . on the parts of both her employer and her . . . *husband.* But whatever it was would have required that she be attending the idle chatter they'd been making, while Temperance's mind had swirled with just one truth: he was here.

Now.

It had been five years since he'd come and found her after that big country estate theft. Five years since she'd ordered him gone, and . . . he'd given his vow to do so.

He'd honored that promise.

Until now.

Why?

I have very specific requirements that only Mrs. Swift might see to . . .

Specific requirements, indeed.

She resisted the urge to grind her teeth.

From across the shop, a handful of the young women lingered at the curtain, watching Dare with wide, dazed eyes.

Alas, he'd always had that effect on women.

I was that girl, too. Captivated. Entranced. Besotted.

After all, he'd had that dazzling effect on *nearly everyone.*

"Mrs. Swift?" Madame Amelie said through a strained, patently false smile. "If you would see to . . . whatever His Lordship wishes?"

Temperance clenched her teeth. Make that *everyone.* For even Madame Amelie proved herself capable of being charmed by Darius Grey. None had ever been able to resist his charm or his smile or his requests. Her miserable employer should prove no exception.

When Temperance still didn't formulate words, the head modiste clapped her hands once. "Mrs. Swift will be happy to assist you."

All the girls at her back sprang into movement, filing quickly from the room so that only the three of them remained.

At last, Temperance found her footing. She gave her head a clearing shake. "Actually, I'm not at all interested in helping *His Lordship*." *What is he up to, pretending to be a marquess?*

Bright color splotched Madame Amelie's cheeks. Yes, because none contradicted her. And even as Temperance knew no good could come from daring to publicly challenge her employer, she couldn't stop the words from spilling out. "And as he pointed out, there are any number of girls who will be happy working with him. Now, if you'll excuse me?" Tugging off her apron, Temperance hung it on a nearby hook . . . and marched to the door, through it, and down the flower-lined path.

With each step she took that put her away from the shop and Darius Grey, the cinch in her chest eased. Until she reached the old Roman road that led to her modest cottage . . .

And the implications of what she'd done hit her.

She turned back and stared at the small shop in the near distance. This was . . . not good.

Where her seamstresses were concerned, Madame Amelie held strict expectations, and tolerated little.

Being called out and defied by one of them . . . and in front of a marquess, no less?

With a groan, Temperance scrubbed her hands over her face. No, the only outcome was . . . she would lose her employment.

She'd always been hopelessly without control of her emotions when he was near.

But not like this.

This shock at finding he had not only survived another trip to the gallows but also returned . . .

Her stomach churned.

There'd once been a time when all she'd wanted in the world was to hear those words from his lips.

She let her arms fall back to her sides . . . and her heart lurched as, in the distance, her gaze collided with him. Marching forward . . . toward her. Those long, graceful, and more purposeful steps carried him ever closer.

And even as everything said "run," this time she curled her toes sharply and made herself stay planted. She'd been running from the thought and memory of Darius Grey from the moment she'd met him. He was the ghost that would always be there, and the only way to have the closure she required was to face him head-on.

Dare came loping over the slight rise, his palms aloft, a grin on his lips.

He always wore a grin.

Even now.

It was a fact she'd always marveled and puzzled over.

"Thank you for waiting," he said when he reached her.

"Did I have a choice?" Temperance quirked an eyebrow. "I expected that you wouldn't stop." And as such, it made far more sense to just hear him out and, more importantly, make *him* hear *her* out. Hear that she'd no intention of resuming any manner of life with him.

"You've always been practical." There was a wistful quality to his murmuring. He reached a palm up, and Temperance recoiled this time, wisely putting a safe step between them.

His touch had always been magic, but she knew all too well the peril in magic.

He let his arm fall to his side. "You have every reason to be upset with me," he said in more somber tones than she recalled ever hearing from him.

"Which reason do you refer to? Your costing me my work?" *Or your vowing to stay with me and then . . . not.* It took a physical effort to call those words back. The pain of those darkest days, ones that had come when he'd gone gallivanting off to steal from some reprobate lord in the country, was still as fresh now as it'd been.

Dare touched a hand to his chest. "Hear me out . . . please."

Please. He'd been the only man she'd ever known in the Rookeries who'd not been ashamed to say "please" and who thanked people. He'd not just taken everything as his due, as all the harshest, most ruthless men in East London had.

It was one of the reasons she'd first found herself so captivated by him.

He'd been an oddity in their world . . . the world that she'd managed to leave behind when she came here and started anew.

Or she'd thought she had. Her gaze slid beyond him to the establishment she'd built a safe, stable future within. And how quickly she'd lost it all. She forced her focus back to him. "I don't see as I have much choice but to listen to you," she said bitterly, resenting him once more for new reasons.

"If I was more a scoundrel than I already am, I'd let you to that opinion and secure your assistance." Dare rested a palm against the gnarled bark of the oak, his arms straining the magnificent fabric of his finely tailored black tailcoat.

And she hated her eyes for being so very drawn to the bulge of his biceps. She worked her stare over his gloriously masculine fr—

He lifted a quizzical brow. Her cheeks heated several degrees as she whipped her gaze firmly, squarely back on his face. And *only* his face.

"You want to secure my assistance," Temperance repeated. She had been so overwhelmed by his return that she'd not allowed herself to think what business he could possibly have with her.

He inclined his head. "Alas, I'd not see you sacked or force your hand."

Surprise brought her eyebrows shooting up. *Impossible.* The seamstress had sacked girls for mixing up the laces. "Are you expecting me to believe Madame Amelie does not intend to release me for . . ."

"For pulling a pair of scissors on a marquess, refusing her orders, and storming out?" He flashed a wry grin. "No, we spoke, and upon hearing me out, she proved agreeable to the promise of not holding any of those offenses against you."

She opened and closed her mouth several times, shock briefly taking her words. *And that is nothing less than stunning . . .*

He rocked on his heels. "What was that?"

"Nothing," she said, unaware she'd spoken aloud. "It doesn't matter."

And yet . . . it did. He could have forced her hand and instead had gone to the efforts of securing her position and leaving her the choice. He'd always been unlike any other person in her life. Emotion stuck sharply in her throat.

Dare briefly palmed her cheek, that touch so fleeting and tender she might have conjured the caress of her own dreaming.

"What do you want, Dare?" she asked quietly.

He straightened from that favorite tree she so loved, which was now just one more place she would forever see him. "I'm a marquess, and I require a marchioness"—he pointed at her—"*you*, at my side."

It took a moment to register what he'd said. A sharp laugh escaped her. "Playing at marquess?" She rolled her eyes. "This is an entirely new approach to thievery for you. If I might give you some advice . . ." She didn't wait for him to ask and granted her guidance anyway. "You just saved your neck. You won't always be so lucky. Playing with the rank of nobleman will only see one result." And she'd be damned if she was around for it. "Goodbye, Dare."

"This isn't a lie, Temperance."

Temperance's steps slowed, and then she stopped altogether. He'd been a thief of much, and capable of using the right words and tone to secure a person's capitulation . . . but he'd never lied. And not to her.

He'd always told her precisely as it was, and even in marrying him, she'd known precisely what he was offering.

She turned back and faced him.

There was a serious set to his always easy features. "This is real."

"What is . . . 'this'?"

"Damned if I even know," he muttered, and she noted those details to have previously escaped her: the slightly panicky glint in his eyes. The restless way in which he balled and unballed his fists. He scraped a hand through those beautiful dark-brown locks.

She stared at him questioningly.

Dare let his arm drop abruptly, and like it was a fancy bench, he motioned to a gnarled limb jutting out of the tree.

She should go.

She shouldn't hear out whatever story this was.

And yet whether she wished it or not, she had bound herself in name and body to this man and, as such, needed to know what had brought him back into her life and why he was now insisting on a real marriage between them.

Her body stiff, she joined him and took a spot on the makeshift bench.

"I was recently caught in a heist." Of course. She couldn't stop the swell of jealousy for that, his one true love. "It was bold and risky, and yet the payout was significant."

"They always are," she said softly. The higher the booty, the greater the risk, and also the greater the certainty that Dare would take the job. It was why she hated that she'd fallen for someone who'd only ever been on a path of danger.

"I'd no other choice." He uttered those far-too-familiar words with the same ease another person might issue a "good morning" or a "hello." That matter-of-fact, straightforward justification he'd always given her. He began pacing. "The sum was sizable, and the person deserved stealing from."

There it was . . . the remainder of that reasoning.

He'd not changed. He never would. A regular old Robin Hood is what he'd always been. Stealing from the rich to give to the poor. And she wanted to hate him for it . . . but she hated herself more for admiring how he cared about the downtrodden when, to the rest of the world, those people were invisible.

"Who did you steal from, Dare?" she asked.

This time, he didn't meet her eyes.

Oh, no. This could not be good. "Who?" she pressed when he didn't immediately reply.

He stopped pacing. "It was an earl."

There was more there. She heard it in his voice, and knew it because she knew this man, more than she wished she did. "Which. Earl?"

He yanked at his cravat. "The Earl of Liverpool."

"The *prime minister*?" Temperance cursed. He may as well have stolen from a damned king or prince. *"Dare."*

He went on over her quiet chastisement. "He's an oppressor who delights in taking rights away from the masses. His household was empty." His mouth tensed. "Or it was supposed to have been. My reports had him retired to the country—"

She cut him off. "Prime ministers don't retire in the heart of the London Season. There were clues painting the operation as a foolhardy one."

The color rose in his cheeks, but he didn't debate her charges. Which any and every other man she'd ever known would have. Dare, however, hadn't been too proud to acknowledge when he was in the wrong. It was yet another reason she'd been so besotted by him. "The clues should have been warning enough."

"I know that now, Temperance."

So why *hadn't* he seen it?

"The fact remains, I was set up."

She tensed as the significance of that finally penetrated. It had been inevitable. When one stole from the most powerful, one secured powerful enemies. Too many knew of Dare and what he did, and though he was a legend, loved amongst the masses, the truth remained that his head could be sold, and sold for fine coin. Her gut clenched. Temperance stood. "Who?"

"I don't know," he said. "A young woman came to me with the information."

A sad smile formed on her lips. He'd always been hopeless where helpless young women were concerned. Someone had used that against him. And yet . . . "What does any of this have to do with your making yourself a marquess?"

"I didn't make myself a marquess." As he spoke, he resumed pacing. "I *am* a marquess."

"You're a marquess. And I take it that is why you managed to get yourself spared from the gallows," she said dryly.

He stopped and faced her. "I know it is far-fetched." His eyes darkened, and she knew the very moment she was forgotten and he was lost in his memory. "I was kidnapped as a child. A tutor turned me over to Mac Diggory."

Hatred burnt through her veins. Mac Diggory. That reviled, most feared, most ruthless of leaders. Dead for some years now, the memory of his evil lived on still. "What?" she whispered.

Dare's gaze fixed on a point beyond her. "I was apparently kidnapped and sold for a sizable sum."

"You're . . ." She couldn't finish the thought.

"A marquess's son."

It defied logic and sense. It was a fantastical story better suited for fiction . . . A small boy taken from his noble family and plunked into the streets, where he'd then risen up to become the Rookeries' greatest and most noble thief. It was also why he had the finest, crispest tones of the King's English. The life drained from her limbs as she sank back onto the edge of her perch.

All these years, he'd been stealing when he should have been shut away and protected in the finest West London townhouse.

"I . . . also, apparently, have a sister. She was born after I'd been taken, and is therefore not really family."

Not really family?

As he spoke so very casually about it, her gut churned and twisted into a thousand knots. She tried to make something out of those words . . . or his face or anything, but he was an unreadable mask. God, how she'd hated that control he sometimes yielded, a power he'd had to keep even her out.

"The *grandparents*"—not "my," but "the" grandparents—"are determined I help form a relationship with her. Help her navigate Polite Society. And, of course, see her settled. I don't know anything about any of that," he said with a frantic little wave of his hand. "Selecting suitors who would make an appropriate husband for her. Who to avoid. Gowns. Dresses." He blanched. "All of it."

What . . . exactly was he saying?

As her mind sought to make sense of all those words, she fixed on just one statement: *help her navigate Polite Society.*

And then it hit her with the same weight of one of her father's unexpected fists to her belly.

"Surely you aren't suggesting . . . ?" She tried and failed to get the remainder of that ridiculous supposition out.

"You are my wife," he rightly pointed out. "Overseeing all this is part of their requirement for me—"

"Their requirement?" she interrupted. "Why would they require . . . ?"

"I inherited a bankrupt marquessate. There are properties, but even so, the earnings have been meager, and whatever there is must go to the villagers." His lips twisted in a cynical half grin. "Even ascending to the rank of marquess, I find myself impoverished."

And if she were capable of laughing, this moment certainly would have been one that merited it. Ever the Robin Hood, he'd not just take from the unknown villagers in need, but would simply add them to the long and ever-growing list of those reliant upon him.

Reliant upon him, just as she'd made herself—she, who'd sacrificed what she'd wanted in a marriage with Dare Grey, convincing herself he might change so that she could be safe from her father.

When she still didn't speak, he cleared his throat. "As loath as I am to take them up on the terms, I've told myself . . . it is just any other job." Only it wasn't. It was one that didn't require him to risk his neck and steal someone else's belongings. He wouldn't see that, however. "I simply have to get in. Squire her about. Get her married. My grandfather will turn over twenty thousand pounds if you and I succeed in seeing the young lady married. After that, you and I can both go back to the lives we've chosen."

She'd long known who he was and how he viewed all his connections. And yet . . . "How . . . very mercenary you sound," she murmured. His cheeks flushed. "It is in all our best interests."

It wasn't in Temperance's . . .

He wanted something that could never be, because of something Temperance wasn't—a lady.

"I'm not part of that world, Dare," she said, determined to disabuse him of whatever madness had sent him here. "I cannot be any kind of chaperone to the young lady . . . or anyone." Temperance might dress them, but she didn't *dine* with them. It just wasn't done.

"Your mother was the daughter of a vicar. You speak the King's English."

"That won't be enough for them," she said impatiently. Surely he wasn't so naive as to think her being able to speak the *King's English* was enough to ensure her entry into Polite Society?

"I'm not from those elite ranks, either, Temperance. We would learn to navigate together."

Together.

It was all she'd ever wanted. So desperately. A dream she'd even allowed herself, only to have it quashed.

My God, please don't . . . do not . . .

Those distant screams of long ago pealed around her mind, and she folded her hands together to keep from clamping them over her ears.

And just like he'd proven her savior in the past, his voice reached through the darkness, and he plucked her from the abyss.

"Despite your low opinion of me, I didn't come here to upend your world, Temperance," Dare said quietly. "I would have you join me . . . of your own volition."

Join him . . .

Those two words, that one thought alone was enough to shatter the reverie.

You always built Darius Grey to be more God than mere mortal. That legend of a man she'd built in her mind was what had gotten her a broken heart.

And she'd believed herself wholly at peace with that . . . only in this moment, with him before her, to find she'd lied to herself. "I cannot be your wife, Dare," she said, her voice somehow steady. And while she trusted that she still had the strength to not break down weeping before him, she stood to leave. "I wish you the best. I wish you every happiness"—because she did; she'd never wanted him to suffer in any way—"and yet, I cannot join you." Nor did she want to.

She couldn't open herself back up to all those old hurts.

He nodded slowly. "I . . . see."

Do you?

Those two words screamed around her mind.

What did he think he saw? Or believe or know?

Temperance began the trek back toward her cottage.

Because he could not know what had become of her in those days. Too much had come to pass. She'd managed to put the shattered pieces of her heart into some semblance of an organ that might beat. To be with him . . . and dream of the life she'd wanted . . . and dream of what could never be . . .

"I did come, Temperance," he said quietly, unexpectedly. "I need you to know that as soon as I returned from the country, you were the first person I searched for."

Temperance whipped about to face him. "You were late," she whispered. *Too late.* "You always were." She shouldn't have needed his saving. She should have been capable enough to take care of herself. And yet that hadn't been the way where her father was concerned. When she opened her eyes, she found Dare's gaze intently on her. "And nothing will change that."

"Sleep on it," he called when she started onward to her cottage. "I leave on the morrow. In the event you change your mind"—she wouldn't—"you can find me at the Black Seal."

Sleep on it.

That favorite, familiar phrase he'd always given her when he'd wished for something from her . . .

A smile formed on her lips before her heart could remind her that she didn't want to remember those happy thoughts of them together. "Nothing is going to change," Temperance said, not allowing herself to look back.

For where Darius Grey and a future with him, any future with him, were concerned, nothing would ever change.

Chapter 6

"You . . . said . . . what?"

Early the following morn, Gwynn sat in the middle of Temperance's bed, on her knees, and stared at Temperance.

Given all Temperance had shared about her connection to Dare Grey, the Marquess of Milford, that should be the part her friend focused on.

"I told him I could not join him," she said, plaiting her hair.

"You are the only woman, Temperance Swift, who'd dare turn out a marquess and reject the life of a noblewoman."

"And what of you? Would any of that matter to you?" She already knew the answer. None would argue her friend had fallen in love with Chance for his funds or rank.

"Of course not." The young woman's gaze took on the far-off quality it always did at the mention of her love. "I don't care if he's a prince or a pauper—he's always a king to me."

Temperance gave her a pointed look.

Gwynn scrunched her nose up. "I see what you're doing there," she mumbled, and tossed a pillow at Temperance.

Managing her first laugh since Dare's resurrection, Temperance caught the feathered article to her chest and hugged it close. Her laughter immediately died. "Either way, I'm not a noblewoman." She was the daughter of a vicar's daughter and the once charming man—turned drunk—with whom her mother had fallen in love.

And . . . there were too many reasons it was perilous to let Dare back into her life again.

"No. You aren't a noblewoman." Gwynn paused. "Though technically, you did marry a marquess, which by default makes you a marchioness by marriage."

"But he wasn't a marquess at the time." He'd just been . . . Dare. And she'd loved him so desperately when he was just an honorable man in the Rookeries.

Gwynn's eyes glimmered. "Ah, but he was always a marquess or destined to the title. You just didn't know it."

Grabbing the same pillow that had been hurled her way, Temperance tossed it playfully back at her friend.

With a laugh, Gwynn caught it to her chest and scrambled to the edge of the bed. "Here . . ." She jumped up and rushed to join Temperance. "Let me." As Gwynn shoved Temperance's fingers out of the way and saw to arranging her hair, Temperance stared in the beveled mirror at her friend.

"I . . . had my heart broken by him." It was the closest she'd ever come to telling anyone about those days that only her brother knew of. And she tried to get those words out, for this woman who was her only friend in the world, and yet . . . could not. Because she was too cowardly to speak them and live those moments aloud.

Gwynn slowed her strokes and brought her hands to rest on Temperance's shoulders. "Be it life or love, a woman's fate is to have her heart broken," her friend said sadly in the tones of one who knew all too well. "You can be with him but cannot because he broke your heart, and I . . ." *Cannot be with Chance* . . . Her friend forced a smile. "But this is not about me. This is about the new beginning the marquess presented you with."

The new beginning. That gave Temperance pause. So shocked, so offended by his reappearance, she'd not considered Dare's offer in the way her friend now presented it. And yet . . .

"I had a new beginning," she said, taking the brush from Gwynn's fingers. "This was it."

"*This?* As in working at *Vêtements Français?*" Gwynn asked incredulously. "A place so trite it literally means 'French Apparel' when there is about as much French in Madame Amelie as in me?"

Temperance laughed again.

Her friend wasn't done. "Or are you referring to working with the likes of Miserable Mrs. Marmlebury? Is that the 'new beginning' you always dreamed of?"

"It was the best that I could have hoped for," she said defensively.

"Yes." Gwynn held her gaze. "Before. But that isn't the case any longer."

Temperance groaned. "You will not let this go." It was a statement.

"No," her friend answered anyway. "Is it permanent?" Gwynn asked, pushing her hands out of the way.

"Marriage is."

Her friend grunted. Her hands flew rapidly as she drew Temperance's tresses into a long braid. "Is that what he wants, then? A real marriage?"

That brought her up short. "He . . . didn't say." For in the request Dare had put to her, there hadn't been talk of a marriage in the traditional sense. Or really, in any sense. Furthermore, he'd not truly wanted to be married to her. They'd struck up a business arrangement, and as such he'd spoken of their rejoining as a partnership so that he could secure funds he required. Temperance grunted. "He didn't say that was what he wanted." There'd been no talk of a reunion or reestablishing the bond they'd once shared. Or . . . more. Oh, he'd been attempting to seduce her into working with him. But that . . . it was different.

Gwynn gave a triumphant little grunt. "I *see.*"

"I'm not going to London, Gwynn," Temperance said flatly. She couldn't bring herself to look at the other woman. "Never again." She'd die before she'd risk coming face-to-face with the monsters of her past. Any of them.

At the long, protracted silence, she made herself glance up.

"I trust, where you lived, and the world you knew . . . it wasn't this new world the marquess has opened for you."

"No," she murmured. "It was . . . the Rookeries."

"This wouldn't be the Rookeries," her friend said gently.

No, it wouldn't. But the location didn't change the fact of who would be with her—Dare Grey.

"This is enough for me."

A sad smile curved Gwynn's wide lips. "You know enough not to believe that lie."

She tensed. Yes, she did. But she'd not be called out on it by her friend. "It's done, Gwynn," she said emphatically in tones meant to end what had never begun as a debate.

Alas, Gwynn proved as tenacious now as she'd been at their first meeting, when they'd gone toe-to-toe over a bolt of ivory lace. "You can say this is enough and that you are content with your life as it is now, Temperance . . . but if that were the case, then I wouldn't have to plead with you to remain silent on your opinion on shades of pink on Mrs. Marmlebury. You would stay silent, do your job, and go about your own business. But you *don't*," she said with a quiet insistence. "Ever." With that, Gwynn turned the brush back over and exchanged it for the forgotten white dress she'd been working on.

Why must the other woman be so stubborn? Why couldn't she just leave Temperance to . . .

Think about yourself . . .

Temperance paused.

And in that she'd proven selfish. Since Dare had put his request to her, she'd fixed on her own hurt; she'd not allowed herself to think about his offer and what it could do . . .

That which she herself couldn't do . . .

She glanced over to where Gwynn was stitching away at a christening gown for one of their clients. Head bent, she attended that task . . . an agonizing, grueling one that, at the end of every day, would see the other woman—would see the both of them—with barely any pence to put in their apron pockets.

With the wages they earned, they'd never leave Madame Amelie's. It was a simple fact. They'd continue on working, earning just enough coin to pay for the rent on this cottage. Rent that her brother helped them afford. The same brother whom Temperance had cared for when he was a small boy had suddenly become the one who helped her, even as he himself knew only financial hardship.

Still wholly focused on her sewing, Gwynn paused to rub at the back of her neck with one hand.

Temperance frowned.

No, they were not getting younger. Their hands would soon grow slower. Their fingers bent.

She spared a look for her palms. They'd always been coarse and rough. Certainly not a marchioness's hands, and that's what Dare would have them be . . . even if for a short while. She balled them to hide the harsh white padding upon parts of her palm.

Then they'd be replaced by younger seamstresses with nimbler fingers, and then where would they be?

Temperance let her hands fall.

She had long ago accepted that this was the best it would ever be. As such, there was a contentedness with her life, a willingness to accept that this was as good as she could expect . . . for her.

But there was Chance . . . and Gwynn. Her brother and her best friend, who'd fallen in love but been kept apart—not by poor decisions or endless divisions between them, but for no other reason than that they didn't have the funds to have a life together. They deserved more.

And I can give that to them . . .

Selfishness had made her look only at how Dare's presence complicated her life.

Her mind balked at the idea of it . . . and yet . . . She pressed her eyes shut.

When she opened them, she quit her spot near a hard-at-work Gwynn and headed for the window. And she, who'd been so adamant that she'd never accompany Dare, thought of what he'd presented—in a new light, and in a new way. She could provide Chance with the ultimate protection and security she'd never been able to fully ensure when he was a child.

"I'll shape the narrative," she mouthed to herself. She would decide what she was willing to give and what she was willing to do.

When presented that way, it was an altogether different manner of thinking.

Why . . . why . . . he didn't necessarily want her to be a real wife to him. A real wife who shared kisses and tender touches and a bed and . . . babies.

Every muscle within her seized up.

Stop . . .

Focus on the arrangement. Focus on what he might give you . . .

Except as soon as the question slipped out, a memory slipped in. *"I want forever with you, Dare Grey. Anything else will never be enough . . ."*

"Forever for me will be short, Temperance Grey . . . because of the life I live. But what time I do walk this earth? It is yours."

Her throat closed up from the long-ago memory, fresh still. *It is yours,* he'd vowed. How soon after they'd exchanged vows, however, before he'd gone off and set to work stealing, leaving her to her own devices?

Nooooooo . . . Please, nooooo . . .

Her agonized screams sounded over and over in her mind, and she fought the urge to clap her palms over her ears to blot out those cries.

Gwynn sighed. "What . . . are you thinking?" her friend asked haltingly, her voice coming across the distance.

Returning to her friend's side, Temperance took her face in her hands and kissed her lightly on the cheek. "That you are brilliant."

Her friend wrinkled her brow. "I . . . thank you?" And then understanding glinted in the other woman's eyes. "You're going," she whispered.

She nodded. "And you're joining me."

Gwynn choked on her laughter. "Now I know *you're* jesting." Her friend gave her head a shake.

"I am *not*." She spoke with a quiet insistence that brought the other woman's gaze back up. "If I go . . . then you shall come."

"Well, that is silly," her friend said with a toss of her glorious golden curls. "I don't belong there. You, however, married into that life."

The other woman was splitting hairs. "You're being deliberately obtuse." Color splotched Gwynn's cheeks, indicating Temperance had hit the nail on the head. "If I am doing this, you are coming with me."

"I can be your lady's maid." Another snorting laugh escaped the young woman as she dipped a graceless, haphazard curtsy.

Temperance gave her a light shove, earning another guffaw from the other woman. "I'm glad you find humor in this, Gwynn," she said softly. "If you join me in London, then you will be near Chance."

The other woman started, her lips forming a little circle. She gave a juddering nod. "Yes!" Taking Temperance by the shoulders, she gave her a light shake. "I will join you." Her expression grew stricken. "That is, if you manage to find him before he leaves."

"Before he . . ." As one, they glanced to the pretty painted porcelain clock Temperance's brother had gifted her for her birthday three years earlier. "Oh, bloody hell."

He was leaving.

Sleep on it. I leave on the morrow. In the event you change your mind, you can find me at the Black Seal.

That was, if he'd not already left. And he'd always been the earliest of risers. Temperance cursed.

Gwynn shoved her gently. "Hurry!"

Temperance took off running.

As she readied the old horse Chance had purchased for them some years ago and climbed into the saddle, Temperance steeled herself.

This time it would be different.

It had to be.

Because there could never be a future with him. Not a true one. *Ever.*

Chapter 7

She hadn't come.

Though in truth, having come here, he'd known all along that the end result would be her refusal.

Nor did he blame her.

For all the passion and love that had been between them, there had been an absolute lack of timing. Their lives had never been synchronous to their relationship.

This time, her presence in his life had been the difference between him earning a fortune . . . and not. Her rejection left him with the task of returning to the duke and duchess and explaining that though there was a wife, the terms they'd put to him could not be carried out. Not in the way they wished.

As such, the only thing he should be focused on was the upcoming meeting and what that meant for him and those monies.

And yet as he guided his chestnut stallion, Bandit, away from the Black Seal and out onto the road leading back to London, he wasn't thinking about the lost funds or the people he might help. Or in this case, the people of the Rookeries, whom he could no longer help.

But then Temperance always had that effect on him—she'd always invaded his every thought and set up a permanent place there. She was the only person who had truly mattered to him. The only person he'd let matter, even as he'd known that with his thievery, he'd no place letting himself get close to anyone. Yes, he helped the masses . . . but he deliberately kept a distance between himself and those he helped because nothing good could come if—when—he failed those same souls.

The steady thump of an approaching mount cut through his reverie.

There was a frantic speed to that galloping horse; the pounding of its hooves drew closer . . . and louder.

Cursing, Dare drew on his reins, and quickly guided Bandit to the edge of the old Roman road . . .

Too late.

A horse barreled over the rise, and—

The blood whirred in Dare's ears as Bandit whinnied loudly. The panicked horse danced wildly under him to escape peril.

Adjusting his hold on the reins, Dare gripped his legs tight to maintain his seat, and kept the mount grounded as the other rider yanked on the reins. That grey mount pawed and scratched at the air before settling back onto all fours.

Dare's heart pounded in his chest as the immediate peril receded. "Bloody hell," he thundered. "What do you . . . ?" His words died as the initial haze of danger lifted and he was presented with the reckless rider.

Her cheeks were flushed, and at some point, her hair had come loose from her braid, leaving her curls to hang in a magnificent tangle about her back, a glorious curtain of dark waves he ached to stroke his fingers through.

Only . . .

She didn't ride.

Dare blinked wildly. *"Temperance?"*

She smiled sheepishly. "I fear I overestimated the timing you would make this morn," she called down breathlessly.

Which meant . . . she'd come, seeking him out. Swinging a leg over the side of his stallion, Dare dismounted. Bandit immediately wandered off to graze in a nearby swath of overgrown grass.

And for the first time in the whole of his life, he, Dare Grey, glib with speech, ready with any necessary response, couldn't get his tongue to form a single word. Not a single one that made sense.

Temperance shimmied down from her horse, but holding on to its reins, she led it over to Dare. "I expected you'd be gone," she said, her words running together. "You always were an early riser, and as such, I went to the Black Seal."

He cocked his head. "The Black Seal?" he echoed, still wholly dazed. She'd long had that effect on him.

She nodded enthusiastically. "The inn?" she clarified.

Were they . . . really discussing the inn he'd just left? "I'm . . . familiar with it," he said slowly, trying to pick his way around not only her presence here but also that she'd sought him out and that she rode and . . .

"A rather silly name, is it not?" she rambled on. "The Black Seal, that is. I mean, if it was Suffolk or Dorset or North Yorkshire or Cornwall"— he struggled to keep up with that cataloging—"I *might* understand 'the Black Seal.' But we are quite landlocked in the Cuckmere River Valley. Why, there isn't even a nearby water."

At last she went silent.

For a moment.

"That is, there isn't a nearby ocean. There are lovely rivers. Just . . . not waters fit for seals," Temperance finished weakly.

"I . . . trust this isn't what you sought me out to discuss? The name of the village inn."

"No." That, however, was all she said. *No.*

She wetted her lips, and he followed the path her tongue took over that plump flesh. And a wave of desire coursed through him, as strong now as it had been the first time he'd spied Temperance, her cheeks flushed with fury as she'd taken on a ruthless street tough who'd been bullying a boy. She'd always been beautiful, but the sight of her as she was now from her wild ride put him in mind of warrior princesses of old, fighting for their countryside.

He'd never seen a woman as fearless. As undaunted.

She proved as much by at last breaking her silence. "You are wondering why I'm here, and the truth of the matter is, I thought we might talk about your reason for coming here."

"Which part?"

Temperance angled her head, the movement sending those heavy black tresses falling over her shoulder. She brushed them back, and how he envied her fingers in that instant. "Were there multiple parts?"

"I . . . uh . . . no." There'd been nothing meaningful about their past, or anything discussed beyond his changed circumstances and his need of her. Which could only mean . . . ? He froze, stopping the question even as it formed on his tongue. For he knew Temperance Grey, knew her pride and her ofttimes contrariness. He cleared his throat and urged her to continue. "If you would?"

"You asked that I return to London and help you, help your sister navigate through her Season."

She stared at him, indicating something was expected of him. "There were other terms presented by the duke," he felt inclined to point out. "If I . . . if we . . ." He motioned between them. Her face revealed only confusion. "Provide an heir to the family line?"

"Provide an heir to the family," she echoed, and then her eyes flew wide, as if she'd just realized what she'd stated aloud. "Good *God.*"

The way she managed to add four syllables into one, and the abject horror etched in her features . . . stung. He'd never imagined a full future with Temperance. Just because of who he was and what he did, and how her expectations were at odds with all that. But thinking she'd be so reviled at the idea of having his babe . . .

His cheeks heated. "Of course not," he said on a rush. "It is why I didn't mention it when I first came to you. I just thought you should know they did present . . . another way," he finished lamely.

Temperance continued to eye him warily. She played with the reins in one hand, and with the other, she scratched her grey mare between the eyes. "What you presented . . . It was not a real marriage." Her already brightly colored cheeks turned several shades deeper.

She'd been clear long ago that a "real marriage" was the last thing she wished for with him. "No, that is not what I'd expected."

"Exactly." Temperance nodded. "As such, when I considered it in those terms, I was able to see that it could prove mutually beneficial to us."

"It?" he asked, slow to follow.

"Why . . ." She spread her palms out. "A marriage of convenience, and I know what you are thinking."

"You couldn't even begin to imagine," he drawled.

"There's never been anything convenient between us . . . or about us, but perhaps this one last thing together can be."

That was what she was agreeing to—a marriage of convenience? It was far more than he'd ever expected . . . and certainly deserved. Nor was it vastly different from what their actual marriage had begun as. And it was also the safest way between them. He still couldn't be a husband to her. Not the kind she deserved . . . and would never have because of him. Shoving aside the wave of guilt, he nodded. "I'm listening."

"I will help you, help your sister, along with the terms of your grandparents' expectations. But that's all." The long column of her throat moved. "Ours will be a business arrangement and nothing more," she went on, all cool logic that would have impressed him if it hadn't been *their* marriage she spoke of.

"Of course," he said automatically. He'd always known there couldn't be anything more between them. Not truly. Not again.

"You should be warned; I'll attend the *ton* events, and host . . ." She didn't want to. By the strained corners of her lips, she no more wished to take part in those events than he himself. "But I don't know anything about them, Dare."

"We'll figure it out together, Temperance."

She nodded. "Yes."

And mayhap that was one of the reasons he so desperately wanted her there. Why it had to be her. Not just because she was his wife in the eyes of England, but because she was of his world. She knew him. They might be strangers all these years later . . . and she a stranger who didn't much like him anymore. But if he was going to be thrust amongst Polite Society, knowing she would be there eased some of the pressure in his chest. A pressure he'd not even known was there until she'd given that assurance.

"But that is the extent of our relationship, Dare," she added quickly, as if she needed to remind herself as much as she needed to remind him. Or mayhap that was only his own imagining. "We aren't friends. We aren't real spouses. We are *partners.*"

A voice—his voice—from long ago echoed at the back of his mind, where he'd kept the memories of them.

Temperance, I'm offering you my name and the protection that comes with being my wife, but that is all I can give you . . . a partnership . . . but not a real marriage . . . There cannot be anything more . . .

"I'm not looking for anything more," he assured. After he received the duke's money, Dare would return to his former life. And she could never accept that. As such, this would only ever be temporary. "And in return? What will you receive out of our marriage of convenience?"

A blush splotched her cheeks. "Funds. I require money." She directed that admission to the hard dirt road.

And as she spoke those words with her head bent, she was once more the proud young woman who'd come to him, asking for his help. Never realizing that she needn't feel shame near him, because he'd only ever seen her strength . . . even in knowing when she needed to ask for help.

He waited, and when she didn't say anything more, he gently prodded her. "For . . . ?"

She lifted her head, and her mouth tightened. And then . . . "I'd like funds. Money."

He waited for her to say more.

Dare narrowed his eyes. "You're in trouble?" He should have known. Why hadn't he known—

Temperance spoke quickly. "No, I'm content with my life as is." *But* . . . The word hovered on the end of her unfinished sentence. "Chance."

Her brother.

She toyed with the fabric of her cloak. "It's an opportunity for me to . . . to see that he has that which he wants."

"Which is?" That question, however, didn't come from the deal they now negotiated, but from a place of caring for who Temperance and her younger brother had once been to him.

"He's a weaver and . . . not very successful. Not yet," she said on a rush, as if she'd felt the betrayal in the simple fact. "But he will be. He is working toward becoming supervisor, and his employer favors him greatly." And yet . . . "Until he does, Chance cannot offer Gwynn more." She spoke as if he knew or should know the woman Chance had fallen in love with. And perhaps he, as her husband and best friend and former love, should. "This would allow them to start their future together," Temperance added hesitantly when he didn't immediately respond.

"I see." Of course she'd put her brother first. She always had, caring for the boy better than most mothers did the children they birthed. That devotion had just been one of too many reasons to count as to why he'd fallen in love with her.

"What about what you want?" The question left him of its own volition, a product of the freedom with which they'd used to speak to one another . . . when they had been friends and lovers.

Color flooded her cheeks. "Are you trying to talk me out of . . . ?"

He held up a hand. "No." He'd have her do that which brought her happiness. And having been separated as they had been, who was he any longer to say what brought her contentment? "I would wonder what you might get out of our arrangement . . . for yourself."

Her frown deepened. "I . . . I have work," she said, backing up a step.

Which would hardly supply her with the funds to see herself settled for life, but she'd not think of that. She'd not ask for more for herself.

Dare closed that distance she'd made with her last step. "With your talent, I always said you deserved more than darning socks," he said. She'd always had a skill with the needle, had even sewn him up on more than one occasion.

Her eyes lit, and for a moment she was the girl he'd fallen in love with back when she'd still had a starry gaze for him . . . before she'd grown tired of his thievery and his commitments to others. Before a harder, more cynical glint had replaced that innocence. "Yes, well, I've asked for what I've asked for."

He'd be damned if she provided for only her brother and his sweetheart with those monies. "Will five thousand pounds be enough?"

She choked, and he patted her lightly on the back. "Th-that would b-be very fair," she said when she was able to properly swallow.

Any other woman might have asked for more. "It is settled, then."

"There is one more matter . . ."

He folded his arms. "Oh?"

"Chance's love, my friend Gwynn. I'd have her join me, and she's agreed to serve in the role of lady's maid. Not that I'll treat her as a servant," she said on a rush. "But rather I'd have her close so that she might see my brother more frequently than she does now."

In their time apart, she'd found a friend. And even while there came a peace and joy in knowing there'd been someone there for her, there was also regret at the reminder of how much time had passed. Of how little he knew her . . . and what had become of her. And also . . .

a reminder that he'd been replaced. She, the one friend he'd allowed himself, had found another.

Her brow dipped. "I didn't expect that would be a problem?"

There was a question there.

"It is not a problem." She'd misunderstood the reason for his silence. "Your friend—?"

"Gwynn Armitage."

"She may join us. If there is nothing else?"

Temperance shook her head. "There isn't."

He gathered his reins. "We'll leave today."

Her eyebrows shot up, and Temperance raced over. "So soon?" she squeaked.

"I left London without informing"—he couldn't get his tongue or lips to make out the words for that old pair who'd presented him with a possible fortune—"them, and there is business I have to see to. Contracts that will finalize the terms laid out." *Is it really about that meeting? Or is it that you fear if she has more time to think on it, she'll back out of the agreement?*

She eyed him suspiciously. "Are they . . . also of the nobility?"

Very briefly, he considered a lie lest she, like him, decide she wanted no part of a contract with the peerage.

"Dare?"

"You might say . . . a duke."

She strangled on another swallow and, this time, waved him off when he made to hit her on the back.

Her horse tossed its head and danced nervously about.

Dare stroked the creature's neck, calming her. "Didn't I say as much?"

"No, you didn't. Not before this."

"I'm sure I did. He is my late mother's father."

Temperance gave him a hard look. "I'm beyond certain I would recall *those* details, Dare."

"Does it *really* matter?" Why, all of a sudden, must it make a difference that he was a lord or that his kin were lofty? And that he despised it?

"Of course it does." She thumped him in the arm with her fist.

He grunted and rubbed at the offended area. "I mean, they are nobility, and regardless of what their title is, they're still all the same. The same class. The same power and—"

"Enough." She gave him another—this time, gentler—tap. "You aren't helping."

He made himself silent.

"Furthermore, it matters, very much. They're of the peerage, and they're your grandparents."

He squirmed. "Yes, well, either way, they're the ones who've put these requirements to me, and I had a meeting on the morrow with my man-of-affairs to work through the details." Dare awkwardly gestured between them. "The details being us . . . and the monies that will come to me"—she gave him a pointed look—"us," he corrected.

"And do you truly believe they are simply going to accept that you've tied yourself to a drunkard's daughter? A commoner from the Rookeries?"

God, how he despised that low opinion she'd always carried of herself. She'd always deserved more. "That isn't all you are," he said quietly.

She waved his words off. "No. That's right. I'm also a seamstress, which, to them, will mark me no different from a woman on the streets. Lords and ladies don't simply accept common street rats into their fold."

His mouth hardened. "Whether they approve or not, the fact remains, you are my wife. And I'll not allow anyone to speak ill of you." Including Temperance herself. Her past didn't matter. It never had. Only in that he'd admired her so deeply for surviving the abusive bastard who'd put her through a hell that would have broken most grown men.

Temperance's lips turned up in a sad little rendition of a smile. "Not speaking those words doesn't change my station. It is what I am."

"You're my wife, and that is what matters. Those were the terms they held me to, and I've . . . *you and I have* . . . fulfilled those requirements."

Temperance sighed. "Dare . . ."

And more than half sensing she intended to pull back on that which she'd agreed to, he spoke before she could. "Is two hours sufficient time to collect your things?"

She searched his face. "You are truly certain this is the only way for you to secure your funds?"

"Aye."

"Two hours is fine, Dare. We will be ready." Hastening over to where her mare grazed, Temperance gathered up the reins.

"Oh, and Temperance?"

She looked back, a question in her eyes.

"There was so much we were unable to get right between us," he murmured, drifting closer to her. "And differences and divides that could have never been bridged." The path of thievery he'd taken, and her resolve to have no part of it, or him, as long as he carried on that life. "And yet you were wrong," he murmured, lightly palming the silken curve of her sun-kissed olive skin. Now dark when it had once been pale from the polluted London sky. He preferred her this way.

Temperance leaned into his touch. "A-about?"

"Not everything between us was inconvenient. Lovemaking we always got right."

Her lips parted ever so slightly, and a gust of the spring air carried her shocked little gasp across the remaining distance between them.

Dare closed it. "If the time comes when you again want me in your bed . . ." Dare left those words there for her, and just as he'd longed to when she'd traced her mouth with the tip of her tongue, he rubbed his thumb along the full flesh of her lower lip. A siren's mouth. The manner of which would send sailors happily into those jagged rocks.

Temperance's eyelashes fluttered, and she moved close to him, and into his touch. "That would be . . ."

A mistake. A danger to them both. Her words hung there, realized by the both of them.

As such, that should be reminder enough. But he'd always been hopelessly greedy where Temperance was concerned.

Swallowing rhythmically, he lowered his head, giving her time to retreat . . . Only she didn't. She lifted her head.

"Let me kiss you, Temperance," he whispered, that soft little entreaty against her mouth.

Her response was instantaneous and glorious, and one he would have sold any soul he had left to the Devil for. "Yes," she moaned.

And he kissed her. As he'd longed to. Lips he'd ached to know once more and had given up the dream of. Now, as he slanted his lips over hers, he remembered all of her, the electric shock of their mouths meeting running straight to his soul like a lightning charge. The aromatic taste of her, honey and mint leaves, the same as she'd taken in her tea, and more intoxicating than any potent alcohol brewed in the Rookeries. Temperance parted her lips, letting him inside, and boldly met each stroke of his tongue, her flesh a fiery brand that scorched him as she commanded their kiss.

The only sounds between them were the erotic rasps of their breaths as they came hard and fast and heavy, blotting out reality and right from wrong, or reason from insanity. All there was, was the two of them.

Dare glided his hands over her, down the small of her back, over the curve of her waist, and then he sank his fingers into her buttocks, dragging her close.

She pressed her body against his.

Neiiiigh. Her mount stuck its enormous nose between them . . . And just like that, the moment was shattered.

Panting, Temperance stumbled back several steps. Her passion-laden eyes formed slow, widening circles. "That w-was . . ."

Glorious. A piece of heaven he was undeserving of.

"A mistake," he said instead.

She nodded vigorously. "A mistake," she echoed. Her fingers shaking, Temperance fished about for her reins.

"Here," he murmured, collecting them in his only slightly steadier palms.

Frowning, she grabbed the leather reins from him. "This will not happen again. Now, if you'll excuse me. I've things I must pack and see to before we leave." With that, she walked off with her horse trailing behind.

He should let her go. It was the wise thing to do. It had always been the course he should have taken around Temperance. Alas, he'd never been able to do what he should around the woman. "Temperance?" he called after her.

Her steps slowed, and she turned about.

"As for making love? It could happen again . . . if you want it, too . . ."

"I've no interest in having you in my bed, Dare Grey," she said, the slight tremble to her words otherwise ruining the crisp quality to them.

With that, she used a nearby boulder to get herself into the saddle of her greying mount and nudged the creature onward.

He stared after her. She'd agreed to accompany him. She was joining him in London when she'd vowed to never set foot in those city walls, and would see him with a fortune when their time was done.

That should be enough.

So why did he find himself regretting that it wasn't . . . more?

Chapter 8

Dare had asked whether two hours were enough for Temperance to pack her belongings.

In her twenty-six years on this earth, she'd never had much to her name. These past few years, however, she'd accumulated more than all the collective ones before them. And still, as it would turn out, she'd needed just thirty-three minutes to pack up all that mattered to her and all she had: Her dresses. The handful of knickknacks her brother had given to her over the years: Her cameo. Her porcelain clock. Her sewing kit.

No, there'd never been much, and as such, packing had been easy. Only, when the knock came, she still wasn't ready.

KnockKnockKnock.

From where she stood at the window, Gwynn peeled back the curtain and peered outside. "He's arrived," she murmured, more to herself. And needlessly.

It was the first time Dare Grey had ever been on time for a meeting between him and Temperance.

A panicky giggle built in her chest at the thought.

Standing in the middle of her small living room with two tattered valises beside her, Temperance bent slightly and gathered the handles.

Yes, the packing had proven easy. It was the leaving which left her stomach tangled up in a thousand knots.

That, and the idea of joining him.

And staring at the door panel, nothing more than a rectangular slab of wood, the only physical barrier between her and Dare, made this—what she'd agreed to—real in ways that it hadn't been.

Sweat slicked her skin.

I cannot do this . . .

She'd been so very sure that she was entering into this latest arrangement with Dare in a coolheaded manner, and yet she'd never been in full possession of her wits and heart where he was concerned.

What if this is different? What if I fall all over again for a man who never wanted a wife and only married me to protect me, and—

A light hand came to rest on Temperance's shoulder, and she jumped. Her panicky gaze went to Gwynn's fingers, life-worn like her own, and the sight of them and that touch managed to ground her.

Her friend stared back with troubled eyes. "I've forced you to do this."

"You didn't." She paused. "You made me see reason, which is altogether different."

Gwynn twisted her hands. "I don't know what drove you and the marquess apart, and perhaps if I'd been a better friend I would have asked that first and put that before everything, but I'm telling you now, you don't have to do this, Temperance."

She'd not fault Gwynn for seeing hope beyond the offer Dare had put to her. "Yes," Temperance said softly. "I do." And mayhap for more reasons than Chance and Gwynn. Mayhap, there could be some sense of closure. That important piece that had been missing all these years since she'd sent Dare away and asked him to never return. And from there, with the money Dare would give her, there'd be funds enough to see she lived a life of comfort—an existence where she wasn't reliant upon Madame Amelie.

KnockKnockKnock.

They looked to the front of the room.

And still, despite her assurances to the other woman and her resolve to join Dare, she could not make herself move. Instead, as Gwynn trotted over to the door and reached for the handle, Temperance called out, freezing her and this moment. "Wait!"

And allowing herself several last, stolen moments, Temperance passed her gaze around the living quarters she'd called home with Gwynn these past years.

Here, she'd retreated and hidden herself away. It had come to represent a place of only new memories, ones she'd made for herself. The Cotswolds had represented hope and anonymity . . . from the father who'd brought her only suffering.

Now, she'd return to the place of it all: London. There, where there was only darkness and suffering and the hurt of old memories. *And him . . . He is there, too . . .*

A black curtain briefly fell over her vision, momentarily blinding her. And she forced herself to blink until the moment passed.

He won't find you in Mayfair. Not as a marchioness . . . He'll never have access to you again . . .

And before all courage deserted her, Temperance nodded. "I am ready."

Gwynn paused with her fingers still on the handle. "We can come back."

No. No, they couldn't. She knew that. Nothing after this would ever be the same.

Gwynn drew the door open and promptly retreated behind Temperance.

Temperance's heart fell.

For it wasn't Dare standing on the stone porch.

What did you expect? That he'd have been there, waiting?

Except . . . she had. Because even with all he'd shared and the agreement they'd come to, she'd forgotten that he was a marquess. And marquesses had servants who knocked on doors for them. And . . .

Gwynn shoved Temperance between the shoulder blades and propelled her forward several steps. She glared at her friend, then looked once more to the servant.

The servant dropped a deep bow. "My lady."

My lady?

Temperance glanced about before it hit her: he was speaking to her. She was the "my lady" to whom he spoke.

"May I offer my assistance?" the tall, uniformed servant asked when she didn't speak.

Temperance shook her head, confusion making her mind move like mud. Was he thinking to spring her from the arrangement she'd foolishly agreed to?

"Your bags," Gwynn said on a loud whisper.

"My bags?" she repeated.

"The carriages are ready, my lady."

"Carriages?" Temperance knew she was parroting back every word out of the pained-looking servant's mouth but was hopeless to help it.

As one, Temperance and Gwynn leaned out and peered around the lanky servant. Only there weren't just two carriages. There were two carriages and a horse. There was that, too.

For "carriages" implied that there were more than one.

"Two?" Gwynn whispered noisily. "What did he expect you were bringing to London with you?" she asked as the servant gathered the collection of assembled bags and started for the carriages.

Temperance's focus, however, was not on those black-lacquer, crested conveyances, but rather the towering figure astride his mount.

The sun radiated down, casting a bright halo of light upon him, highlighting the kaleidoscope of brown and auburn hues of his hair, giving him the look of a fallen archangel.

That had always been Dare, though: a blend between sinner and saint.

"He is . . . quite handsome," Gwynn whispered.

"That he is," she murmured as they fell in step and made one final walk down the length of the walkway to where Dare waited.

"Did I mention he was hands—"

"You did. I know," Temperance muttered. She didn't need Gwynn or anyone to point out that Dare Grey was a specimen of glorious male perfection. His dark-brown hair, slightly tousled, only added to his appeal. Broad shoulders encased in fine wool fabric. She itched to run her fingers down that quality material . . . and test the muscles within.

Dare swung down and started forward, his long, sleek steps eliminating the short divide. He stopped before them, and Temperance opened her mouth to perform introductions.

He greeted Gwynn with a smile. "Miss Armitage, I take it?" He doffed his hat and swept a bow, and Temperance gritted her teeth as Gwynn's cheeks reddened under that gallant display of manners.

"My lord." Gwynn sank into a masterful curtsy.

Temperance frowned. How had her friend learned to curtsy . . . like that?

As the pair exchanged small pleasantries, Temperance hovered there, forgotten. Something hot and unpleasant sat like vinegar upon her tongue.

I am not jealous. She'd grown accustomed to the charm he turned on . . . every woman. Every person, really.

Only that sharp, acidic taste had very much the flavor of jealousy.

"I trust we should be leaving," she said curtly, interrupting them. All the while knowing it was unfair to be resentful of the ease with which Gwynn managed to speak to anyone—a like charm shared by Dare.

Dare and Gwynn's exchange cut off abruptly, and awkwardly.

"Er . . . yes." He beat a gloved palm along the side of his trousers.

Gwynn gave her a light nudge, and Temperance sprang into movement, heading for the conveyances.

"Gloves," she said under her breath.

"What?" Gwynn asked, her shorter legs pumping to keep up.

"Nothing."

He now wore gloves. He'd never donned those articles. It was a small detail to note, and yet another change. One that marked not only the small changes that had befallen him in their time apart but also the station divide that had sprung between them.

She reached the carriage, and found an older, grey-haired driver in wait.

And having been so focused on the greater horror of reuniting with Dare and rejoining him in London, she only just now faced the detail she'd let herself forget—the carriage ride. The last time she'd journeyed in one, she'd vowed it would be her last. Her hands automatically went to her stomach, and she pressed them against her lower belly, and the wrenching cramps that threatened to tear her apart.

She couldn't climb back inside one. Not without remembering all there was about that day and the ones preceding it.

"Is there a problem?" Dare asked, a question in his voice.

"There are any number of them," she whispered.

He cupped a hand to his ear as he'd always done when she'd spoken to herself. "What was that?"

"Nothing," she said now.

Accepting the driver's proffered hand with a word of thanks, she drew herself inside. Gwynn followed close behind, and once again, there was an unexpected stab of disappointment as Dare swung into his saddle.

Of course he'd ride . . .

A different source of envy sluiced through her. What she wouldn't give to exchange the closed-in carriage for the feel of a horse between her legs . . . and the fresh air. She hungered for that, too.

"I never thought to ride in a carriage fit for a queen," Gwynn mused, taking up a spot across from Temperance.

While her friend prattled on about the grand conveyance, Temperance settled onto the plush, luxuriant squabs. She shifted back and forth on the bench. It was more spacious than the workstation she'd left behind at Madame Amelie's, and perhaps she'd be all right, after all. Mayhap this would prove altogether different from the jarring ride she'd suffered through five years earlier. The one that had made it impossible for her to get herself into any other carriage since. And she had tried. A marquess's stately carriage was nothing like the cramped quarters she'd suffered through, with passengers stinking of garlic and spirits and pipes . . .

Do not think of that day . . .

"People like us are destined for run-down hackneys," her friend rightly pointed out, "and crowded mail carriages. The last time I journeyed anywhere was by mail coach."

"Me, too," Temperance whispered. She stared blankly at the heavy gold curtains drawn back at the windows. Her past and present blended.

"Miserable rides, aren't they?"

I hate to send you by mail coach, but there is no other way . . . You cannot remain . . . It is not safe for you here . . .

Her lips twisted in a bitter, empty smile as she stopped fighting the past and finally made herself think about the last carriage ride she'd taken.

Terror, panic, and pain had buffeted her senses; a blessed numbness had prevented her from weeping before the eclectic crowd of passengers.

Gwynn touched her hand, bringing Temperance's eyes open. "But this will be nothing like any ride we've taken before."

She managed a nod.

God willing that her friend proved right.

The carriage lurched into motion, and along with it, her stomach.

And not even twenty minutes later, she'd all the confirmation she required.

"We should stop," Gwynn said for a fifth time.

"I'm fine," she said between gritted teeth, holding on to the sides of her bench and focusing on anything other than the churning of her turbulent belly.

"You are green."

"I'm. Not."

Gwynn peered at her. "I might point out that I can see you and you can't very well see yourself, and so if you could look, you'd see that your pallor is, in fact, very nearly green." The other woman reached for the valise resting beside her on the bench. "I can show you a mirror if you—"

"That won't be necessary," Temperance said weakly. And she didn't know whether to laugh or cry at her stubborn friend's insistence.

At last, Gwynn quieted, and Temperance closed her eyes once more. *Breathe in. Breathe out. Breathe in . . .*

She focused on that mantra, talking herself through her roiling belly. "How long has it been?" she asked in slow, measured tones.

Gwynn consulted a timepiece affixed to the front of her cloak. "Twenty-six minutes, now."

She groaned. "It cannot be just six minutes from when I asked?"

Her friend glanced down at the piece once more, and looked up, beaming. "Twenty-seven now."

Temperance pressed her cheek to the window, the velvet fabric smooth against her face, softening the blow as the carriage whipped her head about. The bumpy ride set the curtains fluttering, parting slightly, and then coming together. And all the while, to keep from throwing up, she stared out at the figure shifting in and out of focus.

Dare.

Regal and tall atop his horse. His cheeks were flushed a healthy red from the fresh air and the pace he'd set.

And I'm green . . .

Reaching up her opposite hand, she slammed it against the fabric, keeping those curtains shut.

"Temperance, you look like you are going to cast—"

Stifling a moan, Temperance glared the other woman into letting those words go unfinished.

Gwynn promptly closed her mouth. "I won't say anything else."

Closing her eyes once more, Temperance shifted in her seat and rested her head along the back of the bench. She refocused on breathing. "Please . . . don't." This was to be her penance, then, for letting Dare back into her life, despite the vow she'd made. There was no other accounting for this misery.

KnockKnockKnock.

The frantic rumble of the carriage wheels slowed, and then the conveyance rocked to a complete stop. Her eyes flew open. She stared questioningly across at Gwynn.

Her friend lifted her shoulders in a little shrug. "I didn't talk." Gwynn smiled. "I knocked. It's vastly different."

She groaned. "What have you . . . ?"

The door opened.

This time, it *would* be him and not a servant.

He'd always been contrary in that. Concern glinted in Dare's face. "What is it?" he asked quickly, moving his gaze over her.

"I'm fine," she said between clenched teeth. Though in fairness, in this moment, now that the carriage had stopped, she *was* fine. And if she were being truthful with herself, she was grateful for the reprieve.

Dare leaned farther inside and peered at her face.

"She's not fine," Gwynn piped up. "She is sick." She motioned to Temperance's stomach and throat, and mimicked retching noises.

"That is enough, Gwynn. Dare—" Except that wasn't what he would be to Gwynn or anyone in London. "His Lordship," she corrected, "has affairs he must see to in London. We cannot *simpleee*—" Temperance's words ended on a squeak as Dare plucked her out of the carriage. "What are you doing?" All attempts at affront, however, were dashed by the glorious spring air, a soft, luxuriant breeze that acted like a balm upon her sweat-slicked skin.

"Business can wait," he said tersely.

Gwynn sighed and touched a hand to her chest.

Temperance rolled her eyes. And here she'd believed cynical, life-wary Gwynn Armitage would be the one person who could prove resistant to Dare's charm.

Easily cradling her against his chest, Dare moved one hand over Temperance, lightly caressing her arms and the small of her back, and this time her belly fluttered for altogether different reasons. "Stop, Dare. I am f-fine."

"She's not," Gwynn called from behind them.

From over Dare's shoulder, Temperance glowered at her friend. "Enough," she mouthed.

Wholly unapologetic, Gwynn winked and disappeared within the carriage.

"I really am," Temperance said as Dare carried her off to the side of the road and through the thick, knee-length grass. He didn't stop until he'd reached an enormous boulder, and with an infinite tenderness, he set her down.

"What happened?"

"I'm f—" He gave her a sharp look, silencing those assurances. Temperance sighed. "Carriage rides make me sick."

"They never did before," he said flatly.

Yes, because there'd been so many times when they'd stolen precious moments together, and he'd put her in a hack to get her home with time enough that she needn't worry about earning her father's wrath. "I do now," she explained in even tones.

"That . . . doesn't make sense. You've taken many carriage rides."

But the day her world had crumbled—the day she'd been beaten beyond recognition and the babe she'd desperately yearned for had been dead from that act of violence—everything revolved around that day.

From that one moment, light had died and darkness had dwelled, and reason hadn't existed for any of it. Her chest seized with all the remembered agony for the babe who had never been. She gripped the sides of her skirts, praying to a God who'd been so very invisible throughout Temperance's life that Dare would let it go. That he'd not ask. That she wouldn't have to sidestep questions about something she'd no wish to speak about. *Ever.* "Yes."

⌘

That was it. That was all she'd say. *Yes.*

When he'd first met Temperance Swift, she'd been a girl of ten, and he a lad of fourteen who'd been a cocksure, overconfident boy believing himself a man who could command the world with a word.

In short order, he'd come to appreciate Temperance as one who'd not be cowed or impressed by him.

Nothing had shaken her.

Only to find at some point in their years apart, she'd developed sickness from carriage rides.

It didn't fit with what he knew of the girl he'd bundled into countless hackneys to help her avoid discovery from her mean, drunken father.

He stared expectantly at her. "That is it? 'Yes'? All of a sudden, carriage rides make you ill?"

She shrugged. "Just 'yes.'" It defied logic. "Nor is it recent, Dare. It's been nearly five years since I've not been able to tolerate them. I just haven't seen you in five years, where you'd know it."

Tension crackled in the air around them.

And he'd have to have cotton in his ears to miss that thinly veiled barb.

His face went hot. She would blame him for their estrangement. When he'd written, and then gone to her? "Let us be clear," he said, taking a step toward her. My God, how many times would they circle around this? "I *came* for you," he gritted out. "I found you. You were the one who insisted everything between us was dead. You demanded I leave. *You* insisted you never wished to see me again." Even as she'd now rewrite the final collapse of their relationship.

The color left her cheeks. "How dare you?" She didn't allow a word edgewise. "Do not pretend as though you came back to have a marriage with me."

Tension radiated along his jaw, and he made himself unclench his teeth. "I told you it couldn't be a real marriage. You knew precisely what I was offering. We were friends who knew what the other might expect." He, however, had anticipated that it wouldn't be enough, that the offer was folly. And yet, even knowing that and all that had come to pass between them, he'd still make the decision again if it meant freeing her from her father's abuse.

Smiling sadly up at him, Temperance hugged her arms around her middle. "How convenient, your definition of a 'real marriage.'"

Heat again splotched his face. He should let it go. He'd be wise to abandon this discourse altogether. Nothing good could come from continuing it. Nothing that would advance the new arrangement they'd come to. "And just what is that supposed to mean?"

"It is just . . . You made love to me, you consummated our marriage, and . . . often. As such"—stalking over so quickly her worn boots kicked up dirt and gravel, she stopped before him, the tips of their shoes brushing—"you can't very well go about claiming that it wasn't real."

She wasn't incorrect, and that dulled the edge of his fury.

"It *was* a mistake, making love to you, Temperance," he said softly, and her lower lip trembled. "I always knew taking you in my arms and bed would complicate any deal we'd agreed to." Which was precisely what had happened. "And yet"—Dare brought his mouth close to hers—"making love to you was a mistake I'd happily commit over and over."

The wind teased and toyed with several black curls, tossing them about her shoulders.

Their gazes locked, and without thought, he slid his focus lower, to her wide mouth. Her breath kissed his lips in the embrace his body hungered for.

"Why did you come?" she whispered, her voice so faint he'd not have heard it had they not been as close as they were.

"You know. I require your assistance—"

"Not now," Temperance said. She lowered her voice, protecting the secrecy of their words. "When I left, why did you even bother searching me out?"

He'd thought himself incapable of being hurt any more by Temperance, but this discovery that she'd not known how much he cared for her . . . "Of course I would have sought you out. You were my wife, and"—*and more*—"you were my friend." That was what hurt most of all about this damn mess that he—they—had made of their relationship. She'd been the only person he'd let inside, close enough to care: a friend, whose happiness had mattered more than his own. And he'd learned firsthand from his connection to Temperance Swift just why he'd been right to never let anyone else in. "You were that, too."

"A friend," she repeated back. A sad little note underscored those two syllables. "It could have been more, though. If you'd been willing to give up thievery, Darius."

Which he hadn't . . . and couldn't. It was a part of him that would always be. And because of that, there was nothing else to say. She, however, spoke as one who believed he'd fully put that life behind him. There was a niggling of guilt that worked around his gut, at letting her to that incorrect supposition she'd made. One that would no doubt result in her hightailing it back to her cottage.

Dare placed himself in front of her. "Very well, you cannot tolerate carriage rides," he said, bringing them back 'round to the discovery that had unearthed old resentments from their past. "The only answer that makes sense is that you won't ride in a carriage."

"We'll return to my cottage, then," she said in deadened tones.

Was hers a question? His chest tightened. "Is that what you wish? Is that what you'd like me to do?"

Indecision filled her eyes. Her lips moved ever so slightly; no doubt on the tip of her tongue was just that, a request to end this before it began. But she wouldn't. Because she'd committed to doing so. Because she'd see herself as a coward for reneging, even though he'd never fault her or blame her.

"No," she said, and that confirmation came as if dragged from her.

He knew this woman so well. And yet how ironic, at the same time, that he should know her not at all. He'd not known of her friendships or of the little yet important things, like how a carriage ride could set her stomach churning. Or that she'd learned to ride.

"I intend to see this arrangement through."

She'd yet again agreed to join him. He'd allowed her now several opportunities to remove herself from the arrangement, and as such, he needn't ask any further.

But he didn't want her like this, feeling trapped.

She'd been that too many times in her life, and he'd be damned if he allowed himself to be one who'd force her into another—albeit different—corner.

Dare dusted the tip of his index finger along the curve of her chin. "Are you sure?" he asked, hearing her reluctance and wanting confirmation that she'd thought through this decision, and that she would take an out if that was what she wished. "Once we enter London, there will be no going back. The world will know you as my wife."

She drew in a shuddery breath. Was it his touch, or horror at the prospect he'd raised? How desperately he wished for it to be the former. "I have to do this." She glanced back to the waiting carriages. "Not just for me, but for Gwynn."

A wave of relief swept through him. One that didn't have anything to do with escaping an explanation to the duke.

"From the ashes of our past, perhaps a future can be born for the both of us," Temperance said.

"We'll ride together, then."

"You being in the carriage will not change my reaction to riding." It would only add a layer of unease, having him in close quarters.

A half grin curved his lips up. "I wasn't referring to the carriage." She followed his stare over to the servant holding the reins of Temperance's horse. "I'll have your mount readied so that you can ride."

"Are you suggesting we ride together?" she blurted.

Dare smiled, eager to restore them to some place of ease they'd played pretend at before. "Unless you'd prefer to ride in the carriage . . . ?"

"No!" she exclaimed. "Thank you. I . . ."

He waited.

"I'm a proficient rider. My brother taught me; however, I don't keep the pace that you set."

He held up a hand. "It is fine. We'll arrive in London when we arrive."

Something glimmered in her eyes, some emotion, some sentiment he couldn't make sense of.

And as he joined her on the walk back to the carriage, he couldn't stave off the questions as to what else had changed for Temperance in their time apart.

Chapter 9

Seated on the carved armchair with Gwynn snoring away, Temperance frantically put her needle to work, trying to distract herself from the thought of her undertaking. The bed pillow she'd tucked under her in the form of a makeshift cushion did little in the way of offering comfort.

Sleep hadn't always come easy to Temperance.

As a small girl, and then as a young woman, she'd learned the cost of slumbering too soundly was that it made one too slow to escape a violent beating from the hands of one's father.

When she'd left London and started anew in the English country-side, different demons had haunted her thoughts and stolen all peace— the loss of a babe, a child who should have never been. Fate had known it, and robbed her of the tiny girl because of it.

She'd never thought to know rest.

And then somehow, someway, she'd learned to sleep. Yes, in some part, the long days and strenuous work at Madame Amelie's were what accounted for the mind-numbing fatigue and exhaustion. But it hadn't been just that. For she'd never worked harder than she had in the Rookeries. No, the gift of sleep was one she'd taught herself. She'd learned to close her eyes and shut out the day's trials and the past and the fears, and just turn herself over to the oblivion that came with unconsciousness.

Or that had been the case.

This night, sleep eluded her.

This time, however, the absolute inability to let go of the day had nothing to do with the past or the heartache of loss or the nightmares of her father.

This time, it was Dare . . . Dare, with whom she was returning to London.

She continued to drag her needle through the pink fabric, attaching it to the pale-green cotton. Whatever scraps had been set for discarding at Madame Amelie's Temperance had rescued, and saved to create something when her time was her own.

That wouldn't be the case when she arrived in Dare's fine London townhouse. There, she'd live the life of a marchioness. A marchioness with a houseful of servants and a duke and duchess whom she and Dare had to answer to. And she'd be expected to attend *ton* events with the most powerful, wealthy, influential members of Polite Society. Her palms grew moist, her fingers trembling slightly, and she steadied her grip.

The idea of being with Dare had been sufficiently terrifying enough that she'd not had time to think of everything their arrangement entailed.

She slowed, her needle hovering along the perfect line she'd just stitched.

Soon she'd be in a position where she needn't rely on anyone ever again. Soon there would be funds enough to see her settled forever. *That* was what she needed to focus on . . . everything awaiting her and Gwynn when she saw through this arrangement with Dare. All she needed to do was suffer about the *ton* for as long as it took for his sister to find a husband.

Given the young woman was the sister of a marquess, and the granddaughter of a duke and duchess, it wouldn't be long at all.

And then Temperance would be free to go on her way and live comfortably forevermore.

And it was all because of Dare.

"Dare the Savior," she whispered into the quiet. The rescuer of innocents. The saver of damsels. That was the role he'd always craved and one he'd carried out with all—including with her. And perhaps there was something very wrong about her for having wanted more from him.

For them.

He'd always wanted to shield her from suffering, just as he had everyone *else* in East London. At first, she'd fallen head over heels in love with him, this dashing, mighty man who'd fought to protect and defend her.

It had been heady and shocking.

She, who'd grown up witnessing her father's frequent beatings of her mother. That same violence she'd also seen carried out against women on the streets . . . So she'd believed that was the only way between men and women.

A bleating snore rent across the small quarters Temperance shared with Gwynn, cutting into her musings. Temperance shook her head, clearing those thoughts, and stared with no small amount of envy at a perfectly rested Gwynn, sprawled on her back with the covers off and her mouth hanging open. The other woman was sleep personified. From belowstairs, the noisy din of the taproom had no impact on the other woman's slumber.

Abandoning all hope of rest, Temperance briefly set down her sewing. She lowered her legs, the cool penetrating her feet. Shivering, she hurried across the room, and as she went, she shrugged out of her night wrapper and exchanged it for another serviceable chemise and dress. After she'd donned her shoes, she gathered up the fabric she'd been working on and headed for the front of the room.

The moment she opened the door, the ungreased hinges squealed.

Behind her, Gwynn sputtered in her sleep, and then her snoring resumed its regular cadence.

Drawing the door closed behind her, Temperance blinked to adjust her eyes to the nearly pitch-black corridor and then froze.

Stretched out on the opposite side of the hall with his long legs unfurled and a leather book in hand, Dare had set himself up. From over the top of that tome, he looked at her. "Temperance."

She dampened her lips and briefly considered retreating back into her room. Briefly.

"Dare." And before she thought better of it, she settled herself onto the floor across from him. At some point, he'd switched the clothes he'd ridden in for a new set of garments. These dark ones were just as fine and flawless. With a book on his lap, he may as well have been a nobleman seated in his office and not a gentleman sitting on the floor of a public resting house.

They sat in companionable silence for a long while, with Dare reading and her stitching fabric into the beginnings of a small throw.

"Unable to sleep still, are you?" he asked, closing his book.

She paused, the tip of her needle piercing the line she sewed, and then made herself drag it through.

Still . . . the assumption was that she'd remained the same all these years later, and she didn't want to remind him that she'd changed . . . in so many ways. It was, simply put, easier to let him to that conjecture.

"I was unable to sleep," she allowed. Drawing her knees up close to her chest, she made a makeshift table of her legs, taking some of the strain from her arms.

"London?"

Temperance stared intently down at her work. "Yes." Why must he continue to remind her of all the ways in which they'd known everything there was to know about one another? So much so that they needn't even speak in complete sentences to know what the other spoke of.

"You won't see him," he said quietly.

Ironically, it was the first time that her unease didn't stem from fear of that monster.

"He doesn't leave the Rookeries, Temperance," he continued on with that same incorrect supposition. "He's become an even bigger drunkard in his old age. He'll drown himself in his spirits."

Unless she'd seen a body upon which to spit, Temperance would never believe anything but that the Devil still walked amongst them. "It's not Abaddon I'm"—*fearful of*—"uneasy about, Dare." Except, mayhap in large part it was. Mayhap she'd just not acknowledged as much until Dare had forced her to. Temperance, however, would be damned if she let him be the root of her fears. Not again. There was nothing he could do that would hurt worse than the pain he'd already brought her.

Dare had always been entirely too confident where her ruthless sire was concerned. And there had been another time when she'd let herself believe in Dare, too. She'd made the mistake of thinking her father had forgotten about her. And that mistake had proven fatal. Tears pricked her lashes, and she gave thanks for the shroud of darkness that shielded those useless drops. She frantically dragged her needle through her fabrics. No good came from crying. If there had, she'd have been healed in those immediate days when she'd birthed and lost her babe. She shoved the needle through the fabric and stabbed the pad of her thumb.

Her breath hissed from her teeth as she dropped her stitchery.

He scooted across the hall. "Here."

It was those tones, those blasted gentle, tender ones, that sent a single tear falling. And then another.

Burying her head in her shoulder, she angrily swiped back the moisture from her cheeks. "It's fine," she said tightly.

Except he reached for her hand anyway, and tugging a crisp white, embroidered kerchief from his jacket, he pressed it lightly against her wound. "It isn't awful," Dare agreed, his head bent over their joined palms.

She stared at the tiny crimson drop as it expanded into a larger, distorted blob. Her stomach revolted. A soundless moan worked its way up her throat.

Just look away, and you needn't see . . . You needn't remember blood upon your person from another time.

Squeezing her eyes shut, she blocked out the sight of it. Except, different remembrances of that sanguine substance had already taken root.

Slick and sleek, so dark it was nearly black. So much of it.

She bit the inside of her cheek.

"There," Dare was saying, and just that one quiet word, spoken in his always-assuring tone, pulled her from the fog of the past.

He glanced up.

Temperance drew her hand back and cradled the injured digit close. As she spoke, she directed the words at the makeshift bandage Dare had arranged from his kerchief. "This world isn't mine."

Dare stared at her questioningly.

"Not this one," she clarified, gesturing to the cramped hall they'd made a meeting place.

Understanding dawned in his clear gaze. *"Ahh."* He scoffed. "This world is as much yours as anyone else's," he said with such affront in his tone and expression, she smiled.

He'd always been offended on her behalf. "It isn't, though, Dare," she said gently. "I've dressed gentry, but never lords and ladies. I don't know their dances or their customs or . . . anything about their ways." And now he'd asked her . . . Nay, she'd agreed to play at marchioness.

Dare shifted, pulling himself around so they sat shoulder to shoulder. And there was a calming peace from that light touch, that shared connection. "This isn't my world, either, Temperance."

She looked up at him. "But it *is*," she said with a quiet insistence. He might not believe it or want that to be the case. "Regardless of how many years you've been away from the *ton*, you were born to this, and that is all that matters to these people." These people . . . whose ranks he now belonged to. Her stomach tightened. As the divide that had always existed between them now proved somehow, impossibly, even greater. "By your own admission, the funds are dependent upon your being seen in Polite Society with your sister."

"And we'll do that," he said calmly.

So confident.

Laughing softly, she leaned against the wall and shook her head back and forth. "Oh, Dare." There wasn't a single challenge he'd not boldly confront. "You fear nothing."

He lifted his broad shoulders in a casual shrug. "What good comes from that?"

"None," she agreed. And she'd once prided herself on being at least like him in this. She, who couldn't countenance carriage rides or the sight of blood. Temperance glanced up at him again. "And yet I've also come to learn that fear is a state that shouldn't be ignored." Reading those premonitions and listening to one's body's inherent unease could prove the difference between life . . . and death. It was an understanding she'd come to too late.

Dare brushed several tresses that had escaped her plait behind her ear. Those strands bounced back, resisting his attempts. Her heart thrummed . . . at the effortless ease of the intimacy of that afterthought touch. He smoothed her hair back once more . . . and this time, the locks complied. Yes, because Dare Grey could manage to tame even her recalcitrant curls. "You've grown more cautious." *In our time apart.*

"Aye." Temperance faced him and met his gaze squarely. "And you've become even less so." He'd learned nothing from his latest trip to Newgate. By his own admission, some unnamed foe had maneuvered him into a noose, and he spoke with only a casualness about it. "You trust that everything will work out."

"Because it will," he said with that same arrogance that pulled another laugh from her.

She lightly knocked her head against the wall. "That isn't how life works, Dare."

"It does for me."

It hadn't for her. "You won't always be so fortunate," she said without inflection. "You will learn that not even you can bend the world to your will. That no matter how much you wish for something"—her gaze slid past him, to the very end of the corridor—"no matter how much you intend to make it be, that sometimes you j-just can't." Her voice quavered as, unbidden, a memory of the babe she'd held all too briefly slipped in. Feeling his piercing stare upon her, she schooled her features. "Polite Society isn't simply going to accept me because you wish for it to be so."

He flashed a half smile. "And you are wrong, Temperance. They'll not only accept you; they'll adore you."

Laughing, Temperance rested her head against his shoulder. "You are many things, Dare Grey, but you've never been naive."

"I don't expect it will be smooth at first, but I trust that we will both win their world over."

He would. That was a certainty. If for no other reason than the charm he oozed and the confidence he possessed, he'd make it happen. In time, however, he'd see that none of this would be effortless in the way he thought it would be. "Good night, Dare," she said gently as she came to her feet.

In one fluid movement, he hopped up behind her. "You will see . . ." She was turning to enter her room when he lightly caught her hand.

Her heart pounded as he guided her back around, and his thick lashes hooded his gaze. And for one moment, she believed he intended to kiss her. *Again.* Her heart beat wildly as she leaned up.

"I don't believe it will be easy. I believe they will revel in our failure," he said pragmatically. "As such, I believe we would be wise to . . . come to a truce during our time together."

When Temperance was a small girl, her father had awakened her by dousing her with a bucket of freezing water. The absolute absence of either passion or desire in Dare's tone and gaze had the same cooling effect. She made herself ease away from him; her back thumped against her bedroom door. From within Gwynn's snoring continued. "A truce," she echoed.

"We've been at odds over much, but we are united in our goal. We will not, however, see this through unless we are working together, and fighting over the past and . . . past wrongs . . . Nothing good can come of that."

Fighting over the past and . . . past wrongs . . . Nothing good can come of that . . .

No, it was why she'd withheld the agony of that loss from him. And there'd been a time she'd resented herself for keeping him from the suffering that haunted her every day.

"That is for the best," she murmured, unsure whether she spoke to his point or to the silent ones that existed only in her head.

Relief swept over his features, and despite herself, despite the agreement they'd just come to, she couldn't tamp down a wave of bitterness. He could simply divorce the past from the present. He'd always been able to separate his mind from his heart, in ways she never had.

"Polite Society will be expecting us to fail. Relishing our missteps," he carried on. "And united is the only way to not only defeat those expectations but also successfully establish ourselves in that world."

How cool he was about this new version of their once passionate relationship. Were they even capable of anything but volatility? They'd only ever alternated between tender, teasing lovers and figures raging at one another over decisions the other person couldn't understand. Could they simply remove the years of history and emotion to achieve the ends they each sought?

Dare held out his spare hand.

Temperance studied those outstretched fingers.

Can you set aside your resentment for his having gone missing when you needed him most?

Except . . . what choice did they have? She reluctantly nodded and accepted his handshake. "I'll agree to a truce, Dare," she allowed when he'd released her palm. Her hand went cold at the loss. "Unless you give me reason not to trust you." *Again.* And there'd been so many reasons to not trust him or his reliability over the years.

His expression grew shuttered. "Good night, Temperance."

"Dare."

She hurried inside her room.

Only it wasn't until she'd changed back into her nightclothes and climbed into the bed, and had the coverlet up to her chin, that she realized he'd never given her any assurances on the matter of trust.

Chapter 10

They didn't make the time Dare had hoped or expected. They'd stopped when he'd intended to push on through the night. Those plans, however, had changed the moment he learned Temperance struggled in carriage rides. He'd not have her ride in the dead of night. Instead, he'd sent her friend on ahead in a separate carriage, while he and Temperance continued at a slower pace.

Which was why it wasn't until late in the afternoon that he and Temperance arrived at his new—albeit temporary—Mayfair residence.

As if they'd been standing in wait, a small contingent of servants filed through the front door and came streaming down the steps the moment he and Temperance brought their mounts to a stop.

Her horse danced restlessly about.

A servant was instantly there.

Only the footman hesitated, looking with wide eyes up at Temperance.

Swinging down, Dare greeted the boy. "I have it, Reuben," he said, waving him off to help hand Temperance down.

The butler hovered in the doorway, his expression . . . pained. Which was . . . interesting, and not just a small bit alarming, given the young man's inability to reveal any emotion before now.

"You have servants, Dare," Temperance whispered furiously.

"Yes," he said as they climbed the handful of steps.

"No," she said, her hushed tones slightly more frantic. Wide-eyed, Temperance glanced at the young men and women scurrying about. "A lot of them."

"Yes."

The butler stepped aside, allowing them to enter.

"Spencer," Dare greeted. Unfastening his cloak, he shrugged out of the article and tossed it to the young man. The servant stumbled as he caught it against his chest. "I take it His Grace and Her Grace have arrived?"

"Y-yes, my lord," Spencer stammered, struggling to right the article in his arms. "I-I took the liberty of showing them to the Opal Parlor." As he spoke, his gaze strayed periodically to Temperance. "They arrived several hours ago."

"Splendid." It wasn't anything of the sort. It was, however, necessary— the meeting to tie up the details surrounding the inheritance the duke dangled over him.

After the butler had stolen another furtive glance in Temperance's direction, Dare relieved him of all curiosity. "Spencer, if I may at this time present my wife, the Marchioness of Milford."

Spencer blanched and lost his hold on Dare's cloak. The garment landed in a whoosh upon the marble floor at his feet.

A footman rushed forward to rescue it.

Spencer's eyes bulged. "The *m-m-maaarchioness*?" When the young butler managed to get the actual word out, he added three additional syllables.

Anger lanced through Dare. "Is that a problem?" He leveled a warning glare on the usually composed head servant.

The other man's small Adam's apple jumped several times. "No?" Dare narrowed his eyes. "Of course n-not?" Angling his body closer toward Dare so Temperance was cut from the exchange, Spencer cupped a hand around his mouth. "Very p-possibly?"

Dare took a step back, closer to where Temperance hovered in the wings, including her where Spencer had sought to cut her out. "Are those questions?" Dare warned in silken, steely tones he reserved for those with whom he found himself on the other end of the dealing table when negotiating for the lives of London's innocent.

His features strained, Spencer tugged at his collar. "N-no?"

From the corner of his eye, Dare caught a young footman rushing over to help Temperance from her wool cloak.

He'd be damned, however, if he tolerated anyone treating Temperance as if she were somehow unworthy. "That sounded like another question, Spencer," he said warningly. At his side, he felt Temperance as she silently took in the exchange.

Spencer glanced briefly past Dare's shoulder, and then when he returned his focus to Dare, the butler appeared a moment away from dissolving into big, blubbering tears. "I don't mean . . . It isn't my intention . . ."

Temperance slid closer to Dare. "Stop it," she whispered.

He bristled. "I've not done anything."

"You're terrifying him."

As one, they looked to where Spencer quaked.

The butler jerked his attention to the cheerful pastoral mural overhead.

She'd call *Dare* out as a bully. "You'd defend him?" he bit out.

"He's not done anything," she said, calmer than he'd ever remembered her. This, this new version of Temperance, who could no longer ride in carriages and got queasy around blood. How many other changes had befallen the both of them in these years apart? And somehow, that realization only sent his anger spiraling . . . with Spencer. With her . . . and with himself.

"I'll not have him treat you with anything less than respect." He hissed out that last word, needing to give life to his fury and frustration.

And wonder of wonders, fiery, hotheaded Temperance met his response with an equanimity and sarcasm. "Because he's surprised?" she said dryly. "Because you didn't mention you'd be returning with a wife, and one so clearly outside your station?"

"You're not out—"

She shot him a look, silencing the rest of that defense.

He moved his gaze over the bronzed hue of her angular face. Any other person would have been offended by the servant's insolence. Another might have been given to tears. And for all the ways in which she'd been quick-tempered, she'd also been possessed of a logic he'd admired her for.

Color filled her cheeks. "What is it?"

He shook his head. "It is nothing." It was him remembering the reasons he'd fallen in love with her, against his better judgment and after vowing to never let someone close.

"And tell me, is *this* your master plan for handling my entry into Polite Society?" Temperance lifted a perfectly formed black eyebrow. She didn't let him get a word in. "Is this how you intend to deal with any and every cut direct I'm given? By calling out and scaring anyone who offends me?"

"No?"

"Is that a question?"

"Yes, then," he said flatly. "That is precisely what I intend to do."

"Oh, Dare." Temperance rubbed her hands over her face and laughed. "Then we are to fail, and spectacularly."

Dare took her lightly by the arm and steered her away from the assembled servants. "You'll be met with respect, or—"

"Or what?" she interrupted. "I told you how I would be received, and yet you think you're going to force people to accept me." She shook her head. "That isn't how the world works. Not this world. Not any world. Those rules are the same whatever class a person belongs to, Dare."

All his muscles tensed. "I'll demand greater treatment of you, even if you'll not accept it for yourself."

A hiss burst from her teeth. "You believe that is what this is about? That I can somehow make people like me and accept—"

"Ahem."

They jerked their gazes back to the forgotten servant. Spencer lifted a gloved palm and waved it slightly. "If I might . . . perhaps suggest postponing your meeting with the duke and duchess?" he asked hopefully. "I can inform them His Lordship is tired from his—"

"No."

"Travels," Spencer finished weakly over Dare.

"We're having the damned meeting." Grabbing Temperance's hand, he propelled them both onward to the damned duke, who couldn't simply give Dare the monies he sought and needed. No, he'd make Dare and Temperance play at domesticity as a proper lord and lady, a role neither of them wanted.

Not unlike their marriage itself.

I don't want you in my life, Dare . . . not anymore . . . never again . . .

"She is going with you?" Spencer called loudly behind them, breaking through the long-ago memory burnt indelibly upon Dare's mind.

"She is, in fact, 'Her Ladyship,' Spencer. Have a care, or you're going to find yourself sacked, and quickly," Dare warned, not so much as glancing back.

Temperance dug her fingers into his. "Stop."

Dare ignored her.

"My a-apologies," the servant panted, slightly out of breath as he struggled to keep up. The man's buckled black shoes beat rhythmically upon the marble floor as he struggled to match the pace Dare had set.

"I said, stop," Temperance repeated, digging her heels in and forcing Dare to either halt or drag her down.

Setting his jaw, he acquiesced. "What?"

"Is this really what you wish?"

"I don't know what you're asking, Temperance."

"Don't you?" Temperance made an up-and-down gesture, motioning to herself. "Is this truly the way you wish to introduce me to a duke and duchess? How you wish to present yourself?" She looked pointedly at his dusty garments . . . and lower to his mud-stained boots. "You should care more than you do, Dare."

He grinned. "Ah, but I don't."

Her mouth remained set in a frown. "That is clear, and yet . . . why? You always took pride in your appearance in the Rookeries . . . Why should it somehow be different here?"

That gave him pause. "You're making more of it than there is."

"Am I?" she insisted. "As it is, being accepted by your grandparents and Polite Society will prove problematic enough, as I'm the daughter of a drunk."

God, how he despised how closely she linked herself and her existence to the miserable bastard who'd sired her.

He lightly touched his forehead to hers. "Temperance, you are more than the circumstances you were born to."

"I know that," she said automatically.

Did she, though? She'd always tied herself and her worth to that vile bastard who'd given her life . . . and her downtrodden mother, who'd died shortly after Dare had first met Temperance. "That is not what I am speaking about, however, Dare. I'm talking about how you for some reason are so very determined to let your grandparents see you and me a certain way." Her shoulders came back. "And you might not care about how you will appear to them"—she wrinkled her nose—"or smell when we're presented, but *we* do."

He faintly sniffed the air, and grimaced. Yes, there was a definite stench of horse and sweat to him.

She gave him another pointed look.

And when presented that way, he was humbled by the realization that he'd not fully considered just how difficult this upcoming exchange would be for Temperance. She, who'd been strong in facing the toughest drunks and street thugs, and as such he'd not let himself think of her as . . . unnerved by meeting with a pair of nobles. "You are not incorrect," he said gruffly.

A relieved sigh came from behind them, which Spencer quickly masked as a cough.

"And you are as obstinate as you've ever been in your failure to concede when you're wrong."

Her lips tipped in the first hint of a real smile since they'd reunited, and his heart somersaulted. He'd missed that smile. He'd missed it so very much and hadn't realized just *how* much until he'd caught that glimpse.

From where he hovered several paces away, Spencer shifted back and forth.

"Spencer." Dare called the other man over.

The servant came running. "Yes, my lord?"

"Please see Her Ladyship to her rooms, and then when she is ready, see she is escorted to the Opal Parlor."

Relief lit up the younger man's eyes. "Yes, my lord." He dropped a deep bow. "My lady, if you will follow me."

Dare waited, watching on as Spencer showed Temperance down the hall. She paused at the end and cast one last look Dare's way, and he tried to make something of her gaze. The distance, however—real and that which had been imposed in their years apart—made it impossible.

After she and Spencer had gone, Dare started for the Opal Parlor. It didn't matter what garments he wore. The meeting was what was import—

He slowed his steps.

That is not what I am speaking about, however, Dare. I'm talking about how you for some reason are so very determined to let your grandparents see you and me a certain way . . . And you might not care about how you will appear to them or smell when we're presented, but we do . . .

She'd been incorrect. This had nothing to do with how he wished for the duke and duchess to see him. And yet there wasn't just himself whom he had to consider. Now there was Temperance. Temperance, who'd done him an enormous favor in setting aside past resentments and differences to journey to this part of England she so hated.

Dare let out a quiet curse, and shifting course, he made his way abovestairs and to his rooms. A short while later, having rinsed with cold water that had been set out in his washbasin and changed into new garments, Dare found his way to the Opal Parlor.

A liveried footman stood stationed at the door and clicked his heels when Dare stopped outside the room. When the young man turned to open the door, Dare waved him off.

"I have it." All this pomp and circumstance and people serving at his beck and call was as foreign as it was unwanted. Per the conditions the duke and duchess had set, he might have to live in this world, but it needn't mean he had to surrender all parts of himself and the life he'd known. With one hand, Dare finished buttoning his tailcoat, and with his spare one, he opened the door. "My apologies," he said as he entered. "I was—"

His words cut off as he took in the unexpected sight.

The duke and duchess sat beside another equally regal couple. Sandwiched between that pair of strangers was another, a slender, pale-blonde young lady. A tray of refreshments sat untouched beside a pot of tea.

Dare opened and closed his mouth several times. "Uh . . . hello?"

At that, the previously frozen room came alive. Everyone set down their teacups, and there came the staggered clinks of glass touching wood.

The unfamiliar trio were the first to come to their feet.

"Darius," the duke boomed. Using his cane, His Grace pushed himself to his feet. He leaned on the marble head, as if the effort had strained his energies. "We're so glad you are back, boy. To finalize the details of our agreement." And for the first time since he'd been reunited with the duke and duchess, Dare found the pair smiling.

Warning bells went off.

"Our agreement."

"That you will marry." The duchess beamed. Clutching her joined fists briefly against her chest, she looked over to the strangers.

Dare followed her gaze to the young woman who'd earned his grandmother's focus.

The lady dipped her eyes to the floor.

Dare looked back to his grandfather. "Forgive me, I'm afraid . . . introductions are required."

"Splendid idea." Her Grace clapped once. Sweeping over, she took one of Dare's hands. "May we present the Earl and Countess of Peregrine. Our families have been closely connected for nearly two generations. Your father and the earl were the best of friends. And your mother was closest with Lady Peregrine above all others." She may as well have been speaking of strangers. "And after so very many years," she said, guiding him across the room toward the young lady, "it brings me the greatest of pleasure and honor to introduce you at last"—she stopped before the serene figure—"to Lady Madelyn Wainwright"—she paused—"your *betrothed*." With that, she joined Dare's hand with the young lady's.

It took a moment to process those last words.

When he did, two thoughts registered at the same time, two *confused* thoughts, neither of which made sense: one, he was holding the hand of a woman who was certainly not his wife, and the other . . .

His . . . *betrothed?*

"My . . . betrothed?" he croaked, his voice pitching slightly up.

"Betrothed," the duke repeated in a joy-filled, bellowing voice. His Grace smiled widely. "Your future wife."

Dare's stomach fell.

Yes, yes, he'd heard his grandparents correctly, after all.

He stared at the small gloved hand joined with his. *Oh, bloody hell.* Dare frantically jerked his palm out of her delicate grasp.

The duke's expression faltered. "Darius? I trust everything is . . . all right?"

Wordlessly, Dare took in the assembly of guests, his grandparents. No. This wasn't all right.

It was a damned disaster.

❦

A short while later, having washed the remnants of travel from her person and changed into her finest dress, Temperance was escorted belowstairs by Spencer.

Periodically, the butler cast strained glances back her way, only adding layer upon layer to her unease.

As they wound their way through the corridors, to keep herself from giving in to panic over her upcoming meeting, she scanned her gaze over Dare's household—and for as long as she lived here, her household, too.

The varnish upon the hardwood portion of the floors added a layer of shine to the monochromatic heartwood flooring and spoke to the wealth of this place . . . which was at odds with the words Dare had spoken about an insolvent marquessate. Ornate, teardrop-shaped crystal dangled from gold sconces. Sconces filled with nub-size candles, those shortened tapers the first telltale indication of the financial state of this household.

If one looked past the initial trappings, one noticed the previously neglected details: the slight fading of the Chinese-paper walls. The velvetlike Wilton carpeting that lined the halls had begun to fray at the edges.

And still . . . despite that evidence of wear and aging, none would ever doubt the grandeur and wealth that had gone into the townhouse.

With every step that brought her closer to Dare's duke and duchess grandparents, Temperance's panic intensified. To steady the trembling of her palms, she smoothed them along the front of her finest dress.

Finest dress . . . ? Even upon its best day, the article she'd constructed of the remnants that had gone unused by one of Madame Amelie's most influential patrons had never been suited to this place. A nervous laugh bubbled up and spilled from her lips.

Spencer stole a glance her way, and she forced herself to draw an even breath.

"Have you been employed long by the marquess's family?" she asked in a bid to break the tension and establish some manner of rapport with the head servant. After all, given her new—though temporary—role within the household, they would be required to work closely with one another.

"I was only hired just shortly before His Lordship's death," Spencer murmured.

"Might I beg a favor, Mr. Spencer?" She reached into her pocket and drew out the note she'd hastily written to her brother, informing him of her and Gwynn's arrival in London. "Would you see that this is delivered for me?"

"Of course, my lady," he said, immediately collecting the missive. He glanced down at the name and address upon the front before tucking it inside his jacket.

There should have been only joy at thinking about her brother's response to discovering she and Gwynn now resided in London. And there likely would have been . . . had she not been about to face Dare's noble family.

Spencer brought them to a stop outside a pair of arched pine double doors. The servant hesitated a long moment, and then with a customary pained expression on his features, he drew the panels open. "Her Ladyship, the Marchioness of Milford."

That pronouncement rang about the otherwise silent room. A silence so heavy and thick the small flicker of fire in the hearth provided the only other sound.

Dare, along with five strangers, stared back at her with horror, and one of those individuals was a young lady . . . a young lady who also stood very close to Dare.

Unease rippled along her spine. The sense of dread that she'd learned to listen to . . . That was now screaming just one single command. *Run*.

She curled her toes tightly and made her feet stay planted.

Clearing his throat, Spencer hurried from the room, and even as he drew those ornate pine panels shut behind him, Temperance caught the relieved sigh.

That click of the doors shutting managed to penetrate across the shocked collection of guests.

"Temperance," Dare greeted. Color splotched his cheeks as he strode over to where she hovered in the entranceway.

She tried to make herself focus on him and find a lifeline in his familiar face and presence. He'd always represented that for her.

Until now.

"What is the meaning of this?" the bewhiskered stranger barked.

The blonde-haired woman clutching at his arm stared with shocked eyes at Temperance. "The *marchioness*?"

"Temperance." Dare spoke in hushed tones. "Perhaps it might be better if we—"

"Who is this woman?" the white-haired gentleman thundered from the center of the room.

The voice, those garments, and the monocle could mark him as only one: the duke.

The regal lady on his arm—the duchess—looked Temperance over. "I am certain she—this—can be explained, Lady Peregrine."

All the while, the pretty young lady took in the exchange with enormous blue eyes.

Temperance's belly clenched. Many times in the course of her life, she had been made to feel somehow less than others. None of those instances, however, could compare with the look in the duke's eyes as he scraped a hard, unforgiving stare over her. Or the feeling of the other strangers gawking at her.

Wordlessly, Temperance glanced about the room. She'd anticipated this meeting would be uncomfortable. Uneasy. Distressing. Many things . . . But not even she could have foreseen this level of misery. Reflexively, she found herself sliding closer to Dare's side.

Lady Peregrine gasped and jabbed a finger at Temperance and Dare. "Who *iiiis* she?"

"I can explain," Dare said with his usual calm, as if he were merely pointing out details on the English weather and not justifying Temperance's presence to a roomful of horrified nobles. "And prior to Temperance's arrival, I was attempting to . . ."

She lifted her chin. She'd not be spoken about or over. Not by Dare. Not by his grandfather. Not by anyone. "I am Dare's wife."

"Who is Dare?" Lady Peregrine cried.

"I believe she is referring to the marquess, Mama," the young lady said in dulcet tones.

"But . . . but . . . he . . ." Lady Peregrine wilted, collapsing into the chair.

"What manner of game is this, Duke?" the bewhiskered gentleman thundered.

"I . . ." And amidst the confusion, Temperance witnessed that which she'd never thought to witness: not only a duke but also one who'd been cowed and silenced by another. "I do not know, but I'm certain it can be explained."

"Come," Lord Peregrine snapped. "We're leaving." Taking his wife by the arm, he guided her to her feet, and collecting his daughter's hand, he led that pair quickly toward the door.

Temperance hurried to step out of their way as they sailed past her.

The duchess set after them, with the duke limping more slowly behind. "Please," the duchess cried. "This can all be . . ." Those assurances grew more faded as she raced to keep up with the retreating trio.

Until all that was left in the room . . . was silence.

Nay, that wasn't altogether true.

Narrowing her eyes, Temperance looked to Dare.

Dare, always unflappable, even in the face of a capture and trip to Newgate, now tugged at his cravat.

"What. Was. That?" she managed to grind out between clenched teeth.

He pushed the door shut.

And the warning bells, already blaring, screamed all the louder.

"There appears to have been a . . . misunderstanding."

She made herself go motionless. "Oh?" she asked, striving for a casualness she didn't feel.

Dare crossed the room, making for a gilded and crystal tantalus. Drawing open the clear, bronze-lined doors, Dare drew out a bottle of brandy and a glass. "It appears I didn't altogether understand the discussion the duke intended to have."

"You didn't tell them you were married."

"There was a misunderstanding," he said as he splashed several fingerfuls into a snifter.

"I know." She bit out those two syllables. "You said as much, two times now."

He swirled the contents of his glass once and then tossed it back in a long, painful-looking swallow. Grimacing, he set the empty glass back down. "I was under the assumption that they were expecting me to take a wife."

"And what were they expecting?"

"The same." Dare grabbed the bottle of brandy and poured himself another glass. "However, there was apparently a betrothal."

"A . . . betrothal?"

"Between myself and . . ." With the decanter in hand, Dare motioned to the front of the room.

Temperance followed his focus over to the doorway the regal couple had fled through just moments ago. The young lady. "Oh," she said, dumbstruck. And all at once, the meaning and the implications of that family struck . . . particularly that gloriously elegant, flawless English beauty's presence. She'd been . . . his betrothed. "She was . . ." And even knowing it as she did, Temperance needed to say it anyway. To give life to the truth. "She was your intended?"

Dare took another drink from his snifter, this time more measured. He nodded. "Apparently. It was a childhood betrothal."

"I . . . see." And knowing all these years there had been another woman meant for him, one who was his social equal, who fit with every expectation of beauty, and who was flawless . . . in every way that Temperance wasn't—in ways that Temperance was broken—suddenly, she had the overwhelming urge to just cry. About everything.

"The duke, however, failed to mention anything about a betrothal. The only statement he made pertained to my being married." He cleared his throat. "Which I am." Dare held her gaze. *"We are."*

As if she'd needed clarification about that great mistake. The thin thread of her patience and self-control frayed and broke. "And at no time did you think to mention anything about me?" she asked, her voice slightly pitched. "You didn't find any moment in which to say, 'I have a wife, oh, and she also happens to have been born in the Rookeries to a drunk and a washerwoman'?" As if a duke or duchess could ever be prepared to learn their beloved, long-lost grandson had gone and wed himself a street thug's daughter? Another panicky giggle climbed up her throat.

"They didn't need to know that," he said tightly.

"Why?" she shot back, propping her hands on her hips. "Because you are ashamed of who I am?"

"Of course not." Exasperation laced his denial. "I've *never* been ashamed of you, Temperance Swift."

She angled her chin up. "Haven't you? You, who always go out of your way to remind me what I'm not. At least I've accepted my origins for what they are."

Closing the remaining distance, he strode over. "Have you? You're the one who finds any occasion in which to mention Abaddon."

She choked. "I do not."

"Or is it simply that you wish to remind yourself of your past because you don't want to let yourself imagine any different future for yourself?"

Outrage drew a gasp from her. "How dare—" The doors were drawn open, drowning out the remainder of that charge.

And the urge to flee filled her again as the duke and duchess swept inside. Not just any duke and duchess, either. Dare's grandparents. The pair's earlier display of emotion may as well have been imagined. For as they entered, linked arm in arm, they may as well have been a lord and lady out on a social call.

The like tension in their wrinkled features and pale complexions proved the only indication that they were not as in control as they portrayed.

A servant waiting in the hall closed the arched double panels so that Temperance was alone with the powerful pair. Although that wasn't altogether true. There was Dare.

And yet where there'd always been comfort in his presence, for the first time in all the years she'd known him, that sense of security was no longer there.

Now there were lies and half-truths and questions.

So many questions.

"Darius." The duchess was the first to speak, as a duchess would. Holding her spare arm aloft, she swept forward with her husband in tow. "I believe proper introductions are in order."

"And explanations," His Grace said brusquely, hammering the bottom of his cane upon the bloodred carpet, garish and wholly at odds in the otherwise ivory-and-pale-white-adorned parlor.

The duchess quelled him with a look. "That will come later."

Temperance took control. "Your Grace," she murmured, sinking into a curtsy the king would have no cause to fault. "My name is Temperance Swift." The woman's brows came together. "Grey," Temperance corrected.

"Greyson," Dare substituted.

Her gaze flew to his. What . . . ?

"Perhaps we might all sit," the duchess recommended in a tone none would ever dare confuse with a suggestion.

All of Temperance's muscles tensed as she took the indicated seat, the one last occupied by the guests who'd run off. Dare's betrothed. Shoving back thoughts of the earlier, wholly composed beauty, Temperance focused on the austere couple settled across from her.

"Now," the duchess began, "come the explanations."

"I'd hardly call what came before proper introductions," Dare drawled. "Only what would I know? A thief scheduled to hang in the Rookeries wouldn't know about proper introductions."

The duchess's whole countenance went a sickly shade of white.

Temperance shot a glare in Dare's direction. Why was he doing this? Only he would endeavor to issue a challenge to a duke and duchess.

Wholly unfazed, he reclined in his seat. "Temperance and I were friends from the Rookeries."

Bright-red splotches formed circles on the older woman's face. Was it the reference to the friendship or the place they'd met? Or both? "Friends," the duchess echoed, spitting it out as if she'd uttered a word she'd no familiarity with and found distasteful. "Men and women aren't friends. It isn't natural." She looked to her husband.

His Grace gave an emphatic and concurring nod. "It isn't natural." He hammered his cane on the floor, punctuating his point with that marble stick.

"We were," Dare said, "and we also married. So one might say we are both friends and husband and wife."

Temperance frowned. He was baiting them. For what purpose?

"When did this take place?" Her Grace pressed, firing off questions.

"Five years ago," Temperance said softly. It had been five years since she'd convinced herself she might be Dare's wife and keep her heart out of their arrangement. All the while, she'd lied to herself . . . She'd failed to acknowledge that she couldn't have taken her heart out of the equation of their union because she'd first fallen in love with him.

"Your marriage"—the duchess turned that query to Dare, Temperance edged out of the questioning—"is legal?" Hope flickered to life in the older woman's eyes.

"It is," Dare said quietly.

"Are you certain?" the duke pressed. "The records?" He motioned four fingers in a half circle, as he spoke. "The officiating? Was it a marriage with actual vows exchanged?" Hope filled the old man's eyes. "Perhaps you signed whatever name you've gone by . . . by . . . where you lived?"

Startled, Temperance jerked her gaze to her husband.

Dare inclined his head. "I . . ." He looked away from his grandfather and over at Temperance. Their gazes locked. "I took care to sign my legal name."

Her mind stalled and then swirled . . . with confusion. He'd . . . signed his legal name. When no one in the Rookeries, certainly not her father, would have been any wiser, ever, he'd still given her his legal name. Why? Why would he have done so? The sole point of their marriage had been to give Temperance the protection that had come from Dare's name that was feared and revered in the Rookeries. She sought to make sense out of why he would have done such a thing.

Unless he really wanted you as his wife . . .

The duke sighed, cutting into those whimsical, nonsensical musings. "And . . . consummated? Was it consummated?" His tone, however, bespoke the resignation of one who'd already accepted the answer before it was given.

I'm going to throw up. Balling her hands, Temperance stared down at her interlocked fingers. She had anticipated being rejected. What she'd not allowed herself to consider was being plainly discussed, and the frantic puzzle of how to disentangle Dare from their marriage in front of her.

Dare covered her joined palms with one of his own, and just that, his touch, both tender and firm, all at the same time, eased the rigidity from her body. "I assure you," Dare said coolly. "Our marriage is a real one . . . in every sense."

Drawing her hand back, Temperance glared at him. "Stop," she mouthed.

The duchess's cheeks fired red. And just like that, all the hope went out of the older woman's piercing gaze. "I . . . see." And by the dejected quality of those two words, the duchess did indeed see.

The duke plucked a kerchief from inside the front of his jacket and dangled it before his wife's face.

Her Grace snatched the article and blotted at the corners of her eyes.

No, *this* was precisely as Temperance had expected the exchange to play out. With many tears and fury from the couple over the fact that their beloved grandson had returned to their world with Temperance at his side. She turned to the duke and duchess. "I'm sorry for how all this has been handled," she said softly. No truer words had she spoken than those. "You've every reason to be angry and disappointed."

Dare lifted a single finger and wagged it. "I'd like to be entirely clear that I disagree. They should only be overjoyed."

"O-overjoyed?" the duke stammered.

Temperance dropped her head into her hands. Why was Dare so determined to botch this meeting?

"You required me to find a wife—"

"You had a bride," the duchess cried.

"One whom I can make my return to society with. And I have."

Dare and his grandparents looked to Temperance.

Sailing to her feet, the duchess beat another retreat to the door. "If you will excuse me?" she asked, and let herself out.

The duke once again struggled after her.

And Temperance and Dare were left . . . alone.

Her *husband* broke the silence. "All things considered, I would say that went remarkably well," he said dryly.

A curtain of fury fell over her eyes. Cursing, Temperance jumped up. "You are enjoying this."

He stood. "Of course I'm not, but sometimes a situation calls for moments of levity."

Yes, it was why everyone in the Rookeries—including Temperance herself—had fallen under his spell. "This is *not* one of those situations." The fight went out of her. She sank onto the edge of the cream upholstered sofa. "You handled this . . . *terribly*, Dare."

He hovered there before starting for the tantalus drink cabinet. "It was always going to go terribly."

How damned matter-of-fact he was. She gnashed her teeth. The hell she'd let him to his alcohol. And furthermore, since when had he begun drinking? Temperance scrambled to put herself between him and those hated spirits. "So you made no effort, no attempt to make this easier for them?" *For me.* "For someone so remarkably smooth and charming in so many things, you really manage to make a blunder of so much, too."

He bristled. "That seems quite contradictory." Dare paused. A half grin drew the right corner of his mouth up. "Charming, am I?"

Her eyebrows shot up. That was what he'd focus on? Temperance jabbed a finger at his chest. "You couldn't have handled this worse if you'd been trying . . ." Her words trailed off. Unless . . .

He frowned. "What?"

"*Of course.* It makes sense."

"What does?"

"You didn't *want* it to go well." Her words came tumbling. "It was as I predicted . . . with you wanting to present us in dusty garments and stinking of horses."

"I changed my attire."

"All along, you've not really wished to meet the terms your grandfather expected of you, and yet the sense of obligation you have to help *everyone* didn't allow you to simply walk away from a fortune. Your behavior, the decisions you made and continue to make, they've been self-destructive."

"Bah, you're making more of it than is there." He tried to step around her, but she matched his movements.

"Am I?" she persisted, breathtakingly beautiful in that show of defiance. She'd always been the only one to defy him. "You wouldn't walk away from all the people in the Rookeries who could be helped with the fortune the duke offered."

He met that statement with stony silence.

"You'd deny you didn't think of them?" Even if he did, she'd never believe him.

Color suffused his cheeks. "Of course I thought of them." It had always been about the people of the Rookeries. "But you"—he gestured to Temperance—"you're analyzing and overanalyzing decisions I've made."

"I don't believe I am, Dare," she said in a hushed voice.

They remained locked in a tense, silent battle. Dare was the first to look away. "You're wrong," he said flatly, and this time when he headed for the liquor, she let him to it. Dare kept his back to her as he reached for a bottle and another glass.

"You have to determine what it is exactly you want more, Dare." She spoke in those same quiet tones she had always reserved for her young brother. "Do you want the funds and future you can use to make life better for the people in the Rookeries"—and for him—"or do you wish to be free of this arrangement with me and your grandparents?" He stared at his still-empty glass. "But you can't play at both." His shoulders tensed. "And I'm not going to sit idly about while you risk losing everything your grandparents are offering because of the internal battle you're fighting." She couldn't. Not when she'd already risked her heart and hopes and future in being here with him again.

And with that, she left.

Chapter 11

That night while the house slept, Dare walked the halls of his newly inherited home.

In the earliest years of knowing Temperance, they had rarely fought. They had been the best of friends, she being the only real one he'd allowed himself in the Rookeries. Not even Avery Bryant had he let in that close.

He'd known the very moment her girlish adoration had faded and she'd become a woman who looked at him with a woman's eyes—disapproving ones. She'd been fifteen, and he'd been heading to Mayfair to steal from a wicked viscount who'd littered the world with bastards whom he didn't take care of. Stealing from one such as that had made complete sense to Dare . . . but had been a decision Temperance hadn't understood.

From that moment, it was as though she had grown up. And they were destined to never see eye to eye again—not on how he lived his life or how he came by the money he did. Gone was the girl who'd looked adoringly up at him and to him. In her place had come a woman—one who knew her own mind and with opinions as big and bold as her spirit. The greatest chasm between them had been about Dare's existence. That which she'd once admired him for, she'd come to disdain.

Over the years, their debates had been fierce and volatile. Ultimately, they'd always found their way back together, where he and Temperance arrived at a truce, an agreement that had ended the conflict and restored them to the friends they'd always been.

This latest truce between him and Temperance, however, had proven their shortest.

Though in fairness, none of this had really gone as he'd expected.

There'd been a betrothal . . . That part he'd not been anticipating.

What did you expect?

As such, Temperance was likely already packed and prepared to leave, and he would be left trying to meet the duke's terms on his own. The twenty thousand pounds he risked losing with her departure should have commanded all his attentions, but it did not.

"Ahem."

That distinct clearing of someone's throat brought Dare's restless journey to a stop.

He turned back and found his butler there.

"I thought to inquire as to whether you required anything, my lord."

"No. That is . . . I am quite well." Clasping his hands behind him, he made to enter his office.

"Ahhhem."

Dare stopped.

Bloody hell. What now?

Spencer hovered in the hall.

The day having been what it had, he should have anticipated he'd not even have peace in this. Clearly, the other man wanted to say something. "What is it?"

"I . . . thought I might offer you my services, my lord."

"I don't require any—"

"I didn't necessarily speak to . . . my regular responsibilities. I have some familiarity with His and Her Grace, as well as their . . . your . . . *family.*"

Dare grinned wryly. "Had there also been a familiarity with the fact that I had a betrothed, along with her parents, waiting for me before I introduced them to my wife, that would be helpful information in the future."

Spencer nodded frantically. "I'll endeavor to do better. I was more than a bit at sea, given the circumstances. I didn't know how to explain any of it in front of Her Ladyship."

"That makes two of us," he muttered under his breath.

"What was that, my lord?"

"Nothing," he said, stealing a glance at the hall clock. "Thank you for the off—"

Only the butler wasn't done. "I was speaking about my tenure with your family." *Oh, bloody hell.* This was how he was to spend his night, then? With a cataloging of the butler's tenure? "If I may?"

Dare followed the other man's gesture to the hall bench, and then it occurred . . . He was asking that they . . . sit. And worse, that request indicated Spencer had no intention of leaving.

He and the butler spoke as one.

"I do have matters of—"

"Thank you," Spencer said and settled himself onto the bench, staring expectantly up at Dare.

The other man had no intention of leaving. Tamping down a sigh, Dare forced himself to sit.

"My role as butler is a relatively new one . . . for me. Not for my family. Although I expect that may come as some level of surprise." Spencer stared back. Something was clearly expected of Dare here.

Lost, however, as to what that expectation was, Dare shook his head slowly.

That appeared sufficient reply enough.

Spencer smoothed his already flawless lapels. "My father served in His and Her Grace's country estate in Yorkshire." Once again, he looked to Dare. Spencer nodded his head ever so slightly.

"I . . . see."

Alas, Dare still saw nothing.

"I've only recently been brought to your London townhouse. The idea was that I would offer some . . . familiarity to you."

He didn't. But Dare wasn't one to deliberately hurt or offend, and as such, he kept quiet.

"There's also the matter of few being willing to work for the household, given the current and questionable state of the finances," Spencer went on.

"And yet you did?" Dare asked without inflection, feeling the first hint of real curiosity since the younger man had begun rambling on about his tenure with the Greyson family.

"I did." Spencer, however, didn't elucidate. "As did the other men and women and their children who've come on staff."

Dare consulted the pair cased enamel watch at his waist. When he looked up, he found the other man's direct gaze squarely on him, a slight and disapproving frown on his lips. Dare made himself release his timepiece. "Is there something you would like to say, Spencer?" he asked bluntly.

The butler laid his palms on his legs and leaned forward. "It is my hope that you will succeed in your new róle here, my lord."

That made two of them. "Thank—"

"For not entirely altruistic reasons," Spencer confessed. "I'm not unfamiliar with the terms His and Her Grace have laid out for you."

Dare rested his folded hands atop his stomach. "Ahh, servant gossip?"

"My own observations," he said evenly.

He'd hand it to the other man; Spencer remained wholly unflappable. It was the first time Dare remembered the young butler being so self-possessed. The servant rose considerably in his estimation, and Dare looked at him for the first time as a potential ally in this place.

"I am not one to question your commitment to being here," Spencer said.

"Then do not."

"However, I've reason to question your commitment to being here."

First Temperance, and now, of all people, his butler. And mayhap, had he truly been of the ranks of Polite Society, he would have sacked Spencer for all-out challenging him. "I take it you're referring to my meeting with the duke and duchess?"

Spencer nodded. "There was that."

Dare's brows came together. "Tell me, is it customary for servants to call out their employers?"

"No." Spencer paused. "In fact, not at all."

"But you are, Spencer?"

"I . . . prefer to think of it as assisting you," the other man demurred.

Dare snorted. "Call it whatever you want, your intentions are clear."

Spencer shifted, the aged wood groaning under that slight movement. "I do not believe they are, my lord. We are not unalike."

Dare repressed a laugh. "Now this I'd love to hear."

"Many are reliant upon your completing the terms laid forth by the duke and duchess."

There were a good many—the most desperate people in the Rookeries. Temperance.

"The servants' livelihoods are dependent upon whether or not you succeed." Spencer's pronouncement came . . . unexpectedly. And just like that, Dare was silenced. "If the funds are not released, husband and wives will be separated and forced to look for employment in different households. As it is," the other man went on, "securing such work is challenging enough. But for families to do so, *together*?" Spencer's mouth flattened into a tense line, and he gave his head a shake. "It's nigh an impossibility. And then there is the matter of ensuring the staff finds placements in households where they will be treated with respect and kindness and not abused by merciless employers."

And Dare was humbled once more to realize how pompous he'd been, thinking the butler didn't and couldn't know anything about what compelled Dare . . . what drove him. "I . . . see." Unlike when he'd given those two words before, this time, Dare did. Spencer spoke of details he'd not previously considered. Nay, not details—people. Yet again more people who needed him to succeed in this endeavor. Dare's palms grew moist, and he discreetly wiped them along the sides of his trousers. So many to help and support . . . and yet further reasons why failure was not an option. "And you are concerned about those people who answer to you?" Dare asked quietly.

"I am," Spencer said instantly. And just like that, a kindred connection, an unlikely one, was born between Dare and his butler. They who were united in common efforts.

"I . . . hear what you are saying, Spencer." And this time, he did.

The young butler dusted his gloved palms together. "Good. Then this has been a very valuable talk." With that, the servant stood, bowed, and took himself off.

Dare remained seated in the hall. He was likely the only nobleman to be called out by his servant, and yet there'd been honorable intentions to the man's doing so. He had looked at Dare and questioned his motives and expressed concern for the people reliant upon him. People Dare hadn't considered in the vein Spencer had forced him to.

Temperance had accused him of intentionally trying to destroy the arrangement he'd come to and free himself.

His sightless gaze settled on the doorway across from him.

What if she'd been only partially wrong?

What if, subconsciously, from the place deep inside that hated everything and anything associated with this world, he'd unintentionally set out to avoid joining Polite Society? What did that say about him as a man who'd committed himself to doing absolutely whatever he could to help the suffering souls in the Rookeries? It marked him as a coward who cared more about his own comfort than he did the people most in need of help.

And that went against all he'd attempted to be.

Coming to his feet, he ventured into the Portrait Room.

Not a candle had been lit, and yet from the enormous frames that hung along the corridor to the walls resplendent in gold satin wallpaper, an artificial light was cast over the space. Dare made the march past various noble figures in powdered wigs. Ladies ridiculously clad in enormous hooped skirts. All the people painted had been frozen in time, as they were . . . his . . . ancestors. And yet it was singularly odd to think that anyone who'd walked these halls had been family.

Because he'd been without family more years than he had been with it.

Dare paused in the center of the room, his gaze locked on one heavy giltwood frame.

Because we do not play in portrait rooms, Darius. We pay our respects to the family who came before us . . .

A child's groan—Dare's groan—reverberated from somewhere deep within his brain.

He stared unblinkingly out across the gleaming parquet wood floors, seeing the tall, smartly dressed gentleman leave . . . so that only a child and a small, delicate young lady remained.

My mother . . . She was my mother, and that boy . . . was me.

Ah . . . but one would never say dancing was playing.

There came his answering giggle.

Dare closed his eyes and let himself see her. The woman he'd not allowed himself to think of in so long, he'd believed her forgotten. Only to find she dwelled there in his memory still. In his mind's eye, he saw her as she winked and took him in her arms, twirling Dare wildly about . . .

Dare forced his eyes open, and when he did, only the dark, empty room met him.

This solitariness was what he'd come to prefer . . . to crave. It was why he'd been content to deal just with Avery Bryant and let no one else closer than his partner. Until he'd allowed himself, against all better judgment, to marry Temperance. He'd convinced himself that he could have the same uncomplicated partnership he did with his thieving partner. But deep down he'd known that could never be the case. He'd told himself what he'd wanted to hear because . . . he'd wanted *her*.

It was just one reason his relationship with Temperance had changed. She'd come to expect . . . to want him to be more than he was or could ever be.

Which was likely the reason he should let her go *now*. Dare could very well strike different terms with his grandparents. After all, he'd negotiated the releases of countless souls with Wylie at Newgate. A duke and duchess so desperate to see glimpses of the grandson they'd once known would prove far easier to bring 'round to his wishes.

So do it . . .

Free her . . .

Free yourself . . .

From somewhere in the townhouse, a shout went up.

And then silence.

Maudlin musings immediately forgotten, Dare snapped erect. He trained his gaze on the doorway. What he'd discovered in the short time since he'd been flung into Polite Society was that any noise was nonexistent in Mayfair; quiet reigned over all. Unlike East London. There, some commotion or another always filled the Rookeries. Some skirmish saw the streets filled with cries born of violence, and the ruthless battles of men and women fighting for supremacy . . . and survival. The hint of battle hung on the air, a state a man had to always be prepared for . . . or ultimately fall to.

But this was West London. As such, when there was no answering cry, he relaxed his shoulders.

And then pandemonium broke out.

"*Helllllllp!* Please, God, help!"

Dare took off racing toward that cacophony.

"How did this happen?" The housekeeper's voice came plaintively. "I'm so *sorrrrry*."

Then one voice of calm broke through the din. "I'm sure this can be explained." Temperance. Fiery of temper, and yet calm and collected when the situation merited.

His heart knocking uncomfortably, and not from the pace he'd set, Dare increased his stride, following the arguing voices that came from the upstairs living quarters. *What in hell?*

"Call for the constable," Lady Kinsley cried, winded, as if she'd been racing across the household.

"I'll not let you," Temperance was saying with a calm that belied the commotion. "He is a boy. Let us—"

"He is a thief."

Dare took the stairs two at a time and went racing onward.

"I've got him," a triumphant servant called from down the hall.

"Let me go." That frantic plea, cried in Cockney tones, familiar, and not just for the street-roughened quality to it.

Dare came to a stop, the sight halting him in his tracks. Ten servants formed a wall of sorts, and Temperance went charging forward, parting that crowd. *What in blazes . . . ?* From over the tops of the heads of the men and women and . . . children in his employ, Dare could see they all collectively brandished various household items, holding those makeshift weapons up and pointing them at Temperance.

Temperance pulled a boy from a servant's grasp, and shoving the child behind her, she wielded her favorite pair of scissors before her. With her cheeks flushed and her eyes burning with fury, she dared anyone to come between her and the boy.

And Dare was briefly frozen by the sight of her. When he was a boy, he'd had a male tutor who'd insisted women were meant to be coddled and protected. Dare's mother had sacked the stodgy fellow, and before he'd been shown the door, she'd told the man the tale of Boudicca, the fearless warrior who'd gathered up her people and led them on a charge of savage attacks upon anyone in their path who'd had problems with the Roman Empire.

His breath lodged sharply in his chest. Temperance *was* that warrior woman of old resurrected, gloriously beautiful in her spirit and passion.

And Dare almost felt bad for the footman advancing now.

Almost.

He opened his mouth to order the young man to stand down—

Too late.

Temperance thwacked the servant's fingers hard with the handle of her scissors.

The young man howled and immediately released the boy.

"Have you no shame?" Glowering at the crowd, Temperance shoved the small street urchin behind her. "He is a boy."

"He is a thief," Lady Kinsley shot back, clutching the folds of her night wrapper close. "He was sneaking into my rooms."

Temperance spoke calmly. "I'm sure it can be explained." She looked down at the small boy, still concealed by the crowd.

She may have doubts about her place in this world they'd been thrust within, but there could be no doubting she was very much, in every way, the lady of this household.

"It can. To a constable." Lady Kinsley looked to Spencer. "A constable, this instant."

Spencer bowed. "As you wish, my—"

"What is the meaning of this?" Dare barked, striding forward. And just like that, the circle parted and silence descended upon the gathering. He stepped into the fray.

"You've invited thieves into our midst, brother," Lady Kinsley said coolly.

Ignoring that attempt to bait him, Dare trained his focus on the small child. His face smudged with dirt, his inky-black hair slicked with grease, he may as well have been any other child in the streets. There was something, however, familiar about the child.

"Wasn't looking for 'er foine things," the child protested. He slid closer to Temperance, and she rested a protective hand on the child's narrow shoulder. "Oi was looking for yar rooms."

Lady Kinsley folded her arms. "I daresay it hardly matters who this person intended to steal from."

Temperance frowned at the other woman. "He is a *child*."

"He is a thief," Lady Kinsley said crisply.

"Not a thief," the boy retorted. "Well, not this time." He glared at Dare. "These yar rules?" the child demanded. "Turnin' out people from the Rookeries? Because Oi was told ya'd see me."

"What?" Dare asked dumbfoundedly. "Of course not. Whatever would make you say or believe that?"

The servants shifted on their feet and made a show of studying the floor.

Dare narrowed his eyes on the group.

Kinsley scoffed. "I take it you know this . . . *person*."

"I don't," Dare frostily corrected. "But that does not mean he isn't worthy of a meeting."

The child wrestled his way from the group. "Well, they wouldn't let me see ya," he shouted. "Been comin' by for six days now. *Six dayyyys.*" And so he'd sneaked in. "They told me Oi didn't get a meeting wit' the marquess an' that beggars only go 'round back for 'andouts." The small boy turned back on the semicircle of servants behind them and cast a glare at the group. "Oi ain't no beggar. Ya 'ear me? Oi do 'onest work." Whipping out a small knife, he brandished the blade.

Several of the maids screamed and squealed.

A young woman hit the ground hard. A footman rushed over to scoop her up.

Swiping a hand over his face, Dare let his arm fall to his side.

Temperance spoke quietly to the child and managed the seemingly impossible—she calmed the volatile little boy. "What is your name?" she asked in the same quiet, calming tones Dare had heard her use countless times when her brother had been near in age to the child.

More cries went up as another pair of servants appeared, dragging someone else over.

"What now?" the butler bemoaned in aggrieved tones.

"I've *goooot* him!" a footman cried, shoving someone toward the gathering.

Dare squinted. *What in hell . . . ?*

Temperance's eyes widened. *"Chaance?"*

Shouldered between a pair of burly servants, the young man—taller but slimmer by several stone—allowed himself to be dragged along.

A gasp went up.

Gwynn, the sweetheart, cried out and went running. "Release him," she hissed, and like a feral cat, she launched her curled fingers at the men holding him.

Rocking back on her heels, Temperance looked openmouthed in Dare's direction.

"Release him this instant," Dare barked, and the servants immediately complied, but hovered close anyway.

"Mr. Chance sent me, 'e did. He told me to come 'ere for the 'elp Oi need. Told me to just give moi name and explain that he'd sent me and that would be enough."

From beyond Temperance's shoulder, Gwynn clasped her hands close to her breast.

"I wanted to see that Lionel made it inside this time," Chance said sheepishly.

Temperance's friend sighed. "There is no one like you, my love."

Chance Swift winked.

"Your friends?" Kinsley drawled, her lip curled up in disgust.

"My family," Dare corrected in cool tones to rival his sister's. "The people of the Rookeries are more family than anyone sharing my blood."

Lady Kinsley flinched, and for a moment he thought that statement had hit some mark . . . but it was impossible. A trick of the candlelight. She pursed her mouth. "Either way, they are intruders. Both of them."

"Well, technically, I am his brother-in-law," Chance ventured. "So perhaps it isn't a crime?"

Kinsley shook her head and looked around the gathering before focusing on Chance. "*Who* is this?"

"My brother," Temperance murmured.

"I found another!" a maid cried.

"Three of them," Kinsley muttered. "Is there *anyone* else here?" she cried out sarcastically as she tossed her arms up.

As one, everyone looked in the direction of the young maid who rushed forward. The girl's arms were filled with a small child. Slightly out of breath, she stopped amidst the gathering. "She was toddling around the hallways."

Silence met that revelation. When no one spoke, moved, or blinked, the servant held the small, dirt-stained girl out.

"Oh . . . my," Lady Kinsley whispered.

Dare's focus, however, wasn't on his sister but on Temperance.

Temperance, who stared with stricken eyes at the child. No more than two or three, and covered in dirt and grime, the babe squirmed, resisting that hold.

And then the child began to cry.

Kinsley was the first to find her voice. "Wh-what is th-*this*?"

And for the first time, the biting young lady possessed sobering tones.

"A choild. Oi take it ya ain't ever seen one before?" Lionel asked smartly.

Temperance seemed to break free of whatever fog had held her frozen. Stalking over, she reached for the wild-curled babe and drew the child into her arms. The child instantly stopped crying.

Dare pointed to his butler. "Going forward, I'm to be informed of whomever is requesting an appointment with me. I'll determine who does and does not receive an audience. Is that clear?"

The young butler nodded wildly. "As you wish, my lord." Giving his hands two quick claps, Spencer managed to clear the gaggle of servants. "Is there anything else you'll require?"

"See that refreshments are brought to my office for me and my guests."

Lionel jutted his chest out. "Did ya 'ear that, Spencer?"

Dare would hand it to Spencer—the other man gave no outward reaction to that insolence from Dare's unconventional guest.

"And milk," Temperance quietly put in. "The babe will require milk."

Dare nodded. "And milk. Temperance? Will you accompany Lionel and me?" There were answers needed as to why Chance had helped sneak a child inside Dare's household.

"But what of me? This is *my* household." Lady Kinsley's cries echoed behind them, growing distant and then fading altogether.

Side by side, with Temperance accompanying them, they made their way back to Dare's office. While they walked, Dare peeked at Temperance. She offered her index finger to the child, who tugged and played with the digit. Periodically, she lowered her thumb, concealing the digit . . . and then let it pop up, startling a little laugh from the girl. And the sight of the two together sent something moving and shifting in Dare's chest. As for a second time that night, he allowed a thought he'd previously forbidden himself from entertaining: a family. One made up of him and Temperance and . . . some nameless, imagined babe. One with Temperance's dark curls and large round eyes and temper and . . .

And it was everything he'd not allowed himself so much as a thought of. People reliant upon him, a thief from the Rookeries, who'd invariably hang for his crimes one day.

Perhaps it was the unexpectedness of one of those small babes about. Or mayhap it was the return of memories of his own childhood. But the yearning for that dream of folly washed over him.

"Why ya lookin' loike that?" Lionel asked on an outrageously loud whisper that brought Temperance's gaze flying over. "Ya look queer. Ya don't 'ave a problem with babes, do ya?" The boy didn't give Dare a chance to answer, but looked quickly over at Chance, who, hand in hand with Gwynn, followed close behind. "Ya didn't say 'e 'as a problem with babes, Mr. Chance."

That managed to break the spell over the smitten couple.

Chance frowned. "Of course Dare doesn't have a problem with children." The lines at the corners of his mouth stretched lower. "At least . . . he didn't." He looked to Dare. "You don't of a sudden have a dislike for—"

"Of course not," Dare said gruffly.

The group reached Dare's office, and he motioned a babe-carrying Temperance on ahead, then Lionel. And lastly, Chance and Gwynn. "Why don't we sit?" Dare said when he'd closed the door behind the eclectic little gathering of people.

As Temperance settled onto the chair, Gwynn went wide-eyed. "Never been invited to sit by a marquess before," she whispered.

Chance clasped her hands in his, then one at a time brought them to his lips for a kiss. "You are more worthy than any woman. Never doubt your place because of your birthright."

The depth of emotion that moved between the couple—love freely passing, and love freely shared—was so foreign to what Dare had ever known. No, that wasn't completely true. They'd once been like Chance and Gwynn . . .

I'm going to marry you if it's the last thing I do, Temperance Swift . . .

His eighteen-year-old voice echoed in the chambers of his mind, paired with her joyous, unrestrained laugh.

His stare strayed over to Temperance, and their gazes locked. They shared a private smile, an intimate one that came from the place of knowing one another.

"Oi'm gonna dirty up yar foine stuff," Lionel blurted.

And the moment was shattered as Dare looked over to the little boy Chance had sent. The child who now eyed the remaining leather button wing chair warily.

Dropping to a knee beside the boy, Dare flashed a gentle smile. "You don't know me, aside from what Mr. Swift has shared."

"'e said yar a good man. That ya loike to 'elp people loike me."

"I like to help people," Dare confirmed. "It was a mistake you were sent away when you did come. I promise that shall not happen again." He flashed a gentle smile. "And I certainly don't care about the furniture and whether or not you or anyone else ruins it, Lionel."

The boy hesitated another moment and then pulled himself up onto the chair, wafting a soft cloud of dirt.

❦

Over the years, Temperance had observed Dare's interaction with all number of people. Where some had ruled in the Rookeries through putting up an armor of coldness, he'd met the people there with kindness. It had been just one of the first reasons she'd fallen in love with him.

And then she'd witnessed him . . . with her brother. When Chance had been just five, Dare had been patient and teasing and kind, and everything Temperance had never seen any man in the Rookeries be toward any child. She'd not even known a man could be that way. After all, her earliest and almost only memories of her own father all included her being viciously beaten or slapped.

Seeing him kneel down beside this ragged street urchin and speak in hushed tones, her heart remembered all over again why she'd fallen in love with him.

And she hated it.

Because it was easier to resent the man who'd paraded her before his duke and duchess grandparents . . . and his former betrothed . . . than to face the man who was so tender and so perfect with little children.

A man who should have children of his own . . .

Oh, God. It is too much.

The child in her arms squirmed, and she relaxed the unintended tight grip she'd had upon the girl.

"Now, Chance," Dare was saying. "I take it you have some manner of explanation about the babe?" Ever so gently, he stroked the top of the child's head.

"It's a girl," Lionel piped in.

The sight of him, so tender with the child, ravaged Temperance's already weak heart.

Clearing his throat, Chance released Gwynn's hand. "He is the younger brother of Joseph Gurney."

At last the reason Lionel was so familiar made sense. He'd the look of his older brother, Chance's best friend from the Rookeries. The pair had hero-worshipped Dare, looking to him to teach them how to thieve.

"And . . . was he caught stealing?" Dare asked.

"No," Chance said instantly. "Joseph followed the honorable path, like myself." Color filled the young man's cheeks. "No offense, sir," he said gruffly.

"None taken."

He'd never been the manner of man to be offended . . . or possessed of an ego. "Gurney is a carder at another mill," Temperance murmured, bringing them back to the matter of Lionel's brother.

Chance's mouth flattened. "Joseph's proprietor is not nearly as kind or generous as Mr. Buxton. Punishing fellow. Cuts wages for imagined offenses, and keeps the differences for himself. He accused Gurney of stealing . . . but he was only keeping what he had coming to him. And now he's stuck in gaol."

And yet . . .

Quizzically, Dare looked to the little girl. "And the babe?"

"She's moi brother's babe," Lionel interjected. "But Joseph's been put in Newgate, and it doesn't look loike he's returnin', and my da didn't . . . doesn't want 'er," Lionel said with a matter-of-factness that made Temperance's chest ache for altogether different reasons.

Wasn't that the way of the Rookeries, though? Daughters were of little value until they were of an age where they could be whored to the depraved . . . or somehow found other skills to justify their existence, as Temperance had with her sewing.

The boy shrugged. "She's just a girl," he added, as if it'd not been perfectly clear as to why the child had been rejected.

"And no less special for it," Dare reminded the boy.

Temperance's eyes filled, and the pair conversing blurred. Dare would have never been one to reject a child because of their gender. Caring for strangers as he did, he would have only passionately loved whatever child had been his.

But then hadn't he shown her that same kindness and regard when she'd been just a girl? When she and all her suffering and the abuse she'd endured at Abaddon Swift's hand had gone ignored or been unseen by the other boys and men in the Rookeries?

"That's why I sent him looking for you," Chance said quietly. "Mr. Buxton has been traveling, and there's been more work for me to see to because of it. As such, I couldn't get away from my work to speak to you myself . . . before now."

And in that desire to look after others, her brother proved so very much like the man he'd looked up to as a father, the one who'd been around since Chance had been the smallest child and had been raised like he were a babe of his own. Her heart hurt for the bond that had been lost . . . between Dare and Chance.

Between her and Dare. If she were being honest with herself, she mourned that loss, too.

She always would.

Dare looked briefly over to the child on Temperance's lap with a tenderness that continued to wreak havoc on Temperance's heart. "What is her name?"

"Rose," Lionel answered. "'er name is Rose."

"Rose," Temperance murmured to herself, and the little girl briefly quieted in her arms. With her bright-red cheeks and the mop of auburn curls on her head, it was a perfect name for the child.

Unable to watch Dare any longer while he spoke to Lionel, Temperance forced her gaze downward to the child—Rose—seated on her lap.

It was the wrong decision.

Enormous eyes so dark they were nearly black met hers. The babe clapped her hands excitedly, and then studied those digits as if they were the most fascinating things in the world.

Temperance sucked in a breath—or tried to through constricted lungs—wanting to run. Wanting to flee. Needing to put the tiny girl down but unable to. She wanted to be free of the crushing weight of pain and regret of what had almost been, and now, what could and would never be.

"Li-Li-Li," the girl babbled over and over, that close approximation of her uncle's name.

"What do you need?" Dare asked in those gentle tones.

Lionel looked once more at Chance.

"Tell him," Temperance's brother urged. "He's one of the good ones."

He's one of the good ones.

And . . . Dare was. He'd lived a life of crime, and yet at every turn, he'd always put others, the men and women and children struggling, first.

Still, Lionel hesitated.

"I knew your brother well," Dare said quietly.

The little boy perked up. "Did ya?"

"Dare taught me and Joseph how to survive," Chance supplied.

Yes, Chance and Joseph had both hero-worshipped Dare. But then so had every last soul in the Rookeries. Even as she'd struggled with Dare's means to help, Temperance herself hadn't been immune to him . . . in any way.

Hesitating, Lionel twisted his hands. "Oi need ya to take 'er. Oi'm a sweep, and Oi can't do it." The boy directed his words at his lap. "Until me brother returns. Moi da?" His voice climbed an octave as he spoke. "'e'll give 'er away, but to people who can't 'ave her. Ya know the people there, Grey. They're bad people. She'll end up dead or worse," he finished on a whisper.

Yes, there was always a fate and future worse than death in the Rookeries.

"Of course we'll care for her," Dare replied without hesitation, and the little boy's shoulders sagged.

Temperance worked her eyes over Dare. He was the only man in the whole of the world who'd simply agree to take in a street urchin's unwanted niece. Nor did it escape her notice that he'd said, *"We'll care for her."* A pairing that would see Temperance and Dare play at that role of caregiver. *It is too much.* Temperance bit the inside of her cheek to repress the piteous moan building in her chest.

Angling his chin up mutinously, Lionel glared about the room as if he resented that he'd had to ask for help. "It isn't for forever. It'll only be until Joseph gets out." And that was where the boy's thin bravado flagged. Lionel's face fell. "If 'e gets out . . ." His voice emerged, whispery soft.

Dare and Chance spoke at the same time.

"He will."

"I promise, he will."

That was Dare . . . issuing promises to free the oppressed. And invariably he'd done so.

"Thank ya, guv'nor. Oi 'eard of ya, Oi 'ave. When Mr. Chance told me to come yar way, Oi'd 'eard about all the people ya've helped." There was so much adoration in the little boy's eyes, a sentiment Temperance had worn in her own eyes more times than could have ever been counted. The same went for most in the Rookeries.

Dare waved off those words. "Helping is what all people should do. The world needs more helpers, wouldn't you say?"

Lionel nodded, and in Temperance's arms, Rose bobbed her head up and down, as if in an agreement of her own.

And as if he'd just realized Temperance was there, holding the babe, Lionel looked past a silent Gwynn and nudged a chin Temperance's way. "Who is this one?" He eyed her with a worldly wariness of a man twenty years his senior.

"My wife."

"Also my sister," Chance volunteered.

Some of the tension left the waif's slender frame. "I can trust her, then."

"I used to look after your brother whenever he'd come to visit Chance." Temperance spoke in solemn tones. "You can trust me, Lionel," she said, understanding those words should and needed to be spoken from her.

"Do you know anything about babes?" he piped in, his voice hopeful.

"I . . ." Her entire body turned to stone. Her facial muscles froze. Oh, God. She was going to break. One more wrong word . . . from him or Dare or her . . . and she'd shatter into a thousand tiny shards.

"She has countless experience," Dare said when Temperance couldn't make herself answer the child.

Temperance tried to get a breath out from her lungs . . . but couldn't. And for a moment, she thought he knew. But he couldn't. Because he'd not known of their babe, and when he'd returned, two months later, from robbing a Kent country estate, it had been too late. And there'd been no babe anymore to mention.

And there'd been no way for her to ever face him again. Not without mourning all she'd lost.

"She raised me like her own," Chance said quietly to Lionel. Her younger brother to the rescue, saving her from the past.

Temperance managed to squeeze that still strained breath out, after all.

"What else do you need?" Dare urged the child.

Throughout the years, many had come to Dare with their hands out, in search of help and support. Temperance, however, had never borne witness to it. Now she took in the exchange, seeing it for the first time, truly. Seeing what had so compelled him to risk his life again and again and again without thought of his own neck. "If either of ya can 'elp me see about . . . freeing Joseph?"

Dare and Chance exchanged a look. "We will . . . ," Dare promised. "Absolutely, we will."

And Temperance was so very grateful that talk of the babe and Temperance and Dare acting as foster parents was forgotten.

"They said ya weren't coming back to the Rookeries. That ya were a fancy lord now."

It was a likely conclusion for anyone to have drawn. Dare's time of living dangerously was at an end, and yet . . . he'd not stop helping. It was why he'd agreed to his grandfather's terms. It was always about others. Never about himself.

He frowned. "Who said that?"

"Me da, and the people in the Rookeries when Oi said Oi was goin' to ya. But everyone? Small told his men, who're tellin' all the boys and girls there ain't any savior there to 'elp us. That free 'andouts from the loikes of Dare Grey are gone, and there was only one choice for all of us."

"Small," Temperance repeated, hate unfurling inside. Once part of Diggory's gang, Small's control of the Rookeries had only grown with the years and that other bastard's passing. He'd always been attempting to exploit the desperate men and women and children there. When her brother had been a boy, she'd fought him on numerous scores to keep him away. And it appeared, with his influence over Lionel, nothing had changed.

Dare straightened and leaned against his desk. "I'm not a man who'd simply quit helping those in need."

Nay, Dare always gave unconditionally, asking for none, when he very well should have accepted support from others. His pride had alternately awed and infuriated Temperance. And that had been the crux of why she and Dare hadn't been able to come together. Because he'd been so desperate, so determined to help everyone that he'd committed himself to a life of danger and thievery, a life that would have only seen Temperance with her heart broken for different reasons.

"I'm one of you, no matter where I live or what title they give me," Dare said. "Is that clear?"

Wide-eyed, Lionel nodded.

A knock sounded at the door, and Spencer opened the panel a moment later.

A maid stepped forward. Studiously avoiding Dare's and Lionel's eyes, the girl hovered by the doorway, steadying the tray in her hands.

"You may enter," Dare called, and the maid stumbled slightly as she rushed over. "If you would set them right on the edge of my desk? That will be all," he said to the girl.

Laying down the silver tray of pastries, bread, cheese, and two pitchers—one with water and one with milk—the servant curtsied and rushed back to the front of the room.

Rose immediately scrambled down from Temperance's lap and ambled over to the food that had been set out. Babbling, the little girl plucked a piece of bread from the tray, and waving it wildly about, she set off to explore.

"Spencer," Dare called to the butler. "Would you see that the nurseries are prepared? We shall also be requiring the services of a nursemaid."

The butler nodded. "As you—"

Gwynn shot a hand up. "If I might . . . suggest that I take on the role of nursemaid? I've . . . some experience with children."

Temperance started. It was the first she'd ever known that her friend had previous connections to children. But then, neither had Temperance shared the many details of her past.

Gwynn looked to Temperance. "Unless you object? I can still help you as you have need."

Dare looked to Temperance, his meaning clear . . . The decision would fall to her.

But that was who Dare had always been, allowing her control . . . a say in her life when in the Rookeries, that was a luxury most weren't permitted. It had been a gift. It still was.

Temperance nodded. "Of course I don't mind. If you are willing, I think that is a wonderful solution for who should care for Rose."

The moment Spencer was dismissed, Lionel sat and stared longingly at the feast before him.

"Why don't you eat," Temperance urged, following Rose out of the corner of her eye as she teetered and tottered on a walk about the room.

Lionel dived into the plate of food. Ripping enormous bites from the loaf, he spoke around his filled mouth. "They don't loike us." The boy swallowed down his mouthful and jabbed the remaining piece of his bread at the doorway. "Yar servants."

"They don't trust us," Dare allowed. "That's a bit different."

And mayhap don't like us, Temperance silently amended. Over the top of Lionel's head, she and Dare exchanged looks. Knowing him as she did, she knew he'd not speak that truth to the child. They ceased with their questioning or comments, instead allowing the child to his meal, likely the first one he'd had in longer than Dare cared to think about, before he got to the rest of the reasons for the child's visit.

Rose drifted closer to the fire, and Temperance flew out of her seat and rushed to gather the girl up. "Pr-pre," Rose wailed in protest.

"Yes," she murmured, balancing the babe on her hip and bouncing her up and down as she'd done with Chance as a child. "It is pretty but also unsafe."

The chubby girl's tears faded to little giggles as the fire was forgotten, and Rose slapped her remaining piece of bread in her tiny fist against her open palm, raining crumbs upon the floor.

Besieged with emotion, Temperance waltzed the child in a small circle.

Feeling eyes on her, she glanced across the room.

Dare's eyes were locked on her. And there was such emotion in that gaze. One she didn't want to explore. Because she couldn't. She didn't want to know anything more about that look of longing there. That Dare Grey, an island of a man with a professed need and want for none, should now stare at her and a little babe—

Tearing her eyes from his, she directed her attentions once more down to the top of Rose's riotous red curls.

When Lionel had a chance to eat enough, Dare straightened and perched himself on the edge of his desk beside the half-empty tray of food. "What else has you desperate?"

Temperance frowned. "He's already indicated his sister—"

Lionel cut her off. "Oi grew an inch." Just like that, proving Dare saw and knew more where people were concerned. As such, he'd known more had weighed on the child. That acuity was a testament to how aware he was of other people's toil.

But then, hadn't he always been the same with her as a young woman? Even when she hadn't borne bruises indicating her latest troubles, he'd known.

"Ahh," Dare said with a dawning understanding.

Returning to the desk, she set Rose down so the child might grab a piece of cheese from the tray. "And that . . . is a problem?" Temperance asked in confusion while the girl nibbled away at the morsel. Most boys, including her own brother when he'd been Lionel's age, had stretched themselves on tiptoes to secure an additional height.

"Yea, it's a big problem." Lionel eyed her like she was daft.

Nearly eleven but with the look of a seven-year-old, any other boy would have sounded more pleased than this forlorn child did. But height was the difference between working and being sacked for the chimney sweeps.

"Oi've been slouchin'," the boy went on, staring intently down at the remaining piece of the loaf in his hand. "They don't know yet . . . but they will. Can't keep it a secret forever." From clogged lungs to fires lit under them and eyes bloodshot and vision damaged, it was a mark of the desperation faced by all in the Rookeries that a child would fear greater being without that work than with it.

And the child couldn't stop himself from growing, either.

"Here," Dare murmured, pouring Lionel a glass of water.

Taking it with his spare, small, dirt-encrusted fingers, Lionel chugged down the clear contents of his glass. "My mum is dead now. Birthin' a babe. An' my sister? She be 'avin' a babe of her own." The boy returned to eating.

So many babes.

In the Rookeries, one of those additional mouths to feed was a burden. It was why Temperance should have been only relieved after the loss she'd suffered. And yet . . . it hadn't been there. There'd been only an aching void, an irrational hungering that had defied the logic of what she should or should not want.

She studied Dare as he sized up his office, and a moment later, he fished a gold timepiece from his pocket and looked down at the object a brief moment.

"Dare," she said quietly, knowing what he intended before he even spoke his next words aloud.

Ignoring her, Dare pressed the valuable into the child's hand. "Here."

Lionel stared down at it, his eyes stunned. "Sir?"

"It is gold. Solid through. This will cover your family's rent forever. You tell your landlord I said as much. And you also tell him if he has any questions about the value or the terms of your rent? He is to come to me."

"Thank ya, sir," Lionel whispered, clutching the piece close to his chest.

He patted Lionel's hand. "None of that."

"Why do ya do it?" the child asked, curiosity in his query. "Ya don't get anything from the loikes o' me, an' ya don't use it for power."

"Sometimes it is just about doing the right thing and helping those who need helping."

Helping. It was what he'd always done. People were acts of charity, and he was the savior of the people.

Just as his offer of marriage all those years ago had been made not because of the love he had for her, but rather because of his desire to protect her. Keep her safe.

Temperance hugged her arms around her middle, warding off the pain of the past.

The little boy's lips formed a flat line. "Oi ain't ever goin' to be able to 'elp anyone. Oi sometimes feel loike Oi'm gonna doi a sweep."

Her heart ached all over again at the forlorn acceptance of a hard fate.

"I was you once," Dare said quietly. "We are all in those circumstances, Lionel." Dare motioned to his office. "Until we're not. And then it is even more our duty to help."

Another knock interrupted the pair, and they looked up as Spencer returned with a young maid, Efa, in tow. "As you've requested, my lord, several of the maids have tidied the nursery and are able to show the child abovestairs."

The girl dipped a curtsy. "My lord," Efa said in heavy Welsh tones.

Temperance's body coiled, and she found herself equally relieved and wanting to cry when Gwynn came forward and retrieved Rose.

Her friend lingered a moment and touched her fingers to her lips, blowing that kiss to Chance.

There was such a longing in Chance's eyes as he watched his sweetheart take her leave, and it was a reminder all over again of why Temperance was doing this. Why she'd let Dare back in her life, despite her vow to never do so.

And now, to have a little babe this close . . . and more, to bear witness to just how tender, how perfect in every way he was with children, proved the universe's cruel way of mocking her.

Carried out in Gwynn's arms, Rose stared over the girl's shoulder at Temperance. Until that pair was gone . . .

And then she was able to breathe again.

"Is there anything else you require, my lord?"

"If you would escort Mr. Lionel to the kitchens? And also, please see that a basket is prepared for him and his family, along with blankets? When you've finished, please have a carriage return him home."

Unable to help herself, she stared on with the same awe of her youth as he fired off those instructions. He was the right man to have been made a marquess. He'd use his ability and power and wealth to help those most in need.

"Yes, my lord," Spencer said when Dare had finished. The butler waited until the boy had joined him.

Chance returned his hat to his head and came to his feet. "I have to go. It is my hope that my employer might be able to intervene on behalf of Rose's father. He is something of a social reformer, and I expect he will help, but it will take time as he's in Norfolk for business."

"We'll find a way, Chance," Dare instantly offered. "When you are free of your work and we are able to talk, we shall strategize what to do."

Emotion stuck in Temperance's throat . . . pride at hearing her brother formulate a plan to help . . . and at Dare being there, as he'd been for so much of Chance's childhood, promising to stand beside him.

The younger man bowed his head. "Thank you. And thank you for helping Lionel—"

"Do not even think of it." Dare cut off the other man. "We'll find out what to do about Rose's da."

Making his goodbyes to Temperance, her brother left . . . and it was just Temperance and Dare, alone.

Silence hung briefly in the air, and an awkwardness hovered there, a first for them.

Dare cleared his throat. "I needed you to stay before . . . for different reasons. For monetary ones related to seeing Lady Kinsley married off."

"And now?"

"Now, there's the babe to see settled."

Oh, God. He didn't know what he asked. She again bit the inside of her cheek, worrying that same bit of flesh. "Dare."

"You were the only one who ever had a way with babes."

This is going to kill me. This was an all-new, unexpected heartbreak she'd never thought she'd have to confront with Dare.

The loss of their babe . . . And now what would never, could never, be for her. Or them.

Say something. It is expected of you here . . .

Her throat closed up. "I only ever did what any other sister would do for her sibling." How was her voice so steady? So even?

"That isn't true," he protested, his voice a tender baritone moving over her like the warmed chocolate he'd surprised her with as a girl. "You were always the one children came to in the Rookeries. You had a way with them. You *have* a way with them."

Stop.

She wanted to clamp her hands over her ears and run screaming from the room. God hated her. There was no other accounting for the dagger Dare unknowingly scraped over a still-raw, still-gaping wound.

"You had a way with them, too," she pointed out more to herself, her voice sad to her own ears. He would have made a wonderful father. If he'd allowed himself another marriage . . . with someone other than Temperance. If she'd not inadvertently trapped him and denied him even that opportunity . . .

I cannot . . .

Pressing her eyes briefly closed, she breathed deeply and grounded herself. "We'll figure out the babe . . . together." Her shoulders sagged slightly. "I may be a woman, but as long as Rose is here, the responsibility should be the both of ours."

"Of course," he said automatically. Dare moved behind his desk and reached for his ledgers.

That was it. *Of course.*

In a world where it was expected that women and women alone would serve in the role of caregiver, he—now a marquess—should accept that role.

It was settled, then.

And yet . . . it was not. Not entirely.

"The timepiece . . ."

"What of it?" he asked when she didn't say anything else.

"Who did it belong to?"

"Me."

Her lips twitched, and she drifted closer, joining him on the other end of the gleaming mahogany desk. "I wasn't implying you stole it."

"Though you would have been right to your assumption," he said with a devastating wink that would have once distracted her.

But that was what he wanted; those were his intentions. A lifetime of knowing this man had taught her as much and made her able to focus. "Whose was it before it belonged to you?"

A muscle moved along his jaw. "The marquess's."

The marquess. "As in your . . . father?"

"I suppose that is one way of thinking of the man," he said distractedly, shuffling through his papers.

"That is the way of thinking of him," she gently corrected.

He briefly paused but continued moving those pages . . . and then he stopped on one. Dare grabbed for his pen and dipped it in the inkwell. He touched the tip against the edge, clearing it of excess, and made several notes in a very familiar-looking ledger.

Wordlessly, Temperance eyed his pen as it moved over the page, as he recorded details about Lionel and the boy's family.

Dare lifted his gaze a tiny fraction, as if he'd just recalled her presence there.

"He was your father, Dare," she said gently.

Some emotion darkened his eyes, turned those irises nearly black. It was . . . a coldness she'd never before witnessed from him, and she shivered. "He was a stranger." With that he rolled his shoulders and resumed writing.

"Do you remember him?" Over the years, she'd asked questions about his family. Who had raised him before he'd found his way to working with Diggory and then Avery? He'd always been vague, offering nothing of true meaning.

He stiffened. "Some," he said tightly.

"Did he . . ." She wetted her lips. She'd always assumed just the downtrodden didn't value their offspring. Now she let herself think that mayhap those powerful lords, too, were as merciless. "Did he beat you?" She managed to get that question out.

His gaze flew upright to hers. "No," he assured her quickly. "He did not."

"You *do* remember him." She pounced on that detail.

Dare let out a sound of frustration. "My memories of him are . . . fine. He was concerned with my schooling and that I be the perfect heir to fill his shoes."

"So . . . he's not a stranger, or worse," she said, not letting the matter go as he so clearly wished. Trying to make sense of this indifference for the man he'd been stolen from. "An ogre like my father was."

"I've spent more years away from my late father than with him, Temperance. And as such, I don't care about a watch that he might have used."

Just as he'd been determined to keep her and everyone else out, he did the same with the memory of the people who'd given him life. "Did use, Dare," she corrected, highlighting that important distinction. "One that your father *did* use."

Midwriting, Dare slammed his pen down in the first break in his temper that she ever remembered of him. Ink splattered his always meticulous ledgers. "Would you have had me let Lionel and his family starve out of some sentimental connection? Because there is none, Temperance." He managed a return to his usual calm. "There is none," he repeated. "Do you know what does matter?" Lifting the ledger, he turned it around, revealing the lengthy column of names.

She worked her eyes over the page of men and women and children—some familiar, more not—of the Rookeries who were reliant upon him. And beside those columns were others, enumerating how much money was needed to provide shelter and food for the individuals listed there. "This is what you intend to do with your grandfather's funds," she murmured. Of course. It fit with who he was. And what he did.

And in doing that, he'd not have to steal. Not again.

"*These* people matter." He jabbed a finger at the top of the page. "Lionel matters."

"But it can be . . . both ways. You can help Lionel and others and still retain connections to the family and life you once knew, Dare."

"I'm sure I could." He lowered his book. "If I had a desire to. I don't." His tone contained a finality to it. Returning his volume of names to his desk, he picked up his pen and resumed writing once more. "I'm not meant to have connections."

"Because you never let yourself have them, Dare," she said softly. With that, she let herself out.

The night of his impromptu offer of marriage, she'd convinced herself that she could be more to him. That they could be more and have more.

Only to learn . . . and accept, too late, that Dare would never let her in.

Not in the ways she wished.

Chapter 12

Dare had never thought partnering with Temperance in a pretend marriage and joining Polite Society, all in the name of twenty thousand pounds, would be an easy venture.

But after she'd said her piece and quietly taken her leave, he was at last forced to acknowledge that he'd not given full consideration to just how difficult it would be in close quarters with her once more.

A woman of moral convictions, the likes of which he'd never known a person could have, she'd shun the acts that most desperate people performed in the name of survival. She'd always challenged him to be more. Wanted him to be more.

And time had not changed that.

But then Dare had always deluded himself where Temperance Swift was concerned. How many times had he thought he could sway her to his way of thinking? Or appease her?

Nay, she was a woman in full control of what she believed to be right and wrong, and they would never meet at a place of like understanding.

The words she'd spoken lingered in the room, staying with him still.

But it can be . . . both ways. You can help Lionel and others and still retain connections to the family and life you once knew . . .

"It is just a damned watch," he muttered into the quiet. A bloody timepiece that she'd gone and tried to make more of. All the items in this household were material baubles. And she'd have him make them out to be . . . more? Because why? The watch had belonged to his father. The father who'd not even wanted Dare as long as Dare had lived there . . .

And certainly not after, when you waltzed off to join Mac Diggory on the grandest of adventures, the voice at the back of his mind taunted.

He stared blankly over the top of his desk. In his mind's eye, his position reversed, he stood there, looking at his father at work. Too busy to pick his head up. Or mayhap it was that he'd been too disgusted.

"It has come to my attention that you've sneaked off to go exploring." There was a slight pause in that steady click of the pen striking the ledger page. "In East London."

"I wasn't exploring. I was—"

His father silenced him with a look. Dare shuffled back and forth on his feet, studying his now grime-covered black boots intently.

"Oscar," Dare's mother said softly. "He was helping. One of the maids has a sister, and he—"

"Took a picnic basket?"

It hadn't really been a basket. A valise, because he'd not really known where baskets were kept, and—

His father again spoke, whipping Dare's head up. "It is enough that he is . . ." Not looking up from his writings, Father waved his other hand. "Him." At last, he looked up, and there was so much loathing, so much disgust, that it hurt sharp in Dare's belly. His father glared. "But I'll not have him leading his brother down the same path of trouble and mischief and irresponsibility. I'll not have two sons as sinners. Is that clear?"

Except no answer had been necessary. His mother's defense hadn't mattered. The fact that Dare had been getting food that they had in endless amounts over to people whose bellies were empty. None of it. All the late marquess had given two jots about was that Dare hadn't been the serious, model heir the marquess wanted him to be. Reflecting back, he could acknowledge his actions as a young boy had not been entirely driven by empathy. There'd also been the adventurous part of him that'd wished to explore.

To see the world.

And what a world he'd seen . . .

Dare tossed his pen down.

God, how he hated this place. For the memories dwelled even stronger here.

So . . . he's not a stranger, or worse . . . An ogre like my father was.

And this time, he couldn't resist the bitter twist of a smile at some of Temperance's parting words. She wrongly assumed that ogres came in only one type and shape.

She was wrong. So very wrong.

Forcing himself out of the past and back to the only thing that mattered—the present—Dare picked up his pen once more. He looked down at the families who were in need of another visit . . . families who required more money, which he'd promised to deliver.

Alex and Dora Smith. Three children.

Natalie Reiner. One son.

Patrick and Patricia Barclay. Five daughters.

The list . . . It went on and on.

And as such, Dare could see only those families, and he didn't give two shites about moral right or wrong. Despite what Temperance had always believed, there were not two sides of this. There were the "haves" . . . and the "have nots."

And taking from the former—even the dead father whom he barely recalled—to feed and clothe the neediest was something he'd never make apologies for.

A restlessness filled him. One that could be satisfied only by doing that which had come easiest to him. The streets of London whispered in his ear, and the need to answer that call was a physical hungering, a yearning so acute to quit this place. If even just for now. To put it behind him and go off on his own and do that which he was truly good at. That which he'd only and always been good at . . .

KnockKnockKnock.

"Enter," Dare called.

Spencer drew the panel open. "You have . . . another *guest*, my lord. A Mr. Avery Bryant."

Shock brought Dare flying to his feet. *"Avery?"*

Avery sauntered in. "The very same, Grey. Given the circumstances of our last meeting and the abrupt reversal of your fate, I'm the one more entitled to surprise." Avery's sharp gaze worked over Dare's office.

In a brave display of boldness, the servant lingered for a moment, glowering at the visitor now doing a circle around Dare's office. "Is there anything else you require, my lord?"

"No, Spencer. That will be all."

Spencer sniffed twice. "As you wish, my lord," he said before reluctantly drawing the panel shut.

The moment Dare and his former partner found themselves alone, Dare took up a place behind his desk.

Avery nudged his chin to where the butler last stood. "Friendly fellow."

"He means well," Dare said, for some reason unwilling to let Avery have that low opinion about the servant. "He's unused to meeting . . ."

"People like us?" Avery supplied with a wry grin.

"People like us," Dare agreed.

His partner looped his thumbs in the waistband of his breeches and glanced around. He whistled. "Though I will say, we don't seem to be the same people. Not anymore."

Dare followed his stare, then frowned. "You're wrong."

"Am I?" the other man asked distractedly as he picked up a white bust of a young lady.

"None of this changes who I am or what I do."

"Doesn't it?" Avery asked, curiosity in those two words. Words that were so very familiar, given Lionel's assumptions about Dare's role in the Rookeries.

"It doesn't," Dare repeated, this time with a greater insistence.

Avery redirected his focus to the bauble in his hand, weighing it in his gloveless palm. "Marble?"

Marble? It took a moment to register what Avery was asking. "I . . ." Dare didn't know. "Believe so," he said noncommittally, refusing to acknowledge that he'd not already taken a full inventory of the household.

Wordlessly, Avery returned the piece to the side table and resumed his silent assessment of Dare's new belongings. Items Dare should already know the value of. He should have inventoried the pieces and sold them off, as had been the initial plan and intent. He'd see to that. Soon. Eventually. As soon as he sorted through . . . his marriage and the duke's terms . . .

As his partner took a methodical turn about the room, Dare returned to his seat and the ledgers he'd been studying before Avery's arrival—or trying to, in vain.

He'd been wholly distracted . . . by her. His wife.

Avery had made his way over to Dare's desk.

"You seem distracted."

Dare grunted. The other man had always seen too much. He shifted on his seat. "It is . . . a lot." The change in circumstances. The new life. The reunion with his wife. And he was drowning under the enormity of it all.

His former mentor–turned-partner grinned wryly. "That it is," he said, wholly misunderstanding precisely what Dare had been saying. "Nice place."

But then they weren't people who dealt in emotion, or anything beyond the physical things to be stolen and sold.

Grabbing the curved back of the wing chair, Avery pulled it out and availed himself of a seat. "I never thought to see you here."

"That makes two of us," Dare said under his breath.

Avery shook his head. "I mean, after Newgate." Avery's lips twisted in the closest rendering of a genuine smile Dare had ever remembered from the man. "You always did have the Devil's own luck."

"Luck," he echoed. "Is that what one calls this?"

A frown chased away Avery's grin. "Don't be an arse, Grey. What do you think any *one* of us in the Rookeries would call this?" He glanced about the room once more, forcing Dare to follow his gaze. "You don't go whining and crying because you found yourself not only spared the noose but also moved up to the West End."

And it wasn't the first time that day he'd been properly chastised . . . and shamed. He looked past Avery's shoulder to the marble bust the man had previously handled. For . . . Dare had bemoaned his state. He hadn't given thought to what he'd gained, but had rather been solely focused on what he'd lost. "You're right."

Avery chuckled. "I always am."

"What brings you here?" he asked, getting to the heart of it. He and Avery were partners, not friends; as such, he didn't believe for one moment this was a social call.

"Been looking into what happened with you. Asking questions . . . about our contacts."

All Dare's senses went on alert, and he straightened in his chair. "And?"

"And the woman who gave us the information about the earl you got caught stealing from?" He shook his head. "She's gone."

She'd run. Or someone had silenced her. Dare cursed quietly. "And did you interview those who knew the woman?"

"From what I've been able to discover, she was just a whore who came to you dressed up as something else."

Everyone had connections, though. Whoever had wanted him gone was still out there . . .

"I'll keep asking," Avery vowed.

And there was no doubting the other man would find out something.

"What else have I missed in the Rookeries?" Since he'd been plunged into Polite Society.

Avery shrugged. "Bartlett Nelson got caught filching a lord's purse."

Dare cursed roundly. The other man would match that revelation with a damned shrug? "Since when did he begin picking pockets?"

Avery lifted his shoulders once more. "All boys eventually find their way to thievery in the Rookeries." He held Dare's gaze. "You know that."

Yes, he did. But he'd also sought to position children as he could into roles where they weren't on the other end of the law.

Who, though, in his absence, had seen to that task? He frowned as a thought slipped in. "You didn't take him under your wing?"

"It was always too much for one person," Avery said in slightly patronizing tones. "You've always known *that*, too."

He hadn't, actually. Dare had believed himself singularly capable of saving those who'd needed saving. Only to acknowledge once more the truth of Avery's words.

"His mum was being pressed by Sparky." Hatred filled Dare at the mention of the gang leader who'd stepped in to fill the void left by Diggory, the last bastard to rule the Rookeries. "He needed the money."

Dare lightly thumped his fist on his desk; the ledgers jumped under that movement. "And you had him steal to help himself?"

Avery surged forward in his seat. "I'm doing the best I can . . ." *With you gone.* It hung there between them. "I'm working with Wylie and freeing those as I'm able."

As he was able . . .

Avery had been the best until he'd trained Dare in his methods. Dare, however, had taken theft to a level the other man had never attempted—by invading the homes of the nobility and racking up a fortune greater than anything they'd found before in the streets. It had been a risk Avery had later attempted and adopted with some skill.

"What have you found?"

His partner's expression was pained. "You don't want to do this. More importantly, Grey? You don't *have* to. Not anymore. Let me handle this. You're free."

Free. This was freedom? He'd traded true freedom for a life of chains. "Who are the latest?" he demanded for a third time.

Cursing to himself, Avery fished into his pocket and withdrew a small notepad. He tossed it over, and as Dare picked it up and flipped through the other man's sloppier notes, Avery went on. "Earl of Moray. Baron Wentnick. And the Marquess of Ashcroft. The last fellow I heard is particularly evil. He and his wife had their own son killed," Avery said matter-of-factly, and not as though he'd spoken of the evil act of filicide. "There's also Baron Bolingbroke on my list."

Dare flipped the page and scanned the names there. "What's his story?"

"He and his parents saw another noble boy kidnapped so they could secure an earldom for him. Goes by the name Maxwell now."

Tension snapped through Dare's frame. There'd been another nobleman who'd traded one life for another. Nay, that wasn't altogether true. As Avery had said, that man had been forced into an existence on the streets. Dare? He'd chosen it.

"You aren't the only Lost Lord. Surely you heard of it?" Avery asked.

"I . . . hadn't," he said, managing measured tones. He closed Avery's sloppy notepad and made to hand it over, but then stopped. "Which one?"

"I'm torn between Ashcroft and Bolingbroke."

It was not flawed logic.

Dare's gaze went to the columns of names he'd assembled of people in the Rookeries requiring help. "I can do one and leave you the other," he said quietly. "I can help."

Avery eyed him like he'd sprung another limb. "You? Thieving still? You're mad." The other man chuckled. "Whyever would you want to do *that*?"

Dare's jaw clenched reflexively. Of course, because the expectation would be that Dare had found his way out and wouldn't need . . . or want . . . to join in those same activities—stealing from society's worst reprobates and giving to those who were truly deserving. "Whyever would I not take part?" he countered.

"Because you're rich," Avery said flatly.

"I'm not, though. Not really." Dare went on to explain the state of the finances he'd inherited and the agreement the duke had laid out.

Whistling, Avery reclined in his seat. "Well, either way, as I see it? You've plenty of stuff here that you don't need to risk your neck to save another. Sell your properties. Sell their fancy things. That'll be enough to last you."

"I'll give it some thought," Dare murmured. Ultimately, however, it wasn't about him. That had long been a distinction between him and his mentor: Dare had been determined to give it all away. Avery had given away only just enough to afford him some power in the Rookeries, and the rest he'd hoarded and held on to for his own security. Having lived the same precarious existence as the other man, Dare would never pass judgment on what anyone did to survive.

Avery came to his feet. "I have to go if I want to be in The Window."

Dare glanced to the clock. "Yes," he said, unable to tamp down envy at the freedom permitted Avery to go out.

The Window, as the other man had called it, referred to the safest hours in which to conduct one's most precarious thefts: the early-morn hours when lords and ladies had returned drunk and tired from their night's pleasures and passed out in their beds. It was at that time when servants stole their all-too-brief rest. And then the household was most unguarded.

Once again a restlessness filled him. A hungering to take part.

"Wipe that look from your face," Avery admonished.

Dare's neck heated. "What look?"

"The only time I ever saw you with that silly, infatuated look on was when you were thinking about Temperance. By the way, I thought she was done with you?"

Yes, because after he'd found her the first time in the Cotswolds and she'd pleaded with him to leave her for good, Dare had returned to the Rookeries and revealed the end of his marriage to Avery. The other man had commiserated with him over brandy he had stolen from some nobleman's household. "I convinced her to . . . help me one more time."

Laughing softly, Avery shook his head. "Always had a way with that one, you did. Always had a way with everyone."

Had it been anyone else, there would have been a trace of envy to those latter words. Dare stared down once again at the notepad containing Avery's latest assignments. He and Avery, however, had managed a perfect partnership, with his mentor having been determined to look after him.

This moment proved no different. "You don't want to do this, Dare. Not again," his mentor said with a gruff gentleness, contradictory sentiments and yet both existing in truth. "And I'm not going to let you venture back out. Your days of that are done."

"As if you could stop me," he called over to his mentor.

With a snort, Avery shoved to his feet. "That much you're correct on." He touched the brim of his hat and headed for the doorway.

Something in seeing his retreat sent panic spiraling. Once Avery was gone, so went with him the link Dare needed . . . craved . . . to his previous life. "I'd start with Ashcroft."

"And here I thought you'd say Bolingbroke."

Because Dare had been a victim of a crime committed by the likes of Bolingbroke. "I'm clearheaded enough to know which assignment is the right one. Mercy is more likely if you're caught stealing from the bastard who'd kill his own son." *Is it that? Or is it simply that you want the privilege of that great theft?*

As he turned, Avery lifted a hand and waved it in parting. "You're not wrong."

"I'm right," Dare called out, earning a laugh from his mentor.

The other man paused at the doorway. "How is she, by the way?"

"The same," Dare said automatically, not pretending to misunderstand who the other man spoke of. "She is the same." And yet different. To say as much, however, would invite an elaboration Dare had no interest in providing.

"Now that I can believe. That one was always a spark."

She and Avery had always had a volatile relationship, Temperance's dislike palpable, an emotion she'd never made an attempt to conceal around the other man. Whereas Avery? Avery had always been amused by her.

Dare stood. "I'd ask you to . . . keep me abreast of the Rookeries," he said, that being the closest he could come to asking the other man to be part of his life still.

"And is that something Temperance is going to support?"

No, she wouldn't. She'd disapproved wholeheartedly of Dare's relationship with the other man, and even more, she'd despised the work they'd done.

The other man chuckled again. "Not that you ever did make decisions based on how she felt about our work." There was no recrimination there, and yet . . .

Dare frowned. Something in hearing the other man put the words *that* way . . .

"Anything else you need from me?" Avery asked, pulling him from those guilty musings.

"Your latest list." At the other man's puzzled expression, Dare clarified. "Might I hold on to it . . . do some research of my own on those households?"

Avery chuckled. "You can take a thief out of the Rookeries, but you can't take the thief out of the man."

Now those were words Dare could find himself agreeing with.

Avery nodded at him. "It is yours."

After Avery had gone, Dare found himself alone once more with nothing more than the ache of regret for what he was missing out on . . . and frustration with this new life he now found himself forced to live.

He studied the four names: men who were all strangers but evil in their own right, and deserving of finding themselves targets . . . Reluctantly, he drew the center desk drawer out and filed the sheet inside.

You? Thieving still? You're mad . . . Whyever would you want to do that?

Dare gathered his ledgers and stared once more at the columns of names: men, women, and children whom he'd given to.

How adamant Avery had been that Dare should carry on in his new, comfortable existence . . . and divorce himself of his past.

And ironically, the pair who'd long been at odds over everything and anything had come together in their opinion . . . of this. For Temperance had been insistent that Dare had to choose one life.

To hell with the both of them . . . telling him who he should or should not be. Or what he should or should not do. Dare knew what his fate and future held. He always had.

Go . . .

The streets called, their whispering potent . . . stronger than the opium the men and women with their tobacco addiction craved.

Go . . .

A voice niggled.

Unbidden, he found himself opening the center drawer and withdrawing the notes written in Avery's sloppy hand.

Do it. Why wouldn't you?

The funds he was here attempting to earn in Mayfair the honorable way required him to give something he didn't know how to give. Dare stared at the page he held in his fingers. While the monies belonging to these men? That money was there, now, for the taking.

Dare snapped his book of names closed and tucked it into the desk drawer.

He stood, pausing to stuff the ripped page into the front of his jacket.

A short while later, he found his way through the all-too-familiar streets of Mayfair . . . and outside the household of his latest *victim*.

A man who deserved nothing but had everything.

This was what Avery and Temperance would have him quit. The only damned thing he'd ever been good at.

The household had been entirely doused of candlelight, leaving the townhouse welcomingly pitch black. Even the heavily clouded moonless, starless London sky complied this night, agreeing with Dare and casting aspersions upon that which Avery and Temperance had urged of him.

Staying close to the stucco unit, Dare withdrew the dagger he'd strapped along his back. He wedged it under the window. The distinct clink of metal striking the wood echoed like a telltale shot. Hanging to the side, he waited, allowing for an errant servant still strolling the halls to investigate any out-of-place sound.

And waited.

Dare straightened and peered into the unlit ballroom . . . recalling a different waltz.

What are you waiting for?

Someone would have come by now had they heard him.

He wiggled the blade back and forth . . . when a little face reflected back within the pane.

Dare jumped.

Heart thudding, he glanced around . . . and then back to the unattended child.

The little babe wiggled its fingers and then beat them hard against the glass.

When no one came rushing to collect the child, Dare hesitated a moment and then rested his palm against the glass.

The child giggled happily. Naively innocent of Dare's intentions or any evil—his father's. His family's.

Dare cocked his head and studied the babe with his thick, dark hair. This boy linked to Bolingbroke.

Dare didn't look at the families he robbed in this light, as having children reliant upon them. He didn't think of them, really, in any way. There were only two truths: the men he stole from were evil . . . and they deserved to lose everything.

Now, this unattended child . . . threw all that into question. This boy, not very much younger than little Rose, whom he and Temperance had taken in that night, had a father. A mother. And a reliance upon the items that filled this household, just as Rose and the children of the Rookeries did. All the families who were dependent upon work here, and who would be split up if there weren't funds to retain them.

The babe tapped his fingers against the glass in a rhythmic little beat.

Dare matched those movements, though his were silent, in the staccato rhythm he tapped.

This was really the first time he'd been confronted with a new reality, one different from what he'd allowed himself before this. Until this moment, it had been all too easy to see the men he robbed not as victims but as sinners deserving of losing out.

He'd not thought of them having sons and daughters. Because to do so would have humanized them. It would have forced him to look at what he did in the same light that Temperance had through the years, as something shameful . . . and wrong.

"Where . . . *issssssss* he?" The cry came close to the room where the boy was, and Dare was jerked back to the moment—the danger in his being here, the risk of discovery. *"Pauuuuul?"*

The little boy looked toward that commotion, and then with Dare promptly forgotten, he went toddling off. *"Ma-Ma-Ma."* The glass muffled the remainder of that call for his mother.

Springing into movement, Dare quit his spot at the Baron Bolingbroke's household and, clinging to the shadows, found his way down the narrow alley and out toward . . . home.

Only it wasn't really home.

He'd never truly had one.

Not since he'd gone off to live in the streets of East London . . . where he'd remained until now.

And there had never been a home again.

Dare quit Bolingbroke's street and continued walking. Time melted away, and he continued on . . . until he found his way back to his townhouse. Spencer stood in wait, opening the door for him. The servant gave no outward reaction to Dare's suspicious nighttime travels, dutiful servant that he was. Dare continued walking, climbing the stairs, and didn't stop until he'd found his way outside a partially cracked open ivory door, resplendent in tulips and roses that had been etched into the panel, two small ponies frolicking at the very center of the beautifully crafted piece. So much loving mastery . . . of something as simple as a door. No detail had been forgotten. Intricate care had been taken for the entryway of this room.

Not so much as blinking, Dare stared at those carvings.

You got me a horse, Mama . . . a hooooorse!

His mother's answering laugh filled Dare's ears.

Why had he come here? This place where his memories were strongest.

He had turned to go when the faintest whisper of song froze him in his tracks.

Tom, he was a piper's son
He learned to play when he was young
The only tune that he could play
Was over the hills and far away.

Dare moved closer, edging the panel open another fraction so he had an unhampered view of the owner of that voice.

Over the hills and a long way off
The wind shall blow my topknot off . . .

He felt drawn to that soft, lyrical melody, soothing and entrancing for its simplicity. Engrossed as she was in the child in her arms, Temperance gave no hint of awareness as Dare slipped in.

Dare had never entertained the idea of being a father. Lord knew he'd hated—and been hated by—his own enough that he'd never romanticized what that relationship was or could be. And then after he'd gone? Well, young boys in the streets didn't think about fatherhood. But he knew the precise moment he'd realized he'd never have and didn't want a child: he'd been unable to scrape by the funds to free seven-year-old Taylor Stephens from Newgate. In the end, he'd watched on, hopeless, just another face in the crowd, as young Taylor had swung from the gibbet for the crowd's amusement, and for a crime of filching figs from a street vendor.

And that was when he knew . . . he'd nothing to offer a child. He'd nothing, really, to offer anyone. Other than money, that was.

Hovering now at the front of the nursery, seeing Temperance cradling a sleeping Rose . . . something shifted in his chest.

Now Tom with his pipe made such a noise
That he pleased both the girls and boys
And they did dance when he played
over the hills and far away.

In her sleep, the child reflexively clutched her finger and suckled, oblivious to the tumult that had been unleashed within Dare.

Temperance held the babe close, as naturally as a mother who'd done it the whole of her life.

Her expression was one of equal parts joy and . . . pain. That emotion at odds with . . . so much.

Her eyes met his over the cherubic babe's head, and their gazes locked.

And just like before, that misery was gone so quickly he may as well have imagined it.

Temperance gasped, her song coming to a jarring halt.

And he found himself mourning the end of that child's lullaby.

Chapter 13

Of all the places she'd expected Dare to be . . . the nursery certainly hadn't been one.

Nor had that been the reason she'd sought out little Rose.

Temperance just hadn't thought she'd find Dare here and have to confront this room . . . and this child . . . and the memories of what had almost been and what would never be, with him beside her.

"I . . . Forgive me," Temperance said softly. "I didn't know you were here." She turned to set the babe down.

"No!" he called quickly.

The babe let out a small wail. Temperance hesitated a moment, her heart twisting at the sound of that plaintive cry. Recalling another . . . weaker, frailer one. Needing to put the babe down, and yet warring with herself for that selfishness. In the end, she was saved . . .

"Forgive me," Dare murmured. And even with that admission, he was stretching his arms out for the small child.

She was saved by the one who'd always been her savior. By the man who'd been everyone's savior. Not just hers. She'd just been selfish to want more parts of him than he'd given to all. Dare bounced on his heels. All the while he lightly thumped the babe on the back until the child quieted. Rocking back and forth, he stroked his hand in little circles.

How many times had she seen him in the Rookeries as he was now? With some adoring mother pressing their babe into the arms of East London's savior. And he'd never rejected that, had simply held the child with a comfort and ease. How many times had he even held her brother as he did Lionel's niece?

Of course, all those memories of him existed before.

This was . . . now. This was an image of him, after . . .

Temperance hugged her arms tight to herself. She tried to get air into her lungs.

Then Rose opened her eyes. She blinked several times as if clearing sleep, or mayhap it was that she tried to make sense of the stranger holding her.

Alas, the little girl proved as hopeless and helpless as Temperance herself—and every last woman where Dare Grey was concerned. She cooed and giggled, batting at his hand.

Dare held his palm up for the little girl to swat at.

Temperance stared on at them, a silent observer in that bucolic exchange.

Her body throbbed with the pain of loss and what would never be.

The little girl squirmed in his arms, shimmying herself lower, and Dare complied. He set her down, and they both watched on as Rose toddled off to explore. And without the shield that the girl had been, Temperance took in those details that had previously escaped her: his coarse dark garments. The cap he wore.

The manner of articles he'd worn . . . *before* he'd claimed his title of marquess.

"You have the look of long ago," she murmured, dread slithering around her insides. And never more had she wanted to be wrong. To be told that she was seeing things and worrying about that which she'd no need.

His cheeks flushed as he followed her gaze over his telltale garments.

Her stomach sank at the confirmation she hadn't wanted, but needed anyway.

"You were . . . out." And yet . . . that didn't make any sense, either. Why should he thieve? He, a man on the cusp of earning twenty thousand pounds and in possession of material baubles that could see him comfortable?

For a moment, she didn't think he intended to answer. "I . . . was," he said gruffly. He wandered closer to where Rose now sat, playing with a pair of metal, painted soldiers. "I went walking."

She bit the inside of her cheek hard, hating the pull stealing had always had over him. Hating the danger he'd willingly put himself in, again and again. "Where. Did. You. Go?"

He stared down at the child in the middle of the carpet, confirming everything she'd feared. "A baron's."

"A baron's," she repeated.

"Bolingbroke."

Quitting her spot at the cradle, she joined him over by little Rose. "Why did you visit him, Dare?" Because she'd have the words from his own damned lips. She'd have him own where he was and what he'd been doing.

Only with his next words, he proved he couldn't. "You know, Temperance."

That was it.

You know.

And she did.

She swiped her hands over her face. "Oh, Dare," she whispered.

A muscle throbbed at the corner of his mouth. "You don't want me selling the contents of this household, and yet you don't want me robbing from those who deserve to be robbed."

He expected a fight. Mayhap even craved it. She'd not give that to him. "You don't get the right to determine that someone should have their things taken, Dare," she said calmly. Mayhap it was simply that

190

she'd uttered those words so many times before to him that allowed them to emerge as evenly as they did.

"His family sold a child to Mac Diggory," he said bluntly. "What do you say to that?"

Her entire body tensed. She heard what he was saying, and yet after all the evil she'd known at her father's hands, still she could not process this depravity.

"He is responsible for some boy having been lost to his family and rightful place. I'm not the only one Diggory purchased."

"Is that what happened to you?" she whispered, her voice breaking. "You were . . . purchased?"

"No," he said bluntly. "I wasn't taken. I was ten and I . . . left. I went freely with one of Diggory's henchmen, imagining a grand adventure: me, living on the streets without my father's disappointment and anger to follow me there."

Her heart buckled under the weight of what he revealed: Dare's first real offering about his past. A past he had clear memories of . . . and memories that were not the grand, happy ones she'd expected.

He took a step toward her. "And everything that happened to me was my fault for it."

Tears threatened, and she gave thanks for the cover of darkness, lest he mistake that moisture for pity and not the regret it was. "You were a boy," she said, wanting to know everything there was about his past. Needing to know more about him than the stranger he spoke of. And mayhap in his speaking of it, Dare could free himself of the chains that still held him.

"I was a boy with an unhealthy fascination with East London." He spoke as one who recited words that had been spoken to him many times before. "A man there offered to show me everything I wished to see of the Rookeries." His gaze grew glazed, distant. "And for several weeks, it was a grand adventure. Me learning to steal and filching bread that I could give to the hungry boys and girls. It was all fun." His expression darkened. "Until it wasn't. Coins were exchanged, and I was passed over to Diggory . . ."

She shivered, unable to let her mind think about the hell he'd known.

Dare gave his head a shake. "Until I managed to get free and go back to . . . stealing and passing things out."

But he'd not returned home?

Rose banged the two soldiers together, clanging the metal and squealing loudly at her efforts. One of the toys skittered out of her reach, and Dare sank to his haunches and returned the item to her care.

Temperance weighed her words. "And . . . what did you hope in going to the baron's?"

"I think that should be fairly obvious," he said dryly, shoving to his feet.

"No, I rather think it is not." It had never been straightforward or matter-of-fact where his efforts were concerned. There'd always been more to Dare's motives. To each decision he'd made about which household to rob or not. Of which artifact to steal or not steal.

Just as she didn't believe it was a coincidence that he was here, even now.

Together, they watched Rose while she played. "Do you know what I think, Dare?"

Lost in thought, his brow contemplatively furrowed, he gave his head a slight shake.

"You could have gone to your rooms unobserved when you found me here. You could have gone before I'd seen you and known where you'd gone and why you were out." She waited until he looked to her, then met his gaze squarely. "But I believe you *wanted* me to know. I believe you wanted me to remind you that this path isn't yours. Not anymore. That it shouldn't be. That you are better than this."

He flexed his jaw. "I *am* this."

"No, you're not," she said, unable to keep the sadness from creeping into her voice. "It's just all you've known, but it's not all that you are."

Rose yawned widely, and Temperance went over to rescue the child from the floor. Taking the toy soldiers away, she returned them to the little bench the girl had retrieved them from. Temperance carried Lionel's niece back to the cradle and settled her into the thick folds of the plush bedding.

The little girl protested, resisting sleep with several little cries.

Temperance rocked the intricately crafted cradle until Rose's eyes grew heavy and then closed.

Soon, little snores filled the room.

Temperance continued rocking the babe and stared on . . . seeing another child there . . . the original one to sleep in that bed—Dare. Back when he'd been the beloved and pampered and nurtured child of a marquess and marchioness.

Her nape prickled, and she glanced back.

Dare's gaze bored into hers.

Temperance's cheeks warmed. "What?"

"I'm looking at how very natural you are doing that. How right you look." Her entire body turned to stone. But he wasn't done. Dare drifted closer. "You deserved that."

Stop.

Except . . . she couldn't get the word out, and he continued torturing her.

"I denied you the right to a real husband and a real marriage—"

"Don't," she entreated.

"A child. You should have had a family in every sense."

And there it was.

Her eyes slid closed.

Had he removed the dagger he always kept strapped to his back and slammed it into her breast, he couldn't have hurt her more than he did in that moment. Temperance focused on breathing, and when the pressure eased from her breast, she opened her eyes once more. "You were very clear in what you offered me. I didn't expect more." *I just wanted it . . .*

Dare stretched a hand up.

Turn away.

Resist.

Instead, she again let her lashes flutter shut and leaned into that touch, anticipating his caress, even before he palmed her cheek.

He slid his hand lower, down her nape, cupping her, drawing her closer.

"Temperance—"

Footfalls sounded in the hall, and he abruptly released her just as Gwynn entered.

Clearing her throat, she looked back and forth between them. Temperance could see a wealth of questions . . . and worry . . . in the other woman's eyes. "Forgive me," Gwynn said and turned to go.

"No. It is fine," Dare called, motioning for her to enter.

As he fetched a small doll from the floor, Gwynn gave Temperance a sharp look. "What are you doing?" she mouthed as she set the cradle rocking.

Looking pointedly at a still-distracted Dare, Temperance gave her head a slight shake.

Dare straightened, and she immediately stopped.

Gwynn took the toy from him with a word of thanks, and even as she deposited it into the cradle, her focus was all on Temperance.

And Temperance proved a coward because, when presented with a deserved lecture from her friend, she opted to follow Dare out.

Silent, no words passing between them, they made their way through the corridors.

Or is it really just that you didn't remain with Gwynn because you want to be with Dare . . . that you are reluctant to let go of the closeness you've just shared?

Ludicrous.

Of course it wasn't that.

Time and time again, he'd proven himself unable to separate from the life of crime he'd lived. He'd never quit steal—

Temperance slowed her steps as something worked around her brain, and then she stopped, whipping back to face him.

Why did you visit him, Dare?

You know, Temperance.

"What is it?" Dare stopped beside her, a question in his gaze.

"You went to steal from him," she breathed as that understanding slammed into her. He'd been evasive as to his intentions, and flippant, but he'd not been direct and blunt about what he'd done . . . which he'd always been. Another might not have gathered that particular detail. But she knew this man. She knew the nuances in how he spoke and what he said with his words and actions . . . and just as importantly, what he *didn't* say, as well. "But you didn't. You didn't rob him."

"What?" Dare's eyes moved around the hall as he looked everywhere but at her.

"I know you," she said softly . . . simply.

He sighed, his gaze sliding past her to the path they'd just traveled. "I went there with every intention to steal from the baron. I brought the blade I use to work my way into residences." As if there might be another instrument in question, he lifted the back of his jacket and revealed the holster there and the blade strapped in. "I jammed it under the sill and worked the window up." Dare wandered ahead several steps, and she moved to put herself in his path.

"What happened?" she asked, not realizing she held her breath until he spoke his next words.

"I . . . couldn't do it," he said hoarsely.

And her heart did an endless stream of somersaults in her breast. Not once in all the years she'd known him had he ever altered his course when it came to his thievery. This . . . was the first time. And it was also the first hint that mayhap he had changed after all, despite his insistence that he couldn't and never would. "Why? What . . . was different this time?"

Dare raked an uneven hand through his hair, knocking his cap loose. "I don't know. And I cannot say that I never will again, but in that moment, I thought of the damned family and the child he has and couldn't bring myself to—"

Dragging him by his shirtfront, Temperance went up on tiptoe and kissed the remaining words from his lips.

He stiffened, and then all at once, his hands were on her.

As she had hers on him. Sliding her fingers under his jacket, she ran them over the contoured walls of his chest.

There, in the hall, for the world to see, with the risk of discovery and passing servants, he pressed her against the wall and made love to her mouth.

Not breaking contact, their bodies moved, him propelling her backward, away from the window and toward her room, but she ultimately led the way. Leading and yet, at the same time, surrendering.

Folly . . . folly . . . folly.

It was a litany, muffled, muted, and then ultimately drowned out by the feel of Darius Grey's mouth on hers.

Except, mayhap if she allowed herself to give in to this once more, she could purge herself of this aching need for him.

Even as Temperance parted her lips, allowing him entry, she sensed the inherent lie in that hope.

The taste of him flooded her senses. Berries and mint, one of those foreign, the other familiar. And she both mourned the small changes that had left him a stranger to her and reveled in the constants that remained.

Reaching past her, Dare pressed the handle and shoved the door open. "Do you want to stop?" he rasped in between kisses.

Her answer came instantaneously, born of honesty and pure desire. "No."

With a low growl, he guided her backward into the room, pausing only long enough to kick the panel closed behind them. "That is the first time I've ever longed for the word 'no' from you, love."

Love. That gentle endearment he'd always had for her sent another fiery wave of heat through her.

The backs of her knees collided with the mattress, and Dare gathered her buttocks to keep her from tumbling back . . . and instead, lifting one of her legs, he rucked the cotton fabric up, that thin material a flimsy barrier that was still much between them. Until it was gone, and she was exposed to him.

The cool spring air was a balm upon her heated skin.

They tangled with their tongues, their flesh coming together in a scandalous dance that mimicked the act which her body truly longed for, hungered to again know.

Desperate to get closer, she wrapped her thigh about him, thrust, and arched. A keening little moan slipped out. Over and over. Those desperate sounds of her desire were swallowed by each kiss.

He'd always known what her body craved, and this moment proved no different. He cupped her buttocks and brought her more flush against him as he guided her down.

The mattress came up to meet her, and she sank into the deep feather folds.

All the while, she met each slant of Dare's mouth over hers. "You are certain," he rasped between kisses. He would be the voice of reason . . . now, when she didn't want reason. "I'd not have this change anything—"

"I'm certain," she said, her breath coming in soft little puffs. Not allowing him to cast any further doubts on this and what she wanted, Temperance dragged him closer. Wrapping her arms about him, she worked her fingers over his back. She tugged his shirt out and wrestled with his jacket. "Why are there so many buttons?" she moaned.

Dare's guttural laugh rumbled his chest as he trailed a path of kisses down the curve of her cheek, and lower.

She gasped as he lowered her bodice and buried his face against her.

His cheeks, rough from the day's growth covering them, scraped and tickled, earning a breathless giggle.

"Still sensitive as you ever were," he whispered, his breath a warm sough upon her skin.

Incapable of words, Temperance's moan gave way to a gasp as he took the tip of her breast between his lips and sucked deeply.

Her fingers tightened reflexively, curling into the long, lustrous strands of his hair.

Then he switched his attention to the previously neglected mound, worshipping the sensitized flesh. He licked at her, flicking his tongue over her aching nipples, and she anchored his head to keep him close, both needing him to stop and wanting the moment to go on forever.

"Dare." His name was a ragged entreaty as she rocked her hips, needing all of him.

"I've waited for this moment for five years, Temperance, and I have no intention of bringing us to a quick conclusion." With that, he tugged her nightdress free at last, and tossed it aside so that she lay naked and fully exposed before him.

She panted, forcing herself to draw away from his kiss. "I want to feel all of you." Rolling out from under him, Temperance came up on her knees and resumed her battle with his jacket. Her hands shook as she freed the last of his buttons. Pushing the wool garment from his shoulders, she threw it over the side of the bed. Frantically, she yanked his shirt from the waist of his trousers, moved her hands under the lawn article, and stroked up and down his sweat-slicked, muscular frame. "I want to see you."

The smile he flashed was the pained, half-pleasured, half-tortured one he'd always worn at the height of lovemaking. That hadn't changed. And she reveled in that realization. And the truth that for everything they'd always gotten wrong, this they'd always gotten right.

Dare pulled his shirt overhead and sent it sailing to join the growing heap of garments at the side of the bed. His trousers followed suit until he was fully naked before her.

Gasping for breath, her chest rising and falling hard and fast, she took in the sight of him. He'd always been glorious, chiseled perfection. Somehow in the years apart, he'd added muscle to his frame: his whipcord-tight, flat belly, the carefully defined lines of his biceps and triceps. Temperance traced a finger over those hard planes, relearning the feel of him. His was a beauty that defied mere mortals and belonged memorialized in the Guildhall Museum he'd sneaked her into for her birthday as a young woman.

She shifted her gaze lower to his length jutting out, high and proud.

Biting the inside of her cheek, she wrapped her fingers around him and stroked as he'd loved . . . and as she'd loved doing.

He groaned, an animallike sound befitting a wounded beast. "It is too much," he whispered hoarsely. His mouth covered hers with a greater urgency, with a passion that danced on the edge of violence.

This time, he lay down and drew her over him so that she straddled him. Temperance sank onto his enormous shaft; her moist channel slicked the way, and closing her eyes, she moaned at the feel of him stretching her, filling her.

How she'd missed him. How she'd missed these moments of passion between them.

Temperance leaned back on her haunches, and he hissed noisily when his length filled her to the hilt.

Then they began to move. She rocked her hips wildly, sliding down and then up. All the while, she stroked her fingers through the damp curls matting his chest. The hair soft and springy against her callused palm. "You are so beautiful," she whispered.

Laughter shook his frame; those reverberations she felt all the way inside, and to her soul. "*You* are beautiful, Temperance Grey."

Temperance Grey.

Oh, God.

She bit her lower lip. "Y-you stole my compliment, Dare." Her body trembled as he continued to drive up into her. Sweat beaded at her forehead and worked down her cheeks, dripping onto Dare's glistening frame.

All teasing faded under the rising tide of their desire.

"That's it," Dare urged, that high praise he'd always issued whenever they made love. He gripped her hips and guided her through each desperate thrust. Until they were moving in a wild, desperate rhythm; Temperance rose and fell over him, crying out as each stroke touched her to the core.

A frantic pressure built and built, pulling her onward to a rising crescendo as he drew her up to that glorious precipice she'd never thought to again fall from. They moved as one, their bodies in exquisite tandem. *"Daaare."* Her voice came pitched to her own ears, dulled by the rapid thundering of her heartbeat. Their pace grew in frenzy; her moans spilled and mingled with Dare's guttural groans, an erotic medley that matched their bodies' dance. The scent of their arousal hung in the air, sweat and musk, evidence of their desire that pulled her closer to a peak of pleasure.

Temperance dug her fingers into Dare's biceps as she stiffened and exploded on a glorious climax. She cried out, screaming his name over and over as she rode him. Bucking wildly, she clung to him.

And then he joined her in her surrender. "Temperance." Shouting his release, Dare grabbed her hips and arched up. As he guided her through that rhythm he needed, he spilled himself in long rivulets. Temperance moaned, savoring the feel of his length as it pulsed and throbbed, and she took all of him. How she'd missed the feel of him . . . of this.

With a gasp, Dare collapsed.

She fell down atop his chest, sprawled upon him with her hair forming a curtain over them.

"It was good?"

"Mmm," she murmured languidly, her eyes shut. Wanting to keep them frozen in this place and moment so that the past and the future could never be. Always. It was always glorious perfection between them—in this.

Except . . . She rested her cheek against his chest. The moment she opened her eyes . . . pretend ended and reality came rushing in. And she was not ready for that. Dare smoothed a palm in light circles over the small of her back, that tender caress so soothing.

Alas, make-believe hadn't ever been for one like her.

Please, do not let him be triumphant.

Resisting the urge to groan, she opened her eyes.

His thick lashes swept low, revealed . . . nothing in his gaze. His features were their usual stoic mask.

And somehow . . . that restraint was worse than any smugness on his part.

She cleared her throat. "I don't wish for this to be . . . awkward."

"This?" he drawled lazily, still stroking her back. His touch . . . delicious, quixotic, and distracting.

Her cheeks warmed. "I don't wish for this to affect how we are around one another. This, of course, changes nothing in terms of our arrangement." *Or our future.*

"Of course not," he said, so instantaneous in his response that her heart squeezed in a way that defied logic. Which made no sense. She wanted him to be unaffected by their lovemaking.

Didn't she?

"This was a mistake," she made herself say . . . for herself, as much as for him.

"Oh, undoubtedly."

Unable to meet his eyes, she reluctantly swung her legs over the side of the bed.

Dare shot an arm out, catching her around the waist.

She gasped.

"But you know I've always been one to make the same mistake over and over," he whispered, placing a kiss against her sweat-dampened shoulder.

Her breath caught on an audible gasp as he filled his hands with her breasts.

He flipped her onto her stomach, laying her over the edge of the bed . . . as she'd so loved.

She closed her eyes and moaned. He remembered.

"Everything," he said, his thoughts always so flawlessly following even her silent ones. He slid a hand around her front and between her legs. His fingers slipped through her damp curls, and he stroked her, drawing a low moan from her lips. "I remember everything where you are concerned," he rasped against her neck, kissing her, trailing his kisses over her. All the while, he stroked her.

She was wicked and wanton. Her scandalous yearnings likely a product of the commoner's blood flowing in her veins, and she couldn't care. The woman he'd been betrothed to, the one he should be married to even now . . . any lady would never be so scandalous. And yet . . . Temperance had never been able to bring herself to care about anything, not when he made love to her.

With her still under him, Dare slipped a knee between her legs, shoving them farther apart.

Whimpering, she clung to the sheets and rocked her hips in restless anticipation, waiting for him to fill her. Arching back to look at him, she pleaded with her eyes and words. "Please," she begged when he still tempted and teased . . . tormenting her.

He slid the tip of his length in, only drawing out her misery.

And then, catching her by the hips, he rammed himself high and deep, and she shattered, screaming his name over and over.

And this time, when she came undone, there was no room for regret. There was nothing but feeling . . . and a perilous longing to live in his arms forever.

Chapter 14

The following morn, Temperance came to breakfast all business.

With her hair drawn back tightly at her nape and her high-necked gown, one would never look at her and imagine the fiery, passionate creature who'd come alive in his arms.

Nothing different may have transpired between them. Last night may as well have never happened, existing instead as longing thoughts he'd carried for so many years. Only the taste of her on his lips and the feel of her skin on his lingered still. Each cry, whimper, and moan of his name as she'd given voice to her passion had echoed in his ears, and he'd happily surrendered his sleep to those memories.

No, it had been real and wonderful. And the most alive and joyous he'd been . . . since she'd sent him away.

A plate of buttered toast forgotten, untouched, and shoved aside in favor of a notepad, Temperance scribbled away. Her pencil flew back and forth frantically over the page, with emphatic clicks of the tip as it struck the page, that same zeal with which she'd always written, and which had always fascinated him.

"As I see it," she was saying, "there are certain areas in which we must become proficient. Many of them. There are dancing and discourse and the rules of Polite Society," she fired off, and he found himself smiling.

She'd always taken charge, and it was just one of the many reasons he'd been captivated by Temperance Swift.

"You're not paying attention," she charged, not lifting her head from those notes commanding her attention.

"I am." *Somewhat.* That was, when he'd not been woolgathering about her.

She finally looked up. "There is also the matter of being *properly* introduced to your sister."

"There'll be time enough for that," he muttered. Now that was a certain way to bring to an end any wistful thoughts—the sister who'd have been happier to see him hang, and who went out of her way to avoid Dare at any and every cost. The same sister he'd now be responsible for squiring about London, and whom his funds were inextricably linked to. *What could possibly go wrong there?* he thought wryly. He schooled his features.

Temperance narrowed her eyes. "What?"

"I didn't say anything," he said, reaching for his cup of coffee.

She put a hand over his, forcing the glass back to the table. "What?"

"One might say she isn't overly fond of me."

"Isn't . . . ?"

"She doesn't like me," he said flatly.

"She doesn't even know you."

"She knows me enough to know she doesn't like me."

Temperance pushed aside her notes and fully attended him. And he had an inkling how her younger brother must have felt all these years.

"She may have taken exception to my not properly appreciating the great Milford line."

With a groan, Temperance buried her face in her notepad and knocked her forehead lightly against the page. "You showed the same arrogance you did with your grandparents?"

"I wouldn't call it *arrogance.*"

She picked her head up. "Call it what you will. You've done nothing to make this easier for either of us." Temperance gave her head a slight but firm shake. "It is done. No good is going to come from dwelling on how you handled the situation before this. We are going to have to begin again."

He moved his gaze over her. In his work, Dare had had dealings with many over the years—men. Women. Most of whom had been facing precarious situations with the law or various gang leaders on the streets. Not a single one of them had ever displayed the military-like control Temperance had.

She blushed. "What?" she asked, a defensive edge lining that question.

Dare made himself focus on the charcoal smudge upon her forehead. "Here," he murmured, lightly dusting that remnant away. "You've pencil here."

Temperance went absolutely still as he brushed the mark from her skin. He stroked his fingers over her brow, caressing her, recalling the night they'd shared.

She trailed her tongue along the seam of her lips, and hunger flared once more. He'd never have enough of her. "W-we should . . . ?"

"Yes," Dare whispered.

Temperance's gaze went to the row of servants stationed along the wall, and with that look, she found the restraint he lacked. Clearing her throat, she angled slightly away, putting a discernible space between them. "I took the liberty of compiling this list." She turned it out for him to read. "And I shall defer to you which matter we might begin with."

1. Proper forms of address

2. Proper forms of dress

3. Curtsying and bowing

4. Dancing

"I feel quite confident in my curtsying abilities—" Temperance punched him lightly on his arm. *"Oomph."*

"Dare."

"Oh, fine," he muttered. "Always serious, you are."

"And not serious enough, *you are.*"

"Fair enough." He grabbed her pencil, circled the item at the very bottom of her list, and went back to his coffee.

She leaned over his shoulder. *"Daaancing?"*

"It is on your list." If he was going to have to suffer through the miseries of Polite Society's norms, he'd begin by enjoying the feel of Temperance in his arms. "By your response, one would think you weren't the one to write it as an option," he said with a wink. Dare made another attempt for his drink.

She again swatted at his fingers. "You promised to take this seriously, Dare."

"I am." Where his motives were concerned, she'd every reason to her doubts and suspicions.

"I'm not making light of this, Temperance," he said quietly.

She appeared wholly unmoved by his solemnity. "Given my work, I've some knowledge of the peerage," she said, her attention trained once more on her meticulous notes. "My experience isn't extensive; however, there was a baroness in the Cotswolds who frequented the shop I was employed at. As a result, I and the other seamstresses were instructed as to how one should and should not speak to lords and ladies."

As a marchioness, Temperance outranked most of the ladies and lords they'd come into contact with. He knew her enough, however, to withhold that particular detail, as it would only unsettle her.

"We shall begin there," she said, placing a little star next to item one on her list.

He frowned. "But I chose this." Wrestling the pencil and note-pad away, he made another circle over the last item. This time, as she grabbed for the pencil, Dare held it beyond her reach.

From over her shoulder, he caught the small smiles from the servants stationed there.

And had they been alone, he'd no doubt she would have stamped her foot as she did when annoyed. "Dare, we have to begin with something we have some knowledge of. We'll need to find dance instructors. In fact, I suspect your grandparents will have the names of gentlemen who might assist in that area, and they'll also likely approve of the evidence you are try—"

"I *know* how to dance."

Her jaw slipped as her mouth fell open. "What?"

This time, he picked up his coffee, free of interruption. "I know how to dance," he repeated, blowing on the hot contents of his glass.

She continued to stare gape-mouthed at him. Unnerved by that look—the one that made him out to be more oddity than man—he took a sip of the bitter black brew. When Temperance still didn't say anything, Dare winged an eyebrow up.

"I . . ." Temperance looked down at her page. "Oh."

"The nobility does not waste time. They start early in instructing their children on life's most important lessons and skills," he said, unable to keep the cynical amusement out of his voice. "Though I'd argue my *parents* would have been best served in having seen me taught how to handle a knife or throw a punch." Instead, they'd given him no talents of any real use or value for surviving in the streets. Everything he had learned, every meaningful skill, he'd either taught himself or learned from Avery.

Temperance lowered her book. "Oh, Dare." Her expression softened.

His neck went hot, and he made a show of drinking from his coffee. He didn't want pity from her. When he'd finished, he set his glass down. "Shall we?" he asked, shoving back his seat.

Temperance stood.

The two servants stationed outside clicked their heels and straightened at their approach.

Dare waved off those extravagant displays from the pair. "No need for any of that."

Moments later, as Dare and Temperance wound their way through the halls to the ballroom, Dare acknowledged that he'd been wrong before. It was awkward between them, after all. This was. They made the journey in silence, a stilted one . . . when it had never been uncomfortable between them. That was what had always confounded him. She'd been the one person whom he'd felt an ease with.

With Avery it was all business and work, and comfortable and safe for it.

With Temperance, he found himself questioning the rules and lessons of thieving in the Rookeries and also wanting . . . everything he shouldn't. That hadn't changed. That had remained a constant, and he feared it always would.

When they reached the ballroom, Dare drew one of the double doors open and allowed Temperance to enter first.

She hesitated before walking inside.

"Oh, my . . . Saints of St. Giles," she whispered. Touching a hand to her throat, Temperance swept forward. Twelve marble pillars, with bases and tops accented in gold, lined each side of the parquet dance floor. Her wide eyes took in every detail, including the seven crystal chandeliers that hung at the center of the room.

As he crossed to join her, Dare took in these newly inherited rooms. The small, carpeted dais showed the same hints of age as the rest of the household. No framed paintings hung on the walls. The sconces were bronzed and not gold. "They are modest compared with most." His voice echoed, inordinately loud in the empty space. "Many I've been inside have marble flooring throughout and—" He stopped himself abruptly, but it was too late to call it back, that reminder of the work he did.

Temperance pulled her gaze back from the glass ceiling overhead, her expression stricken. "I . . . never truly thought of you being in these households," she said softly. "*Before*. Now, I can see you here," she continued in whispery-soft tones he strained to hear, even as close as they were to one another. "Now, it makes sense." Then that was one of them who could see himself in this place . . . in this world. "I didn't let myself think of you inside these homes . . ." She let her arms hang wide. "Inside *this*, because it made the risk of what you did all the more real." Her eyes grew distant, taking on a far-off quality as she left him in thought. And it was the moment he lost her again to his work. "Although the times you were caught by constables and sent to Newgate served as the only reminders I needed."

But then unlike before, where discussion of his thievery left a wedge, this time her features settled into a placidity, and she smiled. "This time is *different*. Before, you'd no choice, and now . . ." Temperance caught his hands and held them in her own. She squeezed them lightly. "You are truly free of that life, Dare." The smile curving those lushly beautiful crimson lips was a smile he'd never seen her wear—ever. One that was soft and free of cynicism or wariness.

And lost as he was in the serenity of her expression, it took a moment for what she'd said to sink in.

You are truly free of that life . . .

It was a conclusion any rational, any sane, person would have reached, but stealing from society's most undeserving and giving it to those who were in need? That was more part of his blood than any title or noble connections. Stealing was how he'd survived, and he couldn't simply disentangle himself from that.

Removing his hands from hers, Dare clasped them at his back and rocked on his heels. "Shall we?"

She nodded.

It was the first he ever recalled her . . . uncertain. This was a new layer of Temperance Swift.

"The first thing to remember about the waltz—"

"The waltz?" she choked out, interrupting him.

"Is there something wrong with the waltz?"

"It is just . . . you . . ." She cleared her throat. "I was thinking something . . ." Temperance stared helplessly back.

And perhaps he was even more a bastard than the world took him for, because he wasn't going to help her. Dare shook his head slowly. "Something . . . ?"

"More distinguished," she blurted.

Distinguished? He tamped down a smile. "Ah, but where, Temperance, is the fun in that?" He drifted closer and looped a hand about her waist.

Temperance gasped; it was the softest, slightest inhalation, and yet headily erotic for the lack of restraint to it. They remained there, chests touching, bodies pressed close. "I-is this proper?"

He lowered his head and their breaths mingled. "Does it matter if it is?" he whispered against her mouth. "Given last night?"

She slapped a finger against his mouth. *"Shh,"* she demanded, glancing about the empty room. "Will I be expected to dance this . . . with other gentlemen?"

And just like that, his plans for their dancing lessons came to a screeching, staggering halt under the image she'd ushered in: one of Temperance locked in the arms of some unrepentant rogue, a rake with a hand too low on her back, and on the curve of her hip. Some scoundrel who was all too eager to seduce the Lost Lord's wife out from under his nose. A gentleman who wasn't a thief of anything but hearts.

"Ahem," he said, clearing his throat. "We could begin first with a country dance, the quadrille."

And damn if the relief in her eyes didn't grate.

"Now," he began, focusing on the business at hand. "For country dances, what you should remember is the movements are a skip-change step with a little jump, and end with your feet together." Humming a tune, Dare demonstrated those steps, slowly, several times, then increased speed so they matched the rhythm of songs played.

Temperance's mouth moved as if she were talking herself through his directions.

"In formal sets, the feet come together, so one doesn't blur the edges as one goes straight into the next figure," he explained.

"You remember . . . so much of this," she said quietly . . . and he missed his first step.

He lifted his shoulders in a small shrug. "I expect it's no different from learning to walk or ride or anything else." Only . . . there were memories there. Ones he'd not thought of: a woman who was a stranger, and yet not. A woman whom he'd not thought about, or of, because there'd been no need for it. But now, with Temperance's observation, that ghost forced her way back in.

It is no different from skipping or running, Darius . . . Come, let me show you . . .

A child's laughter lingered with that of his mother, in these walls still.

"Dare?" A soft hand settled on his arm.

"Fine," he said abruptly. "I'm fine. The quadrille," he said, bringing them back to something far safer—their dance lesson. "You step onto your left foot at the same time you throw your right foot forward, like so." He demonstrated those steps once more, and waited for her to mimic them. Temperance attempted them several times. On the fourth, she was slightly breathless and laughing, with red color in her cheeks . . . and thoroughly entrancing. "It doesn't have to be that far," he said too late, and she completed that step, her leg extended too far out, and she nearly came down.

Laughing, she caught herself against him.

And all the air remained trapped in his lungs, and he wanted nothing more than to freeze her as she was now, blithe and without the cares she'd known. Without the struggles and suffering she'd endured.

"What?" she asked, her breath coming in quiet little rasps. She didn't release her grip upon Dare's jacket, holding on so naturally to him.

"Nothing," he said softly. To say it was anything more would shatter the moment. "Careful with your right foot. If you extend it too far forward and to the right, you can fall."

She pulled away and attempted the steps once more. "Good," he said. "Now, jump, landing on both of your feet, but bending your knees slightly to prevent injury."

Her eyes twinkled. "Who would have imagined dance would be so dangerous?"

It wasn't. Only this woman, and the longing he had for her, represented the greatest peril.

Together, Dare and Temperance went through the steps. Over and over. And then they moved on to the Scotch reel . . . "And at last . . . there is . . . the waltz." He left that there, allowing Temperance to decide whether she wanted to attempt what had once been a scandalous set.

"Who taught you the waltz?"

"My mother instructed me," he said before he could call the words back. Why had he shared that?

Temperance's eyes softened. "Do you remember much about her?"

"Some," he said gruffly, keeping his eyes focused over the top of her head.

"You've never talked about her . . . not to me."

Not to anyone. The mother he'd remembered may as well have died when Dare left.

"If you would rather not?" he said, eager to bring them back to the lesson.

"No. I will."

"It is very much accepted now. Hardly as scandalous as it once was when it first appeared here in London."

"It is scandalous, Lavinia . . ."

"It is merely a waltz, Oscar . . ."

Dare's vision tunneled as he stared straight ahead down the length of the ballroom, and resurrected from his memory was a waltzing pair: a mother and her son of just seven, twirling wildly around the dance floor, a couple gliding in long, sweeping movements, their laughter filling the room, blending until . . .

"What is the meaning of this, Lavinia?"

"He is just dancing."

"Everything he does is outrageous. You shouldn't encourage him more . . ."

That fighting between his parents trailed off in an echo in his mind.

Dare continued staring sightlessly ahead, seeing that image as if the moment played out in real time before him. He'd not allowed himself to think of them . . . for so long. And yet, having been forced back into this household and this way of life meant they were there haunting him at every turn.

"Is it?" Temperance's voice came as if from a distance.

"Hmm?"

"Very much accepted now?" she repeated.

The present came rushing back in a loud whir. "I . . . Yes. From what I've . . . observed." And this time, a memory intruded of this same ballroom . . . only he had stood on the outside of it, his nose pressed against the cold crystal pane as he stared in at a world he'd no longer belonged to.

Feeling Temperance's probing stare and not wanting any questions, Dare shoved off those thoughts and launched into instructions for their next set together. "What one must remember is that the waltz follows a basic box step." Holding his arms in the correct pose, he demonstrated what would be her movements. "Forward left. Slide with the right. And then close, left foot to right foot. Now, switch weight." Dare faced Temperance and found her features a study of concentration. "Your turn."

Her arms hanging at her sides, Temperance stepped forward, then right.

"More of a slide," he murmured. Going on a knee, he took her right leg and gently guided her through the motions.

He froze. His fingers curved reflexively upon her knee, the thin wool of her dress and a chemise all that stood between them. Dare swallowed hard, wanting to resume exactly where they'd left off the night prior.

"Dare?" she asked questioningly, and he abruptly released her.

"Try again," he said hoarsely, leaping to his feet. "Always remember," he instructed as Temperance tested those movements several times. "There is an up-and-down quality to the rhythm of the dance." Although there was a slight bouncing quality to some of those motions, there was even more a natural grace as she mimicked the steps he taught.

"Now back, side, close . . . and you have it."

"I have it," she muttered, practicing once more. "I trust when there is an orchestra and a room full of proficient dancers and a partner that it will be altogether different."

"All of which is easily rectified." Dare held his arms aloft.

Temperance hesitated, and for a moment, he thought she intended to refuse. But then she stepped into his arms.

How right she felt there. And she'd been correct when she'd said intimacy had never been their problem. Their bodies had always moved in a harmony, be it lovemaking or now . . . dancing.

"There's no music," she pointed out, faintly breathless.

Was it from all her earlier exertions? Or the feel of his arms wrapped about her? And why did he so desperately want it to be the latter?

Dare began to quietly sing an up-tempo melody and started them through the steps. Temperance stared down at their feet. She tripped and promptly cursed. Stifling a smile, lest she take it as a sign that he was making light, he tipped her chin up. "Look at me," he murmured, pausing in his song.

"You can sing."

"There're no words."

"It is still singing. You are carrying a tune, and in flawless modulation."

"Music instructors," he confessed, twirling her in a wide, dizzying arc that brought a laugh and, as importantly, an end to her questions.

Temperance stepped on his left foot. "I am terrible at this," she gritted out between clenched teeth.

"You've only just begun, love. Close your eyes."

"I'm not—"

"Close. Them."

And then wonder of wonders, Temperance complied.

"Now, no talking. No questions. Nothing. Just feel the music . . . and movements. And dance."

Together, they glided through the one-two-three steps of the waltz. She stumbled, and Dare tightened his grip at her waist, holding her up, drawing her closer. And when she opened her eyes, so much passion blazed from within those sapphire depths, Dare faltered.

Their legs became entangled, and they came down.

Dare broke her fall, coming down on his back so that she landed on his chest.

Breathless with laughter, Temperance touched the tip of her nose to his. "This is going to prove disastrous."

He rolled her under him, earning another, bigger, fuller laugh. "You dare doubt us?"

"We're on the floor, Dare."

"Yes, well, there is that." He tickled that sensitive place at her side, pulling a squeal from her. She swatted and writhed under him, this game he'd long played with her, once upon a lifetime ago before they'd parted.

"Mercy," she cried between great, heaving guffaws of hilarity. *"Merrrrcy."*

"What?" Dare angled his ear close to her mouth. "I'm afraid I don't recognize that last word, love."

"I take it this is your . . . *wife*? My sister-in-law?" A voice boomed from the front of the room, slashing a blade of sobriety through their exchange.

Dare continued to hold Temperance. Her chest rose and fell in quick respirations.

Framed in the doorway stood the Duchess of Pemberly alongside her granddaughter. Both women wore matching frowns.

And where there were only questions whether Dare belonged to this family, there could never be any doubting that the young woman was cut of the same cloth and shared the same blood as the dour matriarch.

"Your Grace," Dare called from where he still lay on the floor.

The older woman's cheeks turned grey, and she reached about her neck.

Kinsley helped the duchess to her smelling salts.

Temperance pushed frantically against him. "Release me. Now," she furiously whispered.

Sighing, Dare hopped up, and held a hand down to Temperance.

As the pair at the front of the ballroom swept forward, Temperance hurriedly smoothed her skirts and patted her hair.

"You are fine."

"I'm wrinkled," she said out of the side of her mouth. "Your sister?"

"Is not wrinkled."

Temperance shoved a discreet elbow into his side, and Dare grunted. "Stop making light."

"Oh, fine."

The two ladies stopped before him and Temperance.

Kinsley gave Temperance a once-over, wrinkling her nose ever so slightly. "This is where introductions would be best served," she said coolly.

"Temperance," Temperance was quick to supply, with a deep curtsy.

"Hmm. Yes, well, I am *Lady* Kinsley, and you are coming with me and Grandmother."

He frowned. They'd come here and steal Temperance from him . . . and the brief moment of happiness they'd found preparing for their entry to Polite Society? "I'm not aware of any plans—"

"A wardrobe, Darius," the duchess said with a thump of her cane. "Your wife requires a wardrobe."

"For—"

"Grandmother and Grandfather have a dinner party planned."

"To introduce you to Polite Society," the duchess added when no one immediately spoke. "It will be small. No more than sixty guests."

At his side, Temperance dissolved into a strangled fit.

"The sooner you and your wife are introduced, the better off it will be. The gossips will have less stories to invent."

"When?" he asked tersely.

"Saturday evening. The invitations have already gone out, and I'm happy to say there's not been a single rejection amongst the guests."

Of course there wasn't. He might not truly be a lord any longer, but he'd moved stealthily amongst them, through the years, enough to know precisely how they were. They'd not miss an opportunity to have access to gossip before anyone else. "I'll see to my wife's wardrobe."

"And see her properly attired before Saturday?" Kinsley retorted. "You don't have any connections that can secure that feat. Not like Grandmother."

Sending Temperance off in a carriage ride with his ruthless kin? He thought not. "Bloody hell, she's not going."

"Dare," Temperance began.

The duchess's ears fired red, and Dare earned a dark look from his sister. "If I might give you some advice, avoid such language before the dinner party."

Ignoring Lady Kinsley's biting response, Dare focused on the duchess. "She is not going," he said flatly.

Temperance settled a hand on his sleeve. "May I speak with you?"

His jaw hardened. He led her several steps away.

"It is fine," she said when they were out of earshot.

"The carriage. You get sick in them." And he'd spare her that suffering and humiliation in being exposed to his unfeeling *family*.

Tenderness glimmered from within her expressive eyes. "I'm going to have to eventually ride in carriages, Dare."

"Not with them."

"It is a short distance, and I can handle short journeys." She'd always been endlessly brave and proud. "I have to do this."

They locked in a silent battle. With a quiet curse, Dare scraped a hand through his hair. There was no way around this. Whether or not he wished it or liked it, the agreement Dare had struck with the duke required him and Temperance to fulfill certain obligations. "Fine." He bit that single syllable out through clenched teeth.

"It is going to be fine," she promised.

He rested his brow briefly against hers. "Are you attempting to convince me or yourself?"

Her lips twitched. "Perhaps a bit of both of us?"

Dare stroked the curve of her cheek. And for a moment, with the strangers present, the tension of their past melted away as Dare and

Temperance were the young lovers who'd whispered secrets to one another when the world had ceased to exist.

The moment proved short-lived.

As Temperance hurried off to join the duchess and Lady Kinsley, Dare stared after them, wishing he could return to that previous tumble during their waltz, when it had been just them, and only them.

Chapter 15

Journeying from Mayfair to New Bond Street with her new sister-in-law and grandmother-in-law, it was hard to say which part of the day was most miserable: suffering the silent, stark company of each woman or enduring the carriage ride.

No, it was definitely the carriage ride.

Her body lurched with each sway of Dare's elegant black barouche. Sweat dampened her skin, and she discreetly patted back the moisture at her brow.

Unlike her mother, who'd prayed regularly and believed there would be an eternal peace for those who suffered—those like the Swifts—Temperance had never believed in God. She'd never had any real reason to. Living through the hell of the Rookeries, one had *plenty* of reason to believe the Earth, a place of darkness, evil, and danger, had been shaped in the image of Satan. Only to find herself, all these years later, discovering prayer and a hope that there was a God.

Please, do not let me be sick. Please, not now. Not before these people . . .

After she had returned to her rooms, she had ruminated on what Dare shared about his childhood and everything she knew about him . . . in those years after. She had seen firsthand what his life had been . . . and there was only one certainty: if he didn't secure the duke's funds, he'd be lost—forever.

As such, Temperance had risen that morning with a renewed purpose: to see that Dare earned his twenty thousand pounds. Only in doing so would he be forever free of the chains of the Rookeries. She'd even found pride in being the one to lead the charge for her and Dare.

Only to be knocked off-balance once more with the discovery that he needed her help less than she required his. A good deal less.

Of course he could dance. And do so perfectly. With gliding, graceful steps that fell in perfect harmony to a song that he also perfectly hummed, while Temperance had stumbled through the movements and steps.

"I'm not from those elite ranks, either, Temperance," he'd claimed when he was trying to convince her to join him . . . *"We would learn to navigate together,"* he'd said.

All the while, he'd remained wise to Polite Society's customs and ways.

Perfect. Always perfect.

And she . . .

Wholly flawed. Her hands went to her stomach reflexively, and she cradled that useless womb.

Flawed, in every way that a woman *could* be flawed.

Awful.

All of this was . . . awful.

Her stomach revolted against the sway of the carriage ride, and Temperance swallowed convulsively. So flawed that she couldn't even make a damned carriage ride anymore.

He'd tried to spare her from this.

At every turn, he showed himself to be the man she'd fallen in love with . . . and the man she would always love. For his failings and faults and mistakes, he was one who put everyone's happiness and welfare before his own.

And she tried to focus on only that.

Tried to.

Feeling her sister-in-law's gaze on her, Temperance moved her hands away from her belly, and folding them, she rested them instead on her lap.

Her hands clasped firmly, Temperance focused all her energies on one: she stared straight ahead at Lady Kinsley.

This was Dare's sister; possessed of the same dark-brown tresses and a slight cleft in her angular chin, the woman was in very many ways a physical image of her brother. And yet that was where any and all likeness between the pair ended. Dare, who with his effortless charm and ease with a smile, would have never let tension march on as this woman did. This woman, who seemed to revel in the thick discomfort that hung within the carriage.

Lady Kinsley stared boldly back; there was a directness to her gaze that Temperance admired. There was also a coldness to it, too, however. Temperance lifted her chin and continued to meet that unforgiving stare.

She may have been born to a different rank from the woman opposite her; however, people were people. As such, weakness wasn't tolerated or forgiven in any side of England.

The carriage hit an uneven cobble, and she tamped down a groan. *Do not be sick . . . Do not be sick . . .*

And then, miracle of miracles, God proved himself capable of listening to people like Temperance, after all. The carriage rolled to a slow, easy halt.

They'd arrived.

There would be time enough to focus on the misery awaiting her in a posh London modiste's. For now, however, there was only relief that the tense, silent carriage ride had come to an end.

The duchess knocked once on the roof.

A dutiful servant immediately drew open the black lacquer panel and handed the duchess down. He reached back for Dare's sister, but the young woman flicked a palm. At that dismissive gesture, the young man pushed the door shut.

"I do not trust you," Lady Kinsley said the moment the panel clicked shut.

Well, the woman was nothing if not direct and honest. As ruthless as that leveled charge was, Temperance preferred this directness to the veiled insults and innuendos.

"I can certainly understand why, Lady Kinsley," Temperance said. "I'm a stranger, and I'm from the Rookeries. I trust, therefore, you might have reservations about someone of my station."

By the way those thin, dark-brown eyebrows crept up, Temperance's hadn't been the response the other woman had expected.

"However"—Temperance leaned forward—"having had dealings with people of all stations, I can personally attest people of all stations are capable of like cruelty."

Understanding glinted in the lady's eyes. And something that looked very close to appreciation. It was instantly gone. "My grand-parents . . . My mother when she was here . . . living, were desperate to see their grandson and son again. They would accept him back into the fold, regardless of who he is now."

It did not escape Temperance's notice that the other woman hadn't mentioned her father. Questions swirled around Dare's life . . . before. "Your brother," she made herself say.

Lady Kinsley cocked her head.

"That is, you've referred to Dare as a grandson and son, but he is also your brother."

Hate glimmered in the young lady's eyes. "He is no brother of mine. He is, as you said, a stranger, and not to be trusted because of it."

Fury threaded its way through every corner of her person, and Temperance bit the inside of her cheek to keep from hurling a stream of invectives and insults at the woman who'd question Dare. Darius Grey, who'd been a savior in the streets for so many. Even if Temperance could never and would never approve of the work he'd done, she would always respect what he'd sought to do . . . and had done with his spoils. When she trusted herself to speak, Temperance did so in carefully measured tones. "With all due respect, Lady Kinsley, you do not know Dare."

Another person might have been properly chastised. This woman could have challenged a cold slab of stone to a contest and come out triumphant.

"With all due respect," Dare's sister tossed back, "*my brother*, as you would have me refer to him, before he was cut down from a gibbet, was ready to swing for the acts of thievery. Therefore, do not speak to me about, as you call him, *Dare's* honor." She leaned forward in her seat and didn't allow Temperance a word edgewise. "I know people like my brother. Charmers. Scoundrels. Thieves. Glib with words. They can seduce a person into believing they are something other than they are." Her eyes glinted like ice. "But they can't be. They are and always will be thieves, not to be trusted."

What had befallen this woman that she'd such a vile opinion of . . . so many? Including her own brother?

And yet . . . Temperance tried to imagine what it must be like for this woman, to find herself meeting a brother whom she'd never before known. "I trust this is difficult."

Color filled Lady Kinsley's cheeks. "You know nothing about anything."

Yes, there were many times Temperance felt that very way. This, however, was not one of them. "You strike me as a capable woman. Independent. Confident. In control."

"Don't waste your time thinking to ingratiate yourself to me with compliments," the young lady muttered, her color rising.

Temperance hid a smile. "They are not compliments," she assured. "I don't waste my time with flattery. No one from the Rookeries does." That trait had proven problematic during her tenure at Madame Amelie's, when Temperance had been expected to issue any and only pretty words to the clients. "You are well within your rights to feel resentment. I trust it is frustrating to have a person whom you've never met suddenly return." Lady Kinsley's mouth flattened into a hard line. "Your resentment, however right you are to that emotion, is wrongly placed. Dare isn't the one deserving of your anger."

"You come here, simply arriving one day, the bride to my brother's groom, and not even knowing me, you presume to tell me who I should or should not be angry with?"

"You are . . . not wrong," Temperance said quietly. "I'm telling you, your brother did what he had to in order to survive, and I would hope that as his sister you should find some happiness in that, and in his return."

And refusing to engage the young lady one moment more, Temperance opened the door and jumped out.

And then promptly wished she'd never left the carriage. Which would be a first since she'd developed carriage-sickness.

A sea of brightly clad, elegant ladies streamed down the pavement, all stealing long looks and whispering as their gazes caught on Dare's crest and then on Temperance.

Oh, bloody hell.

Temperance's stomach lurched all over again for entirely different reasons. Raising her chin, she sailed forward with all the pride a woman clad poorer than most servants could muster outside the high-end shops. She hurried up the three steps and let herself in—only to be met with more stares.

So many of them.

This is what you agreed to.

Something about having it confirmed here, and without Dare at her side, made it all the worse. It had been one thing imagining herself suffering through this hell with Dare on her arm. With him and his confidence, she'd always believed she could conquer anything. And she was filled with the sudden, powerful urge to weep because of the fact she was alone. Because of the reminder that she'd never truly been invincible, even with Dare's name for protection . . . as he had believed . . . and she had also allowed herself to believe.

Her breath came hard and fast in her ears as the past crept in.

You think you're going to go and marry Dare Grey and I'll forgive that, you whore . . .

Do not let him win here. Not now.

Her father had always been determined to steal her every happiness. He would want nothing more than to see her fail in this.

And it was that reminder, and that alone, which allowed her to bury away the pain of that day and focus on the seamstress fast approaching.

She was . . . the first woman to wear a smile. And it briefly confused and confounded Temperance. "This is my grandson's wife," the duchess was saying. "No expense is to be spared."

"My lady," the young seamstress greeted. "Shall we begin?"

Over the next seven hours, Temperance was undressed, draped, poked, prodded, turned, turned back, and turned around once more. She had more fabrics laid against her person than she'd known had ever existed. She was spoken over. About. Never to.

And when it was done, she found herself discovering a belated understanding of what the women who'd come to her shop had felt like.

A bevy of whispers went up, followed moments later by giggles.

She stiffened and braced to confront those first of no doubt many gossips . . . and . . . found a trio of young ladies, of like pale coloring, laughing as they pointed to a figure seated at the corner of the shop.

Lady Kinsley?

Well, this was . . . unexpected.

Oddly, when she'd agreed to join Dare in London, she'd anticipated being the source of gossip and cruelty because of her birthright. What she'd not expected was that coldness would be reserved for those of their lofty station.

This same woman who sat with her shoulders back but her gaze downcast on the embroidery on her lap bore no hint of the venomous figure who'd called Temperance out so splendidly in the carriage. The busybodies continued with their cruel gossip.

"Well, my mother said," one of the ladies said loudly, "it of course shocks no one that they should find her brother, a common pickpocket, living on the streets . . ."

There was nothing common about Dare Grey. The *ton*, however, would think of him as a common street pickpocket, never imagining that he'd robbed at a grand level that could have seen Dare with houses and riches to rival any lord . . . but who'd instead given it away.

"Scandal follows them all, is what my mama said," another of the pale-faced ladies piped in.

"Well, my mother says the lady not only allowed herself to be seduced by a scoundrel . . ." That last utterance was spoken more loudly than all the others, a statement made with the intention that it be heard. Altogether, the group directed their stares at Lady Kinsley. The lady in question's mouth tensed, and her cheeks fired red. "But she's also carrying his babe . . . That is what my mama said anyway."

This was what accounted for Lady Kinsley's bitterness and resentment, her ill opinion of men.

Oh, that was really quite enough.

"It is unfortunate that your mothers have so much to say in front of you," Temperance drawled.

One of the ladies—the leader of the trio—bristled. "And why is that?"

"Because if they didn't, we'd have blessed silence, as the three of you don't appear to have a brain in your heads."

As one, three mouths fell agape, and the trio's eyes went impossibly round.

The white-clad lady in the middle was the only one to find her voice. "How dare you? Who do you think you are?"

There'd come time enough later to worry about the scandal she'd caused and the powerful enemies she'd found in some peer's daughter. As it was now, all Temperance was capable of was the same Scot's fury her mother had lamented. "How dare I scold three gossips speaking unkindly about another person in public?" She arched a brow. "I'd expect it is a far more egregious offense to be a busybody than the one calling them out." With that, she marched off to assess a pair of ribbons hanging from a clever netting affixed to the ceiling.

"Well!" The only one with a voice amongst them stuck her nose in the air, and with a snap of her fingers that saw the other girls in line behind her, they marched over to three older, plumper versions of themselves.

Temperance tested the fabric of the ribbons, measuring the quality.

She tensed as a person joined her, and then identifying her visitor, Temperance went back to her appraisal.

"You didn't have to do that," Lady Kinsley said tersely.

"No. I don't have to do anything." Well, that wasn't altogether true. She did have to remain here in London and play the role of chaperone to Dare's sister if she wished to earn her five thousand pounds. But even that was a voluntary decision. "I spoke up to those women because I wanted to."

"Why would you want to? You don't even know me, beyond . . ." Beyond how nasty she'd been earlier to Temperance.

Temperance released a pale-blue satin ribbon and exchanged it for an ivory lace one. "I have a greater problem with women gossiping about others than with direct, forthright ones who tell a person precisely how they're feeling."

"Even if said person is telling you she doesn't like you or trust you?" Kinsley asked, trailing close at Temperance's heels as she moved down the aisle.

"I would say there's all the more reason to trust someone who tells a woman precisely how she's feeling. One knows precisely where one stands."

The other woman hesitated. "Thank you," she said gruffly. "For . . ."

Temperance spared Dare's sister from having to humble herself. "You needn't thank me."

And just like that . . . there was an unspoken truce forged between them.

Kinsley stepped closer and spoke from the side of her mouth. "Ava, Anabelle, and Araneid are their names. They are the nastiest gossips, and also diamonds of the first waters. They're very exclusive and live to make everyone whom is not accepted as part of them . . . absolutely miserable."

"Ahh," Temperance said in like, hushed tones. "There is that sort in every end of London."

"Now, their mothers?" her sister-in-law continued to whisper. "They'll invite former lovers, cheating spouses, and the respective others they're cheating with, all in the name of an interesting affair."

Temperance blanched. "That is . . . horrendous."

"And they are amongst the kinder ones," Lady Kinsley stated as fact, examining a violet ribbon.

Those women were amongst the kinder ones? Temperance sighed. This was what she had to face before she managed to secure the funds.

Kinsley spoke, jolting Temperance from those uncomfortable musings. "You didn't ask whether there was any truth to what they were saying . . . about . . ." Her sister-in-law's round cheeks pinkened. "About what they were saying regarding me and . . . a scoundrel."

Temperance tested a bolt of satin that had been forgotten on the table. "It isn't my place to ask you those personal pieces. And certainly not because I'd overheard some horrific women talking about you." She glanced toward the gaggle of gossips. Finding them blatantly staring, Temperance favored them with a glare.

The young women immediately jerked their attention up and everywhere, hastily averting their gazes.

"*Welllll* done," Kinsley said sotto voce. "Are you certain you're not of the nobility? You have the look—"

"I'm quite certain," Temperance interrupted with a little laugh.

"Kinsley, Temperance."

They looked to where the duchess motioned to them at the front of the modiste's. Grateful to put this place, and these women, behind her, Temperance fell into step beside Lady Kinsley, following her out.

When the carriage rocked into motion, to give herself a distraction from the sway of Dare's conveyance, Temperance considered the passing scene.

When she'd agreed to join Dare and assist him in helping his sister, Temperance had been single-minded in her purpose—get the young lady married, secure, and then in turn, secure the funds Dare had promised.

Only . . .

What about Kinsley? What did *she* want?

They were questions she'd not allowed herself to contemplate. Now . . . she did. Really considered it. Did Temperance wish to push the younger woman toward marriage? Temperance, who'd had her heart broken by life and love . . . How could she have failed to consider what the other woman's fate would be?

You put Chance first because he is your brother . . .

And yet, did the ends justify the means?

This time, as the carriage swayed and her stomach lurched, it wasn't strictly the conveyance responsible for that unease. She didn't want to think of Kinsley as a young woman. She was a means to an end. Or that was what she had been. Until Temperance had joined her in the dress shop and seen how she was treated. And then they had talked.

And now, everything was confused in her mind.

She squeezed her eyes shut. *But if she wants to marry . . . surely that is different.* Just because Temperance's heart had been broken, that didn't mean the same fate awaited Dare's sister. Why . . . perhaps she might be like Gwynn and find that beautiful rarest of loves.

And . . . and why did it also feel like Temperance had just tried to convince herself?

She gave thanks when the trip ended and the door was flung open, and fresh air spilled inside.

While the duchess climbed out, Temperance took a moment to discreetly wipe the sweat at her brow. She found Dare's sister staring at her, and abruptly let her hand fall back to her lap. Unlike the cold, angry gaze that had met her on the journey to the modiste's, there was now . . . a softening.

"You get sick in carriages," the other woman remarked.

Pinching her cheeks, Temperance breathed slowly through her nose and exhaled out her mouth. "I take it my reaction was obvious?"

"Well, not at first," Lady Kinsley admitted. The other woman glanced about, then spoke in a conspiratorial whisper. "I get sick on boats."

"Boats," Temperance echoed dumbly. With that revelation, once more Dare's sister unwittingly forced her to see the woman . . . and not the assignment.

Kinsley nodded, and for the first time since she'd met the girl, there was a realization of a different sort for Temperance: just how young, just how innocent she in fact was. "My family would retire to the country every summer, and there would be boat races and everyone loved it, but it was sheer misery for me."

"I've . . . never been on one." She'd done . . . so little. Just like so many children who were raised and died in the Rookeries. She'd seen so little and experienced even less.

"If you hate carriages, you'll hate boats even more," Kinsley said as they descended from the carriage. "On the journey to the modiste's,

I believed you were nervous about the outing or about being with my grandmother and me. But then I saw you at the modiste's and realized if you weren't afraid of the Three A's, you weren't one to be afraid of me and my grandmother or a trip to a shop."

Temperance shared her first smile with Dare's sister.

As they started up the steps of the townhouse, the other woman stopped. "I . . . may like you, after all."

Given what was expected of Temperance and Dare, Kinsley's admission was a step toward their completing one of those terms of the duke and duchess. And yet as she followed behind Dare's sister, it wasn't the money connected to the girl Temperance thought of, but rather the comfortable sense of family that she'd so missed . . .

Chapter 16

One outing.

That was all it had taken for Lady Kinsley to strike a truce with Temperance.

And five days later, the pair had become inseparable.

As such, Dare should be relieved. Working her way into the young lady's good graces would only benefit him and Temperance. That was, after all, one of the requirements laid out by the duke—that Dare cultivate a relationship with his sister.

And yet there was nothing mercenary about Temperance's motives.

But then that had always been what separated her from everyone else in the Rookeries. She would have rather worked harder, for less, in the name of honor and respectability. It was why, with his commitment to theft and flagrant disregard for the law, they'd been miserably ill suited.

Regardless of Temperance's intentions, Dare stood outside the music room, observing the happy pair.

Lady Kinsley played a quick tune on the pianoforte, while Temperance, crouching low, held on to Rose's hands and danced the little girl about in a circle to the unlikeliest of songs—an old tavern ditty, sung in raucously loud tones by Dare's . . . sister.

Be merry my hearts, and call for your quarts,
and let no liquor be lacking,
We have gold in store, we purpose to roare,
untill we set care a packing.
Then Hostis make haste, and let no time waste . . .

He should be relieved. Temperance was doing what he had not and
could not do—form a relationship with Lady Kinsley. That she'd managed the seemingly impossible should be enough. So why, as the outsider of that group, did he find himself wishing he could be part of it?

Because you're bored.

*Because you've nothing else to do, and you really should be out on the
streets, doing what you do best . . .*

This time, those whisperings in his mind didn't have the same convictions they always did.

You should go . . .

There'd be nothing worse than being caught spying.

Peeking in, however, on that happy tableau held him rooted to his
spot, for it was so very reminiscent of long ago. That one he'd seen as a
boy looking in on his parents and—

Lady Kinsley looked up from the keyboard, and her fingers collided
with the keys in a discordant tune. For as much as his sister had come
to like and trust Temperance, there was still only a wariness and dislike
in her gaze when he came 'round. All levity and warmth immediately
faded.

Breathless with laughter, Temperance stopped midtwirl. She followed the other woman's gaze across the room.

Her eyes brightened. "Dare!"

She'd been the only one to ever look at him like that. As if he were
the center of the world.

"I . . ." He tugged at his cravat before he caught Lady Kinsley's
knowing eyes on him.

"Spying, were you?" Lady Kinsley shot back.

Mortification curled his gut, and he balled his hands at his sides. Dare cleared his throat. "I was . . . looking for my wife." Which wasn't altogether untrue. He'd wanted to see her. She, however, had proven elusive these past days. "I thought you and Rose might benefit from a visit to the park."

Surprise rounded Temperance's eyes. "With you?"

Rose clapped excitedly and bounced up and down before plopping down on her buttocks.

His neck heated. "Uh . . ." Had he ever been charming? If so, it was all a distant memory to him.

"That would be lovely," Temperance blurted, and just like that, the sincerity in that wish to be with him and in his company proved buoyant, lifting him up. Picking up the little girl, Temperance turned to Dare's sister. "You must come with us."

No!

For just like that, he came crashing back to Earth. *Bloody hell.* That . . . was decidedly not what he'd intended.

"I'm sure the last thing she wishes to do is"—*join me*—"picnic in Hyde Park," he said quickly as two pairs of eyes swung his way.

Lady Kinsley flashed a smile that none would ever dare mistake for warm. "I'll join you."

"Of course you will," he muttered.

"What was that, *brother*?" Lady Kinsley called from across the music room.

"Nothing. It is nothing at all."

And so a short while later, with the top down on the grand barouche landau, they made the slow roll through Hyde Park, the unlikeliest of gatherings: Temperance; Dare, thief of the Rookeries, seamstress Gwynn, with Lionel's niece seated atop her lap; and the only true peer amongst their lot, Dare's sister.

Temperance tilted her face up toward the sun. Dare watched her carefully for some hint the ride was making her ill, and yet, with her pink cheeks and soft smile, she was a vision of happiness, and he was incapable of looking away.

Breath caught in his chest, he just stared at the sun as it bathed her olive-kissed skin.

"People will wonder," Lady Kinsley said, shattering his focus, "about the babe." She nudged her chin in Gwynn and Rose's direction.

Drawing the babe close, the young maid averted her gaze.

Of course, killer of joy and destroyer of moments.

Temperance sat up. The earlier serenity in her expression gone, replaced with a more familiar somberness. "I . . . Yes. There . . . might be questions," she murmured. "And I'm sorry for that."

Dare frowned.

There were some undercurrents there, ones that he recognized.

Kinsley glanced down at her lap. "It doesn't really matter what they say, does it?"

And unlike the usual tartness that coated her words . . . there was a hesitancy.

Temperance stretched a hand out, covering one of Kinsley's with her own. It was a display of support and comfort . . . and so very . . . Temperance. Thinking of others before herself.

And it drew Dare's attention to that detail which he'd otherwise not paid a jot of attention to—the gossips. There could be no doubting that in this Dare's sister was, in fact, correct. Every passerby, every rider . . . lords and ladies walking alone . . . men and women walking arm in arm . . . all stared as they passed. Their appetites insatiable for the gossip the carriage provided.

Their barouche journeyed through the entrance of Hyde Park and down the graveled riding path.

"This is the time to come out if one wishes to be seen," Kinsley said sotto voce. And there it was once more from his sister, a flash of unease.

Was it at her being here with her East London kin? Or was it . . . something more?

As if she felt his focus, Kinsley yanked her skirts and, lifting her nose, looked off in the opposite direction.

The carriage drew to a stop near the edge of the Serpentine River, and his sister rushed to accept the driver's help disembarking. The girl started off with Gwynn, who carried a basket.

Jumping down, Dare reached for Rose. "She hates me," he said, careful to keep his lips from moving, lest they be read by every last lord and lady present. Reaching back, he helped hand Temperance down.

"She doesn't know you still, Dare," she said gently, taking the babe back from him. They started on the trail after Kinsley and Gwynn.

"She likes *you* fine enough," Dare pointed out, knowing he sounded like a petulant child.

"Because I talk to her," she said simply. "I ask her questions and listen when she speaks." Temperance lowered her voice. "Were you aware there was some manner of scandal surrounding her? That there are rumors she was involved with some . . . disreputable gentleman."

He frowned. "I . . . No." *But I should have been. I should have gathered those details about her.*

"Tell me, at this point," Temperance said gently, "is she anything more than a means to an end for you?"

That properly silenced him.

"I'm not passing judgment, Dare," she said. "I have been of the same frame of mind where Kinsley was concerned. Until now." And yet she'd come to see the same woman who'd been disparaging and rude to her at the start as a friend. It spoke volumes about the manner of person Temperance was. Forgiving. Compassionate.

She touched a hand to his sleeve. "This . . . reunion is impossible for the both of you. Blood does not always a family make, and as of now, that is all you and your sister share. But that doesn't have to be the case, and I'd venture that your grandparents didn't want that to be the case, either."

"Tying a sum to my forming a relationship with the young lady certainly seems contradictory to that goal." And yet . . . neither was that Kinsley's fault.

"Mayhap," Temperance said, shifting Rose onto her other hip as they walked. "Or mayhap they knew you enough to know what compelled you most to try."

Money.

It had always been about money with him.

The means of other people's survival. The means to help.

Rose squirmed, and Temperance made to shift her once more.

"Here," he said, reaching for the child and taking her into his arms. The little girl slapped his face between her hands. And he winced. "You've quite the grip, although I cannot be entirely convinced you've not been put up to that by my sister."

Giggling all the more, Rose again clapped her chubby little palms over his face, briefly covering his eyes and blinding him.

He laughed softly. "Now, *that* was intentional."

His skin burnt, and he looked over.

Temperance stared back, her expression faintly stricken.

He frowned. "I was merely teasing. I don't think Rose would *really* hurt me. Not intentionally." Dare paused. "Now, my sister . . ."

A little laugh spilled from Temperance's lips. The amusement faded from her eyes. "You shouldn't think of it as . . . a chore or requirement." She nodded slightly to the young woman walking ahead of them. "Forming a relationship with your sister. She really is quite . . . kind and witty, and I think you both would learn to like one another if you gave one another the chance to do so."

And then if and when he did, when the terms were met, Temperance would be gone. Pain stabbed at his chest.

Rose jabbed a finger in his eye, and he winced. "Ah." The little girl squirmed and wiggled.

Temperance giggled. "That I do believe, however, was intentional. She wants you to put her down."

How natural she'd always been with children. Nurturing, when for most children in the Rookeries, a fist or a slap were the only touches a boy or girl would know. As she had . . . and yet, for all the suffering she'd endured at her father's hands, she had only loved her brother and cared for him and the others in the Rookeries.

In the end, Rose poked him again and brought him back to the moment. "Well, in the hopes of keeping both eyes, I've no other choice but to comply," he said, gently lowering Rose to the ground.

The little girl instantly took off, toddling as quick as her chubby legs would carry her, onward to Kinsley and Gwynn, now setting out a blanket alongside the edge of the Serpentine.

Dare tried to make his legs move over to that little group . . . and failed.

"I am scared out of my damned mind," he said quietly, that admission one he'd make to none other than this woman. "I don't know how to be with these people. I don't know how to be her brother or a grandson. Or how to be part of their world." All of it was a damned mystery that he didn't want to try to solve . . . because he knew the only outcome would be his failure.

"There is no shame in being afraid, Dare," Temperance said softly.

"But there is." A sound of frustration escaped him. "Thievery, I understand. Threats and danger are things I've learned to develop a mastery of, and a lack of fear. I know nothing of this. While so much is dependent upon my success."

"What of you?" she asked quietly, stepping in front of him.

That brought him up short. He puzzled his brow. "What of me?"

"Once again, you'll not think of yourself . . . but only of all the men and women who will benefit from your efforts." Her hands came up, as they had so many times before, to smooth the front fabric of his jacket. It had always been a tender wife's touch, one he'd not known enough of and never truly appreciated until she'd been gone. "What about the security you might attain for yourself? Or the comforts you might know?" With that she resumed walking.

He frowned, and hurriedly fell into step beside her. "None of that ever mattered to me, Temperance."

"I know that." She paused and lifted her gaze. "But perhaps it is time that it does," she said in the gentlest of tones.

"And what of you?" he returned.

"Me?" she asked, with a quizzical furrow of her brow.

"We're not so very different."

"You and I?" She laughed.

Wryness curved his lips up. "It is a certainty that there's no compliment there."

Temperance stopped beside a narrow white oak and faced him. "We have always been different. That was always the problem."

Dare rested his palm along the trunk, just above her head. "Ah, but I'd argue that it was always that we are the same, and that was the source of the impasse we found ourselves at."

She laughed again. "You are mad." Temperance made to step around him, but he dropped his other palm, framing her and blocking her retreat.

"Am I? You were always responsible for Chance."

"That is not the same," she protested.

"Whose well-being and interests you always placed before your own. Did you not intervene on his behalf at every moment?" Her features tightened. Dare pressed his point. "All your rations went to him, all your funds went to seeing he had an apprenticeship."

"He is my brother."

"Very well." Dare winged a brow up. "Then what of Miss Armitage?"

Those endearing little creases in the middle of her high brow grew as she looked over to where Gwynn stood at the shore, tossing rocks. "What of her?"

"Her hopes for marrying Chance?"

"I don't know what you are saying," she muttered.

"I know. That is my point."

At his knowing stare, Temperance frowned and ducked under his arm. She hurried after Kinsley, Gwynn, and Rose.

"*You've* sacrificed for their dream." He quickened his pace, falling into step beside her. "I've not heard you mention anything about what you want or need for yourself."

"I'm sure I did."

"Other than seeing your brother cared for."

She wrinkled her nose, that hint from long ago of her annoyance. "What else is there to say?"

Dare slid into her path once more.

Temperance stopped on a huff. Planting her hands on her hips, she gave him an exasperated look. "What now?"

"What are your dreams?"

"To see my brother happy," she said without missing a beat. As if the matter were at an end, she fished a cleverly cut piece of fabric from the little satchel swinging on her arm. She proceeded to drag the needles through the material, her skill so flawless she didn't even need to look as she walked and sewed.

He suppressed a smile. "That hardly counts."

"Of course it does," Temperance insisted, another one of those enchanting blushes on her cheeks. Her fingers flew, drawing the thread back and forth through the very edge of the material.

Dare caught her lightly by the forearm, forcing her to stop.

She stared up at him.

"How was your coming to London to be with me, despite your vow not to, any different from my looking after people in society?"

"Because . . . because . . ." She continued to flounder.

"It isn't my intention to question your sacrifice—"

"Good," she said between clenched teeth. "Then do not."

If she were another, he might be deterred. But this was Temperance, whose happiness had always meant more to him than even his own. As such, he went on. "However, I would have you realize that, even as you call me out for devoting my life to helping people in the Rookeries, you have done the same in your life, dedicating yourself to Chance and Gwynn."

"It's not at *all* the same, Dare."

"Isn't it, Temperance?" He leveled a stare on her. "Isn't it?"

Her mouth moved several times.

"Temperance!" From the edge of the shore, Kinsley waved her over.

"You know I'm right, Temperance," he called after her as she hurried off to join the trio on the blanket.

And as he made his way over to that gathering, he was forced to confront the possibility that she, too, had been right about him. What she raised . . . was entirely foreign. An idea he'd never allowed himself— the idea of having a family.

And watching as Temperance lowered herself onto the blanket and Rose pitched herself onto Temperance's lap, for the first time he wondered what it would be to have a future . . . for himself.

⌘

Stretched out on the blanket with Kinsley reading several paces away, Temperance let her needle fly over the small child's blanket she'd begun for Rose. All the while, she periodically stole furtive peeks over at Dare as he played with Rose. The little girl alternated between pitching pebbles at the water and tossing one at Dare.

The girl's aim was terrible, her throw weak, but every time she hurled her tiny missile, Dare would falter and stagger about, as if she'd landed the mightiest blow.

He was, in short, everything she'd known he would be with a child.

And perhaps that is why you shut the door on him that day.

Because ultimately, she'd known she could never be a true wife to him. She'd reconciled not telling him by reminding herself that he'd not wanted a real marriage. Yes, he'd loved her, but he'd devoted himself fully to the Rookeries in every way he couldn't to her.

I would have you realize that, even as you call me out for devoting my life to helping people in the Rookeries, you have done the same in your life, dedicating yourself to Chance and Gwynn.

They weren't the same. And yet those silent protestations felt weak, even to her own mind. For she had given entirely of herself to care for Chance. It was a sacrifice that she would make any and every day, again and again, if she had to.

Wasn't it?

Why must he do that? Why must he take the one thing she'd thought had made sense and throw a thousand questions behind it about what she wanted? About what her dreams truly were. About what she truly yearned for in life.

"I'm worried about you."

She froze in her efforts. It had been inevitable.

The talk with Gwynn was overdue. Temperance had managed to put off the discussion, but with Dare and Kinsley now occupied, there was no escaping.

"You needn't worry," she assured her, continuing to study her sewing. *Liar.* Returning to London and living with Dare had proven even harder than she'd ever anticipated. She'd simply deluded herself into thinking she might somehow be unaffected by him all these years later.

At the protracted silence, she made herself look up. Gwynn stared knowingly at her. "Don't I? You kissed him the other night when I came upon you in the nursery."

"I didn't kiss him." She nearly had . . . and had made love to him after. Heat flared in Temperance's cheeks.

Gwynn stared at her with all the knowing in the world, one that called Temperance out as the liar she was.

Her patience snapped. "Need I remind you . . . *You* were the one who suggested I consider it," she whispered furiously. "You were the one who *encouraged* me to consider it."

"Consider offering him the help he needed. Not . . . spend the time that you do together."

Temperance jabbed her needle through the fabric. "Did you really think that was how this was going to work? That I would be thrust into the role of companion to his sister, accompanying him to events . . . and that I wouldn't be with him?"

It was her friend's turn to color. "I didn't expect—"

Temperance didn't allow her that response. "What? That it would be hard for me? That I wouldn't be able to fully separate the feelings I had for him?" The minute she said it, Temperance wanted to call the words back.

Her friend stared back with a heart-struck expression. "It is because of me."

"Nothing is because of you," Temperance said quickly.

Gwynn, however, wasn't hearing it. "Oh, God." The other woman touched a hand to her lips. "You did it so that Chance and I might have a way to be together."

How was your coming to London to be with me, despite your vow not to, any different from my looking after people in society?

And mayhap in that, Dare had been so spot-on accurate. They . . . weren't different. Oh, in how they went about looking after those individuals they cared about, they were . . . but not in that inherent need to support the ones who were reliant upon them.

Temperance weighed her response . . . and in the end opted to protect Gwynn still with only a partial truth. "I did it for all of us."

"And for that gift, I'll see you left with a broken heart," Gwynn said with a bitter tinge to her voice.

Temperance shivered.

No. She wouldn't have her heart broken again. She couldn't . . . That organ had already been completely destroyed by him, long before this. It couldn't hurt any more than what she'd lost . . .

Their babe.

Gwynn shoved a little elbow into her side, and as one they glanced over to where Kinsley openly watched them. The young lady sailed to her feet and then started for them.

Her friend stood. "I'll leave you to her." Gwynn walked off, but not before she shot Temperance a look that was both warning and knowing.

Abandoning her efforts on Rose's blanket, Temperance rested her sewing on her lap and watched Dare and the babe at play.

"What is it?" Kinsley asked at her side.

For a moment, she thought the always-direct young woman spoke of the exchange between Gwynn and Temperance, and she found herself briefly tongue-tied.

She followed the young lady's stare to the forgotten stitchery. "It will be a blanket for Rose. For when . . ." Her throat closed up.

For too brief a time, she'd had the illusion of a family and the joy of knowing a child.

"For when she leaves," Kinsley murmured.

Temperance managed a jerky nod.

"I shall miss her," the other woman said, staring out as Dare and Rose chucked rocks into the river. "I feel badly about how I . . . reacted to that boy . . . Lionel."

"You found a stranger in your house. Your reaction wasn't unfounded."

"You're being entirely too forgiving. I've never seen anyone treat children . . . any children, with the kindness you and . . . he do." He . . . as in Dare. The girl still couldn't bring herself to fully speak his name. "I assumed it had something to do with my grandfather's requirements for him." The young woman nudged her chin in Dare's direction. "I assumed his coming here today was because my grandfather wished for us to be seen out."

Ah, so the young woman knew about the duke's intentions and efforts. Just how much did she know? And for the bond she'd forged with the young woman these past days, there was a sliver of guilt at not having been up front in what was expected of all of them. Temperance carefully selected her words. "You are aware—"

Kinsley cut her off. "I know enough." Plucking at the corner of the blanket, she stared on at Rose, toddling along the edge of the shore. "But he . . . isn't quite doing anything to earn society's approval or my attention."

And because of that, he'd thrown the young woman's thoughts of Dare as mercenary sibling into question.

"Dare was never one to do what was expected of him." Which was likely why this task he'd been given was so very hard for him.

"It is interesting. He is my brother, and yet you speak of him as one who knows him, and I know . . . nothing about him."

Kinsley fell silent for a long moment, and they sat in a companionable silence while Dare moved on to stone-hopping lessons. "There is a portrait," Kinsley spoke haltingly. "Of my father and . . . *him*."

Him.

As in Dare.

The brother whose name Kinsley could still not bring herself to say.

"He never did that with me," she said, bitterness coating every syllable of that statement. "He rarely did anything with me or Perrin. All he cared about was seeing to his estates. He failed to see the children he had." Kinsley was silent for several moments, and Temperance glanced over. The young woman watched on wistfully while Dare handed stones to Rose to hurl at the water. "Now, my brother, Perrin? He spent time with me like that. When I was invisible, he saw me. He played with me." Kinsley's face crumpled. "That is . . . *was* my real brother."

And Temperance ached all over, from the inside out, with the suffering this family had known. How much damage had been done. How much damage could not be undone. Dare and Kinsley, the siblings who remained, were both hurting.

Temperance considered her words, and when she found them and at last spoke them, she did so with a gentle insistence. "Dare is your real brother, too—"

She'd not even finished when the other woman cut in. "No, he's not." Kinsley drew her knees up and wrapped her arms about them. "Perrin was my brother. He was my friend. He was my confidant. He was my champion. That man?" The young lady's eyes went to where Dare now scoured the ground for pebbles and rocks for Rose. "Your husband? He is a stranger who sees me and sees the money he stands to earn by being my brother." Her lips twisted in a macabre rendering of a smile.

Yes, there was truth to those intentions Dare had. And yet that was not all he was. Temperance didn't believe Dare was blameless in the resentment his sister carried, but there were reasons to explain the barriers he kept up. "I met your brother when he was just fourteen and I was ten." She was aware of Kinsley's heightened focus on her face. "My"—her lips twisted with disdain—"father had me begging outside a scandalous club in the Dials. I didn't realize at the time that he was really intending for some reprobate to . . . pay for me."

"Oh." Kinsley's breath caught on a gasp, and perhaps there should have been a greater sense of shame and embarrassment in Temperance speaking of her coarse, ruthless world. But there was not.

Mayhap if the other woman did learn, she could know some of what drove . . . not just her brother in the Rookeries but all the people forced to live there. "Someone did come up to me that night."

"Darius," the astute other woman murmured.

It was the first time Temperance had ever heard Dare's sister call him by name. She nodded, needing the young lady to know what manner of man he truly was. "I'd my palms out, and Dare came up to me and placed a sovereign in them. 'You're done here,' he said in the finest speech I'd ever heard. I thought he was a prince." Gazing at him, she grew wistful, that meeting so very clear in her mind. "And mayhap he was. He took me to a tavern and used his coin to feed me, and then he walked me onward to London, showing me the places I was best to avoid there. He provided me clues as to which men to avoid." She cleared her throat, not able to elaborate any more for Dare's innocent sister. "He became my friend that night. My champion. My protector." Just as he was for so many others.

Dare scooped up Rose, and holding her under the belly, he made as if to hurl the child into the water. Wild laughter spilled from the little girl's lips, and the sight of it was too much. Temperance closed her eyes and imagined a different child in his arms.

"I don't want a protector," Kinsley whispered. She wanted a brother.

"No." Neither did Temperance. Not anymore. She wanted so much more than that. Gifts that could never be hers.

"I used to want a family," the young lady confided. "I dreamed of one for myself." There it was . . . that word: "dream." "I wanted the husband who would be devoted and a father to our children, and I wanted children who would be happy and loving."

In short, she'd wanted everything she'd never known.

The women went silent.

Nor did it escape Temperance's notice that the young woman spoke in the past tense. "There can still be that." Those hopes that were dead to Temperance could still exist for Dare's sister.

Kinsley's lips twisted up wryly. "Oh, no. I've tried my hand at love, and I want no part of it. Not again."

The gossips' whisperings that day at the modiste's resurfaced in Temperance's mind.

"Yes, they were correct," Kinsley said tiredly to Temperance's unspoken question. The other woman stretched her legs out and hooked an ankle across the other as she continued watching her brother and Rose at play. "I gave my heart where I oughtn't. Nor do I have any intention of making myself an arm ornament for some fine lord, as my grandparents wish."

Temperance stilled. Dare's hopes for that fortune were reliant upon his sister marrying. The same sister who'd no interest in entering into that state. Her mind slowed and then stopped altogether under the realization dawning at the back of her mind.

She sucked in a breath.

"You're thinking of my grandparents' requirements."

She opened her mouth, prepared to give the lie, and yet . . . could not. "I . . . You . . ."

"Yes, I know about their offer to fill Dare's pockets when I marry. Alas, it is fortunate for him that they allowed him an alternative to those funds."

"The alternative," Temperance managed through a suddenly dry mouth.

For God help her, she knew what that alternative was. The staggering weight of grief and loss and fury . . . There was that, too, all roiling in her breast, pounding there so that she wanted to toss her head back and keen from the grief.

Rose raced over. *"Kinnnnneeee,"* the girl cried excitedly, grabbing for the young lady's hand.

Color spilled onto Kinsley's cheeks, and she briefly resisted that show of affection. But even the most cynical couldn't be immune to the babe's charm. "Oh, very well," Kinsley muttered, climbing to her feet. She let the child pull her onward, tugging her along . . .

Temperance sat frozen and watched the brother and sister and the little girl, Rose.

For a moment she thought he'd leave. His body stiffened, and knowing him as she did, she knew he wanted to. He wanted to flee any and all connection, even one that hadn't yet occurred with the woman who was his sister.

But then Rose pressed a fistful of gravel into first Dare's hand and then Kinsley's, urging the pair to hurl those "rocks."

And then, brother and sister began to skip those stones . . . the halting strains of their conversation drifting over.

Tears blurred Temperance's eyes. She'd feared he'd fall back on his old ways . . . the only ways he'd known for so very long. She'd begun to doubt that he was willing to make a go with the family he'd been taken from. Only to see he could open himself to a new way . . . a new life, here in Mayfair.

And with Kinsley's revelation, and the gift Temperance could never give Dare . . . a life that she could never, ever be part of.

Chapter 17

Dare had been without a family for so long he'd not thought he'd missed any aspect of it.

He'd been wrong.

As Temperance, Kinsley, Gwynn, and Rose rushed on ahead through the front doors, he stared after the happy quartet.

It was the singular most terrifying thing in the whole of his life. Belonging to . . . something. And yet there was also a conflicting sense of . . . *rightness* to it, too.

He stared up after them as they climbed the stairs to the nursery. Temperance paused at the top of the landing to look back. She briefly waved before hurrying after his sister. And that lightness filled his chest again.

The moment they'd gone, Spencer cleared his throat. "You have a visitor, my lord," he said as he accepted Dare's cloak.

The reverie from Hyde Park forgotten, all his senses went on alert.

"Mr. Swift," his butler expounded. "I took the liberty of showing him to your office."

His brother-in-law. With the grueling hours he worked, the younger man wouldn't seek him out. Not at this time of day. Unless there was a matter of urgency that merited the meeting.

When Dare still didn't speak, the butler cleared his throat. "That is, *Mr. Chance Swift* . . . Her Ladyship's brother. Should I not have . . . ?" the other man asked haltingly.

"No. You were right to have him wait. Thank you, Spencer." Reversing his direction, Dare quickened his strides, heading for his office.

The moment he entered, he immediately found his brother-in-law.

Seated with his elbows propped on his knees and his head in his hands, Chance tugged at his close-cropped curls. The distressed young man gave no hint that he'd heard Dare enter. Those warning bells blared louder than the ones hanging over St. Mary's.

Dare pushed the door shut behind him with a quiet click; that sound seemed to penetrate Chance's distractedness.

The other man jumped to his feet. "Dare. Forgive me for arriving without any notice—"

He waved off that apology. "You're my brother-in-law and closer than blood. You need never apologize for paying a visit." Urging Temperance's brother back to the chair he'd vacated, Dare claimed the seat nearest him and drew it closer. "What—"

"They're going to hang Joseph," he said hoarsely.

All Dare's muscles seized. "What?"

"They moved up his trial, and apparently it was not enough to deport him. They scheduled him to hang." The younger man's words all rolled together. "And I've not heard from Mr. Buxton. I've no idea if he's even received my note, but I"—Chance swiped his palms over his face—"I don't know how to help him, and then Rose will be an orphan, and Lionel will be left with only his father for protection, which is . . . none."

Here he'd been busy playing at life while others were struggling just to survive.

Dare sat back and considered all those words. Wylie. Wylie was the one with all the control of Joseph's fate.

He firmed his mouth. And there was only one thing that Wylie wanted and answered to . . .

Which meant there was also one person whose help he required . . .

Coming to his feet, Dare called for Spencer.

The butler immediately appeared, indicating he'd been standing in wait. "I require help," Dare explained as he wrote directives on a small scrap of paper.

Spencer examined the instructions written there and then folded them. He tucked the page away in the front of his jacket pocket.

"Do you have any questions?"

"None, my lord," Spencer said, and then took his leave.

While he and Chance waited for the other man to return, Dare resumed his examination of the state of the finances left to him.

From across the room, Chance bent slightly over a globe, spinning the sphere, not unlike the way Dare had as a boy when he'd been waiting for his father to arrive and lecture him on his many failings.

"Did you ever think of going to these places?" Chance murmured.

Dare blinked; it took a moment to realize that the younger man was speaking to him.

"I . . ." He had. All the time. He'd wanted to see not only every corner of London and how the people lived there, but the whole of the world. To discover other people and other places. To explore. It was why, when he'd wandered off with Topher McSally, the street thug who'd taken Dare under his wing and promised to show him the thrill of that world, Dare had believed himself on the grandest adventure. And for a bit of time, he had been. Before his exploration of East London had ended and he'd been passed over to Mac Diggory . . .

"We had a book," Chance said, not pressing Dare for an answer, and bringing him back to the moment. "Just one: *Coryat's Crudities: Hastily gobled up in Five Moneth's Travels.*" A wistful smile pulled at Chance's lips as he stopped the globe from spinning with his finger and then restarted it with the same digit. "Temperance always said Mum had sneaked it free when she eloped with our da, and when he went and sold everything off, she hid it under a loose floorboard . . . And whenever Da was gone, she would just sit there and read it, over and over." Chance stopped the globe with his finger once more and peered down at the location he'd landed on. "Temperance would read to me from that book every night, telling me the world was mine for the taking and that I could be like that traveler . . . honorable. Good. Seeing the world outside of ours, but through respectable means."

Dare smiled. That was . . . very much Temperance. Building up her brother and refusing to imagine a life of crime and sin for him. Just as she'd hoped—expected—Dare would follow.

Closeted away in his office nearly two hours later, waiting with a restless Chance, Dare registered the echo of footsteps in the hall.

And they looked up as Spencer entered . . . with Avery Bryant beside him.

"I found him, my lord," his butler said, faintly breathless, but his voice brimming with pride.

Chance blanched like he'd seen a bogeyman and jumped back.

Avery Bryant grinned wryly. "Still got a problem with me, do you, Swift?" He waggled his eyebrows. "Or was that your sister with the problem?"

The young man frowned and dusted his palms over his lapels. "I'm my own man, capable of making my own judgments," he said tightly.

Dare's butler made no hint of concealing his interest in the exchange, watching the two men as they debated.

"If you'll excuse us, Spencer?"

The servant nodded and then backed from the room, all the while keeping a careful eye on Avery Bryant until he'd gone.

Avery snorted. "Funny to get a request from you, Grey. You got this one who never trusted me"—he jabbed a thumb in Chance's direction—"and your servants don't trust me. But then, mayhap they're the wise ones, and you're the one who never knew what was good for you." He chortled like he'd told the cleverest of jests.

The tight lines at the corners of Chance's mouth dipped. "I don't think it's a good idea he be here."

Temperance certainly wouldn't approve . . . She never had where Avery Bryant was concerned. But sometimes, the end did justify the means. "And what of Joseph?" Dare asked quietly. "Mr. Buxton isn't answering you, and Joseph is set to swing." Chance's cheeks blanched. "Should we not do whatever we need to, to help?"

As they talked, Avery gave no indication he cared either way about the discussion taking place about him and over him. Rather, he continued to assess the same bust he had at his last visit, sizing it up with an expression Dare recognized all too well.

Chance closed his eyes briefly, and then gave a short, tight nod.

Dare motioned to his former partner.

"I have it on authority that you paid a visit to a certain baron," Avery said as he sauntered over.

Dare stiffened.

The other man had known.

"I know. I know everything about the available households. Well"— he nudged his chin—"what did you manage?"

Dare resisted the urge to squirm. "Nothing." It was the second time in his life he'd been forced to admit to leaving a household . . . without. The only time before that had come when he'd gotten himself caught in the act and nearly hanged.

"Nothing," Avery repeated. The other man rocked back on his heels and rubbed at his chin. "You're . . . done, then."

He felt Chance's gaze taking in the exchange.

You're done . . . And it would have been easier and more welcome had there been judgment and not the same relief Temperance had revealed when she'd learned he'd been unable to go through with his last heist. Sweat slicked Dare's palms and entire body as he confronted just how far he'd gotten from his path. "I'm not done," he said, a defensive edge creeping in.

Avery snorted. "There's nothing wrong with it if you are. Like I said before, you should be. Enjoying trips to the park and spending time with your family."

Dare felt his face heat. "You've heard about that."

The other man picked up a paper on the edge of Dare's desk.

Dare plucked the copy of *The Times* from the other man's hands. "It's just gossip. I've no intention of quitting my work. Just . . . perhaps taking a different path."

"A different path?"

He nodded. Only . . . what did that even look like? Could he be the man Temperance thought he could . . . the man she urged him to be . . . and still do that which he needed?

The answer came immediately. No.

While he'd been playing at family, there'd been others starving and struggling. Men like Joseph awaiting a date with the gibbet.

"Grey, it's not a bad thing if you quit. But if you aren't coming back, they need to know that, too. They need to know that it's time to stop relying on you and see to their own needs."

Every word was a blade of guilt, twisting and turning and then twisting back again.

He'd been playing at another life. Playing house here with Temperance and Rose and . . . Kinsley, Dare had enjoyed himself more than he had ever in his remembering. But he'd also forgotten everyone else, too. It was what Temperance wanted. For him to immerse himself in this world and leave the one he knew and wanted behind.

Feeling Chance's stare on them, taking in the entire exchange, Dare cleared his throat. "This isn't why I've asked you here." He motioned for both men to sit.

Dare proceeded to explain about Joseph Gurney and the other man's circumstances.

"Well, what do you need?" Avery Bryant asked when he'd finished.

That had always been the other man's way. Despite Temperance's resentment and mistrust of the street thief who'd trained Dare, Avery Bryant was one who'd quit what he'd been doing and accompany a servant to the other end of London and ask how he might help.

"Wylie," Dare said.

Avery sat back in his chair. "Wylie's gotten more grasping. And you being a marquess now?" He shook his head. "He's going to want even more. Expect it."

"What are his rates?"

"Bribes from a lord?" His partner looped a boot across his opposite knee. "Hard to say. I've heard anywhere from one to two thousand pounds."

Chance promptly choked. "We don't have that to save Gurney."

Bloody hell. "The marquessate is bankrupt," Dare said flatly, never regretting more that he'd not returned when Connor Steele had urged him to. Instead, he'd allowed that wastrel to squander it all . . .

"No Newgate guard is going to believe that, even if it is true."

Except . . . it wasn't altogether true. There were items to be sold. A lot of fripperies and baubles. "You'll handle the transaction?"

Avery nodded. "You write the note, put your seal on it all fancy-like." His partner grinned. "I'll see it gets to his hands, along with the money for the transaction."

Dare reached for a sheet of parchment and proceeded to write.

Chance frowned. "I don't know about this. Perhaps I might try to reach Mr. Buxton once more?"

Both men ignored him. A moment later, Dare had blown powder upon the note, stamped it with his seal, and handed the folded sheet over.

Avery looked down at it several moments before tucking it in his pocket. "Now, the items to sell?"

Chapter 18

"The day . . . was nice," Kinsley said, perched sidesaddle on the wooden, painted rocking horse.

"You sound surprised," Temperance noted as Rose splashed paint upon the little canvas that had been set up for her. After their outing at Hyde Park, they'd taken the curricle to Gunter's for ices, and having since retired to the nursery to explore with the painting supplies, the little girl's life had already proven so much fuller than all of Temperance's childhood in the Rookeries. How she hated that the little girl would soon leave, and then what would the child's life be? Drudgery. Hardship. That was all that awaited her and those like her.

"I never thought of him as a person. I didn't think of him as someone on the streets who'd helped others. Or who might play with babes on a shore. Fathers don't do that, you know," Kinsley tacked on. Her eyes grew sad. "At least mine didn't."

"My father didn't, either," Temperance confided. Any day he'd not been beating her had been a gift. "My father struck me and . . . often." She'd never spoken about the beatings she'd suffered at her father's hand. Of course, nearly every person in the Rookeries had known about the abuse Abaddon Swift's family had faced . . . but she'd not really spoken of it. Only with Dare. "He preferred an open hand. He liked the sound, he would say."

Get 'ere, gel, and take your beating . . .

"I came to learn the sound of his footfalls so that I could avoid him when he was coming. I'd sneak away and hide, and when I did, I would dream of a different life. Yours, even," she said quietly, absently stroking the top of Rose's head. "I never imagined there could be small girls amongst the nobility also wishing for something different for themselves." And yet even through the darkest, worst moments . . . other than escape, what had she ever really wished for? She'd not known . . . anything. The opportunities and dreams available to people of her lot were limited.

Kinsley's eyes flew to hers. "Oh." Her voice came weak. Dare's sister fluttered a hand about her heart. "I'm sorry. I—"

"Please, don't." Temperance waved off that apology. "I only shared so that you might know you aren't alone in your regret of wishing that you could have had a family different from the one you had."

"My father, however, would never have struck me," Kinsley whispered. "How small I must seem to you, complaining about my life."

"Your pain is your pain," she said. Rose brandished her brush. Taking it from the child, Temperance dipped it into a little jar of red paint and then tapped the excess onto the edge. She handed the brush over, guiding the girl's fingers around the handle. "My experience and my pain don't make yours any less significant. It is yours, and you should feel exactly how you feel."

"I do see why my brother married you," Kinsley murmured.

Temperance's heart seized. The other girl couldn't even begin to imagine the perfunctory, businesslike start to their union. Then . . . and now.

An arrangement that had been destined for failure.

Footfalls echoed outside the door, and they looked as one to the front of the room.

A servant drew the door open. "Her Grace, the Duchess of Pemberly."

The old woman swept inside, her gaze taking in first her granddaughter, then Temperance . . . and then Rose. Reaching for one of the chains about her neck, she lifted the monocle to her right eye and peered intently at the little girl spattering paint upon the canvas. "Whatever is *this*?"

Kinsley hopped up. "She—"

The duchess thumped her cane, commanding her granddaughter to silence. "I'd read reports in the papers but brushed them off as mere gossip." She handed her cane off to the maid waiting there. She passed her gloves on to the servant. Reclaiming her cane, she marched forward. "Is this your daughter?" the duchess demanded, the hard strike of her cane penetrating the thin carpet covering the floor.

"I don't have a daughter, Grandmother," Kinsley piped in.

The duchess, however, quelled the younger woman with a look.

Kinsley dropped her gaze to the floor.

Temperance appreciated her sister-in-law's attempt at levity. How different she was from the young woman who'd stormed from her bedroom the night Lionel and Rose had been discovered. And how Temperance hoped that when she left, Kinsley would remain one who was able to see a child from the Rookeries as a child, her life meaningful and valuable despite what the *ton* would have the world believe.

"Well," the duchess began again. "What is . . . *this*?" She motioned to Rose.

Fighting to rein in her temper, Temperance spoke in even tones. "*This* is a child. Her name is Rose."

Her Grace's mouth moved several times before a word emerged. "Rose?"

Kinsley nodded. "Like the flower," she volunteered helpfully.

The duchess's eyes narrowed.

As if sensing she was the subject of discussion, Rose waved her brush wildly about, sending paint splashing. The duchess gasped as red paint hit her square in the chest, turning the sapphire satin a dark shade of purple.

Oh, hell.

Kinsley's eyes widened.

"Forgive me, Your Grace. She is just a child," Temperance gently reminded.

"You've already said as much," the duchess snapped. "I do not need you to tell me she is a child. I can see that. I want to know who her parents are." Fear and horror wreathed that demand.

And then it hit Temperance . . . The duchess believed that Temperance and Dare's union had resulted in a child. And the irony, the painful, soul-destroying irony, was that it had. "She is not ours," Temperance said, her voice threadbare.

The duchess's eyes slid closed, and a breathy prayer spilled from her lips.

Dare's grandparents had not accepted the union as a real one. They were right to their suspicions of her marriage to Dare, and yet that did little to ease the annoyance and outrage that brewed within. Those sentiments felt vastly safer than the agony of before.

From somewhere in the hall came a noisy rush of footsteps and the murmurings of servants.

The duchess frowned. "Whatever is going on?" she muttered, and stalking to the front of the room, she looked out. Perplexed, Temperance peered around the duchess's shoulder. What . . . ?

Four servants balanced an armoire between them and ambled slowly toward the end of the hall.

"What are they . . . doing?" Kinsley asked, completing the very question in Temperance's mind. Dare's sister eyed the flurry of bustling servants. "Whyever would they be moving furniture?"

Temperance's stomach sank. No. *Oh, damn it. Please, please, do not have—*

The duchess shook her head. "I-I . . . do not . . . know."

And by the shock and horror in the duchess's tone, being out of the know was not a state the older woman preferred to find herself in.

From belowstairs, Dare's voice came, slightly distant but clear as he called out commands. "That one . . ."

She gritted her teeth, focusing on her fury and not the disappointment that Dare remained unchanged.

But she already knew. She knew before Kinsley had any inclination of what she'd find. "Lady Kinsley, if I might suggest—"

Ignoring Temperance, Lady Kinsley collected her skirts and bolted.

Gwynn appeared at the door. "What is it?"

"See to Rose," Temperance ordered. She took off after her sister-in-law, ignoring the duchess's commands that they stop.

At the top of the stairs, Kinsley tripped on her hem, but she caught herself against the railing. "Kinsley, please don't," Temperance implored. But the woman would not be stopped.

And mayhap she shouldn't have tried to protect her . . . from the truth.

They reached the foyer and found him down the intersecting corridor. With his back to them, Dare stood in the middle of the hall, directing various servants between two opposite rooms. Engrossed as he was, he fired off orders to several young women. All servants who studiously avoided Kinsley's gaze.

Lady Kinsley stopped so quickly beside one of the open doorways that Temperance ran into her. And the young lady stood, flummoxed, her mouth open and no words coming out.

Temperance caught sight of her brother first: sheepish. Cheeks red. "Temperance," he greeted weakly.

Dare turned.

"What are you doing?" she demanded. Temperance caught his gaze and shook her head, equal parts angry and frustrated. Though she knew. He'd never kept anything. And he should sell it now, after the outing they'd had with Kinsley at Hyde Park? For what purpose? This was a new level of unforgivable.

Just then, another person stepped out of the Opal Parlor, where she'd had her first disastrous meeting with Dare's family . . . and it all made sense.

"If I might suggest you retain this," someone was saying.

Her gaze landed on the familiar man she'd not seen in years. One she'd been so very glad to have never seen again. Only to find her hate for him as strong and violent as it had ever been. "You," she spat.

"At least until we find . . . Oh." Avery Bryant took in the addition of Temperance and Lady Kinsley, and he stopped. "Temperance Grey," he called over cheerfully. In his arms, he held an ivory marble bust. "Or, I've heard it is 'my lady' now?"

"It is nothing," she said between clenched teeth. "You may refer to me in no way at all."

"Friendly as ever," Bryant crowed, and it was all she could do to keep from flying across the room and clawing the face of the man who'd introduced Dare to the dangerous life of crime that had nearly seen him hanged too many times. The one whom Dare still couldn't separate himself from. And she wanted to throw her head back and rail at his inability to help himself and stay on a path that was good for him.

He was working again with Avery Bryant . . . and what was worse, he'd brought her brother into the fold.

"You're no friend of Dare's." He never had been. She teemed with rage. Of course, Dare's having gone to Bolingbroke's . . . He'd have only gotten that information from this one. "And you're most certainly no friend of mine."

"He's helping, Temperance," Chance said in urgent tones.

"Helping?" she spat. "Avery Bryant only ever helped himself."

Her brother came forward with his callused palms outstretched. "They're going to hang Joseph, Temperance."

Her breath caught. "What of Mr. Buxton? I thought he would—"

"I still have not heard from him, Temperance. There isn't time."

So he'd turn to dishonorable means, bribing the likes of Wylie, who'd happily sent Dare to the gallows once. Wylie would line his pockets, and that was only if he didn't hang Dare first. "It doesn't have to be the way," she implored, directing that to Dare.

That seemed to snap Dare's sister from her shock. The young lady glanced from her brother to Temperance, and then ever so briefly to Avery—that hated figure—before returning her focus to Dare. When he didn't immediately respond, she raced over to Avery, who had sense enough to eye her with a proper wariness. Kinsley wrestled the bust from the street thief's hands. "What is going on here?"

And it was a like fury Temperance understood all too well. One that she'd felt and appeared destined to feel where Dare Grey was concerned.

Only silence met the girl's query. Dare's gaze hovered just over the top of his sister's head. The coward. Well, she'd be damned if he didn't tell his sister precisely what he intended.

"He is selling it," Temperance said quietly when Dare refused to answer.

Confusion welled all the more in Kinsley's eyes, and she stared at the bust. "You are . . . selling it?"

When Dare didn't respond, Temperance answered for him. "To help free Mr. Gurney," she murmured. He would bribe a public official, a man not to be trusted, all in the name of saving those in need of saving.

The bust slipped from the young lady's fingers and tumbled noisily to the floor.

He'd not changed. He never would.

And Temperance hated him for it, and more . . . she hated herself for continuing to believe he could be different.

Chapter 19

Dare was always going to sell the contents of the Mayfair household he'd recently inherited. There'd never been a doubt. It hadn't been a question of "if" but rather . . . "when."

Selling extravagant baubles was simply what he did. He cleared homes, stripped them of the clutter, and converted those objects into something important—*money*.

Objects didn't matter. They never had. What came out of them, however? Their value, the money they brought? That was something he cared about. The fortune that could be squeezed out of material pieces was the difference between people living and dying and going without or having food in their stomachs.

That was a lesson he'd come to appreciate from his time on the streets. In the end, everything could and should be sold.

Temperance knew as much. She knew it was how Dare operated.

So how could she still look at him with the disappointment she did now? How, when he'd help Chance free his friend and Rose's father?

And how, when she knows who you are . . . ?

Because she always wanted him to be better. She wanted him to rise above theft and bribery and operate within the confines of the law, failing to see that sometimes . . . there wasn't time.

Kinsley was the first to speak following that revelation. "He is . . . ?" Lady Kinsley moved her gaze between Dare and Temperance. "*What* is he doing?"

Now the lady who lived here . . . He'd not considered how she would respond. He tugged at his collar.

The duchess finally reached the hall. "What is . . . going on?" she asked, faintly panting. The older woman leaned her weight over the head of her cane and struggled to draw breath.

Fabulous. The only one missing was the damned duke.

Dare looked to Temperance, and she jutted her chin mutinously at him. Refusing to help him, she shook her head slightly.

"Perhaps we should adjourn to—"

"The Opal Parlor?" Kinsley spat. She stormed into the room in question, and as he followed reluctantly behind her, she tossed her arms up. "Oh, forgive me, there is no available seating because it is all covered with items from—" Her words cut off on a gasp. The young lady raced over to the row of paintings stacked against one another alongside the wall. "What is this?" Gripping one heavy-looking frame, she struggled to hold the ornate piece aloft. A lord and lady with a boy beside them and a small babe cradled in the woman's arms stared back. "These are the familial portraits," she cried, and quickly returned it to the floor, where she proceeded to flip through frame after frame.

"Things." That correction came automatically, and before he could think about the wisdom of uttering it.

Temperance covered her eyes with her hand and shook her head.

Lady Kinsley's eyes formed tiny slits. "*What?*"

The lady before him might be a stranger, but even he knew to be properly wary of the rage pouring from the stare she leveled on him. Dare gave his collar another tug. "Er . . ."

"Things?" Avery Bryant offered helpfully in Dare's stead. "That's what we call portraits and vases and paintings and crystal. It helps if you think of them all as 'things.'" His partner preened with pride. "Taught him that myself."

Chance winced.

Dare made a slashing motion across his throat, urging his business partner to quit speaking.

The duchess's eyebrows climbed to her hairline. "Who *is* this man? Who are *all* these people?"

When no one rushed to perform introductions, Avery saw to the task himself. "Avery Bryant, at your service, ma'am."

Chance, however, proved wise enough to remain silent under the duchess's scrutiny.

"Your Grace." Rage underlined Lady Kinsley's correction. "She is a duchess, and you will address her properly." She took an angry step toward Dare's partner. "Do you know, you will address her as nothing. You are no one."

"Well, you're a friendly one, aren't you, princess?"

"Avery," Dare said quietly.

His partner grunted. "I know when it's time to leave."

"Do you?" Lady Kinsley shot back. "If you did, you would have left the moment I caught sight of you, you bastard," she hissed, and then she charged.

Cursing, Dare jumped in the way, putting himself between his partner and his sister.

"Kinsley!" the duchess cried, clutching for the chain dangling at her throat that contained her smelling salts.

"Yes, I'm the shocking one, but"—she swiped a hand in Dare's direction—"this one here is letting his thieving friends inside to collect our family's heirlooms."

Avery yanked at his lapels. "I resent that."

"And I'm not . . . really a thief," Chance said weakly. "I work at a mill."

Kinsley ignored Temperance's brother in favor of Avery Bryant.

"I'm to believe you aren't a thief," Kinsley demanded, stepping left and then right in a bid to get around Dare.

"Get. Out. Avery." Temperance's clipped order was one of the only ones Avery had ever managed to listen to.

"I'm leaving. I'm leaving." He looked to the bust lying on the hall floor still. "You want me to take that—"

Temperance stormed over. "Get out," she repeated. She turned to Chance.

Shame marred the young man's features. "I'm so sorry," he mouthed.

She shook her head sadly. "You should go."

Hanging his head like he was still the little boy who'd stolen a loaf of bread and been dragged by the ear by the baker who'd owed Dare several favors, Chance slunk off.

The moment they'd gone, Kinsley faced Dare. "You're taking everything."

"I am selling it." There was a difference.

Temperance gave her head another shake.

"You're selling it," Kinsley whispered. "You're a monster."

"Because I'm ridding the household of items that could bring in valuable coin?" That would spare a man from a trip to the gallows. He opened his mouth to say as much, but Kinsley cried out.

"Yes. That is why you're a monster."

Temperance rested a hand on his sleeve. "Enough," she said quietly to Dare.

"I was right about you. All of you. You're all the same." She looked to Temperance. "And h-her"—Kinsley's voice cracked—"I thought I might even come around to liking you." With that, she flew off, the duchess calling out and racing after her granddaughter, until it was just Dare and Temperance . . . and the army of servants.

Dare eyed the door covetously.

"Don't even think about it," Temperance said, not even glancing his way, inherently knowing what he intended.

She spoke a few quiet words to the young women organizing the things into piles, and the handful of maids rushed off.

She'd claimed she was an outsider, uncomfortable with this world, but there was an ease to how she dealt with his household and the people here.

And yet when they were alone, she leaned against the door panels and just stared back.

He would have preferred her anger and outrage to this silence. Disappointment . . . It burnt from her eyes, so familiar. She'd never accepted how he'd lived his life, and what he'd done. That would never change, and because *he* would never change, it was just one more reason a future had always been impossible between them.

"You disapprove," he said quietly.

"Does it matter whether or not I do?" she answered, offering a question of her own, and really the only answer he required.

The obvious response should have been that no, her opinion really didn't matter. And yet it did. So very much. It always had. Her opinion had always been the only one he'd cared about. And her opinion had also always been the lowest, the one he could never change. "She's a stranger," he said quietly, in a bid to make her understand.

"Dare, the people whom you're so committed to looking after are strangers, too."

And he floundered. "It is different." Did he try and convince her? Or himself?

She pushed away from the door and came closer. "Why is it?" she asked, curious and still absent of her fiery temperament.

"Because she has never gone without," he shouted. "Why should I care whether or not she's distressed at how I secure funds to actually do something meaningful? She has a home and security and should also have material things that can go and feed children who'll never know even a jot of the comforts she's known." His chest heaved from the force of his emotion, and through the tumult, in the greatest of reversals, Temperance remained remarkably composed.

"Tell me, Dare," she said softly. "Your selling off the cherished heirlooms here, Lady Kinsley's and your link to your parents . . . Does this really stem from your resentment over her having lived the life you were deprived of?"

His neck went hot. "Of course not. That is p-preposterous," he stammered.

"Is it, Dare?" She took a step closer. "Is it truly?"

"You don't know what you're talking about. I'm trying to free Joseph Gurney."

"You were giving away your family's heirlooms long before that," she shot back. "You didn't even try to work within the constraints of the law," she said beseechingly.

"There isn't time."

"You are a marquess, and your grandfather is a duke," she cried. "Do you truly think appealing to them isn't the better course?"

"Appeal to them to bribe Wylie?"

"I'm not talking bribery," she said in aggrieved tones as she swept over. "I'm talking about hiring barristers and allowing people to intervene on his behalf. Or asking Mr. Buxton to speak to his fellow mill owners about—"

"Mr. Buxton, who will not even respond to Chance's notes," he hissed.

They locked in a silent battle.

As if he'd be envious of some highbrow lady. He'd been contented with his life in the Rookeries. Hadn't he?

Temperance was the first to look away.

Restless, he wandered over to the kidney-curved ivory bench laden with garments. Absently, he piled the dresses on the arm atop the stack of gowns, and then stopped.

They were gowns that had belonged to another. Nay, more . . . They were gowns that had been worn by . . . his mother. The woman who'd birthed him, and cared for him for an all-too-brief time. Until she hadn't. *Your mother would have you near . . . But it is better for all . . . especially her, if you make yourself . . . invisible.* His throat worked. From that moment on, Dare had seen to his own care.

"So what is the plan . . . to simply get rid of everything?"

"Why should I care?" he cried, spinning around to face her. "Do you think I want anything belonging to a man who knew only shame for me? Who hated me."

Fisting a hand to her mouth, she shook her head.

But he was unrelenting, taking a step closer. "A father who railed at the fact that I'd been born first and not my brother. A father who, when I did try to return, ordered me gone and reminded me that it was better for my mother and sibling if I left and let them be a family without all the problems I brought." Anguish, both bitter and sharp, pulled the remainder of that admission from him. Words he'd never breathed before . . . to anyone. Ones he'd intended to keep only to himself.

The air didn't move; it just hung motionless and suspended.

"I didn't know those things," she whispered.

Because he hadn't shared them. But then mayhap that had always been the problem between them, the reason they'd never been able to make their relationship work: their inability to communicate about . . . everything.

The fight went out of him, and he sank onto the arm of the chair atop gowns that had once belonged to his mother. "When the adventure ended and I was given over to Diggory, I realized what I'd done. I tried to go back." He made himself acknowledge that again—in a different way, the meaning still the same. "He wasn't wrong," he said tiredly, wiping a hand down his face. "When I went off, I chose the life I did. I was selfish and wicked, and I would have only hurt my mother and brother had I been allowed to stay."

She moved in a whir of skirts, sitting beside him on the crowded arm of the chair. "Oh, Dare," she whispered, her voice catching. "You didn't choose this. You were a child . . . one who was deceived into believing the dream of the adventure, all the while being pulled deeper into a nightmare you could have never imagined."

And it had been . . .

Because the food he'd had and the fun he'd had distributing baskets of baked goods to people his father had insisted nobles didn't acknowledge . . . had ended. Instead, he'd been reduced to the same hungry, fearful state lived by every other impoverished child. "I went willingly," he said, his voice empty to his own ears. "I have no one to blame but myself."

Temperance made a sound of protest. She covered his hand with hers and drew it close to her chest.

"You're wrong. This was chosen for you by the man who lured you away and tricked you. And your father . . . He was to blame for you not living in the world you were born to. A world where you could have done the good that your father was determined that you not do. He let you believe you didn't belong here." She lifted her arms, motioning to the room. "And you came to believe it. Because convincing yourself of that was easier than confronting that life went on without you."

Unable to face her and all the truths she leveled, Dare resumed his inventorying of the contents that had been brought down earlier that afternoon. "It changes nothing. The items need to be sold. Gurney needs to be saved, as do so many others."

Temperance spoke in hushed tones. "You don't want to do this . . . collecting cherished possessions and just selling them off without a thought to how other people might feel about it. You're choosing to let him back into your life, which will only end up hurting you."

Him.

He should have known better than to believe she'd let the matter of Avery Bryant's presence go without remark.

"I'm choosing to let him back into my life because of his connection with Wylie." He stared down at the notepad containing the inventory Avery insisted would cover the fees to Wylie for the transfer of the prisoner. "There are people relying on me. Families I can feed." He flipped to the next page in his book. "And his name is Avery. I still have dealings with Avery," he said, not allowing her to erase his loyal partner's name. "He's helped me."

"You always trusted him more than you should," she fired back, not missing a beat. "He's helped you nearly get yourself killed." Temperance came over and plucked the notebook from his fingers, and this time when she spoke, she did so in gentler, almost pitying tones. "He was always about helping himself."

Dare frowned. "That is unfair. I owe him my very existence."

"Precisely, Dare."

He winced.

Temperance wasn't done. "He convinced you that a life of thieving is better than one of honor."

His patience broke. "Honor?" he spat. "Was there honor in your darning damned socks until your fingers bled?" Her cheeks paled, but God help him, he couldn't stop the flow of words. "Was there honor in begging for funds to feed your family? Or in pleading with your miserable landlord for an extension when your father failed to pay the rent on your family's one-room apartment?"

Wordlessly, Temperance handed back his book. She didn't say anything for a long while. At last she spoke. "You aren't wrong, Dare. I *did* humble myself over the years. I begged. I asked for help." He stared beyond the top of her head. "I took assistance from whomever was willing to give it, not just you. I darned socks for mere farthings. There was hardly money in what I did, Dare," she said solemnly. "But there was *always* honor." She thumped a hand against her breast. "I did what I had to do in order to care for my mother and brother, and I can also say that I never compromised myself and my values."

Unlike Dare, who took from the undeserving and gave to the neediest. The evidence of her disdain had always cut like a knife. "Money lets people begin again in new places. It provides them with a roof and a warm fire in the dead of winter. But you had your honor," he asked, unable to keep the disdain from that word. "Did honor keep *you* safe?"

As soon as the charge left him, he wanted to call it back.

Her entire body jerked the way it had the one time he'd witnessed her drunkard father strike her. It had been the first and last time he'd witnessed her being hit, and the memory of it haunted him still. "Temperance," he said hoarsely. "Forgive me. That didn't come out as I'd intended. I respected your decisions, Temperance," he said, needing her to understand that. He'd never understood that pride; he'd fallen in love with her for her honor.

Temperance drew in a deep breath. "You're right, honor didn't keep me safe from him, but neither did that money you so love, either."

"It isn't about me," he cried. "Joseph Gurney was imprisoned."

"And then there'll be someone else. And instead of you finding the right and honorable way to make a difference, you'll go about committing crime after crime, thinking the end justifies the means. And it doesn't, Dare," she said frantically. "It never will."

It was those words that were the answer as to why they had never worked as a couple: his inability to be who she wanted him to be. Who she needed him to be. Who his grandparents needed him to be. Always a failure. Always failing to do that which was right because he was incapable of it. Dare flew to his feet. "And you would worry about some damned timepiece or . . . or"—he slashed his arm toward the floor—"paintings."

She sucked a breath in through her teeth. "That isn't what this is about."

"Then what is it?" he shouted. He needed her to tell him so that it made some sense.

"It's about how you destroy things, Dare," she cried, stalking over to him, her skirts swirling wildly about her ankles. "It is about you making decisions that are poisonous and making a man who is poisonous your partner. It is about you looking after everyone *but* yourself." Some of the fight seemed to leave her. Temperance hugged her arms close to her middle. "We're never going to see eye to eye on this. I'll never convince you that what you did wasn't right. But this isn't about me or you."

"Isn't it? You'll get your brother his happily-ever-after, and I'll get my remaining fifteen thousand pounds."

She winced. "No. Not really, and we'd be wise to remember that." She let her arms drop to her sides. "The person this *is* about is Kinsley. Thus far, you and I have only seen her as a means to an end. And we've both been wrong in that. Your grandfather tasked you with the role he did, Dare, because he wants you to be a brother to her." Temperance nudged her chin in the direction of the biggest mound of belongings in the parlor. "And I'd suggest you begin by not going about stealing the belongings out from under her."

"They are mine to sell, Temperance."

She swept over and gripped him by his upper arms. "You *insist* this life isn't yours, while at the same time insisting the belongings in this household *are*? You don't get it both ways, Dare."

And with that, Temperance released her hold on him and headed for the front of the room. Suddenly, she stopped and faced him once more. "What leaves me truly sad is that I'd begun forming a bond with your sister. We actually spoke to each other in a way that I understood, if not her, what she is feeling. And with what you did here? Inviting Avery Bryant back into your life . . ." Temperance gave her head a forlorn little shake. "You've gone and undone any connection I'd made."

"We just have to see her married," he said tiredly. "It doesn't matter whether or not she likes you, Temperance." Or him. Though for a very brief while in Hyde Park, it had almost seemed as though she didn't quite hate him so much, after all . . .

"She isn't going to marry."

That brought him up short. "What?"

"Your sister, she does not wish to wed."

Shock silenced him. He'd been forced here to London with the expectation and requirement that he see her married. Kinsley had represented the only real path forward to the duke's funds. But that wasn't the only way . . .

Briefly, a thought slipped in . . . of the alternative arrangement, one that would require him to have a real marriage with Temperance . . . a baby. A future together, and the hungering for that imagining was so great it weighted his eyes closed.

Temperance went on to explain, shattering that dreaming. "At Hyde Park, Kinsley shared with me that she doesn't want to marry."

He found his bearings. "She'll marry. She is young."

"She's near an age to my own when you and I were married."

His cheeks flushed hot. "That is different."

"Why?" Temperance persisted. She lifted an eyebrow. "Because you and I need her to marry? Because you want her to?" She swept over. "She doesn't want to, and that is all that should matter."

Or mayhap you can have a real marriage with Temperance . . . one with a child. The memory of her with Rose in her arms slipped in, and a hungering for that vision filled him. Nor did it have anything to do with the terms of his grandfather's arrangement, and everything to do with the idea of being a family . . . with her.

Shaken by the potency with which he craved that imagining, Dare headed for the gilded frames and began stacking them. "Her unwillingness to marry therefore seems to grant me even more reason to sell off the contents of the household, then."

"You still don't understand." Temperance stalked over and lightly wrestled a heavy frame from his grip. She settled it atop the thick stack of dresses. "I think before this exchange, I would have railed at you for the ruthlessness in that thinking." Her lips curled in a heartbreaking smile. "But now I know."

He tensed, not wanting to ask, and yet unable to call back the question anyway. "Know what?"

"You make *every* effort to never have a bond with another person." She spoke beseechingly. "It is why you married me and then left immediately. It is why you took such delight in baiting your sister. Or why you"—she gestured to the stack of gowns between them—"decided to sell everything the moment you had a meaningful exchange with your sister." Each word, accurate in its leverage, hit like a perfectly aimed blow. "And any relationships you *do* have?" Her eyes bored into his, her stare penetrating and one he both needed and yet could not look away from. "You kill, Dare."

Just as he'd killed theirs.

"Is that what I did?" His feet twitched, and he wanted to run. To flee from her accusations, the real and unspoken, ones he'd no wish to explore. "I killed our relationship."

Her response was instantaneous. "That is precisely what you did."

Heat flushed his cheeks. "You were the one who sent me away, Temperance."

"Because you weren't there," she said imploringly.

"I came and found you." And she'd turned him away, leaving him empty and broken in ways that even the separation from his mother and brother hadn't. Done with a past they'd never see eye to eye on, he headed for the door . . . when her words reached him.

"Not when I needed you," she repeated, her voice a faint whisper that he struggled to hear.

Dare sharpened his gaze on her face. Warning bells went off, ringing faintly. What was she saying?

"Chance insisted I leave, but I knew you would return." *And I did. I did.* "My father found out."

He stilled. "We always anticipated he would. That was the plan," he said, faintly entreating. Did he plead with her or himself? He had married her. Her father was supposed to have feared Dare's reputation and influence. "He was to have left you alone."

As if she could not meet his eyes, she glanced down at the floor. "Yes, he was."

He took a step toward her, unable to get the question out, the one that would ultimately explain why she'd turned him away. Deep down, in a place where horror and terror dwelled together, he knew. "It . . . didn't see you safe." His words emerged as a statement, hollow.

Temperance squeezed her eyes shut briefly and sucked in a shuddery breath. She gave the faintest shake of her head, the barest bob of her neck. When she again opened her eyes, a chill scraped along his spine. "No."

Haunted.

In that moment she was a woman haunted, and he would forevermore be tormented by the sight of her as she was, here. Now.

And she must have felt the cold, too . . . for she rubbed her hands frantically over her arms.

He shook his head. He was the coward she'd called him out as. Wanting her to stop. But she continued anyway. Because it was what he deserved. Because it was what she was entitled to . . . his owning the memories of those days after they'd wed.

"He was enraged. He'd other plans for me. Ones that didn't include marriage to you. He wanted me to marry Diggory's number two. My father resented us for thwarting him." Her shoulders came back. "He beat me." There was a peculiar calmness to her admission, one that warred with the tumult ravaging him.

His entire body jerked. "Temperance—"

"Mm-mm," she said, cutting him off, giving her head a more definitive shake. Tears filled her eyes, and the sight of that suffering gutted him. She, who'd never cried before him. Not once. "I need to say this, and . . ." Her voice broke on a sob. He took another frantic step closer, but she held a hand up, staying him in his tracks. "And if you stop me, I don't think I'll ever get the words out."

He nodded jerkily and gave her that which she needed—his silence.

"I was home. Chance came. He urged me to leave. I thought you were coming. I was so s-sure of it."

A groan better suited to a wounded beast climbed his throat and spilled from his lips. *No. No. No.*

"My father arrived." Her voice, her eyes, were deadened. "He beat me." Oh, God. His eyes slid shut, and he wanted to block out each word, each revelation. Each reminder that he hadn't been there . . . when she had needed him.

He'd failed her. He should have been there. What had been more important than her? Nothing. He couldn't even remember the items he and Avery had filched—

"I was with child."

His body went hot . . . and then cold. As through the haze of his own misery and regret and heartbreak, her admission slipped in. "What?" That question . . . his own, came as if down a long, empty tunnel.

She stopped rubbing her arms and stared out, her gaze locked on his chest—sightless.

His body went absolutely motionless. *No.*

It was a single-word litany in his head.

"I was so heavy with child, I was slower."

A piteous moan spilled from his lips. "I didn't . . ." *Know. And isn't that the very point she made,* a voice taunted through his misery.

"I lost the babe." She said the words he knew were inevitable in her telling. "I held her."

Her.

His eyes slid closed.

Temperance continued speaking, her words coming as if from far away. "She was so tiny. Her skin was so clear you could almost see through it."

Forcing his eyes open, Dare stood there, numb, taking each revelation about the child he'd never even known of like the deserved lash it should be.

Temperance touched a hand to the top of her head. "She'd this tiny little tuft of dark hair on her head. This little circular patch."

Dare's throat worked spasmodically. They'd had a babe . . . and that child had been a girl. Something in knowing that made the loss . . . even more. There'd been a little girl, who would have grown to be like her mother, with her fiery spirit and clever wit and . . . Agony shredded the rest of those desperate yearnings. *I am never going to survive this.*

And yet . . . she had. And she'd done so alone. Without him at her side, battling that crushing loss and recovering from the brutal assault her father had carried out. Tears stung his eyes, and he pressed the backs of his palms against them, trying to drive away a pain that could not be dulled.

"There was so much blood. I should have died." Temperance drew in a shuddering breath. "The doctor Chance brought expected I would."

And where was I while she was there, suffering, clinging to her life, having lost our babe?

"He explained I'd never be able to have more children."

The earth ceased spinning on its axis.

And when it resumed rotating, the ground shifted under Dare's feet, and he grappled for something to keep him upright.

My God.

Temperance cleared her throat. "After . . . it all, Chance, he put me in a mail carriage, with money to get to Cotswold. I was . . . sick the whole way."

It was why she could no longer ride in carriages. Now, that aversion made sense.

Now, everything made sense. And what was worse . . . knowing . . . it changed nothing.

Chapter 20

Say something.

Say anything.

And yet he did not.

There was just a thick silence punctuated by the harsh rasp of his breath, that ragged intake and exhale of air the only indication that she'd thrown him into the same tumult that ravaged her now.

He took several steps toward her, and she in equal parts hungered for his nearness and yet could not bear for him to be close.

"Why . . . didn't you tell me?" he whispered.

Temperance hugged her arms tight to her middle once more. "I should have." She'd told herself it wouldn't have brought their daughter back or eased the memories or erased her suffering. She'd wallowed in her resentment of his not having been there when she needed him. Now, Temperance could admit what had compelled her—fear. For the moment she revealed what she had, she would have to own all the ways in which her body was now a failure in a task expected of it. "It . . . was easier not telling you than thinking that you'd reject me."

"You thought I would *reject* you?" he whispered. "I should have been there when you needed me most . . . and I was not."

That was what Dare would focus on . . . his sense of guilt and obligation for not having taken care of her.

Moisture dampened her cheeks, and she touched the backs of her palms to them. *Tears.* At some point, she'd begun crying. When he'd come to her all those years ago, she'd turned him away. She'd told herself it had been because he'd lost the right to share in her grief. He'd not deserved to know. She blotted them several times. "Chance remained behind. He saw to the burial. He kept my father at bay, allowing me the time to make my escape."

It had been the first time, and not the last, when the brother she'd looked after had shifted roles and come to care for her.

"Where?" he asked hoarsely.

"I don't know what you are—"

He glanced over his shoulder at her. "Where is . . . she?"

"St. Abbey. I . . . I've never been. It is an unmarked grave. He could . . . We could not afford more."

Dare caught the back of the chair as if to keep himself upright.

Their daughter rested in an unmarked grave in the Rookeries. His breath rasped noisily. "We were . . . very nearly a family."

She caught the inside of her cheek, hard enough to draw blood, the metallic tinge of it filling her senses. "Yes," she whispered. "Very nearly."

And now, a fate that could never be.

He lifted his gaze to hers, those dark-brown eyes ravaged. "I am . . . so sorry," he whispered.

Temperance, however, didn't want his apologies. She wanted him to understand what his decisions had cost him . . . and what they would continue to cost him if he was unable to change.

"I didn't tell you this to make you feel guilty." It had never been about that. "You don't let yourself form true connections to people. You make every effort to destroy everything that is good in your life. It's why you insist on keeping Avery Bryant in your life." She gave him a sad and, worse, pitying look. "It is why you left after marrying me." Her heart bled from pain. "It is why you are selling items that mean so much to your sister."

With that she started past him.

Stop me.

Say something more . . .

Because surely there had to be some words more than . . . this?

But as she left, there was only silence.

⌘

Dare had lived just ten years with his family. In that time he'd alternated staying at the townhouse or the country properties in Sussex, Kent, and Cornwall. Those memories had begun to lose clarity, time's passage having dimmed them so that the years may have existed as only a dream he'd carried within.

For almost two decades he'd dwelled in East London.

Even after he'd agreed to return and squire his sister about town, Dare had always planned on returning to the Rookeries.

Once his obligations had been met and his pockets lined, he was to have returned to the place that he'd known to be home.

And now, he was back.

Dare strode through the streets of London, a man possessed. He'd walked from Mayfair to East London, familiar streets. And as he stalked through them, he was a man with one intent, one purpose, channeling all his regrets and misery and grief.

I was home. Chance came. He urged me to leave. I thought you were coming. I was so s-sure of it . . .

A babe.

There'd been a babe. A tiny one, too small to survive, but who would have become as strong as her mother.

Not him. Dare wasn't strong. He'd never been. Oh, he'd thought himself so. But she, she had confronted life at every turn and, as she'd said, lived a life that was hard but honorable. All the while, he'd justified his dishonor by the actions of the men whom he robbed.

Dare paused at the end of the pavement, and squinting, he peered ahead.

Drunks filled the streets of East London. They were everywhere . . . But every one of them, they had their own corner. Their own place.

Abaddon had been king of his.

The man slumped with his eyes half-closed, however, bore no hint of a king, but a rat in the streets. Older, greyer, more wrinkled, and more bloated from the alcohol that he subsisted on, he remained largely the same street thug who'd worked for Diggory, feared by nearly all. By the life he'd lived and the spirits he'd consumed, the man should have been dead twenty times before this one.

Of course Temperance would have been correct even in this. The mean bastard was too stubborn to die. His soul was too black for Satan. This was the man. The one who'd hurt Temperance. Countless times. The man responsible for the black-and-blue bruises she'd sported.

At his approach, Abaddon Swift tried to straighten. A silly, spirit-induced smile tipped those fleshy lips up. "As *Oiiii liiiiive* an' breathe. The *marquesssss* 'as returned. Tole everyone it was foolish to think ya'd ever quit the *streee—*"

Dare didn't break stride. He greeted Abaddon Swift with a fist to the face.

Already propped against the wall as he was, Abaddon's head knocked against the brick with a sickening *thunk*; the ferocity of that blow would have sent most men on to meet their maker, or in this bastard's case, the Devil.

Abaddon howled as his already bent nose gave with a satisfying crack. Wiping the back of his ripped, dirt-stained sleeve across his face, Temperance's father smeared blood across his sunken cheeks.

With rage pumping through him, Dare gripped Abaddon by the arms and propelled him back once more, forcing another squeal from the drunk's lips. "Bastard," Dare hissed. "I should have ended you years ago." And yet for all his crimes, he'd not been able to make himself a murderer. Temperance, however, had deserved that of him. She'd deserved for Dare to kill the monster for the violence he had visited upon her again and again. Growling, Dare brought his knee up hard between the other man's legs.

Cradling his crotch, Abaddon went down, collapsing in a heap. Temperance's father writhed and squirmed upon the dank cobblestones.

Dare planted the tip of his boot in the older man's stomach, and all the air left Abaddon on a hiss.

It wasn't enough. With this fierce hungering to end the other man, Dare proved himself very much of this world. This was why he'd been unable to go back all those years ago . . . This was who he was. He towered over Abaddon, reveling in the bastard's pathetic whimpering.

A haze of bloodlust clouded Dare's vision as he drew his arm back again to deliver another blow, the crushing one he wanted to . . .

The other man peered up at him, cowering like the animal he was. Cowering . . . as Temperance likely had as a girl. And in that moment, Dare saw her in his mind's eye . . . defiant and bold and proud, even as she'd taken a ruthless, vicious beating at the hands of the one who'd sired her.

Dare's fist remained suspended.

"I should kill you," Dare seethed. He should have done so years ago. He'd let him live too many times before. If he'd done so, if he'd not balked at having that degree of violence on his hands, his child would be alive even now, and Dare, that little girl he'd never known, and Temperance could have been a true family.

That seemed to penetrate Abaddon's drunken stupor. Fear wreathed his features. "Ya going to finally do it, *theeennn*?"

That was what Dare should do. It was what he wanted to.

He warred with himself.

And yet . . . he'd not have this man's blood on his hands. Not in that way. He slackened his grip. "You can hide, but your days? They are at an end. You'll be dealt with." He'd the influence now to see that justice was done.

"Why *didddn't* ya off me?" the other man wheezed. He spat out a mouthful of blood, and with it went one of his last few remaining teeth. His eyes clenched as he rolled from one side to the next. "Ya 'ad plenty o' opportunities."

Because Dare had convinced himself that their business was different. He'd severed all ties with Diggory's people, had believed the streets were big enough for all of them.

He'd been wrong.

About so much.

Abaddon finally stopped his fidgeting. He lay there so motionless, so still, that Dare peered closer to see if the bastard was either dead or passed out.

Fate wouldn't be that kind.

Temperance's father opened his eyes. "Ya found *ouutt*." Abaddon grunted. "Surprised she didn't tell ya before."

There'd been nothing Dare and Temperance hadn't shared . . . until they'd shared nothing. Dare clenched and unclenched his jaw. However, he'd offer nothing about what was between him and Temperance, not to this man. Whether or not he'd sired her, he was nothing to her.

Turning on his heel, Dare left Abaddon Swift lying on the ground. There'd been no peace or satisfaction this night. Beating the other man didn't change anything. It wouldn't bring back the daughter he'd never known. It wouldn't erase the time and distance that had sprung between Dare and Temperance.

"*Youuuu're* angry with *meeee*," the other man called after him. "*Bee* angry with *yarrrself.* Ya were the one who *leffft.* Ya were the one who *trusssted* all the wrong people."

Mayhap that was what tore Dare up most . . . the fact that the divide between him and Temperance was a product of his own doing. He stopped midstride and wheeled around. "What did you say?"

Abaddon blinked his watery, bloodshot eyes several times. "*Whhhaaat diiiid* Oi say?"

Storming over, Dare gathered Abaddon once more by the shirt-front and dragged him to his feet. He backed him against the building. "What did you say?"

Abaddon blinked and scratched at the thatch of greasy hair atop his head. "*Nottt* sure." His head bobbed sideways, and his mouth fell open.

Soon, a bleating snore spilled from the bastard's lips.

Dare released him, and left him there, sleeping like the dog he was.

Suddenly, the fight went out of him. Dare resumed his restless trek through the Rookeries. Beating the other man senseless hadn't brought any true solace. There could be none anymore.

The memory of everything Temperance had shared, every charge she'd leveled, every heartbreak she'd revealed went with him.

He destroyed . . . everything. It wasn't chance that he put himself in precarious positions and had found himself confined to Newgate at various points through his life. Temperance had seen as much and called him out for it.

And just as she'd charged, it was why, shortly after marrying her, he'd left with Avery Bryant to carry out a series of thefts in the countryside. From a place not even so very deep down, he'd known she'd not have approved, but he'd gone anyway . . . because he'd always made the decisions that had proven the wrong and worst ones.

Dare continued striding onward until he reached the rusted gates of St. Abbey. He didn't stop but passed through those high metal openings that hung forlorn and broken, as untended as the worn, crooked stones within.

Numb, Dare made himself walk onward. As he went, he scanned the tombstones, some with identifying markers. Young children. Old men and women. Other markers had faded with time under the weathering.

And then, there were the others. The ones with no etching upon them, their existence marked only by a blank stone.

Dare stopped beside a random tomb overgrown with moss; the grass had grown, covering most of the stone so that only the smallest bit was visible underneath.

His breath formed a little cloud of white in the cool spring night air. He sank onto his haunches and proceeded to clean the unmarked grave. Tugging weeds and pushing back the earth with his fingers until the stone rose up above the dirt.

All these years, he had believed his life had been one of meaning. He'd seen what he'd done as a noble mission to be that which he'd most needed as a young boy in the Rookeries—salvation.

You don't let yourself form true connections to people. You make every effort to destroy everything that is good in your life. It's why you insist on keeping Avery Bryant in your life . . . It is why you left after marrying me . . . It is why you are selling items that mean so much to your sister.

Ya were the one who trusssted *all the wrong people.*

Those words Temperance had spoken blended with the drunken ones her father had uttered . . . moments ago? A lifetime ago?

Dare scraped a hand through his hair.

What had it all been for?

He'd merely . . . existed. It had been an unwitting decision he'd made to never truly experience life in the hopes that other people might. Because he'd known his worth. Ultimately, he'd known the world was all right without him in it. After all, his own parents had gotten on just fine in his absence. The gift of a family wasn't for people like him.

And yet it was a gift that he'd unknowingly been granted . . . and squandered, as he did everything.

Restless, Dare pushed to his feet and walked a small little circle, staring, searching . . . for her—the child Temperance had been forced to deliver on her own before fleeing so that she might survive.

Tears welled, and this time, in the presence of East London's ghosts, he let them fall.

He wanted a future . . . He wanted a life with her in it. Where the money dangled by his grandfather had represented what he'd craved, it wasn't enough. Not anymore. Mayhap it had never really been. There was . . . her. And whether there was a child or not born of them . . . born to them . . . it didn't matter more than she did.

His grandfather's money would save countless lives, and yet he'd not have it at the expense of all else: his sister, Kinsley, whom he'd been pushing away since he'd discovered her existence. He'd never have let the duke turn Temperance into a broodmare . . . which ultimately was what the alternate route to those funds had been.

He was done stealing and selling himself.

He wanted to begin again.

Nay . . . he wanted a new beginning, with Temperance and his sister.

And yes, his marquessate was bankrupt, but there were connections afforded him now . . . and wealth he could squeeze out of his estates until he could turn it into something more. The help he would provide would be far more limited than that which he'd offered throughout the past twenty years. But there were also people who were reliant upon him who would benefit as well. As Spencer had pointed out, the servants were also men, women, and children whose livelihoods, security, and ability to coexist with their families all depended upon Dare's commitment to this new life.

Feeling a lightness go through him unlike any he'd ever known, Dare wound his way through the dank streets he'd called home . . .

But they hadn't been a home.

Not truly.

Home would only ever be where Temperance was.

Temperance, who'd helped him see the life he'd lived had been one filled with excuses. Who at every turn had urged him to be more . . .

not because she'd reviled him as his father had . . . but because she'd truly believed there was good in him. She'd seen it in Dare, who'd been unable to see it in himself.

When he finally found his way back home, Dare bounded up the steps past a waiting servant and called out a greeting to the boy.

"My lord," he called after Dare.

"Thank you, James," he said, whistling.

"I was told to tell you—"

Pushing the door open, he let himself inside, hungry to see her.

Except . . .

She was already there . . . beside Spencer.

Temperance, in her nightdress and wrapper.

Her cheeks whitewashed.

And . . . she was not alone.

A tall, painfully slim gentleman stepped forward, his uniform distinct. His hat even more so.

And an odd buzz filled Dare's ears . . . as he tried to muddle through.

That which he already knew. Because this wasn't the first moment he'd been in this position. There'd been seven times prior to this where he'd found one of them at his door.

No . . . a voice silently screamed in his head. *Not now.*

"Dare Grey, the Marquess of Milford?" The man spoke in graveled tones, his voice coming as if down an endless corridor.

Dare managed a wooden nod. "I am."

"You are under arrest for the crime of bribery of a prison official."

Chapter 21

There had been any number of places Temperance had never anticipated that she'd be in life.

There'd been the time Dare had sneaked her into the rafters of a Covent Garden theatre, and she'd witnessed the splendor of a musical production.

Or the time he'd taken her off to visit the Serpentine in Hyde Park in the dead of night, under a full moon, and skipped rocks upon that serene surface.

And the time most recently, when he'd escorted her through Hyde Park.

All those moments had blurred together with time meaning little as she sat in the unlikeliest of places, the one place she'd never expected to find herself—inside the residence of a duke and duchess.

Hands clasped before her, she stole another glance at the doorway . . .

Where in blazes were they?

And yet . . .

Temperance again looked to the clock. It had been just twelve minutes.

Twelve minutes since she'd arrived in the dead of night without any form of notice, and demanded to see Dare's grandparents.

What if they won't see me?

Her mind balked at that.

Of course they would. They would, if for no other reason than because she was Dare's wife.

At last, footfalls echoed in the corridors.

The duke and duchess appeared, as properly attired as if they'd just arrived from a ball and not come down from their bedchambers.

His Grace allowed his wife to enter first before following behind.

The appearance of being nonplussed must be something for which they trained those destined to be dukes and duchesses. Or mayhap it was essential training for all those of the nobility: give no outward reaction to anything, regardless of who might arrive unannounced on one's doorstep.

"I trust this isn't a social call," the duchess said in her customary clipped, cool, and droll tones.

Temperance dropped a quick, belated curtsy. "No. Forgive me . . . There is a matter of . . . I . . ."

She'd had the entire ride to prepare what she might say to enlist their support.

He is their grandson. They were determined for him to live. That sobering reminder grounded her.

"Your grandson is in trouble."

Neither the duke nor duchess moved.

At last, they exchanged a look, a long one that may as well have contained a whole conversation that only they two heard. And then the couple found a place upon the pale-blue satin sofa, motioning for her to join them.

Temperance opened her mouth, but the duchess held a finger up, silencing her. "Tea."

What in blazes? Temperance wrinkled her brow. What Punch-and-Judy stage had she stepped upon? "Have you not heard me?" she demanded of the pair.

"My dear, hysterics will solve nothing; tea, however, will solve hysterics, and then we might speak."

And because it was a maddening, illogical philosophy as bizarre as this whole meeting, she claimed the seat across from Dare's grandparents . . . and sat in absolute silence until the moment a servant appeared with a silver tray and the duchess had made a glass for herself and one for her husband.

She turned to Temperance.

The duchess was asking whether she wanted tea? "No."

The duchess aimed an incisive look at Temperance.

That had, of course, been the wrong answer. Tightening her mouth, she accepted the cup handed over and rested it on her lap. "I've come because—"

Another one of those long, flawlessly manicured fingers shot up. *Clink-clink-clink.*

The duchess continued to stir her tea in four and a half more meticulous, perfectly even circles before setting the spoon aside. Raising her glass to her lips, she sipped, and from over the rim, she stared at Temperance.

"Your grandson is in trouble," Temperance repeated bluntly. Perhaps that would break through this maddening indifference.

It did not.

At most, there was just the faintest of pauses, so slight it might have even been imagined, as Temperance expected to find . . . *some* response from the woman.

"Now, what manner of trouble?" she asked, only after she'd lowered her cup back to its neat, floral-painted porcelain tray.

"Dare was attempting to help someone—"

"Your brother's friend," the duchess said, lifting her cup for another sip. A thin white eyebrow winged up. "Was it not?"

Temperance curled her hands tightly. "He is. Joseph Gurney," she said needlessly, that offering useless. A woman like the duchess wouldn't care about those like Joseph Gurney or Lionel. Temperance had always admired Dare. Appreciated what he did for so many . . . But now, seeing how different he was from all these lofty lords who treated the Gurneys and Swifts as invisible—her throat tightened—she loved him all the more.

"I *seeee.*" There was a wealth of meaning to Her Grace's words. Ones that made it beyond clear who was responsible for Dare's current troubles. "And so, Dare was attempting to help your brother's friend, and . . . ?"

What manner of person would choose to make Temperance's visit . . . about this? A wave of futility hit her, a sense of desperation. Her gaze fell to her lap. Her whole life, she'd had control over next to nothing. Why, beaten by her father since she was a babe, Temperance hadn't even had control of her own body. Even as she'd loved Dare, their marriage had been born of her inability to exact change of her own over her existence.

Now she sat before his noble grandparents, desperate. Once more reduced to one without any control.

And as Dare's grandparents stared on, Temperance wanted to leave. She wanted to storm out and say to hell with the duke and duchess and their damned tea and refusal to show emotion. But . . . she couldn't. She couldn't because she loved Dare more.

Firming her resolve, she looked squarely at the lofty pair. "Dare bribed a warden at Newgate," she said quietly. Something he'd done so many times, blind to the fact that people had been plotting his demise. From the last time he'd walked across St. Peter's Square to his arrest this night, someone—possibly Avery Bryant—had been attempting to rid the Rookeries of Dare.

His teacup forgotten, the duke rubbed at his chin. "Hmm."

Hmm. That was what he'd say? A single-syllable utterance that he'd managed to slice in half?

"That is . . . it?" she asked incredulously, casting a disbelieving glance back and forth between Dare's grandparents. "Just . . . *hmm* and . . ." She slammed her teacup down, splashing liquid all over the edge of the dish and onto the gleaming mahogany table between them.

"What would you have us do, my dear?" the duchess asked. "Give in to hysterics?"

"Yes," she cried. Good God, what manner of people were they? "That is precisely what I'd have you do. I'd have you show some emotion. Or give"—she slashed a hand in the handsome pair's general direction—"*some* indication that you care about Dare."

Only the ticking of the clock served as her response. Sixteen and a half precise ticks before Dare's grandmother again spoke.

"And how would that help my grandson?" the duchess asked in her perfectly even tones.

That gave Temperance pause. It wouldn't . . .

"Do you truly think we won't help our grandson, my dear?" the duke said in a surprisingly gentle voice that thoroughly confused.

"I . . ."

His Grace set aside his teacup. "We will do anything for our grandson."

"And yet you'd not give him the funds he was entitled to without strings attached." She couldn't keep the trace of bitterness out of that question.

The duke made to speak, but his wife held a hand up. "Tell me, Temperance," the duchess said. "What do you think he would do if we simply gave him the funds?"

Leave. There was no doubt of it. Dare would have left long ago and happily distributed it all over East London from the Rookeries on to the Dials . . . and would be searching for the next household to rob, to replenish those coffers.

"Strings attached, as you refer to it . . . are sometimes required, if a person cannot be trusted to act in their best self-interest."

And turning to her husband in an indication that the topic was at an end, the duchess spoke. "You'll go handle this."

"I'll go handle this."

Collecting the duchess's hand, the old duke pressed a kiss atop it in an unexpected display of warmth, one that proved the two were not the heartless ones Temperance . . . or Dare had taken them for.

"Thank you," she said hoarsely after the duke had limped off.

And it was the first time since the constable had arrived, demanding to see Dare, that Temperance knew it was going to be all right.

All earlier warmth that had been there at the duke and duchess's exchange vanished.

Dare's grandmother sailed to her feet. "Do not thank me for looking after our grandson. We have always put him first. When his father failed to do so." Hate burnt bright within the older woman's eyes. She knew. She'd known that her son-in-law had sent Dare away.

The duchess headed for the door.

"Oh, and Temperance?" The duchess paused and turned back to face Temperance. "Putting Darius first . . . is something anyone who loved him would do."

And with that not-at-all-veiled meaning there, the duchess left.

⊂≈⊃

Newgate
London, England

Dare had come full circle.

Though it was unclear. Would full circle mark the moment he climbed the gibbet and made that walk to the hangman's noose? Or was it here, on the stone-cold Newgate prison floor?

Sitting on the floor with his back to the wall and his face toward the narrow bars, he stared out.

He'd always had miserable timing.

The worst.

That would remain until he drew his last breath.

There had been he and Temperance . . . as young loves . . . sweethearts who had been pulled down differing paths—he, the path of thievery, and she, one of respectability.

And what did I do? I called her out for bloodying her fingers . . . when all the while, she was doing honest work.

Dare knocked his head lightly against the wall.

So many regrets, and he'd added any number more of them this night.

A figure stepped out of the shadows.

Dare's entire body tensed.

Wylie scraped his wide circle of keys over the metal bars, that clink and clang echoing around the eerily silent gaol. "You know, Grey, you always had terrible timing."

"I was rather thinking the same damned thing myself," he muttered. This was certainly the end . . . He'd reached a point where he'd found himself agreeing with the ruthless warden. "You and Bryant, huh?"

Wylie shrugged. "Struck a better deal."

Struck a better deal.

And with Dare's mentor.

You always trusted him more than you should . . . He's helped you nearly get yourself killed . . . He was always about helping himself.

God, what a fool he'd been.

"You would have been wiser, listening to that old sweetheart that used to get you out of here . . ." Wylie lounged a shoulder against the cell. "Whatever happened to that one? Probably married, she did."

"She did," Dare muttered. "Me."

Wylie tossed his head back and laughed until tears filled his eyes. The warden wiped them back. "Well, you would have been wiser trusting *her* instincts."

"I'd prefer you'd quit talking so I don't have to agree with you any more times this night," Dare said in deadened tones.

The warden glanced down to the opposite end of the hall. "You've company."

Company?

The quiet click of a cane striking the stone floor penetrated through his confusion.

The Duke of Pemberly stopped at the cell.

"Grandfather . . . ?" he whispered, struggling to his feet.

"That man is a lousy one to entrust with your reputation and life." The duke's pronouncement proved an accurate echo of Wylie's earlier opinion.

It is about you making decisions that are poisonous and making a man who is poisonous your partner. It is about you looking after everyone but *yourself.*

"I . . . know that," he said. "How . . . ?"

"Did I find out?" His Grace finished for him. "Your wife." He removed his gloves and stuffed them inside the front of his cloak.

"My . . . wife?" She'd gone to the duke and appealed for Dare's life.

"Never tell me you've forgotten your wife . . . again," the duke drawled.

Never. He never had. He never would. A man didn't forget the reason for his heart's every beat.

The duke stepped nearer Dare's cell. "Come, Darius. It is time to leave this place."

Leave.

It was what Dare had feared the moment Connor Steele had found him and presented him with the opportunity to reclaim his rightful place. Leaving the Rookeries. His role here.

He'd failed to let himself see that he could still do the work he wished to—and make the difference that he wanted to—as the Marquess of Milford.

"And I can just do that . . . leave?"

His Grace thumped the bottom of his cane upon the floor. "I've told you once before that no grandson of mine will hang. And that holds true." The duke released the monocle he still held in his other hand; that little glass cylinder swung loosely at his neck. "But you are certainly complicating matters by making this a regular occurrence."

"How?"

"Your arrest was nothing more than a setup, orchestrated by some uncouth street thug"—Avery Bryant—"and I am a peer of the realm. As such, I've handled the warden . . . who has been accepting bribes over the years, and as such, he found himself in a similarly tenable situation if he didn't agree to release you."

He . . . was being freed. He'd have the opportunity to start over. To begin again. And to do so . . . with Temperance.

There wouldn't be a fortune . . . because he wouldn't force his sister to wed. And there couldn't be a babe because . . . because . . .

Every corner of his soul seized with the aching loss of grief . . . at what he'd only just realized he'd lost long ago with Temperance.

But there could be babes. The unwanted orphans, like what he'd become . . . And there could be a life with Temperance. Together, they would build up what had been stolen and lost in his absence. And together they could bring the change they wished for the world.

"Thank you," he said hoarsely.

"You shouldn't thank me, but rather your wife, who's got a clever head to realize when to ask for help and"—his grandfather passed his monocle over Dare's cell—"which people are reliable enough to turn to."

Avery Bryant.

Dare winced.

He deserved that. He'd realized as much . . . just too late.

Just as she'd been right . . . about so much. Dare had been so determined to do things his way, to help by any means, that he'd been too blinded to see that the one who'd set him on the path of thieving had shifted, becoming the one determined to take him down.

Dare scrubbed a hand over his face.

I don't want it to be that way . . . I want to live a different life. The kind Temperance had urged him to live for years now, and one he'd believed himself incapable of carrying out . . .

Until now.

Before this moment, he'd seen himself through his father's eyes. He'd seen a person who was bad and broken and incapable of anything but a life of sin and strife.

Temperance had opened his eyes to the fact that he . . . was not the person his father had believed him to be. That there was good and worth in him. And he was capable of exacting change . . . in ways that did not involve stealing or bribery, or working with the likes of Avery Bryant and Wylie to bring about that change.

And I want that life . . . with Temperance in it . . .

The duke cleared his throat. "Shall we leave this place, Darius?"

Dare glanced over at the older gentleman, taking in the details that he'd not allowed himself to see these past weeks: the heavy lines around the duke's eyes. The deep wrinkles in his cheeks. He was a man who'd been aged by years . . . and grief.

Dare nodded slowly. "I would like that . . . Grandfather," he said quietly.

Tears filled the duke's eyes, and then patting Dare awkwardly on the back, he led him out of Newgate and onward to the path he wished to make for himself next.

Chapter 22

The following evening, Temperance prepared for her first real entry into Polite Society. She and Dare had not spoken since his return the night prior.

More specifically, they'd not spoken since Temperance had revealed her loss to Dare . . . and he'd returned early the following morn . . . with the duke.

Freed once more.

But then after what she'd shared, what was there to say? After what she'd shared, everything had changed between them; her telling had claimed their ease in being with one another.

What had she expected him to say? Or for them to be? No words from either of them could have changed . . . anything . . . She could not be the one to get him his twenty thousand pounds. Not with her broken body. Nor would she want a future with him that way—a child, if she could have given him that, born for wealth.

He'd always been a man of single-minded purpose. That hadn't changed because of what she'd revealed. Just like he'd always done, Dare was content to make decisions that only left him and the people around him hurting.

We just have to see her married . . . It doesn't matter whether or not she likes you, Temperance . . .

He'd always been chasing money, and it would have been so very easy to resent him for it, had he been driven by his own selfish greed. But it had never been that way with him. Everything he'd ever done had been because of the people in the streets, searching for help in a hopeless world. All the while he'd been helping others, however, he'd deliberately set out to sabotage his own happiness and security.

Not so very long ago, it would have been easy to resent him for all the wrong paths he continued to travel and choose. But that had been before. Before she'd come here and learned all he'd lost . . . and what had truly shaped him.

Now, *he* made sense.

He made sense in ways he never had before—his making decisions that ultimately saw him less safe and never truly happy because he didn't believe himself worthy of it.

And what was worse, knowing as much, knowing why he was the way he was . . . it changed nothing. It didn't make life better for him. It didn't bring him peace with the remaining kin he had alive. And it didn't heal her brokenness.

"Buck up. You look like you're headed to the gallows," Gwynn said as she drew Temperance's gown overhead.

The silk slid in a whispery glide over her hips and then settled in a whoosh at her ankles.

She winced.

"I'm sorry," Gwynn said, horror filling her eyes. "That was the wrong choice of words."

And yet . . .

Temperance's gaze caught in the windowpane. Her expression wasn't vastly unlike what it had been the day she'd gone to face Dare at that hated prison.

"Come. It is simply dinner," her friend went on, mistaking the reason for Temperance's forlornness. "We've been eating since we were born. Perhaps Lady Kinsley will find a suitor tonight, and we can be that much closer to leaving."

And yet . . . that wouldn't happen because it wasn't what Kinsley wished.

And there wouldn't be a babe, which meant . . . there was no money forthcoming by which to help Gwynn and Chance.

In the end, it had all been for naught.

And yet . . . these days she'd spent with Dare? Not once had she thought of the money to be had at the end of their arrangement. Or even really of Gwynn and Chance. She'd simply thought of him.

Gwynn hummed happily to herself.

"Lady Kinsley doesn't wish to marry," she said quietly.

Her friend's little song faded to a slow stop. "What?"

Before she lost the courage to say what needed to be said, she spoke. "She doesn't wish to marry, and . . . so the terms of the arrangement cannot be met. There will be no funds." Which meant there would be that continued impediment between Gwynn and Chance.

Silence.

Thick and heavy and palpable.

Gwynn's lips formed a little circle, and out slipped just one breathy utterance: "Oh." She sat on the vanity chair.

Temperance sank into the sliver of a seat left alongside her friend. "I'm so sorry." Those three words, however, didn't solve the divide that continued to exist between Gwynn and Chance. She bit hard on the inside of her cheek.

Gwynn glanced over. "I want to marry your brother and be close to him," the other woman murmured.

"I know," she whispered, her voice shattered. "I—"

"Hush." Her friend glared at her. "Let me finish. What I was *going* to say was that I want to marry your brother and be close to him . . . but I wouldn't have you sacrificing yourself for me." Gwynn hung her head. "It was wrong of me to ask you to."

"You asked nothing of me."

Gwynn shook her head. "I knew you chose to come to a place you didn't wish to be for me and Chance. I let you do that. And it was wrong."

Temperance cried softly, the tears falling freely. "Why are you taking this so well?"

Her friend dusted them back. "Because I love you. You are like a sister to me. We will figure this out." Gwynn folded an arm around her shoulders and drew her close. "All three of us."

Temperance buried her face in Gwynn's shoulder and wept.

Gwynn patted her and made a clucking sound. "Come. Enough of that. You've the dinner party, and I'd not have you go there with swollen eyes and splotchy cheeks."

"I-I suspect it is too late for that."

"Yes, probably."

A little laugh broke through Temperance's tears. Gwynn hugged her close, and she folded herself in the arms of a woman who'd been like a sister she'd never had.

"Now, where were we?" Humming once more, Gwynn popped up. "We just need several more pins," she said more to herself as she fetched the pins and set to work sliding them into place. Her eyes lit. "Have a look." Pulling Temperance by the hand, she guided her over to the vanity.

And Temperance stood there and simply stared at . . . the stranger before her.

"Oh, my goodness," she whispered. She evaluated her gown with the critical eye of a seamstress who'd designed countless gowns. She had designed and sewn evening dresses for several noblewomen who'd lived in or near Cotswold. The garments she'd created had been made of the highest-quality satins and silks, adorned with the best lace and beading.

Or so she'd thought.

With that stranger staring back, she realized just how wrong she'd been. She'd known nothing about luxuriant material or intricate designs.

"It is . . ." Gwynn's reverent tones trailed off.

"I know," she finished for her friend.

Gwynn stroked a finger along the Austrian crystal beading that dripped from Temperance's cap sleeves. "Look at this tailoring of the material." The other woman spoke with that same reverent awe as she stroked the glorious beading. "This detail," Gwynn whispered.

And while her friend went back to pinning Temperance's hair, Temperance dug deep, looking at what the other woman saw, searching for a shared excitement for what Gwynn spoke about . . . and came up empty. Working as a seamstress had never been a source of joy. No, she'd not even thought about what made her happy, or searching it out, until Dare had urged her to consider what dreams she carried.

And there was a . . . desolation that came from knowing that when she left, that was the future that awaited her. Not one with Dare.

Her heart clenched.

Humming to herself, Gwynn pinned several more curls into place. She made quick work of the remaining pins, hiding them in Temperance's hair. She took Temperance by the shoulders and brought her about to face her. "You belong there." She lightly squeezed her arms before smoothing the fabric.

"I didn't say anything."

"You were feeling unworthy." The other woman paused. "But never forget, you have every right to be here. You're married to a marquess, and that makes you a marchioness and of more lofty station than almost anyone else you'll meet tonight."

How simple Gwynn made it sound. That black-and-white way of thinking, however, didn't match with the strict social stratification that existed.

"Having a title and being accepted into their world are vastly different," she said, letting Gwynn shift her head so she could better reach the other curls.

"You don't need to be accepted there," her friend pointed out from around the pin she'd stuck between her teeth. "Not really. When you are ready . . . you are free to continue on your way."

When she was ready . . . So why did the idea of that future . . . leave her forlorn?

Come, you know why. It is him.

Dare had planted doubts and made her think about things she'd never before considered.

Regardless of whatever came between them, for everything he and they together had not gotten right, he'd been the only one who'd challenged her to look at life as though she should demand more of it for herself. And no matter what had passed between them, when she left and they parted, this time for good, she would miss him. She'd miss his challenging her and his valuing her as an equal.

Tears pricked her lashes.

Her friend stopped. "Again?" Gwynn murmured. "What is this?"

Temperance angrily swiped at those drops and shook her head.

"It is him." Worry filled the other woman's eyes.

"No, it's . . ." Temperance sank onto the vanity bench. "He's done . . . nothing, really. Not anything that he's not within his rights to do." She went on to explain his connection to Avery Bryant and Dare's decision to sell his family's belongings. And his latest trip to Newgate.

When she'd finished, Gwynn sank onto the edge of the bench. "You love him."

Still. I love him still. Temperance dropped her head onto the smooth lacquer surface of the vanity. "It makes no sense." He'd never live a straight-and-narrow path . . . And even if he did, she could still never be a true wife to him. She could never give him an heir or any child. Tears threatened all over again.

"Love doesn't make sense, Temperance," her friend murmured in the tones of one who knew. "If it did, I would have fallen in love with a local villager and not a mill worker all the way in London whom I rarely am able to see." Sighing, Gwynn stroked the small of her back. Pulled to the moment, Temperance stared at the final product wrought by her friend . . . and a stranger reflected back. Gwynn had looped and twisted two plaits about Temperance's head; they formed a coronet of sorts, framed by loose curls that hung about her shoulders and back.

"You shall be the most beautiful woman present," Gwynn murmured. "Now, off you go."

Temperance came to her feet and made the slow walk from her rooms to the main landing.

She would play this part she'd agreed to.

And then after? She would again leave. But she'd never be the same.

These past years, she'd only lied to herself in thinking she was all right without Dare in her life.

When she reached the top of the stairwell, she froze. Temperance's heart knocked wildly against her rib cage.

Long after she was gone from this place . . . and him, this was how she would see him in her mind . . . as he was now: attired in a flawless, midnight wool tailcoat with matching black trousers and boots. A cravat perfectly tied, and the longer-than-fashionable strands of his hair drawn neatly behind his ears.

Hands folded at his back, he paced, those movements precise and focused.

How could he not see that no matter what hell he'd known in the Rookeries, no matter the crimes he'd committed, he was and would always be a king amongst men.

As if he felt her presence there, Dare stopped and looked up.

She knew she'd have to face him again after her revelation and had braced for the stilted awkwardness or discomfort that would be between them.

In this instant, with his eyes on her, however, she was incapable of . . . anything . . .

She'd never given much thought to her appearance. Some women were gloriously beautiful, and others . . . not. She'd been quite content in the latter category. Nor had modesty made her objective. In the Rookeries, being pretty was more a bane, and as such, she'd been quite content to be plain and not the kind of woman to attract notice.

Or that had been the case. With Dare frozen, motionless, his jaw slack and his gaze locked on her, she could almost believe she was beautiful, after all. But then he'd always made her feel special. He'd always treated her as though she were something more than Abaddon Swift's daughter. And being seen by him, this man, had been an aphrodisiac, one that sent the same butterflies dancing in her belly now.

He was the first to break the spell.

Giving his head a shake, Dare bounded over and took several of the steps, meeting her on her descent.

She reached him.

"You are magnificent," he said quietly.

Her cheeks warmed under that praise. "Then it makes me perfectly suitable to be on your arm, Lord Milford." The breathless quality to that reply ruined her attempt at flippancy. He reached for her arm and then stopped.

"I have not thanked you. I'm alive . . . because of you."

"Then we've saved each other, Dare Grey," she said softly.

And as he held his arm out and she linked hers through it, she could also almost believe the game of make-believe they played at—husband and wife. Happy couple. Lord and lady.

He'd spoken to her of dreams, and yet that had really been the only one she'd carried in her heart—him. She would have happily lived in the streets of East London if it had been with him at her side.

They made the journey the length of a hall with a silence between them. As they walked, she ran her gaze over the portraits that hung there now . . .

Temperance slowed her steps.

Dare frowned and brought them to a stop. "What is it?" he asked. "Are you having reservations?"

Yes, she was, but she had been since the moment she'd cornered him in the Cotswolds' countryside and agreed to play companion to his sister. Incapable of words, she walked back several paces . . . and stopped before an ornate gold frame. The portrait within contained four figures: a serious-looking lord and lady, and an equally serious boy. The fourth and last person was a small babe in a long white gown, cradled close in the arms of the woman holding her. Transfixed, Temperance tipped her head. There was an afterthought quality to the way the mother held the child.

The only one with a smile . . . was the babe. Her adoring gaze lifted up to the figures looking out.

Dare's family . . .

Only . . .

Dare's family as it had come to be and existed after he was gone.

All these years, she'd resented him. She'd hated his ability and willingness to shut everyone—especially her—out. She'd not understood him . . . until now.

Now, seeing that portrait, it all made sense.

And for the first time, she looked at what he'd endured, and Temperance saw him . . . For the first time, she understood what had compelled Dare . . . and still did.

"You didn't sell it," she whispered, her voice hoarsened with tears. She looked back and found him there; his hands stuffed in the pockets of his trousers, he rocked on his heels.

When he didn't respond, Temperance looked the length of the hall; the paintings that had previously filled the Opal Parlor had been restored to their rightful places.

He cleared his throat. "I . . . no. I figured there were other things I could sell where I might leave that one." *For his sister.*

Temperance doubled back along the path they'd just traveled. Only . . . it wasn't, as he'd suggested, "just one." She passed painting after painting: of Lady Kinsley alone. Lady Kinsley with an older boy who had the look of Dare—their brother. "You didn't sell . . . any of them." She did a quick inventory of the hall. "There are . . . ten in this corridor alone." Temperance stole a glance over her shoulder to where he trailed after her at a more sedate pace.

"Twelve," he corrected automatically.

He'd always been a cataloger, meticulously counting and tracking all the belongings he pilfered and then sold off.

Except . . .

Temperance stopped at the end of the hall, and frowned as she noted one poignant detail. "But I saw people collecting items and carting them off. What of those?" she asked softly, drifting back to his side.

"What others?"

He knew, and yet he evaded her question. Temperance rested her hands along the front of his jacket and brushed her palms lightly over him. "The portraits that contained you and your family."

Dare grunted. "It made no sense to keep them," he said gruffly, not meeting her eyes.

Her heart ached. "You sold them." Those last links that placed him with the parents and brother he'd had, he'd dissolved.

"Spencer had buyers in mind. He helped me secure them. He was able to fetch a sum for the frame. It'll feed a number of families."

He'd figured out a way to squeeze money out of the household, while allowing Kinsley to retain the connections she had to those heirlooms. It was the first time Dare had held on to anything of value. And he'd done so . . . because of his sister. So much love for this man filled her.

He was not perfect. And yet he attempted to change.

She waited until he finally looked at her. "Your mother didn't stop loving you," she said softly.

His answer was instantaneous. "Either way, I was the child she was better off without. My father was right . . . and I knew it." He stared stonily at that first image she'd studied of the four. "When I came back, I saw them. I . . . One night? I was pickpocketing for Mac Diggory, and I sneaked off." He paused. "To be here. Even though my father had told me not to. I wanted to . . . see . . ."

She started. He'd returned even after his father had sent him away. Her heart twisted at the thought of that little boy trying so desperately to find his way back to his family.

Dare's eyes were locked on that forlorn-looking family of four, and as he spoke, his voice was distant, deadened. "I just walked and walked that night. Even though he said there was no one looking for me. I'd believed him . . . Except that night, I wondered if he was wrong. I found a window—one of the parlors. My mother was playing pianoforte, and my brother was waltzing a little girl . . . a stranger to me." Lady Kinsley. "My . . . sister," he made himself say. "About the empty parlor. They were smiling and laughing, and it was when I knew."

"What?" she asked quietly.

"That I'd been forgotten," he said so matter-of-factly. "Replaced with this new person. That night, I left and swore never to return, because I knew it was what was best . . . for all," he added.

And here she'd believed her heart could break no further where this man was concerned. Tears stung her lashes. "Oh, Dare," she whispered. Every sliver of her soul ached and hurt for the boy who'd stood outside, looking in. Filled with a restiveness, she worked her gaze over the corridor . . . halls he should have been running along throughout his boyhood, and then continued walking through as the rightful heir and marquess. How very close he'd been to escaping the hell of the Rookeries. If only he'd trusted that he'd been missed . . . loved. If only he'd trusted that a mother's love was a bond that could not be broken, even by death.

And once more, he made sense in ways he never had before. She understood him, this man who couldn't truly bring himself to commit to loving and had instead devoted himself to looking after everyone else the way he had needed someone to look after and care for him. He had become . . . what he'd needed. What if he'd stumbled upon every other memory his sister remembered of her heartbroken parents? How would his life . . . How would their lives all have been different?

Color suffused Dare's cheeks. "It is fine," he said, clasping his hands at his back, his gaze still on that family he'd lost.

But it wasn't. No matter the assurances he gave her or himself. He'd been indelibly shaped by those darkest days, and more . . . by what had happened when he'd returned—the father who'd rejected him.

And where his father had been evil, there had been a mother who had missed her son. Who had loved him. And she would have Dare know that.

"Your mother loved you, Dare."

"I know that," he said automatically. "I left when I was ten. Just as I knew my mother loved me was the same way I knew my father hated me . . . But she loved me as I'd been . . . not what I became."

He'd doubted she could love who he'd become . . .

God, how she despised what his father had done to him, the insecurity and doubt he'd placed in Dare's perception of self-worth. He made sense in every way now.

Temperance drifted closer. "You worried she could not separate what you did on the streets," she said, at last with an understanding of why he'd chosen to stay in the Rookeries. "Because your father made you believe that." Taking his hands, she squeezed them, forcing his eyes to her own. "What you did, Dare? You did it in the name of survival. Your parents would have understood that."

"My parents would have had a child who was an oddity, who'd committed horrible acts, scandalous ones that no nobleman could accept from his son."

He'd been so afraid to bring shame upon them, he'd not been able to see . . . His mother would have cared only that he'd returned. Temperance knew, however, to say as much would neither sway his mind nor undo the fate that he and his mother had suffered.

He brushed his knuckles under her chin, and she lifted her gaze up. "Come now, Temperance, you never understood my thievery. Now, you'd make excuses for my actions."

"That isn't true," she protested. "When you were a boy, and I a young girl . . . I understood, Dare. And then even when you were a young man? That made sense to me, too." She shook her head, that action dislodging his touch. "It is that you continued on which I couldn't understand. I saw that you had the ability to do more and be more. It doesn't mean I don't understand why you did what you did as a boy and then as a young man trying to survive." Temperance took his hands once more. "But that is behind you." Her eyes went to his bruised knuckles, and she frowned. "Wylie?"

"No. No." Coloring, Dare freed his hands and tucked them behind his back. "It . . . happened before. I . . . went out."

She stilled. "You went to find him that night," she whispered, knowing intuitively the reason for those bruises. "Did you—"

"I didn't kill him," he interrupted her. "I wanted to, and I should have done so . . . for you. But I proved weak—"

Temperance touched a gloved fingertip to his lips, and then leaning up, she kissed him. "I never wanted you to make decisions that went against your moral fiber. And certainly not for me, Dare. Thank you."

"You'd thank me for not killing him?"

"I'd thank you for doing that which was right."

At the end of the hall, Spencer appeared. They looked to the servant. "The duke and duchess wished for me to . . . inquire as to whether you would be joining your company," he called, his voice strained.

"They're waiting," Temperance said regretfully, sinking back onto her heels.

Dare caught her knuckles and raised them to his lips. "And I'm content to keep them waiting."

Temperance smiled, her heart fluttering as he brushed his mouth over the top of her hand; the delicate silk did little to mute the feel of that kiss. "I know that."

He held his arm out, and she made to slip hers through his, but stopped.

Dare stared at her questioningly.

"She loved you," she said softly. She needed to say that. As a mother who'd loved desperately and lost, she needed Dare to know that. "Whatever evil your father was capable of, your mother loved you. She loved her daughter, your sister, Kinsley, just as she loved the son still with them, but that didn't mean she ever stopped loving you. It didn't mean *she* forgot you."

Such raw emotion twisted his features that her chest went tight all over again. "You can't know that," he said hoarsely.

"I can." She knew better than he ever could understand. That knowledge came from a place of different—but also great—loss. "I only held her a handful of minutes, Dare . . ." Tears welled, and she fought them. "A mother never forgets her child. Ever." The memory of that little girl would remain with her until she drew her last breath. Her heart shuddered and her soul ached with the memory, and she briefly closed her eyes.

When she opened them, she found Dare's agony-filled eyes upon her. Cupping her about the nape, he drew Temperance closer and pressed his brow to hers.

She remained that way, taking the support he'd offered, and for the first time since that tragic night, she wished she'd let him in on their loss . . . because there was a completeness to their grief, one that erased the sense of aloneness.

Dare held her that way, allowing her full control of how much support she wanted and needed. Yet again, he gave no indication that he cared about the roomful of powerful guests no doubt awaiting him—them.

Reluctantly, she drew back.

Still, he lingered . . . His eyes drifted over to the portrait of his parents and siblings.

She waited in silence, allowing him the time he needed to look on at the family—his family—as it had existed without him as part of it.

He turned to her. "I am ready."

And as she slipped her arm through his, this time it felt like . . . mayhap he was ready to face and live his future, after all.

Chapter 23

Since the moment Dare had set foot inside his familial townhouse, he'd thought of nothing but the day he'd eventually leave. He'd craved that moment. Hungered for it with a ferocious intensity.

Only to at last have a sense of . . . peace in being here.

The duke, seated at Dare's left, leaned over. "Your grandmother insisted I speak with you."

"About?" Dare asked, picking up his goblet and taking a drink.

"Propriety. More specifically, etiquette. You were late for your own dinner party, Darius. It is bad form. Now"—the duke leaned in closer and continued speaking in a quiet voice that Dare strained to hear—"I understand it has been a very long time since you followed that . . . etiquette. It will take some getting used to." His grandfather discreetly patted the top of Dare's spare hand.

Once Dare would have taunted the older man for the lesson he doled out. Now, he looked back . . . at himself and how he'd responded to their efforts. How smug and condescending . . . when they were all at sea, as much as Dare had been, with his return.

His family, whose only intent had been to see Dare reintegrated with society.

Nay, not just society—his family. His eyes drifted across the length of the table to where his sister sat, fiddling with her fork and staring at her plate. If it had been about reclaiming his place amongst the *ton*, the arrangement the duke and duchess had held him to wouldn't have had anything to do with Kinsley, or with Dare becoming a brother to her.

"I'm sorry . . . Grandfather," Dare said quietly.

The duke started and cupped a hand about his ear. "Come again?"

"I said I am sorry . . . Grandfather." For so much. For having rejected every attempt the duke had made to be close to him. For having made every aspect of his return to Polite Society . . . so difficult. Dare tried to get the words out, but the duke again patted his hand.

"Fine." Tears misted the older man's eyes. "It is fine, my boy."

My boy.

And in this . . . there was an absolution of sorts.

How very long Dare had been fighting that connection. Fighting *any* bond. It had been just one more thing Temperance had made him open his eyes to. He'd gone out of his way to destroy everything, this relationship included. Had it not been for Temperance, he would have never seen as much.

From where he sat, Dare watched Temperance several chairs away, seated between Kinsley and the duchess. Graceful and elegant, she was a queen amongst mere mortals. She, who'd lived a life of strife and come out on the other side of evil to triumph—and without anyone to save her. Even as he'd wished to be there for her.

She was more woman than he'd ever deserved, and he was a selfish bastard, because he wanted her anyway.

"I want your twenty thousand pounds," Dare said quietly, and his grandfather froze with his fork halfway to his mouth. He was not, however, willing to sell his soul for it. "I've had time to think on it."

"And?"

"And I'm not willing to require Kinsley to marry."

"That is . . . honorable of you," his grandfather murmured, and picking up his monocle, he studied Dare through that round glass. Did he think to search out his intentions? Different motives? "There is, of course, the—"

"Nor will I fulfill the other terms of your arrangement." There'd be no child with Temperance. The pain of that was raw, still . . . and perhaps would always be so. Every corner of his heart ached. Even if she had been capable of carrying a child, however, he'd still not ask or require that of her. "I'll not have my wife be expected to give me a child. She is no broodmare." It was why he'd never really allowed himself to consider that as a real means to the funds.

The duke frowned. "This isn't the place. We can talk on it—"

"There is nothing more to talk about," he said quietly. "We are at an impasse. I cannot"—*nay*—"I will not give you either of what you seek."

He braced for the pressing weight of panic at losing those monies. Funds enough to see so many people in the Rookeries cared for. And yet . . . this time, it did not come. There were other ways. He was not immune to the fact that men born of privilege had greater opportunities available to them. It was wrong. It was unfair. And yet Dare could and would use that for good. Eventually. In time.

"What will you do?" The duke's query emerged, hesitant.

His grandfather held the same fears that Temperance did. And why should he not? Dare had shown no real commitment then, or up until now, to divorce himself of a life of crime and devote himself to an honorable way. "I don't know," he confessed. He briefly studied the silver fork dangling forgotten from his fingers, a piece so fine it could have filled many empty bellies. He slowly set the piece down. "But when I was ten, I chose a life of stealing."

The duke's features contorted, but he made no attempt to silence Dare. As he would have expected any lord would. Particularly with them both within earshot of any number of plummy guests. Instead, the duke angled closer, gripping the edge of the table, as he hung on to Dare's every word.

"At first, it was all good fun. Easy. I was playing in those streets I'd never before visited, let alone knew existed . . ." Then the man had led him along, giving Dare a false sense of security, and ease had left, and

Dare had been forced to confront the real Rookeries. The horror and fear of those earliest days would be with him always. "I knew nothing about East London. Or how to steal or beg, or how to survive." And until Avery Bryant had come along, Dare had paid the price for that ignorance. Mayhap that was what had accounted for his loyalty to one who'd been so singularly bad for him. "I made something out of my time there. No one would dare dispute that the path I lived was a dishonorable one," he allowed. "But I made a future, and I'll do that now." This time, however, the means would not need to be justified by the ends.

And with Temperance at his side, there was no doubting, whatever they had or did not have, there would be happiness.

Now came the matter of convincing her she should trust him again and let him back into her life in every way he truly wished.

❦

He was in his element.

For the better part of the meal, he'd conversed intently with his grandfather. The two of them had spoken long . . . and often. And there was none of the usual coldness in Dare's gaze or smile when he did so with the duke.

Had Temperance not been watching them as closely as she had, she'd have missed the way the duke patted Dare's hand . . . and more, how Dare did not pull away and reject that display of affection.

Emotion wadded in her throat.

He was . . . finding his way here.

Nay, more than that.

He was thriving.

After he and his grandfather seemed to conclude their discourse, Dare went on to speak freely to the guests around him.

This was Dare. Fearless. Charming. Captivating.

In short, he was the very man she'd fallen in love with long ago.

And his perfection highlighted every way in which she was an outsider here.

The long table was resplendent with silver platters and forks and porcelain plates. So very many forks. And he knew precisely the one to use.

And he'd also gathered that she didn't. But he protected her pride still. With every dish, he motioned ever so slightly to the correct utensil for her to use for the given fare.

She loved him for that, too.

She always would.

Temperance proved selfish, for even while she should only celebrate Dare and his achievements that night, never more had her own flaws and station been more on display than they were with him and the other perfect people around them.

And more, to the woman seated beside him—Lady Madelyn. The daughter of an earl, the young lady was not only born to a rank and station that matched Dare's but was also as flawless in every way.

"They are striking, are they not?"

Temperance stilled, and it took a moment to realize those words in her head had actually been voiced aloud . . . by another.

She looked over to her table partner.

Dare's grandmother sipped from her crystal goblet, and over the top of that thin, etched rim, she nodded ever so slightly to the pair in question.

Unbidden, Temperance looked once more.

"She was just a babe when the papers were drawn, but she was always lovely, and he . . . Well, he was always perfection, too." Even if he did live in the Rookeries.

The duchess may as well have given her thoughts voice.

To give her hands something to do, Temperance fiddled with her napkin. Perhaps if she didn't engage, the other woman would stop.

"They were meant to marry."

Alas, the duchess was of single-minded intent . . . She'd a point to make, and Temperance wasn't of the same station as the woman seated beside her, but she knew enough that the duchess wouldn't be silent until she said her piece—contributions or not from Temperance.

"I am . . . aware of that." And had they done so, the perfect young lady would have given him those children with whom he was so very good. The image of that, of what Temperance could never give him and the other woman could, had it not been for her inconvenient presence . . . It was too much . . .

Temperance made herself pop a piece of shrimp into her mouth; it sat, dull and tasteless, about her tongue.

The duchess, however, wasn't done with her. "It is not that I do not like you, Temperance. I do. Very much so."

Her Grace, however, had no reason to lie to her. As such, that revelation proved the greatest of surprises.

"It is merely that Dare and Lady Madelyn? They are so well suited—in personality and companionship . . . and their shared history."

Their birthright: one of privilege and prestige that Temperance would never, ever share a bond over. Her heart turned in her chest.

The duchess was not through twisting the knife, however. "You're also aware that she would have greatly suited him. Her dowry would bring wealth that would further advance Dare's hopes for the people in East London." Sadness wreathed the duchess's words, and that was somehow even worse than the bitterness or anger that had met Temperance at their previous encounters.

For the duchess was correct. The young lady would have greatly suited Dare in every way, and in every way that Temperance could not . . . and never would.

Had the duchess been hate-filled, it would have been easier to resent her, and yet . . . she wasn't. She was simply a grandmother who yearned for what was best for her grandson. She was a woman who wanted Dare to have the life he should, and would, have lived had it not been for that one act of evil committed by Mac Diggory and his henchmen.

"I take it you knew Lady Kinsley would never marry." All the while she kept her gaze on Dare and his former betrothed.

It was why the woman had resented Temperance at every turn. Because she'd seen her as the wife Dare would be stuck with in order to fulfill the terms they'd put to him.

"Yes, we suspected as much. However, it was less about seeing her wed as much as it was about ensuring that someone who was not her horrible cousin was there to ensure her well-being," the duchess confessed. She dabbed her white napkin at the corners of her lips. "It was my husband's hope that there would be more than that. My husband was . . . is of the hope that a child will keep Dare here."

And the duchess, Dare's grandmother, had begun to see a future in which Temperance both remained and provided Dare with the heir and babe to link him to Polite Society.

All the while, she didn't know, could never guess, that was the one thing Temperance could no longer provide.

Pain slashed across her heart as understanding slid in . . . crawling forward with an infinite slowness and then rushing in, all at once: *the funds can never be his*.

Suddenly, the food she had managed to eat that night churned in her stomach, threatening to come up.

"I'm certain you are an absolutely . . . fine . . . young woman, Temperance," the duchess said through that tumult. "My granddaughter, she likes you very much. You are one who showed, in coming to His Grace and me for assistance, that you genuinely care for, mayhap even love, him." *I love him*. She always had. "But Darius? He is of a different world. Now, if there were grounds for annulment?" She pierced Temperance with a gaze, one that Temperance was certain could see inside to the places where secrets were kept. Her Grace sighed. "Think on it, dear . . ." She patted Temperance's hand.

Think on it?

Just like that, as casually as if she'd remarked upon the weather and not a dissolution of Temperance's marriage, the duchess turned and spoke to the guest at her other side—Lady Madelyn's father. The man who should be Dare's father-in-law, and not the likes of Abaddon, drunkard, wife beater.

Numb, Temperance reached for her glass of claret and took a sip. The slightly sickeningly sweet beverage slicked a path down her throat. The rub of it was . . . she couldn't even be resentful, because the duchess was well within her rights to everything she was feeling. What would the noblewoman say if she learned Temperance and Dare had only even agreed to a temporary partnership? Nay, their marriage was one that even if they both wished it . . . couldn't be. She couldn't give him an heir . . . or any child. A wave of grief assailed her, and she wanted to slink under the table and lose herself in the weight of that misery.

Instead, she did the next worst thing.

She looked over at Dare and his flawless dining partner; possessed of gloriously golden curls, a gently rounded frame, and pale-white skin, she was . . . a model of English beauty. The counter opposite of Temperance with her black hair and olive-hued skin and coltish frame.

The young lady said something that earned a laugh.

And jealousy sluiced through Temperance. She took another, this time longer, swallow.

Kinsley leaned in. "Do not listen to her."

Had she heard what her grandmother said?

"I didn't hear, but I could imagine because I know how she is. She wishes for Darius to marry Lady Madelyn. But he's married to you. And she'll accept that in time."

No, the duchess wouldn't. Not when Temperance couldn't be that which Dare needed.

"And do you know why?"

Devoid of energy and numb of emotion, Temperance shook her head.

"Because my grandparents will see what I saw."

"What is that?" she managed to make herself ask. All the while, Temperance wanted to slink from the dining room and continue walking until she found a safe, quiet place removed from the world, and crumple under the emotion that threatened to drown her here before the *ton*.

"They will see that you are good for him. They will see that you have changed him."

Changed him.

"I didn't change him," Temperance said softly, her gaze drawn once more to where he sat speaking to Lord Sinclair, several seats away. Whatever he'd said had brought the handsome, faintly greying gentleman to laughter, that mirth contagious for the other guests around them. "He never really needed changing in the ways that mattered," she murmured for the benefit of the other girl, as much as for herself. "Not inside, not who he really was." He'd simply needed to learn and know that he needn't follow a criminal path to do the good he sought.

Even so, she didn't know if he could ever truly set that life behind him.

"No, he has changed," Kinsley insisted. "When we first met, he taunted me. He went out of his way to do so. Not anymore. And . . ." The column of the young woman's throat moved several times. "He didn't sell them. Not all of them. None of the portraits of my family and I." Kinsley caught her lower lip between her teeth. "And that is because of you, Temperance."

The guest on Kinsley's other side called her attention over, and Temperance was left alone once more. Sitting back, a forgotten participant in the evening's festivities, Temperance was afforded a glimpse of this newly evolved world . . . and how it would be for Dare. There was a family who loved him and saw his good. There was the chance to earn twenty thousand pounds, through marriage to a lady who'd equally charmed Dare's end of the table.

He'd very nearly found his way and, after only a very short time, returned to Polite Society. He would emerge even more triumphant than he had as a thief in the Rookeries.

And sitting there, Temperance knew there was only one thing left to do.

Say goodbye.

Chapter 24

The night . . . had been a success. The guests had been warm in their welcome of him and Temperance to their folds. It had been a wholly unexpected response from members of the peerage, which was no doubt in large part a product of whom the duke and duchess had chosen to enlist support from.

And yet for the triumph the night had in fact been, through it he'd been singularly aware of Temperance—somber. Unsmiling. A shadow of who she'd always been . . . even in the face of every horror she'd suffered at her father's hands.

The moment the house was empty and quiet, he set out in search of her. Expecting to find her where he invariably did every night—in the nursery.

Only this time, she didn't sit beside little Rose's crib.

Dare found her in the Opal Parlor . . . that room that had been eternally a source of conflict between them. Standing at the window with her back to him, she gave no indication that she'd heard his arrival.

Unnoticed, he used the moment to observe her. She'd not removed her evening gown, the silk clinging to the wide curve of her hips and the generous swell of her buttocks, making her already narrow waist impossibly smaller.

"The night was a success," she said quietly, shattering the illusion that he'd been the only one aware of the other's presence.

"Yes."

Pushing the door closed behind him, Dare joined her at the window.

There'd always been an ease to their silence. They'd never been a couple who'd needed to fill voids of silence. They'd been as comfortable with nothing more than the quiet of being with one another as they had jesting or teasing or talking about anything and everything.

Something in this, however, felt . . . *different*. Unease whispered up and down his spine.

"I spoke to my grandfather," he said, wanting to get to the heart of it.

At last she faced him. "I saw you conversing." Her eyes moved a tender path over his face. "I am so happy that you and he have found a way to be a family."

A family.

Only there was just a partial peace with his grandparents. Temperance, a life with her, represented all he sought in a family.

"I explained that I'll not sell my sister to marriage, not even for his fortune."

A smile formed on her lips, and she smoothed her palms down the front of his chest, that wifely gesture the more automatic and beautiful for it.

"I didn't do that because of me," he said, mourning the loss of that tender caress as she let her arms fall to her sides. "Nor do I believe I was truly capable of seeing how ruthless I was in my approach to my . . . family." It was still foreign, thinking of Kinsley and his grandparents in those terms. Mayhap it always would be. He did see now that he couldn't have a relationship with them . . . unless he tried. "I did it because of you."

She made a sound of protest. "You're wrong. You would have eventually come to see Kinsley. It might have just taken you a bit longer."

She didn't give herself enough credit for all the ways in which she'd changed him . . . for the better.

"And . . . did you speak to your grandfather about his other terms for you?" She briefly dropped her gaze. "Did you tell him we could not have a child?"

"No." He saw the way her body tensed, and yearned to take her in his arms. "I didn't tell him, Temperance, because that was never his business . . . or anyone else's. I was *never* going to ask you or make you a broodmare for some arrangement. I wouldn't whore you or myself."

"And definitely not now . . . knowing what you know." She turned, angling her body and shutting him out. Her features, reflected in the window, were a mask, and terrifying for their absolute blankness.

Panic rooted around his chest. She was shutting him out. Pulling away. And he'd be damned if he let her. Dare tried again. "I told him that we wouldn't answer to anyone about the topic of babes, because it did not matter. Because it doesn't, Temperance." He paused. "*You* matter. Having a life with you matters."

Her back tensed.

Dare drifted closer and lightly touched her shoulder, bringing her about to look at him. "I'm telling you, the funds? They do not matter." He moved his gaze over every cherished plane of her face, willing her to see that truth. She was the only thing that did matter, a future with her.

"You don't mean that," she countered. There was a slightly elevated edge to her voice, one that urged caution and told him the wrong word uttered would be a costly one. "You know the good you can do with that money. You've been plotting and planning all the ways to use it. You don't just abandon that. Not you." She drew in a breath, and when she spoke, she'd reclaimed her earlier composure. "So do not pretend like they don't, Dare."

That had been before.

Before he'd let himself to a vision of a future. Before he'd allowed himself to see that maybe he was worthy of one, after all.

He forced himself to speak with a calm he didn't feel. "You are right. That money could be used for good." Her gaze flickered away from his. "But there *can* and *will* be other ways for me to secure those funds." Her eyes darkened. "Honorable ways," he hurried to correct. "Ones that don't require me to steal anymore. I'm done with that way of life, Temperance."

He wanted a new start, a life with an intent and actions that were *both* honorable.

And for a moment, he believed he'd penetrated her reservations. The hope and happiness in her revealing eyes proved fleeting. "I wasn't enough before, Dare," she said softly, "and I've even less to offer you." *Now that there couldn't be a babe.*

His heart knocked uncomfortably against his rib cage. *I am losing her.* Because he'd never shown her that she was more important to him than even the role of savior he'd taken on. He closed his eyes. He'd charmed his way out of prison, any number of hangings. He'd had the words to navigate the complexities amongst men battling for supremacy in the streets of East London.

But God help him . . . he didn't have the words to keep her.

"I don't want anything from you. I just . . . want *you*," he said hoarsely.

A single tear slid down her cheek, winding a meandering trail, and somehow the solitariness of that lone drop proved more devastating for the finality of it. "The money will always be between us—"

"To hell with the money, Temperance." The avowal exploded from Dare, but she continued over that interruption.

"The money that you won't have, married to a barren wife. And you'll regret not having that money, and you'll resent that I couldn't give it to you." She brought her shoulders back. "I cannot be a real wife to you."

"I do not care that we cannot have children."

Sadness glimmered in her eyes. "I've seen you with Rose. I know that is a lie."

Dare ran a hand over his face. "You're right." She jerked, and it was all he could do to not take her in his arms and hold her tight forever. "I wanted children. But I wanted them with you. I wanted girls with your spirit and boys with your wit and strength."

Tears slid down her cheeks, and with shaky hands, he brushed those drops back. But they continued coming. And he'd been wrong before—this endless stream of grief was lash after lash upon his soul. "But, Temperance, I did not, and I do not, want those children more than I want you," he implored, willing her to see. "*We* can be a family. You and I. And if you desire it, we can have children other ways, and they will still have your spirit and strength because *you* raised them."

She dropped her eyes to his cravat. "Not in the ways that will make them your legitimate heirs." And there was such a quiet acceptance of that, he spun away from her.

"To hell with the marquessate," he cried, his voice echoing in the stillness of the room. "To hell with it," he repeated.

"You don't mean that. People rely upon you as the marquess. You know that . . . and you wouldn't ever abandon them." Temperance drew in an agonizingly shaky breath. "I cannot stay, Dare."

She couldn't stay with him? Why didn't she say that which she truly meant?

Panic and desperation swirled, and he took a step away from her, pacing, and then made himself stop. He faced her and leveled his gaze on her. "Is this what you want?" How was he so calm? How, when he was falling apart inside? "To leave me?"

Please don't let it be what you want.

She bit down on her lower lip. "This is what we both want," she whispered.

"No," he said sharply. "You don't get to do that. You don't get to speak for me and tell me what I want or need."

She held his gaze. "I don't want to be with you, Dare."

His heart lurched, and he frantically searched his gaze over her face, looking for the lie. Needing to find it. "I don't believe you."

"I sent you away before," she pointed out, that snapped utterance striking like a spike to the chest.

And she'd had every right to send him away. He'd failed her. He'd failed at their marriage. Whatever his motives, he'd put thievery ahead of her . . . all the while knowing precisely how she felt about the *work* he did.

He'd lost the right to her love and a real union.

And he proved a selfish bastard still because he wanted her anyway. "We're married, Temperance, and that doesn't just . . . *sto-op.*" Desperation lent an extra syllable to that word. "I want to fight for us and—"

"There are grounds for a dissolution of our marriage."

He stared blankly at her. Surely she was not saying . . .

"I'm barren," she said, misunderstanding the reason for his silence.

He rocked on his heels, the earth moving out from under him. She'd thought . . . all this through.

"I spoke to your grandmother," she said softly, as if in confirmation of his unspoken thoughts. Temperance glanced briefly down at the floor. "After the dinner party, we talked in private."

"She had no right to that, Temperance," he hissed. "None at all." That most intimate detail about Temperance's past and her inability to conceive was information she needn't ever explain to anyone, and certainly not the damned duchess.

"I wanted her to know it, Dare." Temperance looked him squarely in the eyes. "Because knowing would allow her to help us see the marriage dissolved so that you can . . . begin again."

"I don't want anyone else," he cried, desperation breaking down the little self-restraint and control he had of himself in this moment. "I only want *you.*"

"And as you said to me before, you don't get to decide that for the both of us, Dare." She smoothed steady palms down the front of her gown, that glorious piece that he'd forever see her descending the stairs in. "This is what I want."

And with that calm, quiet utterance, she exited quietly from the room, and took his heart with her.

Chapter 25

One week later
Mayfair
London, England

In the following days, Dare oversaw his estate business. He met with his man-of-affairs and solicitors and spent hours upon hours learning the ins and outs of his properties. He learned what the previous marquess had done to bankrupt them, and he also discovered the path of solvency the properties had been on, long before some dissolute, distant relative had inherited.

Dare's father had never done anything to modernize the title. Dare's brother, however, had. He'd ventured into the *scandalous* world of trade and attempted to bring changes to properties that had been within the Greyson family for the hundreds of years before. And now Dare had stepped in where his brother had left off.

Between his new work and the lack of thievery, his life had become what he'd never expected—mundane.

Oh, he'd be lying to himself if he said stealing didn't still call to him. It did. That hungering to slip inside and steal would always be with him.

Not because of the items and wealth to be had, but rather because of the feeling it had brought him.

An urge that he couldn't and never would understand that was sated by stealing.

Perhaps it was the familiarity of it. Perhaps it was the hungering for some manner of control in a life in which he was largely without.

Joseph, since being freed, had returned and claimed Rose, and with that so, too, had gone another connection to Temperance.

He missed his wife. God, how he missed her. Even full as his days were with his business and saving lives, still not a day passed where Dare did not think of her. Where he did not miss their battle of wits. Or her smile. Or her laugh. Or just everything about her.

Seated across from Dare, Spencer looked up, a question in his eyes.

Dare gave his head a shake. "Forgive me," he said, motioning for the young servant to continue.

"As I was saying," his servant went on, "I've gone ahead and cataloged those items which were purchased by that man." *That man*, Dare had come to learn, was how his butler had taken to referring to the previous Marquess of Milford—the one who'd held the title between Dare and his late brother. "These are all free to be sold with no worry of emotional entanglements." He turned the book around for Dare to look over.

Dare passed his gaze over the meticulous columns. "If you weren't such a damned good butler, I'd say you'd be better served as my man-of-affairs."

"Thank you, my lord. I've also taken notes on items which do . . . or might . . . hold sentimental value for their connections to your late brother and parents, but were purchased . . . after . . . after . . ." The other man let his words trail off.

"I left to live in the Rookeries," Dare finished for him. "It is what happened." And though there would forever be a crushing weight of sadness and loss that had come of that dark decision, neither could

Dare bring himself to regret it . . . because then there never would have been Temperance.

"Very well, then, my lord. I marked the items prior to your leaving, and then those objects that came after."

Dare collected the heavy leather tome and proceeded to flip through the pages. Not an item or artifact had been left off the other man's impressive notes. Everything had been meticulously cataloged. "I don't deserve you, Spencer," he said with all sincerity.

Color filled the servant's cheeks. "We were once friends, my lord."

Friends?

He stilled.

My father served in His and Her Grace's country estate in Yorkshire . . . I've only recently been brought to your London townhouse. The idea was that I would offer some . . . familiarity to you.

"Holy hell. *Spenceeer?*" he whispered. The son of his family's head butler in Leeds, Spencer had been a playmate and friend to both Dare and his brother.

The other man bowed his head. "My lord."

"I didn't . . . I . . ." Words failed.

Spencer cleared his throat. "A great deal of time passed. We were boys, and I go by my family name now, and as such, I wouldn't expect you to remember me."

But . . . Dare had. He'd spent his life burying memories deep down in an attempt to forget everyone. It had been altogether easier to forget them than think that they'd forgotten him. It had been just one more thing Temperance had helped him see.

That was why Spencer had been devoted when Dare hadn't deserved it. And why he'd been committed to helping Dare and saving the Milford estate.

The office door opened, and Kinsley swept in. "Dare. Spencer," she greeted as the servant jumped to his feet and bowed.

"My lady."

"If you'll excuse us, Spencer?" Dare requested.

"Of course." The other man proceeded to gather up his things.

It was the first time since he'd returned to his family's fold that Kinsley had sought him out . . . about anything. Upon Temperance's departure, Kinsley had settled into her days looking after Rose . . . until the child had gone.

"You wished to speak with me?" he began when Spencer showed himself out.

"About your wife. You should go to her," Kinsley said without preamble.

He blinked wildly. "I beg your pardon?"

"Don't beg mine. Beg hers." Kinsley plopped onto one of the wing chairs. "I trust Grandmother is responsible for Temperance feeling as though she had to leave. Grandmother means well, but she has never been one to truly understand matters of the heart."

His sister spoke as one who knew. And it reminded him of all the ways in which she was still a stranger . . .

"Well?" Kinsley lifted an eyebrow. "I expect you have something to say."

"Temperance . . . chose, and she didn't choose me." There were no more humbling words he'd ever admit, ones that had ensured he'd remain forever broken. Dare glanced down at the official-looking pair of envelopes that had been resting at the corner of his desk for the past three days. "I . . . would respect what she wants." He'd only ever taken where she was concerned, committing an emotional theft greater than any other robbery he'd ever carried out.

"She loves you," Kinsley said simply. There was a brief pause. "Though I'll admit that it's not entirely altruistic, sisterly devotion on my part." Sadness paraded across the young lady's face. "I . . . miss her very much."

"I miss her as well," he said gruffly. It was the first real, meaningful admission he'd ever brought himself to make to his sister.

Kinsley glanced down at the envelopes. "You are not done with her. Not just yet."

No. But . . . soon. He couldn't, however, bring himself to make that admission, not because of Kinsley but rather for what it would do to him emotionally. In the end, another knock came, saving him from answering.

Spencer entered with Avery close at his heels. "Mr. Bryant to see you," he said coolly.

Bryant . . . the only guest whom the always unflappable butler had never bothered to feign a politeness for or over.

All Dare's senses went on alert. The visit was long overdue, but not unexpected. He'd been anticipating it. "Kinsley, if you'll excuse me?" he said for a second time that afternoon, trading one guest for another yet again.

Kinsley climbed to her feet.

"What, no introductions?" Avery drawled with his usual dry humor.

Kinsley blushed, and it was the blush . . . the hint of danger, and the sign that he'd be wise to keep his sister far away from the likes of Avery Bryant.

His partner stepped aside as Kinsley passed by him.

"You've become a protective brother in your old age. Never thought I'd see that," Avery said with a laugh. Crossing over, his longtime partner availed himself of the same seat Kinsley had just vacated. "I've already paid visits to Moray, Wentnick, and Ashcroft." His partner withdrew a heavy packet from inside the front of his jacket and set it down at the corner of Dare's desk . . . directly beside the envelopes. "Made out quite well, I did," the other man said. "I secured nearly two thousand pounds from Moray's flatware alone."

Dare steepled his fingers together and stared over at his partner, the man he'd known since he was eleven . . . the same one who, just three years older than Dare, had shown him everything he knew.

Who'd revealed every secret and helped Dare build the future and career he had.

"As I understand it, Bolingbroke should be vacating his London townhouse," the other man was saying. "He and his wife are expecting another child."

"What do you intend to do?" Dare asked, watching his partner closely.

"What I always do." Avery shrugged. "Or perhaps I should say what 'we' always do." He looked briefly in Dare's direction. "Of course, I'm happy to cede the assignment to you. I've never been greedy where you were concerned."

No . . . Avery hadn't. It was why Dare had remained partners with him longer than any thief in the Rookeries worked with another.

"And given the bastard's crimes and the . . . personal connection, it would be only right to leave the honors to you."

Dare simply stared at him for a long while, watching as Avery picked up the packet, opened it, and went on to silently read contents he no doubt had already memorized.

"Why did you do it?" Dare asked quietly.

The other man stopped reading and looked up. "I already told you, because of the fact you were—"

"Was it the money? The desire for power?"

Avery stilled. The other man glanced briefly down before meeting Dare's focus once more. "I don't know what you're talking about," he said carefully, setting the packet down.

It was Avery Bryant's only tell. That half-of-a-second look away, so quick that if one blinked one would miss it, and also, one Dare knew because of how damned close he'd been to the thief.

"You bastard," Dare seethed. "You betrayed me, connected yourself with Diggory's remaining thugs, struck a deal with Wylie . . . all to see me hang. Why?" he whispered. *"Whyy?"*

"You don't know what you're talking about," Avery snapped. He reached for his packet, and Dare caught the folded sheets, beating the other man to it. His former partner glared. "I took you in and taught you everything I knew, and allowed you to become what you did, and this is how you repay me?"

"Is that why?" Dare asked quietly. "Because I surpassed you, and you finally saw a way to reclaim the power you'd been without for so long?" Now it made so much sense. The other man's attempts at getting Dare to settle into his life hadn't been the encouraging words of a friend. They'd been the greedy attempts of a man protecting his territory. "Tell me you didn't work with Swift. Tell me."

Avery flattened his mouth into a tight line.

Oh, God. The bottom fell out of his stomach, as he had confirmation of everything he'd only just suspected. "You did."

"Abaddon Swift controls the streets Mac Diggory once did. It was nothing more than a business decision, Dare."

Nothing more . . . than a business decision.

He'd partner with the man responsible for killing Dare and Temperance's baby . . . who'd beaten Temperance endlessly as a young girl. A curtain of black rage fell across his vision, momentarily blinding. "Get the hell out," Dare said when he trusted himself to speak. Avery had kept him alive when by all rights he should have been dead, and that was the only reason Dare let him live now. "Abaddon's already been rounded up by the law and will be serving his time far away. Unless you care to join him, I suggest you get yourself from my sight and never come near me or mine again."

The color slipped from his former partner's scarred cheeks. "You would just . . . end our friendship."

"We were never friends," Dare said. "We were partners. I've had only one friend, and it wasn't you."

Stiffly, Avery rose. "I've always done what I needed to do in the name of survival. You should not only know that already but also understand it."

"I'll never understand you or any of the decisions you've made." And he'd certainly never forgive them. He tossed the packet at the other man, and it hit Avery square in the chest.

His former partner caught those pages and looked down. "How did you . . . ?"

"Figure out it was you?" he supplied. "The clues were always there that you were poison to me; I was just too blind to see it." And he wouldn't have, had it not been for Temperance opening his eyes to it.

Shoulders slightly slumped, the other man started for the door.

"Avery?" Dare called, and his former partner wheeled about. "It was a trap, wasn't it? Bolingbroke?"

For a long while he thought Avery wouldn't comment or respond, but then he nodded ever so slightly.

"You were pushing it too hard," Dare explained, answering the unspoken question. "Get out," he said quietly . . . and the other man, his partner in crime, left.

There should be bitterness and pain and hurt that came from that betrayal. And yet, he felt nothing where Avery Bryant was concerned. There had only ever really been one person whom Dare had trusted. One person whom he'd wanted in his life. And yet, he'd been so very afraid of having her there.

No, it was as he'd said to the other man: only one person had ever mattered, and now Dare had just one thing left to do—give her everything she wanted.

Chapter 26

Temperance's fingers ached.

And her back and her neck. Those, along with parts of her arms she didn't even know the names for.

In her short time in London, she'd somehow forgotten the degree of toil and strife that came with a seamstress's job.

No, it was just that she'd *let* herself forget those miseries.

But then perhaps this was to be her penance for having failed Gwynn. For having dragged the other woman all the way to London, bringing her so very close to the grandest hope she carried in her heart, only to then dash it with the truth of Temperance's own selfishness. Either way, her friend had said nothing about their having to return and beg for their work back.

Even as they'd not been replaced. Even as there were no finer seamstresses in the Cotswolds.

Gwynn, who'd been more loyal than Temperance deserved, and who'd been only understanding that the hopes she'd carried for them to be their own women had died with Temperance's decision.

Except, was it really disloyal? The terms the duke and duchess had presented Dare had ultimately taken the decision away from Temperance . . . even if she'd wanted to give him a babe.

And I wanted that . . . I wanted that so very much. To be a mother to the very manner of child Dare had envisioned for them, strong and witty and spirited. And the pain of that would never, ever go away. Not just to have that child . . . but to have her or him with Dare.

Dare, who had cradled little Rose and—

"Hullooo . . . Miss *Swiiiift*, I'm looking for more of that pretty pink fabric."

No, she'd been wrong. This was to be her penance.

"Yes, Mrs. Marmlebury," she said, hurrying to fetch the garish satin in question.

Her friend caught her gaze across the shop.

"Pink?" Gwynn mouthed, and then from behind the old widow's back, she pulled a face as if retching, and Temperance managed that which she'd never thought to accomplish again—she laughed.

A slew of horrified stares went to Temperance.

Oh, bloody hell.

Madame Amelie swept over.

Oh, bloody, bloody hell.

"Is there something funny, Mrs. Grey?"

Actually, there had been. "No, madame."

"Do you find your work here amusing?"

Absolutely not and never. "No."

The woman's eyebrows snapped together. "Yes?"

Why don't you tell me what the damned answer is? she silently raged.

Her employer leaned in. "Then I suggest you have a care with your laughter. I will see to Mrs. Marmlebury."

So Temperance was to be *punished* . . . for laughing.

Temperance hurried into the back and sat at her tiny little station. She grabbed the partially completed day dress and her needle, and resumed sewing. This was fine. She'd prefer the physical misery of putting her body through this work to having to suffer through the likes of Mrs. Marmlebury. It was only a brief reprieve. After all, this was to be her future . . . But she would take those breaks from horrific clients when and where she could. From out on the shop floor, the bell jingled, announcing the arrival of some other unkind harpy.

Temperance jabbed her needle into the fabric and let the rote motions take over as she saw to the dress.

She'd forgotten what it was to be free in any way, capable of even just laughing without censure and condemnation. Just like she'd not been able to have an opinion on colors of fabrics or types or cuts or . . . anything. Only Dare had ever encouraged her to live freely, without constraint, and without apologies. He'd never expected her to answer for how she felt.

And those had been gifts.

She'd not realized as much until she'd fled. Temperance had left trying to protect him. Only to find that she really had been trying to protect herself from the fear that Dare would one day reject or resent her. When challenged by his grandmother, Temperance had allowed herself to be weakened by a sense of her failures as a woman. Only . . . she wasn't a failure. She wasn't broken. She had time to see that now. In those moments when she'd stated her intentions to leave, he'd been adamant that her inability to have children didn't matter. He'd spoken of the possibility of theirs being a different type of family.

And she wanted that.

All of that . . . with him.

But he'd not come for her. That truth was with her daily . . . along with what it meant. What it truly meant about his thoughts on a future with her.

He . . .

Her nape tingled with awareness.

Impossible.

And yet—

"Hullo, Temperance." His voice washed over her, that deep baritone, honeyed and warm; it would forever haunt her sleeping and waking thoughts.

"D-dare," she greeted. She made herself lower her sewing, but God help her for a coward, she could not turn. She could not face him.

Her heart thumped hard and fast.

He is here.

She briefly closed her eyes but did not rise or turn to face him, for fear that when and if she did, he'd disappear.

She knew why he was here, and she'd allow the reality of that to sink in after she just embraced his presence.

How she'd missed him.

Dare stopped at her shoulder . . . and remained . . . silent.

He'd not allow her to her cowardice, then.

Temperance shifted slightly in her seat, turning on the bench and looking up so she could meet his gaze.

She could make nothing out of it.

His eyes were serious and solemn when they'd always before this contained a teasing glimmer or spark.

"Joseph Gurney has been freed."

Of anything he might have said, of anything she'd expected he might utter, that had not been it.

"I managed to locate Mr. Buxton . . . who proved as your brother expected he would be: horrified at the circumstances surrounding Mr. Gurney's imprisonment. He's something of a social reformer, an abolitionist, and . . . he wishes to reform the prison systems. He's invited me to take part in his efforts." Dare twisted his hat in his hands. "He said given my title and . . . the life that I've lived, that I might help make meaningful change in London."

Her heart swelled. "That is . . . wonderful." And she meant it. At last, he would have a new beginning and, more, the future he deserved. One that she would never be part of.

"And . . . those portraits? The ones of my family that you said I was wrong to sell. You were right. Getting rid of them did not erase the regret I felt in leaving my family. Nor did it erase the love I had for my mother, or the love she had for me. I . . . purchased them back. All of them."

Tears filled her eyes, and she blinked them back. "That is . . . also splendid, Dare." He'd come all this way to tell her that? Surely that meant something about his being here. Surely that meant—

Wordlessly, he set an official-looking envelope down atop the forgotten-until-now gown.

Blankly, she looked down at it. *What is this?*

Except she already knew. Just as she'd known with a woman's intuition that he'd been near, she knew with a sickening dread what was contained within. Because their time together hadn't been finished until this was done. *This* was why he'd come.

His features were a mask that revealed absolutely nothing. "You said you wanted an annulment. My grandfather secured the necessary signatures."

Yes. Yes, she had. For him.

This was why he'd come, then. Not to share in the joy of what his life held in store. But to sever what their life together had been.

With surprisingly steady movements, she picked up the packet, broke the seal, and scanned the pages. She'd known what would be contained within, but seeing the words inked in black and stamped in various places left her frozen in her seat, unmoving.

"It . . . is done," he said quietly.

After she'd lost her babe and her marriage had fallen apart, she'd thought her shattered heart was incapable of breaking any more. How much was there left to give?

Only to find even more agony could be squeezed from the still-beating organ.

She bit the inside of her cheek, welcoming the sting of pain for the distraction she needed.

It is done.

"That is, it is done . . . if you wish it." Dare laid another packet on her table, and she stared at it before making herself pick it up and . . .

She gasped. "What is . . . ?" Temperance tried and failed to get the words out.

"Five thousand pounds, as was promised," he said quietly. "There should be funds enough to share as you would with your brother and Miss Armitage . . . but I've it on the authority of Mr. Buxton that he will name your Chance as his mill supervisor." Words escaped her. Dare cleared his throat. "My grandfather had time to reflect upon what I said. He made the decision to not withhold those funds, and as such, I'd have you take them and . . . and do with them as you would."

Women such as she weren't permitted dreams. They worked and then they died, and if they were fortunate, the end wasn't as painful as their living days had been. And now, he'd give her this. "I don't know what to do with this," she whispered.

He sank to a knee beside her seat and cupped her cheek. "You *do* with it whatever you wish. If it is a trip to see the world, book your passage. If it is that you want nothing more than to have a parcel of land that is yours and retire forever, then you do it. *I* do not want an annulment."

Her heart paused in her breast.

"But I want you to have a choice. I want *you* to at last decide what it is you want your future to be." Tears filled her eyes. "And God, Temperance," he whispered. "I just want to share in whatever those dreams are . . . with you."

Her breath caught on a little sob, and he angled her head so their brows almost touched. "I love you," he said in ardent tones. "You are all I ever wanted but was entirely too afraid to admit because I didn't believe I was worthy of being loved."

"You are," she said through the emotion clogging her throat. "You always were." And she'd failed if she'd made him feel somehow less for all he'd been to so many . . . including her.

"I know that now. And Temperance," he went on, capturing her falling tears with the pads of his thumbs, "I realized that because of you. You are my every happiness. You are my purpose. You are my heart. But I'd not have you for those reasons . . . not because I need you. But rather, because you need me and want me, too . . ."

Temperance's shoulders shook from the force of her silent weeping. His beautiful visage blurred before her, and she closed her eyes in a bid to clear the moisture so that she might see him. So that she might ascertain that this moment was real. On shaky feet, she stood. "Children . . ." She managed to get out that one word.

His expression softened, and he gazed upon her with such tenderness and warmth that she fell in love with him all over again. "Children do not make a marriage, Temperance." He straightened. "A husband and wife together do. If you want children with me, boys or girls or both, who've lived the harsh lives that you and I once did, then I'd have that with you. And if that is not your wish, then I am content with that, too. Because your happiness is my happiness, and that is all I want. For you to be—"

Sobbing, Temperance rushed into his arms. "I love you."

Dare caught her to him; gripping her tight about the waist, he just held her close. "I love you, Temperance," he whispered, placing a hard kiss against her temple. "Marry me?"

"Yes," she managed between tears that had given way to uncontrollable, joy-filled laughter. Catching him by the nape, she dragged his face close, but he pulled back slightly, withholding that kiss she so desperately longed for.

"I'll not let you go this time," he promised. "I left you once, and I'll not make that same mistake again. I—"

She touched a fingertip to his lips, silencing the remainder of that vow. "That is good, Dare Greyson, because I've no intention of letting you go this time."

And with that, she kissed him and welcomed the rest of her future.

Acknowledgments

The idea for Dare and Temperance's story came to me in the middle of a theater performance of *Hamilton*. I was seated next to my brilliant editor, Alison Dasho, who thankfully had a pencil in hand for me to jot down my notes and ideas, and talked with me—during intermission, of course—about my vision for this book. I'm so grateful to her for allowing me to tell this tale, and for offering her invaluable guidance along the way about this and all plots percolating in my mind.

About the Author

Photo © 2016 Kimberly Rocha

Christi Caldwell is the *USA Today* bestselling author of more than ten series, including Lost Lords of London, Sinful Brides, The Wicked Wallflowers, and Heart of a Duke. She blames novelist Judith McNaught for luring her into the world of historical romance. When Christi was at the University of Connecticut, she began writing her own tales of love—ones where even the most perfect heroes and heroines had imperfections. She learned to enjoy torturing her couples before they earned their well-deserved happily ever after.

Christi lives in Southern Connecticut, where she spends her time writing, chasing after her son, and taking care of her twin princesses-in-training. Fans who want to keep up with the latest news and information can sign up for her newsletter at www.ChristiCaldwell.com.